Hidden in Full View

A Novel Out of Africa

Samantha Ford

Published on Amazon Via KDP
All Rights Reserved.
Copyright © 2023 Samantha Ford
(ISBN 9798871720912)

No part of this book may be reproduced or transmitted in any form or by any means, graphic, electronic, or mechanical, including photocopying, recording, taping or by any information storage or retrieval system, without the permission in writing from the copyright holder.

The right of Samantha Ford to be identified as the author of this work has been asserted in accordance with the Copyright, Designs and Patents Act 1988 sections 77 and 78.

This is a work of fiction. The characters and their actions are entirely fictitious. Any resemblance to persons living or dead is entirely coincidental.

******

Also by Samantha Ford

The Zanzibar Affair

The House Called Mbabati

A Gathering of Dust

The Ambassador's Daughter

The Unexpected Guest

A Widow in Waiting

Amazon Reviews

"This is simply the best book I've read in a very long time. This talented lady brings Africa alive. Wilbur Smith you have some competition…"

"A cracking good story with a totally unexpected twist at the end!"
John Gordon Davis – author of Hold My Hand I'm Dying

"Having read all Wilbur Smith's books, this author ranks up with the best of them. Best read I've had for years!" Peter C. Morgan

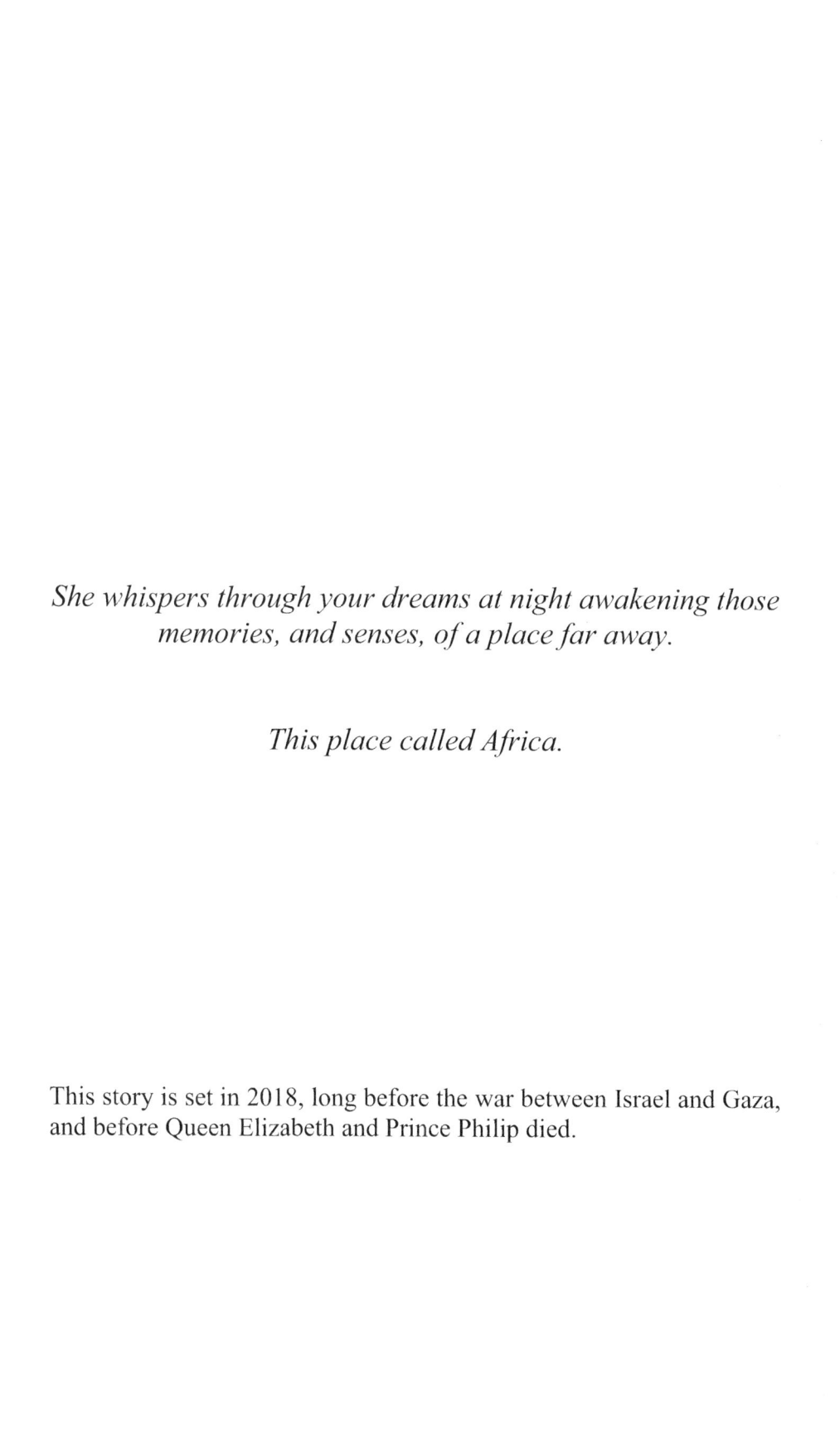

She whispers through your dreams at night awakening those memories, and senses, of a place far away.

This place called Africa.

This story is set in 2018, long before the war between Israel and Gaza, and before Queen Elizabeth and Prince Philip died.

Chapter One
England
2016
Zelda

Zelda Cameron looked up when the front doorbell rang. She lifted the parcel from the dining room table and made her reluctant way to the door.

Fleetingly she wondered if this was the right thing to do. What would the repercussions be when the parcel reached its destination? She hesitated, then shrugged her shoulders. Everything has a destination she reasoned with herself. She was reaching hers and all she could hope was that this last gesture would go some way to put to rest something that had haunted her for so many years. Decisions made with emotional haste, she thought bitterly, often had disastrous consequences.

The night before she had brought the two cardboard boxes into her sitting room, going through the contents meticulously. The briefcase open on the table in front of her. The fire threw shadows across the carpets, softening the outlines of her furniture and the heavy curtains, taking the chill from the room, illuminating the soft pastels of the paintings on the wall. One by one, she threw her personal documents, photographs, and letters into the waiting flames. What was left she laid carefully in the briefcase, tears wetting her cheeks.

Her lawyer would have only what she would like him to have. The rest she had now destroyed. Now no-one would know anything about who she was, and what part she had played in the terrible events that had followed.

She glanced briefly at the open briefcase and its chilling contents, her stomach tight with anxiety as she lowered the lid and locked it.

That would be enough. That was all she was prepared to leave.

*****

The courier placed the parcel in the box behind his seat, adjusted his helmet, mounted his bike, then roared off down the road, heading back to London.

Zelda watched him go then closed the front door and walked shakily over to the window, gazing out over the expansive lawns and ancient oak trees, now shrouded with grey, looking like black skeletons, their bare branches reaching out into the mist as though they were trying to find their way past and through it. Much as she was feeling herself now.

February always felt like the longest month of the year, a dead month. The festivities of Christmas and New Year's Eve a distant memory, the challenge of a new year ahead with all its pitfalls and triumphs and the price tag attached. She had paid her price in advance and knew she would not be here to see another February. Or, she thought bitterly, another September when the flowers arrived with their chilling message of death. But that had been years ago now. He had stopped tormenting her, taunting her for what she had done to him and how he was repaying her for it. She had always hated lilies, the flower most associated with funerals.

Now she watched the soft English rain as it swept across the manicured grounds of her cottage garden, leaving a haze of grey in its wake. In many ways it reminded her of the family farm, in the Eastern Cape, on a cold winter's morning before the sun seared through the clouds and spread its warmth and light across the arid landscape. In the late afternoon the thorn trees threw dark paths over the bush and briefly bathed them in gold before sinking behind the mountain range leaving only a fiery red sky.

The trees there on the ridge were flaming silhouettes casting long shadows through the trees and farmlands, the light diminishing before darkness swiftly fell and the cool night air enveloped the farmhouse and the land around it.

High above the stars made their appearance, only a few at first then, when the sky was as black as velvet, the rest were revealed in all their glory, unimpeded by town or city lights, a glittering rolling carpet of unimaginable beauty almost blocking out the blackness of the night. The moon back lighting the outline of the surrounding trees.

*****

Zelda turned her head and looked at the painting above her fireplace. To some it would seem to lack the fire and colour most people appreciated in a piece of art. But to her it was as valuable and precious as the country she had left behind.

Winter was different in Africa, stealthy, bringing a sharpness with non-reflective cutting edges. Gone was the softness and blurred edges of the distant mountain range, the featheriness of the branches of the trees. Only the seductive whispers of a cooling night, reflecting the ageing of another year as it was and as it was becoming.

There was the farmhouse, where they had played as children. The windmill standing on triangular stilts creaking and groaning. The blades generating the wind, glinting in the harsh sunlight, pulling the reluctant moisture from the dry cracked earth, pumping life-giving water to the farmhouse, the animals, and gardens.

There the aloes were spiky and green and spread through the front lawns of the house. Tenacious, red, white, purple and orange bougainvillea draped themselves over the spacious wrap around veranda and up the sides of the dirt splashed white walls of the homestead, the agapanthus adding a dazzle of purple and blue.

Leopard trees with their leaves as delicate as lace, and slender white trunks allowed dappled sunlight to filter through as they shaded the veranda.

The artist had captured the essence of the homestead perfectly. The façade of the house was reminiscent of the old Dutch homes in the Cape.

The isolated homestead was a long building embellished in soft white, the central gable prominent and simply decorated with its twisted cement leaves. Creaking steps led up to the heavy wooden entrance door. The roof thatched, the large windows with their dark green frames and shutters.

Slightly distant from the main house the long low building housed the staff and their families, the windows smaller but the frames painted the same dark green. In a manageable fenced area, the staff grew their own vegetables, safe from their few goats and chickens. Large barns, for storage and repairing farm equipment, stood to the right of the staff quarters where numerous farm dogs found shelter from the heat.

The life-giving water nourished the fruit and vegetables. The huge herds of sheep provided the meat required to make the elderly old farm self-sufficient. There were no shops nearby, only vast tracts of land as far as the eye could see.

In the Spring the land was an artist's palette of purple and yellow flowers, mauve daisies with their yellow centres, and wild sage with its pungent scent, with a backdrop of impossibly high blue skies and brooding grey mountains in the distance.

Zelda stood up and went into the kitchen to make some tea, then changed her mind and poured herself a glass of wine. Going back to her chair she looked at the painting again as her memories crawled back.

The farm was two hour's drive from the small town of Molteno which had barely changed from its inception decades before. The town was simple, a garage with a Wimpy Bar next door, a modest supermarket, a few restaurants, including a steak house. A pharmacy, two banks and, of course, the Dutch Reformed Church and not much else.

But Molteno was famous for two things. The snack most South African children had been brought up on – Ouma's Rusks were made there and had been for decades; and for sheep farming which gave the town its rough and ready appearance. This was a farming town and didn't aspire to be anything else. The main road running through it was tarred but the roads spiking off it were gravel.

The roads out to the hundreds of farms in the area were mere tracks, rutted with teeth rattling corrugations in the summer months, and deep mud and potholes in the cold and wet months.

There was a modest school in town which, when they were old enough, they attended. When the children reached high school age they went to a boarding school in Queenstown, about one hundred kilometres away.

Zelda, when she left school, began her teaching career in Queenstown. In the evenings as she drove home, she would pass small villages built close to the town itself. Each dwelling round and thatched, with tendrils of smoke rising in the sunset. The African children with their big liquid brown eyes, their teeth white against their round faces waving and laughing and calling out as they ran alongside the road, their bare feet throwing up puffs of dust, pulling their toys behind them.

The toys were simple and hand made from discarded wire coat hangers, rusting tins, and cardboard boxes, which the children fashioned into cars and carts bringing hours of play into the world they knew, with no expectations of anything else.

There was always something to celebrate in their simple village life – dancing, braais, weddings, and funerals, which went on long into the night, the firelight flickering, throwing shadows over their glowing faces.

The singing of the women as they washed their clothes down by the river spreading them to dry on the hot sun-baked rocks. The children would play in the water, splashing, laughing and shouting at each other, oblivious to the brutal sun beating down on them. Oblivious to any future they may be part of as they grew into young adults.

Young girls helped their mothers with the laundry, their hair plaited with brightly coloured beads which whispered and clicked as they bent from their waists and scrubbed at their clothes, pounding them on nearby rocks to remove stubborn dirt and stains.

Bare footed boys looked after modest herds of goats and cattle nibbling on the dry grasses, their feet already hardened, crisp and cracked with callouses.

Zelda took a sip of her wine and smiled. Such a simple life then so many decades ago. Would it be the same now, she wondered, with all the dramatic changes South Africa had gone through? She doubted it.

As planned, she had manoeuvred a meeting with her future husband, Paul Cameron, a young English doctor, in Queenstown and married him. With the two children they were now a family. A family she had carefully prepared for. When Paul was offered a partnership in a thriving practice on the outskirts of London, he had snatched the opportunity to return to the country of his birth, taking his family with him.

*****

Life was different here in England. She was glad she didn't live in London anymore. Zelda had been overwhelmed with the contrast of the vast city and her simple upbringing on an isolated farm in Africa.

Coming into London by train the houses were small and boxy, all looking identical from the outside, their gardens a narrow strip, living cheek by jowl with their neighbours. Rusting iron chairs, overturned tricycles and wheelbarrows with tired looking garden sheds and unkempt gardens. The city was a cacophony of noise; traffic, trains, televisions and blaring music vibrating through the walls, planes roaring overhead from various London airports, couples arguing and screaming at each other, babies wailing, packed underground trains and stations, and the high streets teeming with people. She had hated her new life in London and all the troubles it had brought with it. The loneliness. She had wanted to turn and flee back to the land of her birth. But that would have been impossible, utterly impossible.

There was no turning back.

Zelda missed the sunset silhouettes of animals coming to drink from the rivers and water holes, the rasping cough of a leopard, the spine-chilling distant call of a lion reverberating through the darkening bush. The rivers bathed in a red light from the dying sun. Elephants moving into the mauve light of another coming day, then swallowed up in the rapid fall of darkness and becoming one with their land, treading lightly, silently. Only the crack and rustle of a fallen tree in their path. The silence of it all. The quietness of the bush as the day wound down and night approached.

Zelda felt a tightness in her chest. No point in looking back. Never again and no-where else could Africa be recaptured or replicated. But she was part of that great continent, it was in her blood, in her very soul. She had let it go but never forgotten it and knew without doubt, it was where she should be. Where she belonged, where she wanted to be. Where she had made her innocent, but disastrous mistake.

Having to leave Africa was punishment enough for that.

Her garden cottage here in England was some miles out from the picturesque village of Larkstown, with its duck pond, village green, hump backed bridge and colour washed cottages. She hoped it wouldn't suffer the demise of other villages in rural England which now housed few permanent residents.

Living in a remote village held little appeal for people working in cities around England. There was money to be made from leaving the places empty and cashing in on holiday lettings. The post offices, local butchers, bakers, small pubs, and libraries, normally the heart of every village community, had gradually closed, the village church bereft of worshippers. The graveyard only a whispered reminder of what had gone before.

Soon it would all be over. Her mind once again wandered back to her childhood as she stared at the painting on her wall.

She wondered, briefly, if she might leave any kind of footprint behind in Africa. An imprint of herself on those warm dusty bush paths. A shadow of who she was then, running free and wild around the farm; full of hope and dreams as the world awaited her with its cruel ability to crush everything, to stamp on these hopes and dreams and leave only bruised petals with their brief lingering fragrance and memories of another time and place.

The wind would blow gently through the long wavering, lion coloured, grasses and cover those little innocent footprints of her and her brothers with dust, as though they had never been.

There would be no imprint left of her here on hard roads and pavements in another land. Only an empty step, like millions of others, lost in a sea of discarded chewing gum, puddles and cigarette butts. No imprint at all. She would leave nothing behind. Her dust, her ashes, would be scattered in a place only known to one other person.

Her solicitor had been given explicit instructions which she knew he would follow to the letter. Two years from tomorrow, the man she had entrusted with her secrets and speculations would hopefully retrieve her couriered parcel with its shocking contents.

The man would not know her name. She knew she could trust him; his name had appeared briefly in articles she had read in the *Telegraph*. He would know what to do, where to look. He had made a career out of it.

It was a lot to ask of someone who lived thousands of miles away on another continent. But if anyone could find the answers it would be him.

Zelda heard the familiar sound of the purring of a vehicle, the crunch of tyres on the driveway.

He was back.

Every September, over four consecutive years, he came with his funeral lilies. He had stayed for an hour, or so, going through the details so she would be constantly reminded of the consequences of her actions.

But tonight, something was different. It was February. Why had he come back again now after all these years of not seeing or hearing from him?

She stamped down the fear she had always felt when she heard his vehicle. He could not hurt her now. It was all over. All of it.

Zelda knew what he had come for. But he was too late.

Briefly the headlights of the vehicle pierced the dark mist and lit up the quiet and dark pebbled driveway leading to her home, its lights sweeping briefly around the sitting room searching for her.

She had been planning this for months. She had made her own decision before any more damage could be done.

Zelda began to feel a warm glow from the pills and the wine. She felt her body relax and closed her eyes as they misted over and blurred, the knocking at the door receding, the shape of the room distorting. The wine glass dropped soundlessly to the carpet from her limp hand.

Somewhere in the distance, she thought she could hear the melodious clear voices of the African women as they swayed in time with their singing. She could smell and hear the soft crackle of the fire burning, shooting blood red sparks up into the star-studded sky, the wisps of grey curling then dissipating.

She heard the soft clapping of their hands, a traditional sign of welcome, their voices were beginning to fade. But she could see them clearly as they beckoned to her. She turned towards them.

The greyness turned to blackness as she followed the sound of their singing and returned to the place she had yearned for. The place she had always called home.

"I'm sorry," she whispered to the empty room. "I'm so terribly sorry…"

Chapter Two
London
2000

Joe McNeil lay on his bunk in a drug infused stupor. Through the grimy filth of his port hole, he could see the thick grey mist further obscuring his view of the equally grey River Thames as it made its sluggish, but treacherous way, through the estuary and out towards the North Sea.

The old, dilapidated barge, partially hidden in the reeds and detritus of the river, rocked silently at its moorings. The interior dimly lit by a single flickering bulb. The air rank with the clouds of dope permeating everything.

He had been buying and selling drugs since he was fifteen. He had grown up on a council estate where life was rough. The people were rough too. Always looking for an opportunity to escape into another world. Joe provided that other world with his wares.

He had hit the streets of London when he was eighteen and didn't look back. There was an endless demand for what he was selling and in that vast city there were plenty of ways to avoid the cops. Plenty of ways to avoid getting busted.

He had lived a squalid life until he managed to make enough money each month to be able to afford the low rent on the rapidly deteriorating barge a mate of his owned.

His mate was doing time in prison and wanted a lowly rent whilst he served his sentence. Joe was happy with that. With the money he made, and the government benefits he collected each month, he could afford it.

His buyers knew where to find him down here on the Thames. But it was by appointment only. Hidden from prying eyes.

He heard the thud on the deck and groggily sat up, pushing the ashtray under the bunk and covering the spent joints with a blanket. It didn't sound like cops; he would have seen their flashing lights if they were about to do a raid.

But to be sure he pushed the opposite port hole open to let out some of the noxious fumes alongside the contents of the ashtray.

Cautiously he climbed the short iron rung step, lifted the hatch, and peered out into the dark night. Nothing.

But he had heard something.

There were no pretty potholders full of brightly coloured flowers on his barge. No comfortable cushioned seat to sit in and admire the views of London and its surrounds, no attractive designer lamps hanging from hooks. No, just a couple of black plastic bags full of empty take-out boxes, crushed beer cans, and other rancid rubbish.

Joe looked around and that's when he saw the dark shape of something in the corner. Cautiously he moved towards it, the shape moved, trying to get up. He jumped back in fright.

"Help me. Please help me…"

He edged closer. By the dim light which came from his quarters he could see it was a young girl, her wet hair plastered to her head, her body bruised and bleeding, one eye half closed. She was naked except for a brief pair of panties.

He stumbled back down the steps and wrenched the dirty blanket off his bunk then hurried back and put it around her. Hauling her to her feet he manoeuvred her down the step and into the tepid warmth of his cabin and lay her on his bunk, the blanket puddled around her body.

He stared at her. "Who are yer, luv, wot you doin' in the bleeding river at this time of night?"

The girl was moaning, moving her head from side to side, trying to say something.

He bent his head and tried to listen. "Black, black…"

"Is that yer name, luv, is it Black?"

The girl sighed, her lips fluttered then she lay still, her head stopped moving her arms and hands went limp. Her blue swollen eyes now stared ahead.

Panic stricken Joe gave her a nudge. He'd seen dead bodies before. But this girl had snuffed it right here on his bloody boat.

The last thing he wanted was to call the police and have them swarming all over the place. He already had a criminal record and served a couple of years for dealing. The police would probably accuse him of killing this girl. They would search the barge, turn it inside out and find his stash of supplies for his customers. Before he knew it, he would be back in the slammer again and for considerably longer than the last time.

Jesus! His already muddled brain tried to think of what to do next. He had no alternative. He stared at her tanned body, noticed she carried no weight, her muscles were well-toned. She must have been a healthy young thing before she snuffed it. He peered at the small tattoo at the top of her hip. He had seen plenty of those in his short lifetime but nothing like this one, just a funny shape with a black outline.

It was foggy and dark outside. Where the barge was moored, partially obscured by sodden rushes and other detritus from the flowing river, there were no lights anywhere. He switched off the single flickering bulb. Now there was no light at all.

He grasped her under the arms, pulled her off his bunk and dragged her back up the step. He looked around carefully. There were no patrol boats around. No other movement of other boats, no-one walking around in the fog at this time of night, no-one who could see his hidden disintegrating barge.

He hauled her to the side of the barge and carefully manoeuvred her over the side, grabbing her slippery ankles as he slid her body slowly and soundlessly back into the river she had appeared from. He watched as the strong current pulled her away from the tangle of branches.

Then she was gone.

He rubbed his wet shaking hands on his filthy jeans. Job done. Problem sorted.

Chapter Three
London
2016

The driver carefully manoeuvred his vehicle through the crawling traffic on the Earl's Court Road. The wet road reflected the taillights of the cars in front, the rain fell relentlessly.
The crowds scurried along under umbrellas shrouded in raincoats clutching their shopping bags.

Lights from the many cheap restaurants threw a cheerful warming glow on the wet pavements outside.

He glanced from left to right; there were hostels and cheap hotels wedged between charity, quick print, hardware shops and take-out places, their international flags dragged flat by the wetness, hoping to entice all the international tourists and businesspeople filling the city, who hadn't already booked one of the thousands of other hotels available.

There were numerous pubs and wine bars, but he thought the whole road was beginning to look tired, grubby, and run down. Backpackers, students, and young tourists came in their thousands to the Earl's Court Road, from all over the world, looking for cheap accommodation and their first tantalising taste of London.

The plan he had set up, years ago, had served its purpose. Soon he would retire to somewhere warm and disappear. He was looking forward to it.

There were still some loose ends he had to tie up. Things he still had to do to ensure his future dreams and plans. Getting rid of the bitch was one of them.

He had always hated her; from the moment he met her.

Hundreds of people went missing every day in the UK. In his opinion people who ran away either had something they were trying to reach, or something they were trying to avoid.

What if she had kept notes? Well, they probably wouldn't make sense to anyone and who cared now, years later, what had happened? He certainly didn't. Even so he needed to make one final trip and destroy anything which may implicate him sometime in the future - and that included her.

*****

He drove alongside the river Thames and stopped in one of his favourite spots under a bridge. He got out and wandered down to the river's edge. It was high tide now and although the river looked placid and benign, he knew there were dangerous strong currents hidden beneath. Those powerful tides could overpower even the strongest of swimmers and sweep them out into the icy North Sea.

Not a keen swimmer himself he could imagine the terror of helplessly being swept out to sea. He replaced that thought with one of the calm and tranquil beaches of another country. He could take his pick – he could go anywhere. He was still relatively young, only in his late forties. He had his whole life ahead of him. He knew exactly where he would be heading. He wanted to assess the damage he had caused.

It was all about the hunt, the chase. He had caught all of them.

He rubbed his cold hands together and blew on them, wrapped his scarf around his neck, took a last lingering look at the river, smiled, then turned and walked back to his vehicle.

Chapter Four
London
2016

The office of solicitors, James Barrington-Smith and Associates was on a side road off Kensington High Street. James Barrington-Smith had signed for Zelda's package. Going back to his desk he had unwrapped the parcel and looked at the two envelopes and locked briefcase.

Zelda had been quite clear with her instructions. One letter and the briefcase were to be delivered to her bank's safe deposit facility where it was to remain for two years after her death. Thereafter James Barrington-Smith was to have the other letter delivered, by hand, and signed for by the recipient personally.

James had buzzed for his secretary. "Ah, Christina. Please take this briefcase and letter down to the bank and have it lodged in Mrs Cameron's safe deposit box as per her instructions."

James Barrington-Smith turned back to his computer, pulled up the following years daily planners and inserted the date for the delivery of the letter, as instructed, to Mr Harry Bentley at the *Telegraph*.

He frowned slightly. Zelda Cameron had been his client for over ten years. He had processed her husband's estate when Paul died ten years ago and drawn up Zelda's will. The parcel had arrived, prior to her sudden death, almost as though she had anticipated it.

James had become rather intrigued with this client over the years. She had had a fine mind and an eye for the smallest detail. He was, he admitted, curious about the briefcase and her instructions to him. But he would carry out his final duties to her by adhering to her wishes and winding up her estate.

Given he knew there should have been obvious beneficiaries he had found it odd she had left nothing to anyone. When asked she had looked at him, her large dark brown eyes steady on his face.

She had put her head on one side and given him a bleak smile. *"One wants nothing and the other wants it all – it's best to do it this way."*

The garden cottage in Larkstown was to be sold and the money from her carefully chosen investments and the proceeds from the house, were to be donated to a charity in the country where Zelda Cameron had been born and brought up. The contents of the house could be sold to the new buyer, or failing that, auctioned off. Whatever was left would be donated to a charity in the local village.

Something else about her bothered him. But he was never able to quite put his finger on what it was. Sometimes he felt she was shielding herself from something. Not quite telling him the truth about her circumstances.

When she left his office after their various appointments, he felt as though she had never been there.

She had been cremated, as she had wished, and her ashes delivered to a church in London. This, too, he had found puzzling. Why not have her ashes scattered in the same graveyard as her late husband? Why had she instructed him to wait two years before having the letter delivered to Mr Harry Bentley at the *Telegraph*?

Locking the other letter in his safe he had reached for her file and started the procedure for winding up her not inconsiderable estate.

He calculated his commission for handling it. Feeling suddenly more cheerful he decided he would dine at his club this evening, all further thoughts of Zelda Cameron dissipated from his mind.

Chapter Five
London
2018

James Barrington-Smith checked his weekly planner. Two years had passed since the death of Zelda Cameron. It was time to carry out her final wishes. He went to his safe and retrieved the letter addressed to Harry Bentley at the *Telegraph*.

He buzzed his secretary, Christina. "I need a courier to deliver this letter, by hand, to Mr Harry Bentley at the *Telegraph*. He must sign for it personally, not the security, not his secretary. It must be handed to him and only him."

*****

The courier parked outside the building which had housed the offices of the *Telegraph* for decades and made his way to the front door.

Since the 2015 attack on the French satirical weekly newspaper based in Paris, *Charlie Hebdo*, where twelve members of the publishing team were brutally murdered at their weekly editorial meeting by Islamic extremists, every newspaper and magazine publisher in London had ramped up their security.

Anyone delivering any parcels, any courier, or visitor was confronted with an extremely sensitive security system, more sophisticated than at any airport in the country. The Telegraph was no exception.

The courier removed his helmet and gloves and presented himself to the security officers. "Delivery, sir, for Mr Harry Bentley?"

The security officer held out his hand. "No need to go inside, mate. Just put the letter through the scanner and it'll be delivered to Mr Bentley."

The courier shook his head. "No can do, sir. This letter must be delivered to Mr Bentley. Those were my instructions from the solicitor. He must sign for it personally. It's a legal thing apparently."

The security officer shook his head. "Sorry, mate. I'll ring through to his personal assistant and she can come down and take delivery."

Again, the courier shook his head. "Nope. Mr Bentley must sign for it himself. Those are my instructions."

Harry Bentley, the editor of the Telegraph looked up with a frown at the knock on the door. He disliked being interrupted in the middle of his weekly meetings with his top staff members. His secretary gave him an apologetic smile.

"Sorry, Harry. There's a courier downstairs who is most insistent he has a delivery for you, but he won't hand it to security, or to me. You must sign for it personally. Apparently, it's from a firm of solicitors in the city."

Harry sighed, stretching his navy-blue braces in irritation. "Sorry chaps, give me five minutes. I'll be right back. It's probably a subpoena, or someone wanting to sue us for something or other. So, nothing new there."

But Harry was wrong.

Something far more tantalising lay within the letter. The tentacles of which reached back over forty years in another country far away.

Chapter Six
London
2018

Harry Bentley took a sip of his coffee and hooked his thumbs around his braces. He glanced out of his office window and watched the pedestrians on the pavements enjoying the first of what hopefully would be the beginning of some early Spring sunshine.

As always, the traffic was heavy with red buses, black cabs, vans, refuse trucks and an endless stream of cars and motor bikes weaving in and out as they all strived to reach their destinations. In the distance he could see Green Park where people would be sitting on the benches or strolling along with their dogs; mothers, or au pairs, pushing babies in prams or state-of-the-art pushchairs, joggers side-stepping in and around anything in their path.

Harry sighed. He quite fancied a walk into the park himself. It had been a long hard winter with brutal winds and floods, but today looked like a decent day to be out and about.

But walking around in the park was not going to fill the column inches of his newspaper. He turned back to his desk and picked up the hand delivered envelope embossed with the company's name. James Barrington-Smith and Associates.

He slid his thumb nail underneath the flap at the back and withdrew another envelope and a note from James Barrington-Smith himself.

Dear Mr Bentley,
I have been instructed by my late client, Mrs Zelda Cameron, and entrusted with her final wishes. One of which was to ask you please to forward the enclosed letter.

The recipient of the letter will know where to find the man my late client wished to contact. I do not have any idea who this person is, but she assured me your journalist would know where to find him.

For this person to carry out the last of her final wishes it will be necessary for him to come to my offices and collect the keys to her safe deposit box, in person, with the appropriate identification.

I thank you for your time and hope the above request will not be of any inconvenience.

Yours most sincerely,
James Barrington-Smith.

Harry sat back in his chair and smiled. It had been quite some time since he had received a proper letter in an envelope – cards at Christmas, yes, although they were down to a trickle with the e-cards available now.

He folded the note and looked at the other envelope.

It was addressed to Mr Jack Taylor.

Jack Taylor was his top investigative journalist and had worked for him for over twenty years. He had lived and worked in London, starting out as a cub reporter on the *Telegraph*. He had a keen eye and a nose for unusual stories, and a dogged ability to follow leads until he unearthed the truth and ran the story to ground.

Jack also had another gift. There was a calmness, a way about him which evoked trust. In the world of hard-nosed, intrusive, and aggressive journalists who would do anything to get a story, using every ploy available to trick someone into saying something they didn't mean, then using it against them.

Jack didn't operate like that. He used the gifts of compassion and caring he was born with. He knew he would get his story, but he had a different way of going about it. He genuinely cared for his fellow human beings, for what they had been through, or were going through and they sensed this.

Even when he had chased and uncovered the perpetrator of a crime, someone who had crossed the line of humanity and entered a different world, he tried to understand the motives behind the crime or crimes. Even the bad guys recognised something in him, not all of them, but some. There was always a reason why someone had taken a life.

Jack had always wanted to be a journalist, his parents had hopes for him to become a lawyer, a scientist, or a doctor. He had had an excellent education at Eton and Cambridge, but Jack had set his heart on story telling.

He had been an avid reader and watcher of the news from an early age. He liked to work things out. Why did people do such diabolical things to each other? How did people get away with what they did? How could people disappear without a trace? How did the ones left behind cope with such terrible grief and loss?

Jack became fixated on knowing there was an answer out there somewhere. People did not just disappear. Someone always knew something. Murder was about motive – a reason to kill. There was always a reason for one human being to kill another. He went after the reason.

Over the years he had worked his way up to the position of Senior Crime Reporter and his success rate with digging out the truth in cold cases had been the envy of his colleagues. Now he was at the top of his game. Respected by everyone in the newspaper industry.

Jack knew everyone was entitled to their own life, to make choices, good or bad. He mostly got the guys who had made the bad ones. The bad choices which led to doing bad things to mostly decent people. They lived with their secrets and lies and sometimes took those secrets and lies to their graves with them. But there were other cases where they had thought they had got away with murder. Until Jack Taylor started digging around years later.

Jack accepted an event couldn't change, but the understanding of how it happened could. It took a keen eye to trawl through police statements from years before. Sifting through the case files often contained a secret or two to cracking a cold case. It was all there if you could find it. A discrepancy, a hidden clue in a contradictory statement, an investigator's handwritten notes in a margin. Re-visiting a witness, speaking to detectives who had worked on cases and could recall the details years later, some with surprising accuracy. Especially if the case had never been solved and they had been intimately involved with it.

Jack also had many contacts all over the country, especially in London, they trusted him, even though most of them had served time in Her Majesty's prisons or were just hovering above the legal limits with their underground activities. He knew the value of a secret depended on who you were trying to keep it from and that a sequence of conclusions was based on a chain of assumptions.

Three years ago, a British woman had gone missing in South Africa, the daughter of a diplomat. Sir Miles had been an old friend of

Harry's and wanted his best journalist on the case to try and find his daughter.

Harry sent Jack.

The story was a cracker. But the price Harry had to pay was that Jack, having tasted a new life in South Africa, wanted to stay there.

Not wanting to lose his top journalist, Harry had agreed Jack would be his man in Africa, digging out stories, following leads and contributing a weekly column for his thousands of readers who had tasted the expatriate life abroad, and the many who had lived in Kenya, Uganda, Tanzania, Zambia, Zimbabwe and South Africa. His columns were extremely popular.

Jack had a different way of looking at things. His column wasn't just about big houses, swimming pools and house staff, or the races, polo, top restaurants, award winning wines or the social life of the chosen few. His stories were grittier, and the readers loved them. Whisking them back in their minds to a life they had left behind. Bringing back memories through his written words, evoking emotions buried long ago. And the insatiable longing to go back to those times.

Jack's time in Africa had produced some spectacular stories out of Kenya, Zimbabwe and South Africa. Over and above tracking down what had happened to the Ambassador's daughter. There had been two others. One had Jack travelling to Zimbabwe trying to unlock the story of a young child who had turned up at a luxury game lodge in the bush, in the pitch dark, having survived days in the dangerous terrain on her own. Then the peculiar circumstances surrounding the death of a prominent diplomat in Kenya.

Now Harry stretched his navy-blue braces, already smelling another possibly intriguing story. He looked at the tempting envelope in front of him. The desire to open it was overwhelming. But Harry was from the old school of newspaper men. Journalists had to be enquiring and curious by nature to follow leads and taking no prisoners when it came to a story. That's what newspapers were all about.

But Harry would never open a letter addressed to another person. It wasn't something one did.

He knew Jack was taking two weeks to travel around South Africa, making new contacts, familiarising himself with that vast country and getting to know the towns and cities and the people who lived there.

Harry would courier the letter to him. He knew the postal system in that country left much to be desired and house deliveries were almost unheard of. Most people had a post box number. But Harry was taking no chances.

Whoever James Barrington-Smith's client might have been, they had gone to a lot of trouble to get in touch with Jack, via him. Who knows what the keys to the deposit box would reveal?

Who was the man Jack would have to find? How was he linked to James Barrington-Smith's deceased client. Zelda Cameron?

Harry picked up his phone. He would call Jack and let him know there was a couriered letter waiting for him at his favourite pub – The Inn in Hazyview, a town near the world-famous Kruger National Park. The Inn belonged to a friend of Harry's from his London days. Hugo.

Hugo has been a top tour operator selling safaris to South Africa from the UK. For years it was a tough job trying to persuade people to go on safari during those turbulent times in the country. Then Hugo decided he would give the whole thing up and go and live there himself. He bought a run-down old house, added rooms on over the years and turned it into The Inn. One of the most frequented water holes for humans in the whole of Hazyview.

Harry would address the letter to Jack at the Inn.

Chapter Seven
South Africa
2018

Jack Taylor had started his journey of exploration in the Limpopo Province which took its name from the mighty sluggish river which provided an informal border between South Africa and Zimbabwe.

Having struggled through the potholes and fought his way through the traffic in the town of Tzaneen he had decided to turn around and begin his long journey from the north to the south of the country. He wanted to learn more about his adopted country. He wanted to meet people of all races who called this place home, whether they be farm labourers or farmers themselves, blue collar workers or captains of industry, it was the only way he would be able to immerse himself; he wanted to see how and where they lived.

Tzaneen, in some ways, reminded him of small towns in Kenya, with the teeming traffic, honking taxi bus drivers, music blaring from shops, and endless traders with their wares on display stacked on wobbly tables on the pavements, exposed to the harsh sunlight, exhaust fumes and dust from the relentless traffic. This, indeed, was the new South Africa.

Before the changes came, the area was famous for its production of tea and fruit including mangoes, bananas, tomatoes, and avocados. But politics and labour relations, plus squatters and land grabbing, had changed all of that. Farmers sold up and moved further south and the fruit and tea withered and died on the vine.

Jack called in to a local supermarket in Tzaneen to stock up with water and snacks before heading south. He filled his supermarket basket and wandered past the large frosting chest freezers displaying various meats. He frowned and lifted a bag of something he didn't recognise, but was intrigued by, then hastily dropped it back when he recognised the feet and still crowned heads of dead eyed chickens.

As he traversed this vast country, it presented him with the golden savannahs of the Free State, vast swathes of flat land, wheat, maize, and sunflowers shimmered and rustled in the heat of the February sun. There were great gaping gorges and dizzying, heart-stopping mountain passes.

In Mpumalanga he had gazed at jaw dropping canyons offering spectacular views of mountains and valleys, soaring eagles and thundering waterfalls punctuating the stillness.

Occasionally he saw troops of baboons emerge from the rocky outcrops of the bush, like a group of school bullies, slowing down to let them cross with their swaggering gait and arrogant glances, and the odd humble tortoise making its ponderous way across the highway. A tortoise was protected by the law and if you ran over one you could be in big trouble. He wondered briefly how the conservation people could work out which driver had squashed a tortoise but left that unanswered.

It was a land of magnificent striking contrasts with no earthquakes, tsunamis, or volcanic eruptions. He followed the main highway which snaked from the border of Zimbabwe to the tip of Africa.

Whenever possible he would detour off on to lesser roads, sometimes dirt roads, dry with rutted corrugations, small stones and gravel pinging on the chassis of the car, a cloud of dust hanging motionless behind him, exploring the hinterland where it was wild and dusty with open scrub lands, livestock farms and elderly rural towns. Quite unlike the sleepy narrow country roads of England where the only traffic you were likely to meet was a hay laden tractor, a herd of sheep, or a massive truck carrying sheep or cows to the abattoir.

In these South African rural towns he stayed in quaint guest houses, simple but more than adequate. He would wander through the town and talk to shopkeepers, residents, restaurant owners and anyone else who had the time to talk to him. Time meant nothing in these sleepy towns where everyone seemed to know everyone else. But it was in the evenings, in the local pubs, where he got the real feel for his adopted country.

Everyone was friendly and eager to talk to the posh, good looking, English journalist with the wild blond hair and big engaging smile. He listened to conversations about politicians, the state of the energy supplier, Eskom, the weather the crops, the past and the future.

The farms were mostly owned by Afrikaners who inherited them from their fathers and grandfathers before them. They came into town for supplies and a beer or two before heading back to their isolated farms and livestock.

They all knew each other and stuck together having little or no time for an English journalist, but a few of the younger ones were polite enough.

Some had accepted the changes thrust upon them by a new government. But some had not.

It had been a turbulent time in their history – the Boer war in 1899. It was a vicious scorched earth policy perpetrated by the British. Boer farms were torched, their crops and homesteads sent up in smoke, their livestock shot, their women and children herded into concentration camps where twenty-eight thousand of them had died of malnutrition and disease.

Small wonder, Jack thought, they had a long and bitter memory of that time. Much like the Jewish people who also had long and bitter memories, even to this day, about the Nazi's during World War II. The stories were handed down through the generations and entrenched in their DNA.

Orania was such a place. A place he had been keen to visit, it would make a good, but controversial, story for his newspaper. Orania was a small settlement, south of Kimberley, owned and run exclusively by white Afrikaners for white Afrikaners, with a population of around two thousand people. No Africans lived or worked there. Every job was done by Afrikaners, be it shelf stacking in the general grocery store, or cleaning the floors of the two schools, a hospital, and other places of business. Outside of the town of Orania there were big circular fields of lucerne and wheat, irrigated with huge overhead mobile sprinklers. Well-padded cattle and sheep grazed somnolently in paddocks.

Beyond was the Orange River supplying an endless source of water to the area and its surrounds. Outside the town was a modest hotel for visiting guests to Orania, a supermarket and several big sheds with cars and trucks parked around. Here panel beaters, blacksmiths, and garages serviced farmers for miles around the district.

Orania had its own currency, linked to the South African Rand, it had its own newspaper and radio station. There was no crime, therefore no police station. Disputes and petty offences were resolved by the local committee made up of homeowners. They produced their own electricity with no need to rely on the worsening situation with Eskom, they grew their own food and produced everything themselves – they were totally independent and self-sufficient, needing nothing from the outside world and asking for nothing in return.

The town of Orania itself, had its own shops, hair salons, a library, post office, schools, restaurants, a local bar or two and plenty of Dutch Reformed churches, all run by their own people. They even had their own flag which smacked vaguely of the old pre-apartheid era.

Jack knew there were many arguments for and against such a community in the new South Africa. Some saw it as a blatant slap in the face to the new government, others tried to understand. Others fully understood.

The Jews, he thought, were like the Afrikaners in many ways. The state of Israel existed today only because, so many years ago now, a handful of Jews worked hard and lobbied and agitated making a nuisance of themselves. The world thought it was a fool's errand – demanding a Jewish state, just as the Afrikaner had for Orania, on a continent of hostile Arabs. The Jews were powerless – they had no army, no infrastructure, no money; they were a decimated people. But a handful of Jewish leaders kept struggling and agitating for it until the British threw up their hands in despair and granted them a chunk of Palestine, the size of the Kruger National Park.

From a journalistic point of view, there were emotional similarities between Orania and the state of Israel. He would tread carefully with this story. But it was a story he wished to include in one of his columns.

The Afrikaners who lived in Orania, vehemently denied the place had racial connotations but rather it was a community determined to protect its culture, to ensure the Afrikaner, who had already lost his country, his flag, his national anthem and identity, wouldn't be lost in the breathlessness of time.

They were fiercely proud of their people, their history and the huge part they had played in building South Africa with its excellent infrastructure of national highways, bridges, mines, railway lines, state buildings, world class vineyards, and the hard-working farmers who had toiled long and hard on their farms to provide food, fruit and wine for the nation and international markets, over the many years they had run the country.

Jack had been intrigued with the little town of Orania with its old Dutch styled buildings, neat roads, impressive churches, and shops. Children played and ran around; people there left their homes unlocked and everyone knew everyone else, just like the old villages in England. It had been like taking a step back in time. Although he was aware, even in England, under the surface, there were places seething with unwarranted prejudices.

The people he had spoken to in Orania, were polite and friendly but cautious, he was a journalist after all, with their comments on how they lived and what they hoped for in the future. They felt safe living there with their own people, their own language, and their own culture. They were a deeply religious people putting God, the bible, and family above all else.

Slap bang in the middle of South Africa? How long would a whites-only community survive? Radical politicians denounced it as racist.

Jack, with his objective journalist's mind, could see the arguments both for and against Orania, it would make a provocative article for his weekly column in the *Telegraph*.

He thought about how he would shape and mould his article about Orania as he drove steadily on. His sunglasses were filmed with dust, the sun blinding, despite putting down the sun visor the air-conditioning in the vehicle struggled against the heat of the sun as it blazed through the windows.

Sometimes he could go an hour on a secondary road and not see another vehicle. He passed African villages where the children waved and smiled at him; not for the first time he speculated on how many Africans had fabulous white teeth, given to them by nature, unlike the Americans who paid an absolute fortune on getting their teeth fixed from an early age to ensure they also had perfect teeth.

There were individual traders on the sides of the road waiting for a vehicle to stop and buy their fruit and vegetables balanced on wobbly plastic crates. Women with their babies strapped to their backs in cloth pouches, bundles of firewood perfectly balanced on their heads, making their stately way back to their villages.

There were plenty of dogs foraging for food, with ladders of ribs outlined through their dull, patchy coats. Bony cattle grazed on the scrub land sometimes standing still in the middle of the highway and refusing to move. Donkeys pulling two wheeled wooden carts, trotted daintily along the road, the carts full of fresh produce, livestock, firewood, building materials or young children.

Some of the bigger towns were home to large houses surrounded by spikes, electric fencing, and alarm systems. A sharp contrast to the small rural towns he had visited.

The Karoo was a vast swath of vast open spaces and a distinctive landscape, in the distance he could see isolated farms. Simple windmills glinting in the sun turned squeaking and groaning like old men, as they lifted the reluctant water from the baked earth; the land peppered with sheep, goats, fat cattle and ostrich.

In its isolation Jack felt it had almost a sacred feel about it and seemed to go on forever. Miles of endless miles of nothing but natural, silent, scrubland. At one point in the late afternoon, he had felt himself become mesmerised by the long black ribbon of highway in front of him and felt his lids grow heavy, his eyes starting to close.

He had jerked himself upright and pulled over at the first available picnic site, of which there were plenty, and well signposted, some kilometres before they appeared.

He parked under a solitary tree which also shaded a white cement table, decorated with bird dropping as were the two half-moon cement seats. He stretched his arms and legs and sipped from his bottle of water. Surrounding him was complete and utter silence except for the engine of his car ticking as it cooled and the soft rustle of an old plastic bag entangled on a bush. It felt surreal, as though he was the only person left on the planet.

Jack walked over and wrestled the faded plastic bag, its branding bleached by the sun, away from the thorny bush and deposited it in a large open refuse basket behind the table.

Hundreds of flies rose from its depth, buzzing angrily at the disturbance, then descended back amongst the leftovers from other drivers who had passed the same way.

After a while he began to feel uneasy with the silence. Climbing back into the unforgiving heat of the car he turned back onto the highway, increased the volume of his music, always classical, pulled his seat into a more upright position, and drove on, looking forward to seeing some signs of life.

After slowly navigating unnervingly steep escarpments he was astonished at how the landscape changed as he entered the Western Cape.

The province was lush and green, like being in another country. Vineyards stretched for miles around surrounded by majestic mountains shimmering in the heat, and there was Table Mountain its mighty outline blue-black in the distance, brooding over the city in all its majesty, unchanged for thousands of years. His destination was Cape Town; he would spend a couple of days there.

He knew it well from the many visits he had made over the past three years and the few short months when he had lived there. Then he'd make his way back to Mpumalanga and his home in Hazyview.

Before reaching Cape Town, he turned left off the highway and headed for the quaint town of Arniston which he had heard so much about. As he approached the fishing village the strong wind blew a dusting of blond sand across the road, and he could smell the sea.

He spent two days there, staying in a modest guest house which, he was told, used to belong to an old fisherman but had been converted. The village was famous for its lime-washed simple fisherman's cottages, blinding in the hot midday sun, with their thatched roofs. A backdrop of craggy cliffs, rolling sand dunes and the intense blue of the sea lent itself to long walks, which Jack indulged in.

On one of his long walks, he spotted a lone fisherman, the stillness of him, as the sun began its descent into the sea, smearing the surface with red and gold. He paused to watch him standing on a rock with his simple line dipping in the sea.

Jack had lifted his hand in greeting and walked towards the old man whose face was creased and dark from the hours he spent in the sun and with most of his teeth missing, his skin lined like an old walnut. He told Jack his family had been fishing and living here for over fifty years. He had never ventured out of his village and had a serenity about him which Jack envied.

No doubt, he thought to himself, the simple fisherman had no time for Facebook or the internet, or anything else which wasn't connected to his simple daily routine of catching fish and looking out over the cliffs, the sand dunes and the mesmerizing sea which gave him all he needed or wanted. The end of the day would bring the fresh food to his table to feed his family.

After spending an hour with the friendly fisherman who seemed to have all the time in the world for a chat, Jack returned to his guest house having booked a table for one at a local restaurant who specialised in fresh fish straight from the sea that morning.

He was well satisfied with his journey; it had opened many windows for him as to the diversity of this enormous country and the people who inhabited it. He was fully aware of the poverty, lack of educational facilities, homelessness, high unemployment, and crime.

He had seen the squatter camps, the homes made of iron sheets and cardboard, skinny dogs with their heads down, tails between their legs, searching for scraps of food, the washing hanging on bushes, the plastic bags and other rubbish strewn everywhere. They were tight communities there, riddled with menace and crime from desperate forgotten people.

Often, when he had lived in Cape Town, he had stopped for a red light and seen the desperate 'poor whites' as they were called, holding up pieces of cardboard begging for money, for food, for a job, for anything to relieve their impoverished lives. There was no place in the new South Africa for people who had little or no education.

The changes had been swift and brutal, and they soon began to realise there was no place for them anymore.

Oddly enough, he had never seen white people in Kenya desperately standing at traffic lights begging for money on the couple of trips he had made there.

Here in South Africa, he always kept a plastic bank bag in the cup holder of his car full of Rand notes, he found it impossible to drag his eyes from the desperation in theirs. He felt guilty even sitting in his comfortable air-conditioned car with places to go, restaurants of his choice to eat at and a decent roof over his head. It wasn't much but he hoped a few bank notes would at least assuage the hunger and provide a little temporary help for these people. Even so he felt uncomfortable as the lights turned to green and he drove off.

These people, these poor whites, didn't slump and call out with their hands outstretched, begging for money; they didn't tap on car windows – no, they stood tall and proud as they held their pieces of cardboard in front of them with as much dignity as they could possibly muster on an empty stomach and an empty future.

The people who had everything money could buy and the people who had very little. He wondered which end of the spectrum were the happiest, and their levels of hope for the future.

As was often the case, white South Africans with money and power chose to live in their own bubble of whiteness. They had their generators and solar panels, which they could well afford. Life was not so disruptive. Within that bubble, social standards were set. Through them you were invited to dinner, bridge, tennis, and sundowner parties. Day trips on luxury yachts and weekends at luxury game lodges. The country had changed of course, but it was still, to his mind, the laager mentality, with a token nod to the new elite and powerful African players who had, legally or otherwise, earned their place in the social pecking order.

Then there was the expatriate community. Some had chosen to stay; some were here on contracts. The expat was a 'tribe' unto itself. They lived an elevated lifestyle here. Glorious inexpensive Cape wines, relatively inexpensive food, compared to where they came from. Large houses in expensive suburbs, swimming pools, big cars, house staff, and a glorious climate with long summer days. A far cry from back home. They were non-political as, after all, it wasn't their country. If things didn't work out, they could always go home.

The problems of the country, the corruption, and the crime, of which they were all too aware of, and took note of, made them meticulous with their security. As for the ever-increasing power cuts well, 'just a spot of bother, old chap. The generator will kick in any minute now. Anyone for another gin and tonic?'

The rainbow nation was in full swing with or without those expatriates, who took much from the lifestyle of the country but gave little back.

Chapter Eight

Jack drove along the dirt road leading to his cottage just outside of Hazyview and close to the Kruger National Park. His windscreen was splattered with the white smeared debris and blood of dead insects, the sides of the car spattered with dried mud and dust from the final leg of his journey.

Home had never looked so good.

He parked his car under the jacaranda tree, then gratefully got out and stretched his aching back. The silence after the steady thrum of his tyres, the sound of the engine and all the traffic noise was like balm to his battered senses.

It had been a long journey. He retrieved his bags from the boot of the car and made his weary way to the front door of his cottage. He could hear the gurgle of the stream at the bottom of his garden. The right-hand wall was covered by a riotous tumbling of blood red bougainvillea.

Near the stream a frangipani tree was in full bloom, its delicate white flowers flushed with yellow inside, its heady perfume lingering in the air.

The interior of his cottage was cool, the thick stone walls keeping out the heat. But, even so, Jack turned on the air-conditioning and switched on the fan which slowly gathered speed, curling the corners of books and magazines as it dispersed the torpid air.

The room was spotlessly clean, no thanks to him. Winnie, his Zulu cleaning lady, came in once a week and cleaned up after him, hissing and muttering at his untidy ways but always with a cheerful smile. She called him Mr Yak, as so many others did here, unable to pronounce his name correctly.

He was used to it now.

Every two weeks the garden service came and kept the garden under control, cutting back the foliage and debris of fallen branches from the stream at the bottom of the garden.

It was a simple cottage, but well-furnished and open plan. The patio was his favourite spot. Two large oak trees bent over the tin roof shading the outside furniture, the tin roof creaked as it expanded and contracted under the heat of the day and the cool of the approaching evening. A blush of apricot clouds threw brief shadows across the brittle dry grass.

He threw his bags on his bed, hauled an ice-cold beer out of the fridge, kicked his shoes off and tip-toed over the red-hot tiles of the patio. The lawn looked as though it needed water. He turned on the hosepipe, retrieved his beer and took a long swallow then flopped into the plump cushions of a white wicker chair stretching out his long legs with a sigh of satisfaction. He rolled the cold can around the back of his neck and then down his throat, feeling the iciness of it against his over-heated skin and the roof of his mouth.

The sprinkler puffed and clicked softly as it sprayed arcs of water over the parched garden, the sound was soporific. He lifted his swollen feet and perched them on the wooden railing and sighed with relief, waving a listless fly away from his face.

It had been an excellent trip and given him plenty to think and write about. He would get stuck into that tomorrow, but right now he was going to relax and watch the squirrels scampering across the lawn tails puffed up like parasols sheltering their bodies from the sun.

His phone rumbled and he glanced at the screen – Harry.

He sighed regretting the intrusion. "Hello Harry! I've just got back to Hazyview. Fascinating trip, some good stuff for the newspaper. Feeling a bit knackered to be honest. What's up?"

Harry grunted. "Sitting in the bloody dark and its only four o'clock. I hate February. Bitter out there."

Jack grinned. "Lovely here. Just having an ice-cold beer looking at the sun going down over the bush, knowing it will be up and blazing merrily tomorrow morning!"

"You are a cruel and insensitive man, Jack. Anyway, old chap, something has come up. Something quite interesting."

He told him about the letter which had been couriered to him by the solicitor James Barrington-Smith.

"It seems his deceased client, a Mrs Zelda Cameron, wants you to find some chap. There's a letter addressed to you, which I had a hard time not opening. I had it couriered to the Inn, no point in sending it to Jack Taylor, 'somewhere in the bloody bush where the sun always seems to be bloody shining," he said, a note of sarcasm in his voice.

"Hugo will pass it on to you, okay? I want to know what the lawyer wants and what he wants you to do. I need another story Jack, so get on with it will you? Also, the deadline for your weekly column is coming up. Looking forward to a good one after your wanderings. Must dash, train to catch. Cheerio."

Jack took another sip of his beer. No way was he going to get into his mud-spattered dusty car and drive into Hazyview to collect his couriered letter. He had had enough of driving – it could wait until tomorrow.

He called his mate Piet Joubert. Piet picked up on the first ring.

"Hey, Jack, where are you? Still pounding along our magnificent roads looking for old aunties and *okes* who want to complain about power cuts and the state of our corrupt government, hey?"

Jack smiled into the phone. "Nope. I'm at home. Christ, it's a huge country. I sometimes forget the sheer size of it! It was a fascinating trip. I have loads to write about which will keep Harry twanging his navy-blue braces with glee."

Piet sounded hopeful. "Come across any interesting stories we can get stuck into - any we can get our teeth into? Bodies buried in shallow graves, missing wives, or children? Deserted ghostly farms where the inhabitants have mysteriously disappeared from? Maybe you were hijacked or robbed?"

He sighed. "Guess not, hey. Well here, my friend, most of the tourists are packing up and heading for home. It would be good to have something else to chase instead of moaning tourists who complain about not seeing the big five within ten minutes of their first game drive.

"*Jeez*, Jack some people have no patience, especially the *bleddy* Brits and Germans. Always complaining about something. *Shoo*, I love my job, man, but why come on safari if you're scared of anything that moves? Spiders, geckos, anything with hairy legs or great big flapping ears?

"One German guest phoned reception to say there was a crocodile in her room. Went to calm her down, checked out the room, you never really know what might have sneaked in from the Kruger looking for a quick swim in the hotel pool. Told her I had looked everywhere and there was no crocodile anywhere. Then she pointed to the wall and there was a gecko, minding his own business just looking for some mozzies to eat for his dinner. *Ag*, I suppose if you didn't know it probably did look like a miniature croc…glad she didn't spot that big bugger of a rain spider trying to hide behind the curtain! *Jeez*, Jack, I'm thinking it was more fun looking at dead bodies than dealing with hysterical guests. At least dead bodies don't whine and moan all the time."

He sighed loudly. "So, my friend, let's meet up for a beer later, you can tell me all about your trip? Don't go writing rubbish stuff about my country you hear me, Jack?"

Jack stifled his laughter. "Okay. I wasn't planning on doing any more driving today. But as it's you wanting to buy me a beer, I'll see you later."

He went to the fridge and pulled out another beer. He was looking forward to meeting up with his mate. Ex-Detective Inspector Piet Joubert didn't have what you would call a sunny disposition. He had been side swiped when the new government had come into power and took early retirement before moving into private practice.

Jack had met the grumpy detective in the small dusty town of Willow Vale in the Eastern Cape when he had been following a cold case involving a missing child. Although antagonistic at first towards the British journalist, then based in London, Piet had been intrigued because that case was one of the very few Piet had been unable to solve twenty years previously.

They had formed an unlikely alliance as they worked together, the Englishman and the Afrikaner, but the case had been solved. Piet had been offered a job as Head of Security for the hotel they had stayed in and accepted it, along with a good salary, a pension, medical aid, and a neat furnished cottage set a little away from the main guest cottages.

Since then, they had worked on other cases together. Despite this Jack knew little about Piet, apart from his years working for the South African Police. Piet never talked about his family, or his childhood and Jack had never intruded on this. If Piet wanted to disclose that part of his life he would, in his own good time. He had been married, this Jack knew, but it had ended in divorce, and he had no children, only the worst tempered and possibly the ugliest cat Jack had ever encountered.

Piet had the pure rich blood of an Afrikaner running through his veins and never let Jack forget it. Taking a swipe at the Brits at every opportunity and muttering about the Boer war. He was one of the best detectives Jack had ever worked with, with excellent contacts throughout the country, mostly in the police force, past and present, or with policemen who had retired and gone into private practice either as private investigators or working for security companies who were popping up all over the country as the crime rate soared. Piet's contacts were a constant in the ever-changing political arena and a sea of change. He used them ruthlessly when necessary.

Jack had decided he didn't want to live in a city again and beautiful though the Mother City was he had chosen to live in Franschhoek, an hour from Cape Town, in the valley of the vines. Although he had loved the French feel of the town, he found the summers brutally hot and full of tourists from all over the world. In the winter, when the last tourist left town, the place was practically deserted.

He had been to Hazyview on a couple of occasions before he decided to make it his home. He liked the bustle of the town, the never-ending international visitors from all over the world who had come to stay at the luxurious private game reserves and others who chose the Kruger National Park for their safaris. Whatever their choice the game was prolific. The bush laid out before them in all its staggering, unpredictable, beauty.

The town was a portal to all the abundant wildlife. The shops reflected the tone of the town with its boutiques selling all things safari, hats, belts, boots, shorts and shirts. There were boutique galleries featuring wildlife art, carvings of wild animals and African inspired jewellery, tour operating companies, travel agents, restaurants, bars, book shops, game rangers picking up and dropping off tourists from their guest houses and hotels – yup! The town had a unique buzz all of its own and Jack loved it. London was becoming a distant memory.

He had been invited to parties and braais, in Hazyview, and he'd dated the occasional girl in town but nothing long term – he had been down that road twice before and firmly decided life without a relationship was far less complicated and allowed him to do what he loved best – chase stories. Chasing women was far more complicated.

Now the air was cooling, he wriggled his tired feet as he watched the blood red sun disappear behind an acacia tree in the distance, the sky shot with red, pink, and gold.

On the opposite side of the stream a dik-dik, a tiny antelope, made its delicate way down to the water to drink. It paused and looked around, its tail flickering like a faulty light bulb, the sinking sun dappling on its dark burnished coat, as it bent its head to drink.

The leaves of the old oak trees feathered above Jack's head as the twilight descended around him, the only other sound was the orchestra of the night tuning up, the screeching, hooting, chirping, and rustling of night birds and insects. The frogs down at the stream would soon follow.

In the distance the hills with their craggy outcrops of rocks were bathed with a blush of apricot pink.

Jack stood up and stretched his aching back. Time to meet up with Piet. He would grab something to eat at The Inn.

Chapter Nine

Jack pulled into the car park of The Inn. There were plenty of other cars already there and as he closed the door a roar went up from the crowd inside. He doubted the roar was in honour of his arrival — there must be a big rugby match on.

He looked up, a brief shadow blocked out what was left of the sun. The sky was suddenly filled with bulging bloated purple clouds. A storm was coming. He hoped it wouldn't cause a power cut. Eskom was more than capable of doing that without inclement weather.

The one thing he knew was the interruption of power during a big rugby match, when the Springboks were playing, could drive even the most docile fan into a frenzy of incandescent fury. But Hugo, knowing his customers, had installed a big generator.

Jack pushed through the noisy crowd and made his way to the bar. Perching on a stool he tried to catch the eye of Hugo, the owner. Hugo was wearing one of his bright flowery shirts and a pair of frayed shorts, his feet were, as always, bare. He had his usual cheerful grin on his tanned face.

Pushing past the other busy barmen he made his way to Jack lifting his arm in greeting and brandishing an envelope.

"Hey Jack. Good to see you again! This came by courier for you – I signed for it - hope that was alright? I forged your signature. Let me grab you a beer and some snacks. Be right back."

The Springboks scored another goal, and a deafening roar went up from the crowd watching the big screen in the corner of the bar. He felt something nudge his thigh and looked down into the big brown eyes of a young Labrador.

Jack reached down and stroked the dog's head. "Hello Hope. How did you find me amongst all these people? How are you?"

Hope's golden tail swung back and forth with a rhythm all its own. Jack reached for a strip of biltong on the bar top and offered it to her.

Hope didn't blink as she swallowed it then looked soulfully at him shifting her eyes towards the dish of biltong, hoping more would come her way. It didn't.

With a reproachful look at Jack, Hope threaded her way through the legs of the crowd watching the game. When the Boks scored again, a roar went up, Hope joined in with a long howl. The guys loved this furry fan and rewarded her with whatever snack they had to hand. Anything would do as far as Hope was concerned. She loved her food whatever form it came in.

Hope was Piet's dog and was supposed to be an extension of his security detail. But the friendly dog, with a smile like a dolphin, preferred to keep her eyes on the people in the bar and on the guests who sat outside their rooms enjoying sundowners and snacks – especially if there was biltong around. Everyone loved her. Piet had given up trying to discipline her. Jack had read somewhere that in time, dog and owner started to look like each other, but he had a hard time believing it.

Piet certainly did not have a beguiling face or a smile like a dolphin – quite the opposite in fact. Maybe in time he would lighten up a bit, but he doubted it. Piet was Piet, grumpy or otherwise, but he had a fine mind, honed by years of experience as a detective, watching and reading other people. They were a good team when they worked together on various cases.

As part of the security team at the hotel, Hope was sadly lacking in skills; she loved everyone and didn't have a mean bone in her body to chase dodgy looking people should any of them be staying at the hotel. But her public relations credentials were without question. Guests loved to see her walking around with the Chief of Security, ex-police detective Joubert.

Jack felt the hearty thump on his back and steadied his glass of beer. Piet pumped his hand and gave him a big smile, not quite dolphin like, but close.

"Good to see you, my friend. Nice to have you back."

Piet leaned on the bar next to him, he took off his battered cap and placed it on the counter. His dark green uniform uncreased despite the heat outside, the epaulettes on both shoulders glinting in the fading shafts of sunlight coming through the windows of the bar. He was solidly built with not an ounce of fat on his muscular body. His cropped dark hair tinged with grey at his temples, his dark blue eyes fringed with thick eyelashes any woman would kill for. He glanced around the crowded room his eyes skimming the crowd, missing nothing.

"Hey Piet. That was one hell of a drive, I have to say. Gave me a different perspective on the whole country – it's massive! Sometimes I didn't see another vehicle for a couple of hours. But it's good to be back. I'll have plenty of stories to give Harry for the newspaper. That should keep him happy."

Piet glanced at the slim DHL envelope propped up on Jack's half empty bottle of beer. "What's this then? Someone knows your favourite hangout, hey?"

Jack reached for the envelope. "It's from Harry. Some solicitors in London had it delivered to him personally. I haven't had a chance to open it yet. I've just got here. Harry said a solicitor wants me to find some bloke. Let's have a look."

Jack tore off the opening and found the envelope inside addressed to him, he ran his thumb along the flap and pulled out another envelope and looked at it incredulously.

"Well, well, it seems I won't have to look far. It's for you?"

Piet lifted his eyebrows in surprise. "For me? Why would some English solicitor be looking for me?" He looked slyly at Jack. "Not as though I have a lot of British friends... just you, and only because you found me in Willow Vale and needed a bit of help with your investigation…with that case you couldn't solve on your own."

Jack handed it to him, ignoring the jibe. "Dunno. Look and find out. Perhaps some nice British person has left you a ton of money? A relative maybe?"

Piet scowled at him. "Don't talk *kak*, man. No-one ever left me anything only my ex-wife, she left me her bad-tempered *bleddy* cat, waste of time that cat, ugly as all hell, spent all its days spitting and hissing at me and leaving fur everywhere. *Nah*, don't know any Brit who would leave me any money. None of my relatives would be mad enough to go and live over there when they could stay here, now would they? Anyways, I don't have any relatives. Only my sister who inherited the folks farm up in the Eastern Cape."

He paused looking at the envelope. "Well, whoever sent it to me is not aware of my elevated status to Chief Security Office at this here hotel. It's addressed to Detective Inspector Joubert…"

Jack had his eyes on the envelope Piet was holding. "Maybe it was someone from here who went to live in the UK. Come on open it and see."

Piet tore open the envelope and pulled out a single sheet of handwritten notepaper.

'Dear Inspector Joubert,
I instructed my solicitor, Mr James Barrington-Smith, to contact you two years after my death. There was a reason for this time frame which will become clear to you in due course should you decide to help me.
What I am asking you to do is complicated. It is a story that goes back many years. I did something which, with hindsight, was wrong. If I had chosen a different path… But it is too late now to change anything. But not too late to try and find out what really happened, hence this letter to you. The British police came up with nothing. But to be fair, thousands of people go missing here in the UK every year. Some turn up. Some are never found.
My solicitor has been instructed to give you, personally, and no-one else, the key to my safe deposit box in London. Inside you will find something which I hope will interest you enough to pursue what is now called a cold case?
I have enjoyed Jack Taylor's stories in the Telegraph, I have been an avid reader of this newspaper for many years. I know you have worked with him on several cold cases. I didn't know where to find you, but I knew Jack would.
You must come to England to obtain the key to my safe deposit box. My solicitor has been instructed to pay for both yours and Mr Taylor's plane tickets and any other expenses which you may incur. I have put his address and phone number at the bottom of this letter.
For a mother to lose her child is the cruellest cut of all. Are you still a mother when your only child dies? In some circumstances acceptance of that loss does come, but only in time. The hardest thing of all, for any parent, is not knowing what happened – where is their child now?
An unanswered question which will haunt them for the rest of their lives. Just one of the many children who disappeared off the face of the earth. But it is true that somewhere someone has the answers…someone knows what happened.
People don't know how to deal with grief – that's why death is so shocking. It's an emotion we were never told about. Something we were never taught how to handle. Each person handles it in a different way not knowing when the terrible loss will abate or how long it will take.
Yours sincerely,
Zelda Cameron.

Piet, wordlessly, handed the letter to Jack who read it quickly, already feeling the familiar fizz of excitement snaking down his spine.

He looked up. "So, what do you think Piet – fancy a trip to the UK? You've never been there, have you?"

Piet frowned at him. "Never been out of the country, so, no, I haven't been to the UK, nor do I plan to go there no matter what this Zelda person has to say in her letter."

Jack grinned at him. "But you do have a passport, have you not?"

Piet nodded. "Look Jack, this Zelda person, she might be talking rubbish. She might have been a bit gaga when she wrote this," he flicked the letter disdainfully with his finger. "It's madness to rush over to your country just on one letter, written two years ago, promising nothing but a few jumbled words about someone who is missing. *Nah*, not going, my friend. I need more than this," he flicked the letter again, "before I even think about getting on a plane and flying for twelve or so hours to a country, I have no desire to visit. Notwithstanding the *bleddy* awful climate and a bunch of people who talk about the weather all the time. *Nah*, not for me. Never felt warm and fuzzy towards the Brits, as you know…"

Jack grinned. "Come on Piet. I know you're intrigued. This Zelda took some time and trouble to track you down. It's an all-expenses paid trip – what's not to like? Ah, yes, of course, you don't like flying do you…oh well, like you say, I guess it's not worth following up. You'll have to let the solicitor know yourself as the letter is addressed to you."

Piet scowled at him. "It'll be a waste of time, I'm telling you. We need more than this to get me interested, you understand what I'm saying? Anyways, I like it here. I like the open spaces, the animals, the weather and the people, our own food. I'm too busy now. There are still plenty of tourists in the hotel. Need to keep my eyes on everything." His voice trailed off.

Jack looked at him innocently. "Hey, listen. We have open spaces in the countryside in the UK. Okay the weather can be somewhat erratic, but the people are nice and friendly. We have wild animals same as you have here."

Piet leaned forward. "Listen to me, my friend," he hissed. "I hate zoos and circuses. Hate to see wild animals kept in cages. As for a circus? They should be shut down, banned. *Jeez*, Jack, in the wild elephants don't walk on their hind legs. They don't dance around to music, holding each other's tails wearing pink frilly skirts and stupid hats on their heads – it's a *bleddy* disgrace, it's humiliating and degrading for such a magnificent beast."

He snatched at a piece of biltong on the bar. "Elephants should be in the bush, plodding around with their families, covered by dust, treading the ancient traditional paths elephants have travelled for hundreds of years. They should never be in an enclosed cement cage with a chain around their leg," he said angrily.

Jack held up both of his hands. "Whoa. Okay Piet, wild animals, or not so wild animals are out then. Forget I even mentioned it. I think this letter is worth following up. Could be quite a story behind it. This Zelda person needs your help. No doubt she had the means to employ a private investigation company, but no, she specifically wants you and it makes me wonder why?"

Piet read the letter again. "Let me think about it, my friend, but don't get your hopes up, hey."

Piet grabbed his old baseball cap off the bar counter, rammed it on his head and strode out of the room, Hope following closely behind. He left the letter on the bar.

Jack watched him leave. It was the flying bit Piet didn't like. But he had seen the glimmer in his eyes when he had read the letter addressed to him. Oh yes, Piet was interested all right. He just needed a little more persuading…a little more enticement.

He cursed himself for bringing up the subject of wild animals. Piet could be difficult, this was true, but Jack hadn't expected to hear how passionate he was about the subject of zoos and circuses. Wild animals wandered freely in the Kruger National Park, almost on Piet's doorstep so to speak. He agreed with Piet, zoos and circuses should be banned outright in every country.

The rugby match was over, and the bar had gone quiet. The All Blacks had won. After all the pumped-up adrenaline during the rugby match the figures at the bar looked somewhat deflated as they discussed the result and held a post-mortem on the game. Blaming the Irish referee for everything which had resulted in the Springboks not winning the match. The Springboks had thrashed the All Blacks on many occasions over the years, but this wasn't one of them.

Jack finished his beer, scooped up the letter and made his way home. He would grab something to eat from the freezer and microwave his dinner. He was tired.

He sat out on his patio and thought about the letter from Zelda Cameron as he watched the storm building up in front of him.

The storm choreographed its own dance. The crescendo of thunder, lightning, and rain building to an almighty climax, the sheets of rain its final curtain call. Mother Nature, the *prima donna* of the show, performing throughout the valleys, mountains, rivers, and deserts of Africa. Her four-legged audience, silent and watchful as they sought shelter beneath the trees and bush.

The animals, although used to the fury of storms, would wait to hunt and kill. They submitted meekly. Waiting for the storm to blow itself out in its own time and at its own pace.

Jack read the letter again, feeling the chill in the air from the now passing storm, leaving only the soft patter of rain on his tin roof.

Zelda Cameron's request to collect whatever it was from her safe deposit box seemed simple enough. The problem was it had to be Piet who accessed it.

Somehow, he had to persuade Piet to make the trip to the UK. A place he had never had any inclination to visit.

Even the tantalising contents of the letter weren't enough to overcome that.

Chapter Ten

Jack spent most of the next morning writing up his notes on his trip before breaking for something to eat.
He scraped the last of his microwaved meal from his plate and took it through to the kitchen. He checked his watch. The UK was two hours behind South Africa at this time of the year. Which made it four in the afternoon there.

He sat down outside and pulled the solicitors letter from his pocket; he dialled the number in London.

"James Barrington-Smith and Associates," a bored female voice drawled.

"Good afternoon to you. I'm calling from South Africa, my name's Jack Taylor. I'd like to speak to Mr Barrington-Smith if I may?"

"Please hold, Mr Taylor. I'll see if he can take your call."

Within seconds Jack was put through. "Ah, Mr Taylor. It's good to hear from you. May I ask if you managed to trace the man my client was looking for?"

"Indeed, I have. He is a retired Detective Inspector, he used to be with the police here. Name's Joubert. I gave him the letter. He's a little reluctant to make the journey to the UK now. He's head of security at a hotel, so a busy man at this time of the year. It's high holiday season here in South Africa. But I'm available to come over. Perhaps if I obtained Power of Attorney from Mr Joubert that would suffice?"

There was a slight pause. "This does present some difficulty, Mr Taylor. You see my instructions are to hand the keys to the safe deposit box to this Mr Joe Bear and no one else. He has an unusual name, does he not?"

Jack stifled his laughter. "Actually, Mr Barrington-Smith his name is pronounced *Joubert*, *Piet Joubert*."

Barrington-Smith sounded a little flustered at getting the name wrong. "My apologies, Mr Taylor. Yes, Mr Joubert is the only one I can hand over the key to," he paused, "when do you think he would be able to travel?"

Jack thought the answer would probably be never. "Mr Barrington-Smith perhaps you could give me a little more information about Mrs Cameron. It's a lot to ask for both of us to fly over there on the strength of a rather cryptic two-year-old letter. We both have full-time jobs, I'm sure you understand.

"Does it have anything to do with how she died perhaps? How old was she? Can you tell me that? Clearly, she had a husband at some point. Where is he now? Can you tell me anything further so we can perhaps make an informed decision based on some credible facts?"

"Mrs Cameron was in her seventies and her husband died some years ago. I'm afraid I have no other information I can give you over the telephone, Mr Taylor. Mrs Cameron didn't disclose the contents of her letter or what is in the safe deposit box. I do know it is a briefcase but the contents within I cannot speculate on."

James Barrington-Smith sighed, sounding irritated. "I am anxious to close this final chapter of Mrs Cameron's life. I was instructed simply to arrange two first class tickets and meet all your expenses here in London."

Jack grinned to himself. If one had to fly seven thousand miles there was no better place to be than up front on the aircraft. Plus a few days in a first-class hotel might go a bit of a way to persuade Piet to make up his mind.

Jack cleared his throat. "Very well, Mr Barrington-Smith, leave it with me. I'll have another chat with Mr Joubert and see if he can free up a few days to fly to London."

"I would very much appreciate that Mr Taylor. Good afternoon."

Jack looked down at his dead phone. Not the friendliest of people, typical public-school boy. Jack took a sip of his coffee. He rather fancied a trip to London. He could introduce Piet to Harry, who he had never met. They could spend a weekend with his parents in the country. Get the key to the safe deposit box and see what secrets the briefcase held. Must be important if Mrs Cameron had been prepared for two first class tickets and all other expenses paid? That was a big investment.

Mrs Cameron was prepared to pay a high price for Piet to collect the briefcase and find out what it contained. Jack's gut instinct was this might lead to a rather intriguing story.

Firstly, Piet didn't like flying and secondly, he had, so far, had nothing good to say about the UK or the people who lived there, as for the weather? Well, Jack thought to himself, this time of the year, the end of February, could be a little unpredictable. But there might be a few sunny days. What better person than himself to show Piet a little of his old country. Introduce him to the delights of the English way of life.

He would give Piet a couple of days to think things over; nothing the man liked better than a possible new case to follow, a good story to sniff out. Despite what Piet had said he would be intrigued why some woman in the UK would seek him out, know his name and want him to travel to the UK and retrieve a briefcase from a safe deposit box.

Chapter Eleven

Jack was sitting at the quiet bar in the middle of town. He had spent the day writing his columns for the newspaper. Now he sat, rolling his beer mat back and forth across the bar counter as he tried to work out the best way to persuade Piet to take the all-expenses paid trip to London with him.

There was no point in going on his own as Zelda Cameron's letter had been extremely specific. The keys to her deposit box would only be handed to Piet Joubert in person and for this he would have to provide identification.

Jack had noticed the man sitting a couple of bar stools down from him. He was probably in his mid-fifties, maybe a bit older, wearing khaki shorts, safari boots and an expensive looking pale cream shirt. He seemed deep in thought and hadn't looked up when Jack took his place at the bar.

The barman had taken advantage of having only two customers to deal with and was quietly polishing the glasses and tidying up the row of bottles and wiping down the mirror behind the counter. A wide-screen television was on, but muted.

The man took a sip of his beer and then bent his head into his hands. Jack watched him in the mirror. The man was clearly upset about something.

Jack turned on his stool. "Hey, are you okay?"

The man dragged his hands down his face and looked at Jack with a tenuous smile. "No, not really. But thanks for asking. Just a lot to think about now."

Jack gave him a hesitant smile. "Look, my name's Jack. How about joining me for a drink. I'm a good listener. It helps to talk to a stranger sometimes?"

The man hesitated for a moment, then held out his hand. "Graham." He shifted up a few bar stools and sat next to Jack.

"Are you from around here Graham?"

"No, I live in Cape Town. Born and brought up there. I've just had a couple of days in the Kalahari and the Kruger before heading back. Came to say goodbye," he said softly, almost to himself. "My parents used to bring my sister, brother, and I here in the school holidays. It's always held a big piece of my heart."

He took a sip of his drink. "Where else in the world am I going to see what I've just seen? I was driving slowly along in the Kalahari when out of the bush a huge herd of springbok arrived from no-where. The whole sky seemed to be a teeming tawny yellow. They were leaping and bounding, ears up, tails up, following their leader and when they saw my vehicle they flew – literally flew. Flying in arcs, forefeet up hind legs streamlined, golden wide-eyed creatures with white bellies and fluffy tails and exquisite horns, the earth thundering from hooves. There seemed to be dozens of them. Then the last one flew across the road and disappeared. Took my breath away."

He wiped his sleeve across his eyes. "Almost like they were saying goodbye to me as they flew away…"

Jack smiled at him. "Goodbye? No plans for another safari then?"

Graham stared into his glass of beer. "No. We're leaving the country. I've sold my house. My wife doesn't want to live here anymore wants to go home to the UK. She's English with a British passport, so not difficult for me to get residence there. It's where you're from isn't it, Jack. I recognise your accent."

Jack nodded. "Yes. But I live here now. Been here for a couple of years. Best move I ever made. Love it here."

Graham sighed heavily. "I don't want to leave. This is my home. I'm fifty-five, it won't be easy to start a new life in a new country and leave everything that's familiar behind.

"The hardest thing will be to leave my family. My elderly parents, my brother and sister, my cousins and aunts, my buddies, most of them I've known since my school days. It's a big move."

Jack shook his head in sympathy. "Not easy I know. I did it myself, coming to live here. But I don't have a wife and kids, just my folks. But, hey Graham, it won't be so hard to keep in touch with family and friends, not with all the technology these days. I'm in touch with my buddies all the time. The UK isn't so far away, just a twelve-hour flight and you can be back here in a flash."

Graham was quiet for a few seconds. "That might be so. But I don't want to leave my country. I don't want to leave my people. I like the wide-open spaces, the bush, and the animals. I love sitting out on my stoep, with a glass of ice-cold wine, watching the sun go down, watching the stars at night. Cape Town is beautiful; I've loved the place all my life. I've watched it grow over the years."

Jack nodded and let him continue.

"Yes, the political face of the country has changed. There's a lot of things wrong with this place as I'm sure you know, Jack. The years before the new president was elected were long and bloody. Terrible things happened, tribe fighting tribe, riots, the usual stuff…the crime here now, the destruction of the infrastructure here. The criminals raping companies like Eskom, Transnet, SAA, leaving them to die a slow and heart-breaking death. But one thing the politicians and criminals can't take away is the enduring beauty of the mountains, the valleys, rivers, the sea and the sunsets…they'll remain the same for all time, as they have always done. Can't be bought and sold by anyone." His voice trailed off heavy with despair and regret.

Jack swiftly changed the subject. "So, what line of work were you in?"

"Investment banking. I made a ton of money. Had a lovely house in Constantia, full of art and antiques, a huge wine cellar, gorgeous garden, latest model Mercedes in the drive – all gone now. Times got tough in the markets; South Africa had always been at the mercy of hard currencies worldwide. Then came the financial crisis and the company closed."

He took another sip of his beer. "I had to sell the house," his voice faltered. "We rented a cottage outside of Cape Town, but it didn't work out. I have two daughters in their teens now. My wife worries about their safety and their future. She said she was leaving the country whether I liked it or not. So, what choice do I have? Lose my wife and daughters, or go with them to the UK? At least there the lights stay on all the time, unlike here…bloody Eskom."

He pushed his glass to one side and signalled for his bill. "No doubt I shall be able to get a job stacking shelves in a supermarket. We can't afford to buy there, not with the exchange rate, but no doubt we'll find something to rent. Probably some area like Wimbledon, lots of fellow South Africans live there."

He held out his hand. "Nice to meet you, Jack. Good luck in South Africa – you'll need it. If things don't work out you can always go home, can't you?"   Jack shook his hand, seeing a brief flash of resentment in his eyes at someone who had more choices than he would ever have.

"Remember this, Graham. The lights may be on in the house in another country. But it doesn't mean anyone's home.

"Moving memories and familiar possessions into a new place, making it look just like home, is one thing, but when you turn and look out of the window it will be unfamiliar.

"Keep in mind you can always come back to Africa, too. It'll be here, waiting for you."

Jack watched him pocket his change and make his unsteady way out of the bar.

Jack tapped his beer mat on the bar counter thinking about Zelda Cameron's letter to Piet. Clearly, she had lost her child at some point.

The hardest thing of all, for any parent, is not knowing what happened – where is their child now?

Jack had been confronted with many cases of missing persons during his career. It was well-known if a missing person, especially a child or young adult, isn't located in the first forty-eight hours of being reported missing it is unlikely they will be found alive. Seven years later, under the legal system there, in the UK, that person would be missing presumed dead. But the case file was never closed.

Young people, he mused, were unpredictable, parents think they know their children – but they don't. Don't know what they're planning, what they're thinking, what their dreams might be. Who they have met and not told their parents about.

He took a sip of beer. Children, he knew, died all the time, and left unspeakable grief behind. A child with a terminal disease held a different resonance. It gave parents the time to adjust to the inevitable. Gave them time to prepare. No mother wanted to see her child suffering and in pain.

What exactly had happened to Zelda's child? And why wait two years before contacting Piet? Why Piet?

A missing child leaves a crippling legacy of life or death. It was the not knowing, the unanswered question which bite into the hearts of the ones left behind.

*****

Jack wasn't surprised to see Piet's car pull into his driveway. Judging by the expression on his face as he made his way towards him, Piet had a lot on his mind and Jack thought he might know what that was.

"Need a beer, Jack?"

"Sure. I have one cooling for you. I was expecting you. Where's Hope?"

Piet threw his battered cap down on the table and sat heavily in one of the chairs. "*Ag*, that dog, Jack. Seems to spend all her time in the bar these days, worse than you, hey! If she's not in there she's sniffing around the guests for a reward for all her patrolling around the grounds, which, I hasten to point out, she does little of, not the perimeters anyway. More like a *bleddy* door to door salesman."

He took a swallow of his beer and smacked his lips in appreciation. "Hot one today, hey? Must be over forty degrees."

Jack nodded as he wiped his forehead with his sleeve. "Okay, Piet, what have you decided then about the trip to the UK?"

Piet studied his safari boots for a long moment then looked at Jack. "See here, my friend, I joined the police because I wanted to make a difference. To put things right when they were wrong and help the community in any way I could. To catch the bad guys and shove them in the slammer. Police work became my whole life; helping people is what I did then. It's in my blood.

"This *auntie* in England needs help." He grinned at Jack. "Obviously, the British police are unable to offer this help, or don't know what to do with whatever the problem seems to be – that's why they need a South African to sort the whole thing out. How can I resist a challenge like that, hey? Show them where they are going wrong, or went wrong?"

Jack didn't respond and looked at him blandly. "Absolutely right, mate, my country needs you to solve whatever problem Zelda Cameron has, or rather had. I take it I can now book the flights then?"

"*Ja*, I've cleared it with Hugo, the hotel is quieter now. Shaka, my chief Zulu security guy, can easily handle anything that comes up – he'll just stick his spear through someone he doesn't like the look of – finish and *klaar.*"

"I'm assuming that means something along the lines of done and dusted?"

Piet tipped his bottle and drank thirstily. "Whatever. Anyways, Hope will be well looked after, she won't even miss me. I've fired her from the security detail, my reason being, as I explained to her, she isn't, and never has been, an asset to the team. She eats too much and doesn't attend to her duties. I think her career challenge might have been not security but rather public relations. Hugo will look after her whilst I'm away, so long. His regulars love her.

"So, Jack. I'll leave the travel arrangements to you. Too busy myself. Just let me know the details. Not looking forward to the flight, I have to say. But someone needs my help. It's what I do. You can tag along if you like."

Chapter Twelve

Jack tapped on the door of Piet's cottage, the door was ajar, and he heard Piet's muffled voice telling him to come in. He found him in the bedroom, clothes scattered on the bed, his scruffy safari bag open. Hope was curled up in her basket looking decidedly unhappy.

"Hey, Piet. Just checking you haven't changed your mind about our flight tomorrow?"

Piet stuffed some more clothes into his bag without looking up. "Nope. Not looking forward to being squeezed into a seat made for a kid, for twelve *bleddy* hours either. But we have a job to do, all expenses paid you said. Might be a bit of a case to crack, who knows."

He ran his hand down the back of his neck. "*Jeez*, not sure what to pack now. Don't have thick clothes for crap weather. My boots should be okay though."

Jack stifled a laugh. "Listen here, mate. You're going to need some warm jumpers and a good coat, plus those safari boots of yours might be able to cope with the bush but they sure as hell won't look too good after a few days of rain and puddles. Plus," Jack's eyes surveyed the clothes on the bed. You won't need your shorts, that I can promise you!"

Piet looked crestfallen. "Too bad, my friend, I don't have jumpers and I've never owned a warm coat. Waste of money in Africa. Not buying one for just one trip. Where the hell would I find one anyways? Its summer here, nothing in the shops to cope with freezing weather," he pointed at his boots and frowned. "What's wrong with these boots? They can surely cope with a bit of rain now and again. Works here."

Jack tried to look concerned. "Tell you what. I've got plenty of warm weather gear and a spare coat. Shoes won't fit you though. Let's go back to my place and I'll kit you out, and, um, you're going to need something slightly bigger and sturdier than that ancient safari bag.

"I can lend you a suitable suitcase. Oh, and don't even think about bringing your gun with you. The Brits are a bit funny about guns, unlike America…you must have all sorts of paperwork and permits, so the gun is a no go. Anyway, you won't need it. England is a peaceful place, you know, green and pleasant land and all that?"

Piet gave him a sour look. "Don't give me all that bullshit about green and *bleddy* pleasant lands, my friend. If it's so great, why did you come and live here, hey? Your country is as dangerous as this one only on a larger scale. We don't have terrorists blowing up teenagers at concerts, or blowing up trains, buses, and restaurants here, that's for sure. Don't expect me to get on a bus or an underground train, you hear me?"

"Come on Piet. You've had your fair share of bombs going off all over the country during the so-called troubles, during the transition and before. Okay, not on the scale perhaps as in other countries around the world, just sayin'."

"That was in the past, my friend, now we are known as the murder capital of the world, not sure how anyone worked that out."

"Exactly, you're going from the murder capital of the world to dear old Blighty, where terrorists are rare, and guns are rarer. What's to worry about?"

Piet gave him a look that didn't seem filled with confidence. "Come on, let's go and have a steak – doubt whether I'll get a decent one in your country…"

*****

Piet and Jack joined the queue of passengers waiting to board their flight. Piet was muttering and complaining about the crowd, the long queues at security, the removal of shoes, belts, the emptying of pockets, the security wand going where no wand should ever go and anything else he could think of. Jack knew it was all about trying to hide his nervousness about the long flight to London.

They boarded the plane and Jack handed their boarding pass to the smiling flight attendant who gestured to her right. Jack led the way into the first-class cabin and found their leather armchair seats.

He turned to Piet with a nonchalant look. "Window seat for you Piet? Or would you prefer the aisle?"

Piet was beaming with delight, an unusual countenance for him, at the spacious seats that looked like armchairs. Nothing like what he was used to on the few flights he had taken, in economy, where the seats were squashed together and uncomfortable and all on offer to eat was a tiny bag of peanuts and a fruit juice in a cardboard container with a straw stuck to the side.

They stowed their hand luggage in the overhead then spread themselves out as the flight attendant hovered, ready to see to their every need. Once they were settled, she brought glasses of champagne and a generous plate of canapes.

Jack lifted his glass. "Here's to a good trip then, Piet. I think you might enjoy this flight. You even get to sleep lying down with pillows and a duvet, have a proper dinner with knives and forks and a decent breakfast before we land."

Piet stretched his legs out and looked around contentedly. "Only thing to beat this, my friend, must be Concorde which, unfortunately, is no longer flying."

Jack pulled the in-flight magazine from the pouch in front of him. "Yeah, now that's one thing I wish I *had* experienced. I was in London when Concorde made its final flight. There were three of them, a sort of final fly past. A salute. Wow, what a sight it was and very emotional, I have to say. Concorde used to arrive at Heathrow from New York, every evening at six. You could hear it coming before you saw it, that throaty roar. Imagine three of them on a formation farewell. Fantastic aircraft. We won't see that sort of graceful design again, I can tell you."

Piet rummaged around in the seat pocket in front of him then tried out all the buttons in the arm rest. "Wasn't safe though was it, my friend, that's why they grounded the entire fleet. No-one in their right mind puts their life in the hands of one person.

"That's what I don't like about flying, see. I like to oversee my own life hey. At least I can see what the pilot is up to this end of the plane, see if he looks worried or anything."

Jack decided not to say anything about the fact that since 9/11 the cockpit was locked. Only the crew knew the password to get access before the flight.

The flight paused at the end of the runway before gathering speed and roaring off before lifting into the dark skies. Johannesburg glittered below them but only briefly. Jack wasn't sure if Eskom had turned the lights out or they had disappeared behind cloud cover.

He glanced briefly at Piet who clung to the armrests, his knuckles white, his old baseball cap pulled low over his tightly closed eyes. Jack smiled. Not everyone liked flying, it was true, but personally he loved it.

They reached their cruising altitude, and the planes interior lights sprang to life. Jack loosened his seat belt and pushed his seat back. "Hey, Piet, are you asleep or did the take-off frighten you to death? How about a drink? Calm you down a bit?"

Piet lifted his cap and looked around warily. "*Ag*, nothing to it really. Feel safer up front than down the back. I'll have a beer."

Piet loosened his safety belt and pressed the button in the armrest, his seat tilted silently back. He stretched his legs with a sigh then felt around in his pocket and pulled out Zelda's letter.

"Now, Jack, let's work out a plan of action here. I spoke to my old friend Bertie, to see if I could find anything about this *auntie* Zelda Cameron. But, of course, he needs a lot more information before he can start digging about in any database. We don't even know if she was a South African for a start." He paused as the flight attendant placed his beer in front of him and a plate of *hors d' oeuvres*, then handed him a menu with a gracious smile.

Bertie was one of Piet's personal contacts. He had worked with Home Affairs, the government department who monitored all entries and exits from South Africa and who had a database containing the identity number of every person who was a permanent resident or a citizen of the country, or a visitor. Personal and private information which was closely guarded and not available to the public.

Bertie had once been a part of the old government, but when it changed, he too was shunted to one side to make room for the less experienced Africans who were eager for jobs under the new regime.

However, the new government recognised his skills and computer expertise, and he was employed by them on a private basis which meant, as far as Bertie was concerned, he could share information with the likes of Piet who he trusted and had known for many years going back to when Piet was a serving officer with the police department.

Plus, Bertie had contacts all over the world, other computer experts with access to their own government databases. Getting information on people through other governments was a long-drawn-out affair, with a lot of red tape and form filling required.

Bertie and his mates around the world had formed a private club where they shared information when required. All members had to agree as to who the information could be shared with and only individuals in their private capacity would be given sensitive government information.

People who could be trusted and had a history with one of the members. Information about births, deaths and marriages, criminal records and such like was shared. It worked well for all of them and cut through any legal or other government hurdles.

Piet put his letter to one side and studied the menu with the British Airways logo on the cover. "So far, Jack, I like what I see with this British Airways. Good looking woman waiting on me hand and foot. Good food on the menu. Well, it sounds good but haven't tasted anything yet…nice comfortable seat.

"Pity South African Airways is in trouble, or I would have insisted we fly with them. *Ag*, it's a shame, hey, one of the best airlines in the world brought to its knees by corruption and greed."

Piet shook his head in despair. "Anyways, what's the plan of action here?"

Jack helped himself to a round biscuit with fresh salmon and cheese then took another one. "Tomorrow is Friday, so I thought we should check into the hotel, freshen up, then I'll show you around London and introduce you to one of the finest capitals in the world. Full of history and fantastic architecture. I want you to see Buckingham Palace, Houses of Parliament, all the famous streets, Westminster Abbey and so on. I want you to get a feel for the size of London and show you what we might be up against if we must go digging for information."

Jack chewed thoughtfully on his fifth salmon and cheese snack. "I thought we should take the weekend off and I'll introduce you to my folks down in deepest darkest Somerset. That way you'll get a taste of the English countryside in all its glory."

Piet didn't look particularly enamoured with the plans so far. He didn't want to be a *bleddy* tourist. He'd had enough of them at the hotel.

Jack blithely continued with his plans. "Then on Monday we go and meet the solicitor, Mr James Barrington-Smith, pick up the keys to the safe deposit box and take things from there. No point in checking in with Harry before then. He'll want to know what we find out. Okay with you?"

Piet grunted. "Sounds okay, I suppose. Not bothered about being a tourist though. Seen enough of them to last me a lifetime. What sort of things does your mom like to cook?"

Jack frowned. "Oh, just traditional English food. You know, roasts, pies, puddings that sort of stuff. Why do you ask?"

Piet looked at him from under his thick eyelashes. "I don't want that spotted dick stuff, or," he paused, "frogs in a cake."

Jack gave him a puzzled look then laughed out loud. "Oh, you mean toad in the hole?"

"Yup. Sounds disgusting, man, not eating any frogs in any hole. I know French people like the legs, but no ways am I eating any frog, in a hole or out of it minus its legs or otherwise. Or sausages made of blood or *bleddy* jellied eels. *Eish!* You English eat some funny stuff, hey. Still haven't worked out what faggots are, but I have a good idea. Hope British Airways don't dish up any of the dodgy stuff for dinner."

Jack flicked through the in-flight magazine. "You eat some pretty revolting sounding stuff where you come from, mate," he said without looking up. "I mean what about those mopane worms? They sound disgusting. Not to mention the delicacy you call *Walkey Talky*? Even the Brits wouldn't eat the heads and feet of chickens when they can eat the proper part, its body. Stuffing flying ants into your mouth whilst they're still alive. As for a Smiley, well it would turn anyone's stomach! I mean, who would want to sit down for dinner and stare at the whole head of a bloody sheep, complete with grinning teeth and staring eyeballs? Afraid not, my friend. Bit barbaric by anyone's standard.

"Some of the stuff you may consider a gourmet meal would never make it to the glossy foodie magazines or feature on any cooking programme. Not even the French would touch the stuff. They would leave the kitchen, aprons over their head, and run screaming into the streets."

Piet grinned at him. "Yeah, okay, what can I say? But I'm still not eating any of your dodgy food, you hear me?"

Chapter Thirteen
London

Refreshed after a comfortable night's sleep on the flight and a full breakfast of bacon, eggs, tomatoes, and sausage (Piet prodded it and looked at it suspiciously before taking a bite). Piet and Jack made their way through Immigration and Customs, collected their luggage, and joined the queue for a taxi.

Although the sky had been grey and overcast when they landed. A watery sun had appeared as if to welcome the extremely reluctant Piet Joubert to London.

Piet looked through the windows with interest as the black cab made its way up the motorway, into the heart of London and their hotel, the Draycott, situated in Chelsea. The solicitor had booked two rooms there for one week. Paid for in advance. Should it be necessary, their stay could be extended.

After a hot shower, they both unpacked then met for coffee in the comfortable and cosy sitting room overlooking a private garden. A cheerful fire crackled and spat in the centre of the room.

"Room alright, Piet?"

Piet, still wearing his scruffy cap and one of Jack's thick jumpers, nodded.

"*Ja*, it's okay I suppose, looks comfortable with a nice view over the garden. Well, that patch of green with a few dead bushes, if that's what they call a garden here. So far, so good, my friend. But couldn't understand a word the taxi driver was saying. Where was he from. Poland or somewhere?"

Jack smiled. "He's a Londoner, a Cockney, they have a language of their own. Salt of the earth, as my old man would say. It's not easy to become a cabbie in London. They spend four years cycling around every street in the city. They must know every restaurant, nightclub, famous shops. It's called The Knowledge and it's a tough test to pass.

A lot of them give up but the ones who make it through, well, you won't find a better taxi service in the whole world."

Piet frowned. "Why don't they use GPS, like everyone else then. Why *bleddy* cycle around in *kak* weather for four years?"

"It's a tradition, Piet. London wouldn't be London without the black cabs. They've been going for over a hundred years. Cabbies are highly respected and proud of the knowledge they've earned over those four years."

Piet waved his hand in the air dismissively. "Whatever. Wouldn't get into a taxi in South Africa. Even if the driver had spent four years driving around Jo'burg on a bike. Wouldn't last a week in that crazy traffic anyway his bike would be nicked in the first two days. Far too dangerous. Taking your life in your hands doing that. Like flying. Now, when does my guided tour start? Did you hire a car or something?"

Jack shook his head. "Nope. We're going on a red London bus with no roof. It's a sightseeing bus for tourists, complete with a tour guide who will point out all the places of interest. It's the only way to see any world city, in my opinion. They do all the work, and you get to see the very best the city has to offer."

Piet looked despondent. "You're coming as well, so long? With all these funny accents around the place I might not understand what this tour guide is talking about. Not keen on that idea, my friend. Besides, someone might decide to blow up the bus. Like they did before."

Jack grinned at him. "Nothing like a bus ride around London on a sort of sunny day. Only way to see London as far as I'm concerned. You won't get blown up; I promise. That was a long time ago. Bring your coat, the one I lent you with the hood. If it starts to rain, I don't want you muttering and complaining more than you normally do, okay?"

*****

Piet crouched in his seat, sheltering from the weather, the rain dripping of his sodden baseball cap. The trip on the red bus was interesting enough, but London was far bigger than he had imagined, with its small, cobbled roads running like rivulets off the main streets, its passageways dark and shadowed. Yes, the buildings, the architecture, hundreds of years old, were impressive. They had nothing like this in South Africa. In comparison their history was young.

He watched the crowds of shoppers on Oxford Street, they moved like an endless wavering line of determined safari ants. He noted the homeless people huddled in doorways, sometimes with a dog lying next to them.

Here in the UK, they too had their share of poor and homeless people. But unlike South Africa, here the homeless could get food from soup kitchens, find shelter from the bitter weather at night in shelters, according to Jack.

All provided by various charities, churches, and the government.

Some of the young people he saw seemed to have a uniform of sorts. Jeans, or track suit bottoms and hoodies, anonymous in their grey and black apparel.

They moved aimlessly along the pavements seemingly with no destination in mind. Their faces devoid of emotion or purpose.

He wrapped his coat more closely around his body, feeling the icy outside air clinging and penetrating the marrow of his bones. Something he had never experienced before, or ever wanted too again.

Trying to find something or someone, trying to find a lead or two, would be a big challenge in this city. The crowds were endless, the cacophony of noise from cars, buses, motor bikes, black cabs, delivery vans and trucks. The never-ending road works, the scaffolding around buildings being built or renovated, the jack hammers, bin lorries, the sirens of the emergency services. The constant gathering of stop and start, slow-moving traffic.

He could find his way around Johannesburg and Cape Town with no problem, but this was something else altogether. His contacts would be useless here, although he knew Jack had a good network which he had built up over the years when he had lived and worked in the UK.

Not for the first time Piet wondered why this Zelda Cameron wanted him to come to London. But here he reluctantly was.

He turned to Jack. "See here, Jack, enough of the rain already and I'm freezing my butt off up here on this *bleddy* bus. Don't need to have any more of a history lesson. I'm done. Let's get off and find a pub where they sell decent beer. I'm hungry, but I don't want any funny food, you hear me, my friend. *Jeez,* all this noise and traffic, is doing my head in."

Jack squinted at him through the rain, wiping his wet face with the back of his hand. "Good idea, mate. Can't say I'm enjoying this much myself. Let's hop off at the next stop and get a bite to eat. There's a pub in this area I think you'll enjoy."

Piet wiped his wet sleeve across his wet eyes. "Hope it's an old pub, Jack. Not one of those fancy gastropubs. Long as I can see what I'm eating I'll be happy."

Jack stood up. "It's not that new, I think you'll like it. It's about four hundred years old. But the food is traditional, and the beer is good. Come on."

Chapter Fourteen

Piet and Jack, having had an early night, boarded the train at Paddington Station for their weekend in Somerset, Jack's family home. Piet seemed unimpressed with the vaulted ceilings and history of one of London's oldest railway stations. He looked grumpy.

Seated in the first-class carriage Jack opened his newspaper and shook it. "Ah, Piet. Nothing like a proper English newspaper to read in first-class. If Harry were paying out of his budget, he would go ballistic. But as its Mrs Cameron, covering all our expenses in England, well, no problem."

The train pulled smoothly out of the station; Jack was soon absorbed in his newspaper. Piet looked out at the rain smeared window, his heart sinking at the thought of a rain sodden weekend deep in the English countryside. He feared his safari boots would not be up to the challenge.

He suddenly had a great desire to be back home. Somewhere out in the bush where there was only silence. He imagined himself sitting alone around a campfire in the bush, sausages and chops sizzling on the grill. His sleeping bag ready and waiting in the back of his truck. The vast skies above him silent and watching as the stars appeared, one or two at first, then a carpet of never-ending bedazzlement as the rest made their appearance. The roar of a lion in the distance, the belly laughs of the hippos as they made their way out of the water to forage on the land during the night. The cackle and giggle of the hyena. The lonely call of an owl.

He brought himself back to the present, shrugging off the unfamiliar warm coat, throwing it on the seat opposite. He stared out of the window.

The grey sprawl of London with its endless view of back yards of dark sooty houses, back-to-back gardens, identical fences and washing lines. Some strewn with discarded tricycles, prams, cheap overturned pushchairs with their rusting wheels and ragged seats, the children long gone; pieces of broken furniture, a rusting supermarket trolley.

Others were equally neglected. As though they had given up competing with the endless procession of trains entering and leaving the main station. The smaller towns on the outskirts all looked the same to Piet. The pubs looked all the same as well.

He imagined customers sitting with grim determination, clutching their pints, staring into the depths wondering what had happened to their younger, single, freer selves, beaten into submission by the reality of their now lives.

How easy it must be to get hemmed in, locked in, buried in stifling routine and mundane concerns. Each day the same as the one before and the one ahead.

Africa may have its problems, he thought, but to walk on a beach at the end of a sun filled day, watching and hearing the crashing waves, the heady fresh salty air singed with the smell of kelp. Sitting at a beach side café with an ice-cold glass of wine or bottle of beer, well, that to him was more of a life.

Even if you had had a bad day at the office your spirits could only be lifted by the sheer beauty of it all.

Through the rain-streaked windows, London was left behind and gave way to earth tones of cultivated land and drab farm buildings, with the occasional glimpse of grand houses, hidden and shrouded by hundred-year-old trees. Arrogant with age as they stood amidst vast lawns and ancient forests.

Centuries old villages filled the windows for a few seconds. A post office with a bright red post box outside, no doubt redundant with the new technology.

A pub, the station with packed parking lots and the obligatory dark stoned church with its steeple. The crumbling leaning tomb stones, green with age, the etchings to loved ones barely visible after decades of wind and rain, nestling in its ancient grounds. One or two village shops and used car lots with their wilting bunting strewn across the forecourts.

Then the miles and miles of fields, isolated farmhouses, the bare twisted branches of trees bereft of leaves and the endless frost hardened fields, sometimes with only a lone stately manor house for company. Shrouded in sweeping fog and drizzle. Even the horses in the fields looked miserable as they stood in the rain, heads down, wearing thick coats to keep them warm.

Jack rustled his paper and glanced out at the fields. "Bit like the Karoo don't you think, Piet?"

Piet gave him a sour look and grunted. "No, it's not. Nothing like. Time you got some glasses, my friend…"

Piet slumped in his seat. Why did so many South Africans choose the UK to come and live here? Why give up the green rolling hills and mountains, the endless sweeping coastlines, the vast spaces, the dazzling sunshine? The way of life they had been born into.

Sure, London and the countryside he was travelling through had a sense of timelessness about it, he would agree on that. But what good was timelessness if you only had a limited amount of it yourself?

He would prefer the rough and tumble, the unpredictability, the colour, and the pulse of life which throbbed through the arteries of his own country.

Yes, his country was corrupt, crime was soaring, the infrastructure was crumbling, the power cuts never-ending, but the country had a vibrancy about it. There was a challenge which the people of the land rose to meet. An acceptance that, yes, Africa was far from perfect, but the government, no matter how they tried to change things, could never stuff up the enduring beauty of the continent.

The smell of it, the feel of it, the sense of the people that this is where they belonged, where they wanted to be. They couldn't screw around with Mother Nature in Africa. She did what she liked when she liked. The lady and her assets were not for sale.

Jack shook his newspaper and folded it in half. "Ten minutes, Piet, then it's our stop. Bit of a miserable day. I can see by your face you're not impressed by the journey through our green and pleasant land. I agree, it's a bloody awful miserable day."

*****

Piet had found Jack's parents warm and welcoming. The family home was impressive, the main gathering place was the kitchen, where a cheerful fire, set in the wall created instant warmth.

Piet immediately relaxed. After a hearty roast lunch where he recognised everything on his plate, he joined Jack and his amiable father for a walk in the countryside, along with the three family dogs who were overjoyed at the prospect of running through the grey and bitterly cold, darkening afternoon.

Even the dogs, Piet noticed, were wearing additional coats against the elements.

Piet crunched through the frozen leaves and brittle grass; Jack's scarf wrapped around his frozen face. Cognisant Piet was unused to this kind of weather, Jack and his father kept the walk short. Then made for the local pub.

Jack and his father chatted away to each other and passing friends, bringing Piet into the conversation where possible.

After an hour or so, Piet excused himself and wandered over to the end of the pub and warmed himself by the roaring fire, along with five dogs with the same idea. He sipped at his beer counting the hours before he could get back to London and open the *bleddy* safe deposit box.

Jack's father leaned over. "Is Piet alright, son. Why doesn't he come back here and join us?"

Jack smiled. "He probably feels a bit out of his depth. He's a loner. He would rather be sitting out in the middle of the bush with a lamb chop and a nest of *boerewors* on his own fire, surrounded by wild savage animals and blood-sucking mosquitoes; that would be his idea of good company. But despite the expression on his face, he's probably quite happy, staring into the flames and thinking about his next move."

*****

Piet looked at the five dogs stretched out and warming themselves by the fire. All Labradors, obviously a favourite choice of the Brits. He hadn't realised they came in all sorts of shades, shapes, and colours. But just like Hope, they were nice and plump. Probably had the same relentless hunger as his own dog.

He could feel his toes and feet starting to thaw. He looked down at his ruined safari boots. He'd had them for years; at the end of the day, at home, he would bang them together to remove the bush dust and they would look as good as new. He shook his head. Sadly, they had not survived the testing rigours of the English weather.

Chapter Fifteen

Piet and Jack presented themselves at the offices of James Barrington-Smith at nine on Monday morning.

His secretary led them through to his office and closed the door quietly behind her.

The solicitor rose to his feet, shook their hands, and indicated they should sit. "Thank you for coming gentlemen. I trust your journey was pleasant. The hotel comfortable? Dreadful weather this time of the year, something I'm sure you're not used to Mr Joubert," he said cheerfully.

He shuffled some papers on his desk and sat down, his hands clasped together on the desk. "May I ask you, Mr Joubert, for some form of identification, as per Mrs Cameron's instructions?"

Piet frowned with irritation as he pulled his ID document from his pocket. He stared down at his ruined safari boots and waited impatiently for the fussy solicitor in his expensive suit to get on with things and give him the *fokkin* key to the deposit box.

He noticed Jack's familiar jiggling foot and knew he was just as impatient to get the briefcase open and see what was inside.

Barrington-Smith returned Piet's ID card and sat down. "Perhaps you would care to partake of some tea or coffee, gentlemen?"

Piet felt his patience begin to fray. "See here, Mr Barrington. We have come a long way at your request, hey? Seven thousand miles, in fact. Please hand over the key and we can be on our way. No need to come back here is there?" He stood up.

*****

Barrington-Smith hid his annoyance at not being addressed by his correct full name. The South African was impatient and, in a hurry, not mincing his words. A rough sort of fellow, Barrington-Smith thought to himself. Not familiar with the correct protocols of how things were done in the UK. Lacking in the etiquette which should be accorded to a legal chap like himself.

As for the scruffy baseball cap, well, it would have been courteous of him to take it off on entering his office.

But rough though he appeared to be, with his strong South African accent, the solicitor could see he was no fool. His eyes had scanned the room and its sole occupant as soon as he had entered the office.

Jack was enjoying the conversation immensely. The fusty old-school solicitor was way out of his depth with Piet taking over the entire proceedings. The police officer in him, there for all to see.

Piet held out his hand. "Key and the address, sir?"

Barrington-Smith opened his drawer and handed over a small key and a card.

"One key for the safety deposit box and the address of the bank. Here is a letter signed by me, requesting the bank to give you access to Mrs Cameron's safety deposit box. You will need to identify yourself again, Mr Joubert."

Jack stood up and held out his hand. "Thank you for your time, Mr Barrington-Smith. I trust we will find all the answers to our questions within the box. You seem unable, or unwilling, to answer the questions I put to you when I called from South Africa."

"That is correct Mr Taylor. I have followed my client's instructions to the letter. I have nothing further to add. I shall expect your final expense account when you have finished your business here in the UK, accompanied by the relevant receipts and your bank account details.

"I should point out that in my considered opinion Mrs Cameron's wishes have been carried out, as per her instructions and I consider the matter closed. Good day to you both."

Jack turned around to leave and found Piet had already gone.

Chapter Sixteen

Piet and Jack, having hijacked the intimate hotel boardroom, now sat together around the modest boardroom table. The battered leather briefcase in the middle of the table.

There was a soft knock at the door before the waiter entered with a tray of coffee and sandwiches, then departed just as quietly after Jack had signed the bill.

Piet rubbed his hands together, blew on his cold fingers and reached for the briefcase. He glanced at the single card, looking at the numbers of the combination lock they had found perched on top of it in the safe deposit box, then moved both dials on either side. The case snapped open, and Piet flipped back the lid. Jack leaned over expectantly.

There were three envelopes. One large and bulky and two small ones; one addressed to Piet. The other addressed to Zelda; and a square biscuit tin with a faded picture of the Houses of Parliament on the front.

Using a knife from next to the pile of neatly cut sandwiches, minus their crusts, Piet slit open the envelope addressed to him and withdrew a single sheet of writing paper, recognising her handwriting from the previous letter he had opened in Hazyview.

Zelda.

Jack remained quiet, he sat back again, munching on his egg mayonnaise and cress sandwich, taking sips of hot coffee. So far this was Piet's case. He could hardly contain his curiosity as to what lay within the envelopes and square tin box.

Piet read the letter carefully, then re-read it before handing it over to Jack.

Dear Inspector Joubert.
Two years have passed since I last wrote to you. Now you are reading my final letter - one of the most difficult I have ever had to write.

The contents of the large envelope and the tin are deeply disturbing, but, as a policeman I am quite sure you have seen worse in your career. That's why I chose you to follow this trail I have left behind.
Over three hundred thousand people go missing every year in England. Some of them are found, some return of their own free will. Some are never seen again. Some have personal reasons never to be found.
Four young girls went missing between the year 1997 and 2000. Anna-Marie Cloete, Chantel Jameson, Elizabeth Balfour, and Suzanne Clifton. They seemingly vanished. They each took a flight to London and were never seen again.
This briefcase does not belong to me. It was delivered to me by someone with impeccable credentials. He too was powerless to do anything about the person who was involved with these girls.
I, of course, have nothing to fear now. I am dead. However, there are people still living, who could be greatly harmed and deeply affected by what happened all those years ago when the girls went missing. But it goes back further than that. I was involved from the very beginning.
You may well be frustrated and possibly angry that I cannot give you any more information other than what is contained in this briefcase.
The man who entrusted it to me, not the owner, carries a heavy burden of guilt as he is unable to reveal who it once belonged to. It is his cross to bear, as it is mine.
The reason I instructed my lawyer to send these papers and the briefcase to you two years after my death, is because the person I hold close to my heart will have returned from his hiding place.
He is still in danger, if he still alive, with the knowledge he must hold within. The owner of the briefcase knows where to find him but feels safe enough after all this time. However, I have now handed this over to you Inspector Joubert. I know you will pursue this story of the missing girls and then this person I loved so much will once again be in danger. The person who is responsible for the girls' disappearance, and I fear, their murders, is still out there somewhere.
I know exactly who the owner of the briefcase is, and like him I also carry a heavy weight of guilt for the part I played.
You will find no trace of me. I have destroyed all my personal papers.
Zelda.

Jack re-read the letter then passed it to Piet who was watching him, waiting for his reaction.

Jack's forgotten coffee cooled. "Jesus, Piet, what have we got here then? A letter from Zelda? Full of presumptions, accusations, and possibilities but not very much to go on. Sounds like none of these girls was her daughter who we previously thought she was looking for."

Piet grunted and reached for the second envelope, opened, and addressed to Zelda, with no date on the envelope or the letter he pulled out.

My dear Zelda,
We have discussed the missing girls but have been unable to do anything.
The person responsible left the briefcase for me to find. So confident was he that I could never discuss it, or the contents, with anyone.
I shall be leaving London for an indeterminate time, to a place where no-one will find me. I shall be safe. However, I cannot take the briefcase with me. I cannot take anything with me. Therefore, I have no choice other than to leave it with you. My suggestion would be that you go through the contents then keep it in a secure place. Perhaps your solicitor might suggest a safe deposit box?
We are both in great danger. I will be safe for a while, but I fear for your safety. He will come looking for you once he realises I have gone. Where else would he look for his briefcase?
May God bless and watch over you.
My love to you as always.
You must seek help from a trusted person.

Piet passed the letter to Jack then carefully pulled out the envelope and the tin box.

Pushing the now empty briefcase to one side he opened the remaining envelope and shook the contents out onto the table.

They both stared at the faded photographs of what could only be the four missing girls. On the back of each photograph was the name of the girl.

Finally, Piet reached for the old biscuit tin and carefully eased off the lid. Inside were four dark blue velvet pouches, drawn together at the neck by a piece of thin gold braid and more photographs.

Out of habit Piet patted his pockets and withdrew a thin pair of latex gloves; he handed Jack another pair. "Don't know what we're going to find in here, my friend, but there might be some prints, you never know. Not likely after such a long time, and anyways we've got our prints all over everything else already. Let's see what we have here."

Jack looked up from the photographs, his journalist's mind skimming and absorbing the information on the four girls. All blonde with long hair, all young in their teens or early twenties, all very attractive with their wide smiles and big eyes. They looked full of life, happy and healthy.

Piet shook his head. He had seen a lot in his career, but the innocence of these young girls who had come to Britain to start the next chapter of their lives, full of excitement and anticipation... Jack could see it had hit him hard.

Piet opened the first velvet pouch and withdrew a thick hank of long blonde hair tied together at the end with a tight circle of cotton. He sucked in his breath then breathed out slowly, laying it carefully on the table. Next, he withdrew a colourful beaded necklace with a pattern of the new South African flag. This he placed alongside the long hank of hair. He tipped up the pouch and it delivered its final piece of evidence. A small square of a tightly packed piece of paper. Opening it carefully he spread it out on the table: One word was written:

Chantel.

Piet's stomach turned over as he clinically looked at what was in front of him.

He opened the remaining three pouches, each with a hank of hair Careful to align them with their correct name, their photograph and piece of jewellery. A black and silver ring belonging to Anna-Marie, a beaded hair clip belonging to Elizabeth and an elephant hair bracelet belonging to Suzanne.

Jack examined the contents of each pouch, the blood draining from his normally tanned face. "What do we do next Piet? The owner of this briefcase must have known all four of the girls, and clearly got close to them," he gestured at the table.

"The parents must have reported them missing to the police. This could be of great value to their investigation. I think we have a possible serial killer here.

"We need to hand these things in – let them re-open the cases. It's the right thing to do, Piet, and we should do it. This is not just a story to be followed up. In my opinion it's a clear case of murder. The case will be ongoing, the files kept open...there will be a file on each of these girls somewhere in the archives."

Piet sat at the table silently, carefully returning the evidence to each pouch. Then he spread out the other photographs in front of him and looked steadily at each one of them. Turning them over he saw the girls' names on the back of each one. These were original photographs.

Each one featured one of the girls with either what he presumed was a mother, a father, or both. All smiling happily, their arms around each other. In the case of Chantel, he could see it was taken on a beach. Table Mountain looking silent and accusing in the background.

He handed them, one by one to Jack. "That's why Zelda Cameron was looking for me," he said softly. "Because these girls were all South African. I think Zelda Cameron was also a South African. She wants me to find out what happened to them and why. The British police would have been on the back foot from the start. But it's our starting point, Jack."

Piet looked carefully at each photograph committing the girl's faces to memory, then placed them back in the tin. He reached for one of the sandwiches and poured himself another cup of hot coffee. He tapped his fingers on the lid of the tin, deep in thought. Then unexpectedly he clasped his hands together and bowed his head.

Jack had always found moments like this a trifle awkward. Overt gestures of faith were rarely seen in the world he was brought up in. Most Afrikaners, he now knew, were deeply religious people. They were brought up on the Bible, lived by its parameters and rules. Out of respect for his old friend, he remained silent.

A few moments later Piet stood up abruptly and went over to the window which opened to the gardens outside. He threw them open and took some deep breaths. He stared out for a few moments and then turned back to Jack, his face like thunder.

"We need to start at the beginning, my friend. The beginning is Zelda Cameron, she is involved in all of this. But you tell me the *bleddy* solicitor *oke,* wouldn't give you any details about her?"

He slammed his fist on the table. "Well let me tell you this Jack. He will give them to me unless he wants to end up in a whole pile of *kak!"*

He snatched another sandwich from the now depleted plate. "This Zelda Cameron turned to me, a South African ex-policeman, not that she realised I had retired, not by choice I can tell you that much, so long. But she reached out to me because the police over here came up with bugger all.

"We're taking over this case, my friend. I am not turning this evidence over to the Brits. That I can tell you right now. We will do it my way. I'm taking these girls home and you and I will start digging for information from there."

He bit savagely into his sandwich. "I have many contacts there, people I can turn to and find out where this story started. You have the same network here on this soggy island of yours. Together we will crack this case together, not so?"

Jack looked at him with alarm. "Watch your blood pressure Piet, you look as though you're going to explode. Okay, I'll go along with you on this one. Together we can work faster than any police force, without all the red tape, the bloody data protection crap, and the endless waiting for information.

"Your mate Bertie will be able to track down the families of these girls…the police must have been involved from this end and they will have a file on each girl with any other information.

"Hey, where are you going?"

Piet had rammed his cap on his head and shrugged into his coat. "I'm going to see that *bleddy* solicitor in his fancy suit, and this time he's going to give me some answers about Zelda Cameron. Finish and *klaar*.

"You stay here Jack. I play the policeman better on my own, he might not be so forthcoming with a famous journalist in the same room. Leave him to me for half an hour and I'll come back with the information we need to get moving."

With that he slammed out of the room. Jack smiled to himself. He would have given anything to have been there when Piet kicked the door down of Mr Barrington-Smiths hallowed office.

He pulled the photographs and Zelda's letter towards him and set to work. Chasing a story. He fumbled under his thick jumper and felt for the notepad he always carried in his shirt pocket.

His mind was churning as he made notes and took photographs of everything in front of him with his phone. He looked up and saw he had been working for two hours; outside it was getting dark. He glanced at his watch. Only four in the afternoon. He sighed. In Hazyview the sun would still be shining.

He called Harry and told him what they had found in the briefcase.

"See here, Harry, can you get someone to do some back research on the stories of the missing girls? I need some dates and anything else they can find that would maybe link them, apart from the fact they all came from the same country.

"Someone needs to check anything similar over those four years. We might have mentioned something in our own newspaper about these missing girls during those years. One of our journalists might well have come to some conclusions of his own which could help. Maybe he found a link somewhere."

"I'm on it, my boy," Harry boomed down the phone. "Let's meet here at three tomorrow. There are a couple of people I would like Piet to meet. I'm looking forward to meeting him myself. Then we can go and have drinks at my Club and discuss the way forward."

Harry cleared his throat. "I would have remembered the story if all four girls went missing at the same time, but as it was over several years. I'm afraid I don't remember and would have no reason to. As you well know thousands of people go missing here all the time. It might make the front page if the person was famous, or the family was in some way, but even so, a bigger story would have wiped it off the front page and relegated it to another page for a day or two. Then it would have been forgotten.

"Unfortunately, in most cases a missing person doesn't even get a mention, as you well know."

Harry adjusted his matching navy-blue bow tie. "I have a dinner engagement tomorrow evening, but perhaps you and Piet might like to dine at my Club, my treat. I think Piet may enjoy the atmosphere there."

Jack snorted. "At the moment Piet isn't enjoying anything. Not the weather, not the country, not the food and not the bloody solicitor – nothing. He's not in a good mood, I can tell you. He'll be in a worse one when he gets back from his second visit to James Barrington-Smith!"

Chapter Seventeen

Piet Joubert walked straight past the solicitor's personal assistant, despite her protests, and opened the door to Barrington-Smith's office.

The solicitor looked up, expecting to see his personal assistant, his heart sank when he came face to face with the South African. He regained his composure quickly, although Piet was now leaning over his desk his knuckles white against his tanned hands.

He leaned back slightly. "Mr Joubert, an appointment is normally made if you wish to discuss anything with me. As you can see, I'm rather busy now," he gestured around at his immaculate office and bare desk. "Perhaps tomorrow would be a more convenient time. My personal assistant will make an appointment to suit you?"

Piet lowered his head and narrowed his eye. "Now, see here Mr Barrington-Smith. I'm here now and here I will stay until you will wish you had never got in touch with me in the first place."

James Barrington-Smith leaned back a little further. "Perhaps you would care for some tea Mr Joubert?"

"I want answers, sir. You can forget about the tea.

"Now listen to me closely. Mrs Cameron requested me to come to this country because she needed some help with a private matter which we have now discovered in the package she left for me. She wanted a person from her own country, someone she could trust. That, sir, is me. I may be a retired policeman, but I am a practicing and licenced private investigator."

"Jack Taylor asked you some simple questions over the phone. You requested he call you and this he did. However, you seemed unable or unwilling to help him out with any information about Zelda Cameron, or, come to that any information about her husband except the fact he's dead."

He took a deep breath. "It's possible the police may become involved with this. Should there be a link, which I believe there is, they may wish to call on you?"

Piet sat down heavily. "Now. You drew up Mrs Cameron's will, therefore it is likely you drew up her husband's as well. To do this, and as you are clearly the Executor of Mrs Cameron's estate, you will have copies of the death certificates. I would like these and any other information you have, including where Mrs Cameron was buried.

"Secondly, you will furnish me with details of her last address before she died. Also, if her death was suspicious in any way and I have reason to believe it may well have been. I would need information on the postmortem if this was the case. Are we quite clear on all this so far, sir?"

*****

James Barrington-Smith had often thought about taking a holiday in South Africa, going on a longed-for safari. Now he was having second thoughts. Surely not all South Africans were as abrasive and demanding as this one who was breathing like an angry buffalo barely taking breath?

The mention of the involvement of the police was a little distressing, he had to admit. Perhaps it would be in everyone's interests if he gave the damn policeman what he wanted, then perhaps he would go back to his own country as soon as possible, no doubt leaving him, on behalf of Mrs Cameron, with a large bill.

Silently he retrieved Zelda's file from his mahogany bookshelf and opened it. He removed a few sheets of paper and rang for his assistant.

She brought the copies back a few minutes later. Piet glanced at them briefly. "What about the information on her husband I asked for? Copies of the death certificates?"

Barrington-Smith looked at Piet, his eyes hostile. "Mr Cameron's details are confidential. By law, I have no obligation to give any information about him to you, or about any of my other clients.

"I have given you a copy of her will simply because it would be available in the public archives, after probate had been completed. There is nothing I can do about that. You will also have a copy of her passport, which I was under no obligation to give you. But in good faith I have because she obviously wanted you to do something for her."

Piet continued. "What line of work was her husband in and when did he die? Where is Mrs Cameron buried? You wound up her estate. Were there any beneficiaries? If so, who were they?"

Barrington-Smith sighed deeply, feeling a cluster headache forming around the back of his neck. "Mr Cameron was a doctor. But I cannot disclose where he practiced or give you any further information. Mrs Cameron was cremated, her ashes placed with a church in London, as per her request. She died of natural causes.

"There were no beneficiaries, as you will see when you go through her will. Everything was left to a charitable organisation somewhere in South Africa. The Gift of the Givers if I recall. I followed her explicit instructions as the law requires in this country, Mr Joubert."

Piet slapped the papers against his palm. "So, you're telling me she had no children then. Is that correct?"

"I said there were no beneficiaries."

Piet glanced at him and stood up. "Thank you, sir. If I have any further questions, you can be sure you will hear from me."

James Barrington-Smith stood up, smiling tentatively. "Perhaps you would be good enough to share with me what you discovered in the briefcase? It has always rather intrigued me?"

Piet glared at him. "I'm afraid that's highly confidential information, sir. I have no obligation, by law, to share any of it with you. Good afternoon."

*****

Barrington-Smith reached into the drawer of his desk and retrieved a bottle of whisky and a glass. His hand trembled as he poured himself a more than generous helping.

Mr Joubert was a touchy sort of fellow. He reminded him of the school bully at his very expensive public school. Perhaps the South African was carrying some sort of history on his shoulders – him, and his people, now a minority group in the new South Africa; perhaps being somewhat abrupt was part of his persona. He was a rough chap alright. But there was no denying he was highly intelligent and tenacious.

Perhaps, James mused, feeling steadier as the whisky coursed its way through his bloodstream, he should look at Kenya for his safari. He looked out of his window, then frowned – perhaps not.

He had read somewhere that gay people were not very welcome there, illegal in fact, to enter the country as a couple. Or was it Tanzania or Uganda?

He couldn't remember. He had some difficulty in remembering things about Africa. They kept changing the names of their international airports, their flags, names of their towns and sometimes the names of the country. It was all frightfully confusing when one wanted to plan a safari.

Perhaps he and Malcolm should just go to France instead. The food was good, they both spoke French and, most of all, the French didn't give a damn who you were, where you came from and what you did. If you could speak reasonable French, you were accepted. If you didn't, well, they were quite intolerant towards the English. Downright rude in fact.

Chapter Eighteen

Piet and Jack had dined at their hotel, then retreated to the sitting room to discuss the information they had now assembled.

Piet patted his pocket for his glasses and put them on, then pulled them off and threw them on the table. "Waste of time those *bleddy* glasses. Can't see *fok* all."

Jack retrieved them and gave them a quick clean with his handkerchief before handing them back. "Here, try them now. Nothing a good clean can't sort out. You should try it some time."

Piet grunted and put them back on and pulled his notes towards him, Jack did the same. "Okay. Zelda Cameron was born in 1942, which would have made her 74 when she died." He pushed the copy of her passport over to Jack.

"Unfortunately for us it's a copy of a British passport. If it had been her South African one, we would have found a wealth of information from her identity number. So far, we have no idea of her maiden name, but I'll get Bertie onto that at a later stage. Don't want to get him involved until we have a lot more information for him to work with, it makes him a bit cranky. At least we have a photograph of her now. Not a good one I have to say. Looks very ordinary. Her husband was a doctor, but I have no idea exactly when or where he died. Some years ago, I would imagine. No copies of the death certificates for either of them."

"No worries, Piet, I can easily get copies of both death certificates. I have contacts as you know,"

Piet glanced down at Zelda's letter. "This part baffles me. *'However, it goes back further than that and I was involved from the very beginning,'"*

Jack shook his head then glanced at the photograph of Zelda. "Admitting she was involved from the very beginning, well, it could mean anything including she was somehow implicated in the disappearance or possible murders of these girls. Certainly, she had a hand in events somewhere along the line."

"Also, who wrote the other letter warning her she was in danger?" Piet asked.

Jack drummed his fingers on the polished table. "I can't even hazard a guess at this stage. But we'll find out once we start digging into her past. This copy of her will looks simple enough, can't see anything there to raise any red flags.

"Her request to be cremated is straightforward but why she would want her ashes to be sent to London is a bit of a mystery. Also, here she requested no flowers. I could find the undertakers who carried out her wishes, but I can tell you right now, with all this data protection nonsense they won't give us any details. Only next-of-kin get that information, and it doesn't look as though she had any. No beneficiaries either. Everything went to various charities.

"We need to find her birth and marriage certificates. Get her maiden name."

Piet nodded and took a sip out of his can of beer, ignoring the expensive crystal glass which was supposed to accompany it. "Everyone looks like a murder suspect in their passport photo. Don't know why the authorities won't allow people to give a big smile, might cheer the immigration people up a bit – they always look suspicious and unfriendly, same as customs officials. Like they don't want you and your foreign currency in their country and have a bad smell under their noses when they look at you.

"Anyways, I have Zelda's last known address in a place called," he looked down at the spelling of the name, "Larkstown. Do you know this place, Jack?"

"Not well, but I've heard of it. Small village not far from London, popular with local tourists who like a sniff of an old English village with hump-backed bridges and quaint thatched houses.

"I think I should follow that up, Piet. English people don't like folks knocking on their doors asking questions, especially if they have an accent like you have. Might think you're German. Those retired types also have long memories… more likely to open up to me. The local pub would be a good place to start."

Piet glanced at him. "Yup. Maybe try and find something more out about her husband. He was a doctor, maybe he knocked the girls off. He would know how to do it and get away with it. You might come up with something useful. I've seen enough British television to know about nosy neighbours, all that twitching of curtains, so long. Someone might remember something about our Zelda. Worth a go, hey."

Piet looked at the letters again. "Also, this friend she mentioned, clearly, she loved him, or was very close to him, maybe even related to him. On the other hand, the letter to her could have been written by a woman. Not sure where to start with that one. See what you can sniff out."

Jack glanced down at his notes. "I've asked Harry to get some research done on the four missing girls. Might not come to anything after all this time, but let's see what they dig up."

He took a sip of his wine and pushed it to one side as he flipped through his notes. "I need to use a contact of mine here. Bill Watson, ex-police detective, retired now, but would have been on active service when the girls went missing. We need to get more details from police files. Not going to be easy. Also, we don't want to alert the authorities to the fact we are going to chase this story."

Jack gathered his papers and notes together. "I'll get hold of Bill, see if he can use some of his contacts to pull the files for us. We need the names and addresses of the girls' parents in South Africa for a start. They would be in their sixties now, maybe even older. It's likely the parents kept reminders of their lost children. Might pick up something there."

Piet tapped the table with his bottle. "It's also highly likely the parents of these missing girls contacted the South African police to report their girls went missing en-route to London. I'll follow that lead up. The South African Embassy here would have been notified; not sure how helpful they'll be after all this time. Bugger all they'll tell me if they know my police background, but it's worth a shot, not so?"

Jack rubbed his eyes, aware he too might be needing glasses sooner rather than later, not that he was going to admit it to anyone. "We need to know if the girls had siblings, where their parents are now, what schools they went to, who their friends were, if they had boyfriends etc. When did the parents realise their daughter were missing? What was the time frame before the police were informed of their disappearance?

"My other question, which the parents may be able to answer, is this. The parents obviously gave the UK police photos of Anna-Marie, Elizabeth, Suzanne, and Chantel when they disappeared. But how the hell did a possible killer get hold of these other photographs we have here? The more informal ones of them on the beach, not the classic end of term ones?"

Jack flipped a page of his notebook. "I believe we can discount the possibility of the girls moving on from the UK, and the parents knowing nothing about it. If the girls had British passports, they would have had no problem travelling to and around Europe. However, if they had South African passports that would have been impossible as they would have to have a Schengen visa.

"For overseas flights you must be at the airport at least two hours before take-off. Also, at such a milestone in a girl's life the parents, or at least one of them would have seen them off. A whole new chapter in their child's life was opening. They would have been there. None of those girls missed their flight. We need to find out which airline they were flying. My money is on either South African Airways, British Airways or Virgin."

Piet nodded in agreement. "That's your job then, my friend. Assuming the girls were going to go to university here, and I'm only assuming this because of the similarity in their ages. They no doubt went to good private schools in South Africa. But we need dates, my friend, dates. With your posh accent and good looks, although your hair is a bit scruffy, well, you'll be able to get more information than I ever would, not so?"

Piet crunched his can of beer up and rolled it to one side, ignoring the droplets it left on the highly polished, no doubt, valuable antique table.

"*Ja*, like I was saying. To put your child through university here you must pay three times as much for being an overseas student. So, we must assume they came from privileged monied families.

"These four girls, although they disappeared over the course of four or five years, came to the UK around the same time of the year as each other, that would have been September; ready for the intake of new university students. Like I said we need definite dates of when they left South Africa. Normally after Matric which is November, December, students spend a gap year working as waitresses, or whatever. Some travel abroad, some do internships. They would have already applied, before they matriculated, for a place in the university of their choice and been accepted.

"We must assume these four girls probably stayed in Cape Town, or at least in the country, did odd jobs, had some fun, met up with their mates from school and basically had a good time before they were due to leave the country and settle down to some serious studying."

Piet smothered a yawn; it was coming up for midnight and he was tired. "I'll use some of my contacts with the police, all shoved out now, of course, but they still have their own contacts in the new South Africa. Need to find out if they got involved in any way to trace the girls. Have my doubts, hey, the country was under the new government. They would have had their hands full, not only with pushing aside good decent Afrikaner policemen, to make way for the new guys, but with all the violence and crime that continued after Mandela picked up the reins of the country.

"Plus, hundreds of white South Africans fled the country, thinking the end of the life they had known would spiral into anarchy. It won't be easy."

Jack also yawned. "Okay, time for bed. I'm knackered. We're meeting with Harry tomorrow at three. He's looking forward to it. He suggested after the meeting we have drinks at his Club, then dinner. He won't be joining us, not for dinner, unfortunately. Okay with you?"

Piet looked at him warily. "Suppose so. What can I say? Never been to a fancy English gentleman's club. Know all about them though. Ancient posh *okes* drinking port and smoking big cigars, rustling their newspapers, and ignoring everyone else, looking bad-tempered. Most of them suffering from gout and hobbling around with walking sticks. They let women into those clubs, Jack? No, I thought not."

*****

Jack was making mental lists in his head, prioritising who he should contact and when. He closed his eyes trying to recapture something; something skittering through his memory, nudging it into action.

He turned the bedside light off, for once without any assistance from Eskom.

Chapter Nineteen

Piet and Jack went through the security at the offices of the *Telegraph.* Piet looked around with interest as they made their way to Harry's office. A huge room was filled with journalists pounding away at their laptops in individual pods, shouting down telephones, calling out to each other as they gathered the news and articles for the next edition of the newspaper. In the background huge television screens rolled endlessly with news from around the world.

Jack knocked on Harry's door and let them both in. Harry stood up beaming a welcome at his favourite journalist and the now legendary retired Detective Inspector Piet Joubert.

A little overwhelmed by the boisterous welcome and handshaking, Piet looked at one of the most respected and well-known editors in the entire country.

In front of him he saw a tall man in his early seventies, with a full head of silver hair swept neatly back. He wore his distinctive statement navy-blue braces, Piet had heard so much about, with a bow tie to match. His deep blue eyes accentuated by the whiteness of his hair and his traditional attire.

"Good to meet you, finally, my dear chap. Welcome to London and the hallowed offices of my newspaper. Now, let's sit down and discuss what looks like an intriguing and possibly excellent story. All expenses funded by the elusive and mysterious Mrs Zelda Cameron, right, Piet?"

Piet nodded. "Yes, all funded by her but only here in the UK. Then it's out of your budget, Harry."

Harry shrugged and turned to Jack. "About time we had a visit from you, my boy. Been far too long. Let's get on with things, shall we?"

Harry's personal assistant placed a large tray in the centre of the boardroom table, removing a separate pot and a plateful of biscuits in front of Piet.

"For you, Mr Joubert. *Rooibos* tea and some Ouma's rusks. Lots of South African products available here now, trying to keep up with the thousands of South Africans who hunger not only for familiar things to eat and drink but also for the memories they evoke."

Piet beamed at this thoughtful gesture and murmured his thanks.

Harry sat back, hooking his thumbs behind his braces. "We've gone back through the archives of our newspaper and found nothing. No mention of any missing girls over the time frame you gave me. Unfortunately, the disappearance of your girls made less than a ripple as far as the media were concerned at the time.

"The crash of the Air France Concorde was big news. Zimbabwe was news when Mugabe started to confiscate farms from white owners, worst snowstorms in fifty years here, Mad Cow disease, earthquakes, floods, and famine. The fall-out of the marriage of Prince Charles and Diana. Politics, of course, and the scandals that go with it, celebrity marriages and divorces and so on. But the biggest global story at around the time your girls went missing was Nelson Mandela.

"His release from prison and the negotiations that went on which led him to take up the reins as the first black President of South Africa. He was the darling of the media with his famous voice and smile. Unshackling his people from decades of the hated apartheid regime.

"People all over the world had been demonstrating for years, demanding his release. There was little or no sympathy for the future of the white people in that country."

Piet scowled at Harry. "End of a lot of things, Harry, including a lot of careers for a start. Including mine. But whatever, all over now, not so?"

"The point I'm making, old boy is this. One white girl disappearing during that time, or rather four going missing without forming a recognisable pattern, was not worth a mention in your newspapers or ours. As far as the press in your country was concerned, if they even ever heard about it, the girls had left the country on their way to London. So where was the story? Likewise, even though I'm sure the parents of the girls reported them missing and the police reported it to their British counterparts, where was the story for the press?

"They all arrived in London, confirmed by immigration authorities, and then disappeared. Still no story."

Harry took a sip of his coffee and munched on his chocolate biscuit. "Sorry, you chaps are on your own with chasing this one. Between the two of you I'm sure you'll follow the trail and find out what happened to those four girls. I'm expecting a terrific story from you, you hear?"

Jack and Piet looked at each other. Piet hauled the battered old briefcase onto the table, opened it, and laid the contents out on the table. Careful to ensure each hank of blonde hair was matched to the right piece of jewellery and the name of the girl. Plus, her matric photograph dressed in her school uniform.

Harry sucked in his breath having now been confronted with what was clearly not four old stories about four girls who went missing from another country. But a clear case of possible murder and a serial killer.

He stood up and walked uneasily around the table. "This could be a tricky one, chaps. Clearly all this information does indeed point to a possible serial killer. It should be handed over to the police immediately. The cases need to be re-opened, and the perpetrator pursued. It would be the correct and legal thing to do," he said innocently.

He sat down again casting his eyes over the letters, the photographs of the girls and the contents of the four velvet pouches.

"However, I know you two are a good team, you move fast. Both of you have contacts in the countries involved. My feelings would be to pursue this on your own initially and only bring the police in when you have solid proof.

"Legally, we are bound to inform them. But as they know nothing about the briefcase and its contents, I'm going to back you both.

"The police budgets and manpower here are stretched to capacity at the moment…" he glanced at Piet. "I know finding out what happened to these girls is close to your heart, Piet. So, let's run with it shall we? I've appointed someone here to dig deeper and focus on the story, his name is Stefan de Villiers, a fellow countryman of yours.

"He was involved with the case about the little girl who pitched up at the game lodge in the dead of the night."

Piet and Jack nodded. Stefan, they now knew, was a good journalist. He would be an excellent choice for their current situation.

Harry looked up at the knock on the door. "Come!" he shouted. The door opened and Stefan De Villiers appeared.

Piet and Jack stood up. Stefan was thirty-six, nice looking with his dark floppy hair, clear grey eyes a warm smile and the solid build of a rugby player.

He shook hands with Jack then turned to Piet, breaking into rapid Afrikaans as he pumped his hand.

Jack sat back down. "English, guys, please. Harry hasn't a clue what you're talking about and you know he likes to know everything. Hey, Stefan, we want you to look at the contents of this briefcase which has been entrusted to Piet. See what you think."

Stefan's smile dissipated as he studied the contents on the table. "*Jeez,* what the hell have we got here?" The colour leached from his face as he stared at the four hanks of long blonde hair. He looked at Piet.

"The four missing girls, right Piet? Harry mentioned you were interested in them."

Piet nodded. "*Ja,* and we're going to track down the bastard who took them with everything we have. Jack will cover the UK with his contacts. I'll be digging deep in South Africa. That's where this story began."

Between them, Piet and Jack filled Stefan in on what they knew so far, and how they had acquired the old, battered briefcase.

Stefan, wordlessly, pulled out his phone and took pics of everything laid out on the table. Then read the two letters.

Harry quickly intervened. "Listen, Stefan. As we all know this information should be handed over to the police. However, we have decided Jack and Piet should run with it and then, when they have solid evidence and only then, the police will be informed.

"They won't be happy, but Jack and Piet are more likely to solve this than the British police. The story begins in South Africa and that's where Piet wants to start. No need to involve the police here at this point."

Harry ran his hands through his silver hair. "This means, Stefan, no-one outside this room needs to know anything at this stage. Clear about that?"

Stefan nodded. "Understood. Anything you guys need, let me know. I'll see what I can come up with here. Christ, I haven't seen anything like this before. Tragedies and scandals, yes. But a possible serial killer who collects trophies, makes my stomach turn to acid, especially as they were South African girls.

"The letter from Zelda Cameron is disturbing, likewise the other one warning her of the danger she was in. But who wrote it?"

Stefan shook their hands again. "I'll get onto it straight away. Good hunting, my friends." Shaking his head, he left the office.

Harry glanced at his watch. "Right, chaps, let's go to my Club and have a drink. I think we all need one."

Carefully Piet, placed everything back in the briefcase and put it under his arm.

His team was in place, just like the good old police days in the Eastern Cape. Jack would use all his contacts in the UK, and he would use all his in South Africa.

Like a jigsaw puzzle they would have the outline, the frame of the puzzle in place. All they had to do was filter through thousands of other pieces of accumulated information until they finally had the full picture.

Chapter Twenty

Harry hailed a taxi outside the offices of the newspaper. "Where to, Guv?"
"Whites Gentlemen's Club."
Piet was surprised at the name of Harry's club. Was it for whites only then? As they made their way through the heavy traffic, Piet looked around. If this club was whites only then it would be London's best kept secret, judging by the massive cross section of people he saw. People from all over the world who had made the UK their home. Although Piet couldn't understand why. He was nevertheless intrigued.

Harry paid the cabbie and gave Piet a few moments to inspect the ancient façade of the building. "One of the oldest private gentlemen's clubs in the country, my boy. Opened in 1683, so it's a bit old even by our standards. Now, sorry about this, Piet, but your thick coat and equally thick jumper will have to be removed. They have a high standard of dress code here for members and their guests – jackets and ties are *de rigeur.* Tradition, my dear chap, tradition. Very important in this changing world. One must keep up standards."

Piet looked down at Jack's borrowed clothes. "Don't have anything fancy other than Jack's clothes, Harry. Probably won't let me in, then. Never mind, I can find a nice friendly pub somewhere where they'll accept me, hey? Maybe a Nando's where I can get some decent grub?"

"Absolutely not, my dear fellow. I called ahead. A tie and jacket will be made available by the concierge. It will be my pleasure to have you as a guest here. Come along."

Now sporting a jacket and tie, Piet sat uncomfortably in his rigid chair, the old briefcase wedged between his feet. Fortunately, the concierge had not noticed the sad state of his safari boots or perhaps, seeing the look on Piet's face and hearing his thick accent, had chosen to ignore them.

Piet looked around the room with its traditional dark wooden panelling, brass studded deep leather chairs, round tables seating groups of expensively dressed members who were probably wearing handmade shoes. The gloomy portraits on the walls of unsmiling, no doubt heavily titled gentleman and royalty of past members.

Miserable looking sods, he thought to himself. Entombed since sixteen *voetsek,* whatever year Harry had mentioned, in artificial light and no doubt a cobweb or two with their strange hairstyles and clothes.

No business talk was allowed at the club, Harry informed him. "So, what are we going to talk about then, hey?" Piet replied. "Not the *bleddy* weather, I hope. It's enough just seeing it."

Harry roared with laughter, garnering some looks of strong disapproval and irritated shaking of newspapers from his fellow members. He decided he liked Piet and his blunt ways. A refreshing change from most of the people he mixed with, always so frightfully politically correct, careful not to offend, but not when it came to politicians, oh no. Damn good detective as well.

After an hour talking about nothing, except world affairs, Harry stood up. "Must dash, have a dinner appointment. By the way, jolly good wine cellar here. Good luck with your story chasing. And Jack, keep the bloody expenses down when you get back to South Africa, you hear me? As Piet reminded me, Mrs Zelda Cameron won't be footing any bills once you both return to South Africa. I need this story and sooner rather than later. Regards to Hugo when you see him. Cheerio then."

Piet tugged at the unfamiliar tie around his neck. "Listen, my friend, this *bleddy* tie feels like a hangman's noose. Those portraits are making me depressed, hey. I don't even want to think about what they serve up in the dining room. Let's get out of here and find somewhere a bit more friendly. I don't like your hairy jumper but it's a damn sight more comfortable than what I'm wearing now. I'm out of here – you coming?"

Jack had known when Harry mentioned his club that Piet would hate it. Now he stood up, waited for Piet to hand back the tie and jacket before shrugging on his jumper and heavy coat. Then they stepped out and Jack hailed a taxi.

Piet sank back into the deep seat. The city was already dark, the brake lights of all the thousands of vehicles caught up in the snaking traffic reflected on the wet roads.

"Like these cabs, Jack. Must be thousands of them here. Seems when you lift your arm, wherever you are, one appears from no-where. Anyways, hope you picked a good restaurant. A place we can have a decent steak or ribs or something. Then we should head back to the hotel and plan for tomorrow, hey. See who's going to do what?"

Jack knew of a place on the Kings Road, not far from their hotel, where they served good food, although expensive, but, hey, Mrs Cameron was paying. They should be able to get a steak there and a decent bottle of wine as they made their plans for the following day. That would cheer Piet up.

As they entered the restaurant a smiling waiter sidled up. "Table for two, sir?"

Piet turned around and looked behind him and scowled. "Are you seeing something I can't see? You see more than two people?"

Jack's heart sank. Piet had had enough of the challenges of the day and was not in the mood for anything other than a decent steak. The highlight of his day had probably been Harry's assistant bringing him some *rooibos* tea and some bloody Ouma's rusks, which, as far as Jack was concerned, were a serious health hazard to your teeth.

Jack nodded to the waiter. "Sorry, my friend here has had a bad day. Yes, table for two, thank you."

The slightly mollified waiter seated them at their table overlooking the King's Road, handing them their menus.

"Perhaps I may ask sirs, if either of you have allergies to the following; if you have challenges with any food products, for our chefs to meet your every need? Are you allergic to peanuts, tree nuts, eggs, milk, wheat, shellfish, soy, or sesame? Lactose or Gluten intolerant perhaps?"

Piet rolled his eyes and slumped back into his seat. Then sat abruptly forward. "Listen here, my friend," he hissed. "The only challenge I have here is with you."

Piet looked at the menu. "Bring us a rump steak, rare, and the *bleddy* chips, okay. Alright with you Jack?"

Jack nodded, hugely entertained by his friend.

Piet turned back to the waiter. "Bring proper bread. I don't want anything with seeds or bits of currents stuck in it, and full fat butter to go with everything else, you hear me? Make it snappy, we're hungry. Whilst you're at it, we'll have a bottle of South African Merlot. I see here you have wines from all over the world, Australia, California, New Zealand, and France and only a pathetic selection from South Africa.

Tell your manager to forget about the *fokkin'* peanuts and such like, and up the selection of South African wines, hey?"

They watched the waiter scuttle away with as much dignity as he could muster, probably wishing he had perhaps chosen a different career path.

Jack grinned at Piet. "Lighten up, Piet, poor sod's only doing his job. It's been a difficult day, I know. The wait staff must ask all these questions lest you slide off your chair and roll around the floor, frothing at the mouth with an allergic reaction. "We live in times of suing for absolutely anything. People go through their lives waiting for an opportunity to make big bucks from insurance claims. It's how it is today."

The waiter delivered the bread and Piet examined it closely to see it didn't have bits of fruit or nuts running through it. He ripped off a piece, slathered it with full fat butter, sprinkled it generously with salt and stuffed it into his mouth.

He chewed contentedly. "See here Jack. Our girls didn't have the opportunity to eat at a restaurant like this. They were never asked about what they liked, or didn't like, whether they were allergic to anything. They never had the choice. They were possibly murdered and, in my book, all this ridiculous, politically correct *kak*, is neither here nor there. All this are you allergic to *bleddy* this or that, it amounts to *nothing* where I come from.

"Posturing, that's all it is, like the poncing waiter who doesn't give a shit whether we enjoy our dinner or not. Hope he's not expecting a tip because he's not getting one."

He helped himself to another piece of bread. "*Nah*, I want to go home, Jack. Find out what happened. When I want a decent cut of meat, I'll go to the local Steers or Spur and get it there, without all the health threats, delivered by a waiter without a phony French accent to ruin my dinner. You hear what I'm saying? Ah, here comes the steak, with or without all the perils of eating a mouthful of meat."

He peered at the rich yellow sauce cascading down the side of what he considered a very small steak indeed, then carefully scraped it off, alongside some suspicious looking green decoration. But the chips looked okay.

"Need to get back home, Jack. I'm done here. I'm not happy or comfortable hereabouts."

Jack nodded. "Okay. I'll stay here and follow up with my contacts, take a day or two in Larkstown, see what I can find out. I'll get hold of

Bill Watson, my police buddy and see if he can find anything about the girls. You go home Piet, work your end. I'll sort your return ticket."

Piet looked at Jack across the table as he chewed his steak. "You know something, Jack? The present contains nothing more than the past.

"I'm going home and taking those girls with me. We're going to find out exactly what happened to them – you and me Jack. We're going to find this bastard; we're going to hunt him down. You might not want to be around when I find him…"

Chapter Twenty-One
Cape Town
2018

Anna-Marie's mother watched the waves rolling in and out from her Sea Point flat. It was the only constant in her life. The only thing that never changed, no matter what was happening in the world. No matter what had happened in her own life.

No-one trains you to be a mother, she mused as she sipped her tea People tell you how it will be, how enriching. How a child changes your life forever and you nod and say yes, I can't wait etc. etc. but you have no idea how irrevocably your life is going to change.

The sheer force of love erupts from deep within you when that child is born. The instinct to protect is fierce and unyielding. The killer instinct in you bubbles to the surface from a place hidden from you, unknown to you until now.

You will kill to protect your child.

Twenty-four hours a day your mind and instincts are honed to protect your child. You are constantly on guard, alert to any perceived danger. This feeling is unlike anything you have ever known. Like a wild animal with its young, you stand guard. Ready to kill and attack anything or anyone who poses a threat.

The years, of course, pass swiftly by. The baby becomes a toddler then a child. A gangly pre-teen, then a teenager – and still you watch over them, alert to any danger as you watch your child stand tall and walk out into the world, away from you; but the child will always be your child no matter their age or where they travel to. Still, you try and protect them when you know, deep inside, your job is done. The joy and happiness, however, stays deep within you.

There is nothing redemptive about the loss of a child, no valuable lessons learned. It is too big, too overwhelming. Impossible to articulate. It is a bleak, overwhelming physical pain, shocking in its intensity. Every time you think you might have moved forward a step or two it swells back, like a tidal wave, a tsunami, to drown you once again in the shocking reality.

She took another sip of her tea. Hope is the worst thing you can wish for. Hope is the moment before they tell you the truth. Hope is a set-up, the bait, an illusion – then they, the authorities, the police, take it from you. You are left hollowed out with nothing left inside to take you any further.

When I'm asleep, she thought to herself, I am neither happy nor unhappy. I feel nothing at all with the dawn of yet another day. Then, a few seconds, before the nightmare of her loss brutally returns. Not one day passes when I don't think of her. My protection at its most vigilant was not enough. I wish I could sleep forever.

All those years have been taken away, snatched away from me. They were all for nothing.

Anna-Marie has gone. Someone took her.

Chapter Twenty-Two

The next morning Piet and Jack met for breakfast and a final meeting before Piet flew home that evening. Jack noticed with amusement Piet's suitcase, or rather the one he had lent him, was packed and ready to go at the entrance to the hotel's front door. Piet was keen to leave London and head back home, even though the flight was not until the evening.

They spent some hours in the dining room going over the case and planning their strategy. Jack would arrange to meet up with his old police inspector buddy, Bill Watson, and hopefully retrieve from the archives the four case files of the missing girls. It was a long shot but one he was going to take.

After that he would visit Zelda Cameron's last known address and spend a couple of days in Larkstown. There he would use his journalistic skills to try and find friends or acquaintances who might have known her.

Piet would use all his years as a policeman to gather as much information as he could about Zelda's links to South Africa and would take it from there.

Once he had retrieved the addresses of the girls when they lived in Cape Town, he would do some groundwork then hand it over to Jack to follow up. He didn't think private schools, which undoubtedly, they would be, would like an ex-policeman sniffing around. They guarded their reputation fiercely to justify their eye-watering tuition and boarding fees. A good-looking British journalist with the right accent would have better luck than he would.

Piet stabbed at the yolk of his poached egg. "It's going to be a tough one to crack, Jack. No bodies. No proof of anything – we have nothing to go on right now, absolutely nothing. But we start at the beginning, twenty years ago, if not earlier and follow the trail, not so?"

Jack nodded. "Victims of a serial killer, if this is what we have here, usually have something in common. The killer picks their victims based on shared characteristics. Now all we have is all four missing girls were blonde, young, and South African. So how had the killer gone about hunting for them? Was it because he was from there. How could he have known where they came from? How did he get the photographs of Anna-Marie, Elizabeth, Chantel, and Suzanne?

"Where did Zelda Cameron fit into all of this – because she most certainly did."

"That, my friend," Piet said quietly, "is where we are going to start – with Zelda. Forty years ago, when she left her homeland."

Chapter Twenty-Three

Jack phoned Bill Watson. They had worked together on cold cases in the past and become firm friends. Their friendship based on trust and confidentiality.

"Good heavens, Jack. Haven't heard from you for some years. Heard you left the newspaper and went to live abroad somewhere. Good to hear from you!"

"Still with the *Telegraph,* Bill, but working out of South Africa now." Jack briefly filled in his old friend on where he was and what he had been up to and what he needed now. "How are things with you? How are you enjoying your retirement?"

There was a slight pause. "To be honest, Jack, I'm not. I'm bored out of my mind. I decided golf was not what it was cracked up to be and I was useless at it, did my back in as well. As for bowls, well forget it. I'm not a gardener of any note, it would appear. So here I sit.

"I looked at joining a security company, but they want big burly types with military backgrounds, preferably Russians and Poles. You know how it is, no loyalty to anyone. Only the ones who are paying them vast amounts of money. They don't exactly stick to the letter of the law either, doing what must be done when it needs to be done. Seems I'm too old to be effective whichever way I jump."

"You were one of the finest detectives I've ever worked with, Bill, and I mean that. You picked up things others had missed. You'd be an asset to any company lucky enough to take you on."

"That may be, Jack, but not helping me now. My wife died four years ago, terrible blow to us. But I have my daughter, Zoe. Don't see as much of her as I would like, but there it is. Sold the house after Sheila died and I now live in a flat in Islington, not a bad part of London. At least there's a bit of life around me rather than sitting in a house in the country looking at my unkempt garden. Anyway, enough of me."

Jack cleared his throat. "I might have something for you Bill. I need some help with four girls who disappeared over twenty years ago. I need information which, for me, will be difficult to get hold of. What do you say?"

Bill didn't hesitate. "What do you need, Jack? I'll help you, of course. So, tell me about these girls?"

Jack gave him the details he had so far. "Bill, I also need information on this Zelda Cameron, like exactly when she entered the United Kingdom and who with. Also, I need to access the missing persons files on the four girls. I need to know what the police did. What they found when the girls were reported missing. Can do?"

Bill cleared his throat. "Give me the name of the girls?"

Jack flipped his notebook open. "Anna-Marie Cloete, Chantel Jameson, Elizabeth Balfour, and Suzanne Clifton. They all disappeared between 1997 and 2000. Do you need anything else Bill?"

"Nope. That's all I need to pull the appropriate files. My daughter Zoe joined the police force and works in the archives. Shouldn't be a problem to lend her old man a hand, make copies of them, strictly against police rules of course. I'll have a look through them and meet you tomorrow."

He named a pub in Islington, and they arranged to meet there the following evening.

*****

Bill and Jack met at the pub in Islington. Bill was big and burly, his greying hair cut into a short crew cut. "Good to see you, Jack. Let me get some drinks then you can tell me more about the case you're chasing."

Bill returned with the drinks and took a long and satisfying gulp of his. Then opened the four slim files he had brought with him.

He frowned. "Finding missing persons is a massive headache for the police, as you know. Thousands go missing every year. Being from overseas makes it even harder. Not like one can pin a picture of the missing person on a tree in the area they came from and hope someone would recognise them and come forward with information.

"But let's give it our best shot. Can't say I recall these four South Africans going missing. But I have copies of the files here, which you can peruse at your leisure. I've already read through them, nothing much there, apart from the dates they arrived and a brief investigation."

Bill sipped his beer. "I did a bit more digging for you. Forty years or so ago, two boys came into the country with your Zelda Cameron. It was all legit. She was married to a Paul Cameron, British citizen, in South Africa, and all four of them arrived in the UK."

"Birth certificates, marriage and death certificates, Bill?"

Bill shuffled through his files. "I don't have the marriage certificate from South Africa, or the birth certificate for Zelda Cameron, but I do have the names of the two boys, Tinus and Marius. Nothing suspicious, they looked like a perfectly legal family entering the UK. Of course, forty or so years ago the sort of technology we have today wasn't available. So, immigration only gave the paperwork a cursory glance.

"Zelda Cameron died on February 27th, 2016.

"Now let's look at the four girls. In each case the police here launched an extensive search, as you will see in the files."

A police siren screamed passed, and Bill paused, watching the police car looking a little wistful, then continued. "All the girls flew from Cape Town to Heathrow on direct flights, obviously not the same one. All four of them on their way to different universities here in the UK.

He tapped the files in front of him. "They arrived in London, all the dates are recorded here, then went through immigration and customs and obviously made their way to the arrivals hall and took the Heathrow Express, a coach, a bus, or the tube to get to their booked hotel. Except they never checked in. Each girl had planned, according to their parents, on spending a few days in London before making their way to university."

Bill ran his hand over his short hair and continued. "The police checked with the various accommodation outlets in Earl's Court Road where each girl was booked in by their travel agency in Cape Town. This information came from their parents who the police obviously worked closely with once the girl had been reported missing.

"The thing is Jack, not one of the four girls ever made it to their hotels. The police took into consideration that the girls had other plans their parents didn't know about. Meeting a boyfriend who had other accommodation available. But what we have here is four girls, all en-route to a different university, who never made it to their accommodation, that's an odd fact. Too much of a coincidence."

Bill was quiet for a few moments. "As you will see, Jack, when you go through these files, the consensus was that the four girls had somehow been snatched at the airport. It's impossible to believe all of them would have made an alternative plan to run off with a boyfriend, for instance."

Jack listened carefully as Bill continued. "The police did an intensive investigation after the first girl disappeared. Anna-Marie Cloete, aged nineteen. They questioned the security staff at the airport, people who worked in the various shops and restaurants, the check in staff, immigration and customs, cleaners, catering staff. It was an intensive investigation, but they came up with absolutely nothing. Hardly surprising when you think of the thousands of people who enter the country from all over the world."

Bill tapped the files in front of him. "I asked Zoe to check if any other girls from South Africa, apart from these four, had been reported missing, under the same circumstances, over the past fifteen years or so. The answer was no. It looks as though our potential suspect has gone to ground. Or he's in prison, or better still he's dead.

"You need to factor in 9/11 here. After that, every country in the world ramped up their security at airports, draconian efforts to keep the bad guys out. No more cursory glances at the paperwork, no. Documents were scrutinised, countries worked together, sharing information. Your man might have found it a lot harder to get information on girls after 9/11.

"That's why he dropped out of sight. It was too risky to try anything at the airport with all the tight security controls now in place."

He looked at Jack. "So, tell me what you have got on this case, Jack? Why are you following it up now?"

Jack told Bill about Zelda and the briefcase she had left. Then he scrolled through all the photographs he had taken of the contents and handed over his phone to Bill.

Bill showed no emotion until he came to the velvet pouches and their contents. He hissed through his teeth as he went back through the photographs.

Jack waited a few moments before he spoke. "These four girls, Bill, are connected. There was someone waiting for them, who took them. The contents of the briefcase are irrefutable. We think someone killed all four of them and left the proof of what he had done."

Bill sighed deeply. "You know, Jack, you should report this to the police. You have evidence of what may have happened to these girls. You can't go out there on your own with your South African counterpart, Piet Joubert? You have here, it would appear, a serial killer,

103

who has a penchant for young South African girls. The police need to know about this Jack, they really do."

Jack rubbed the side of his face. "I know. But Piet feels differently, and I agree with him. The two of us can work more quickly on our own. We have useful contacts.

"To open this case now, something that happened years ago, with all the proof we have, will take years within the British police system. We want to follow up ourselves; then present it to the British police."

He grinned at Bill. "They might even be grateful we did all the groundwork."

Bill didn't smile back. His brow furrowed as he thought through the evidence Jack had shown him. "All this happened over twenty years ago, right? In those days they didn't have the developments we have today in forensic science and technology. Serial killers are caught much sooner today. Identifying which unsolved murders could be attributed to a serial killer is the hardest thing to solve. This looks like a case in point."

Bill, once again, ran his fingers through his short hair. "Serial killers tend to have an exceptionally good grasp of other people's emotions and are quick to pick up on any vulnerability or weakness to convince their potential victims into doing things they normally wouldn't. That's what he saw in your four girls."

Bill took a sip of his beer and wiped the froth off his upper lip before continuing. "This is what I think happened.

"He saw young girls who were vulnerable. They arrive in London, full of excitement, they're off to university with all the fun and promise that holds. The airport is crowded with a lot of flights arriving, from all over the word; thousands of people; it's all heady stuff for a young girl. I remember Zoe as a giggly teenager, Jack. She was living for the moment, not thinking clearly or responsibly. They don't think for a second anything bad can happen to them.

"The girls go through all the formalities at immigration and customs and then head for the exit. Suddenly they're on British soil, on their own, in crowds of other arrivals and they're a bit overwhelmed, uncertain, don't know what to do. It would be easy for a predator to be a friendly Samaritan and offer to help them.

"Having read the files and the interviews with their parents, none of the girls had expected to be met at the airport. Nothing had been arranged by the travel agency or their parents. The girls were to take the

Heathrow Express and then a taxi, a tube or bus from there to their accommodation.

"So, the question remains. How did this person know their names, and which flight they were on? What they looked like?

"The biggest problem the police had was the same problem the South African police had. The girls had left their country, which was definite. They arrived in London, that they knew from immigration. Then they disappeared."

Chapter Twenty-Four

Piet Joubert arrived back in South Africa and drew in a lungful of the scent of Africa. He had never been more pleased to be home, back in the land he loved. He stood for some moments as the other passengers swirled around him heading for the arrivals hall and allowed the warmth of a February morning to penetrate his tired back.

He took the domestic flight back to Hazyview and was pleased to see the ever-smiling Zimbabwean receptionist, Blessing, from the hotel, waiting for him. On the drive back to the hotel Piet peppered Blessing with questions on any security incidents at the hotel which might require his ongoing attention.

"No, Mr Piet, all is well. Shaka the Zulu is watching everything, most of the guests have left for their places far away. It is quiet everywhere now. Winter is coming here and the rains. Our guests are not liking the rain."

Piet heaved his suitcase from the back of the vehicle and made his way to his cottage. He could hear his dog, Hope, barking in anticipation of his arrival.

He opened the door and Hope circled him, her tail whirling like a windmill, she bent and picked up the first thing that came to hand, one of his slippers, and ran around and around him.

"*Ag*, Hope, I know you're pleased to see me, but you're making me dizzy!" Hope dropped the slipper and rolled over onto her back, beside herself with seeing her owner again.

Piet bent down and rubbed her tummy. "Yes, I'm pleased to see you too. Now come on, I need to unpack, take a shower, then go and check the premises. You think you can manage that, my girl?"

Piet had put the briefcase on a side table with a stern warning to his dog it must not be touched under any circumstances. He had had an answer ready for customs should they have searched his luggage, but they didn't. It could have been a tricky situation if they had.

He took a quick shower and changed into his security uniform, looking with despair at his ruined safari boots, but he put them on regardless. They still felt damp.

Piet checked the premises then perused the list of guests on the computer, assisted by Blessing. Then made his way to the bar. It was busy, as usual. Hugo, the owner, raised his arm in greeting. "How was your trip, Piet. Enjoy the green and rolling pastures of my old country? Beer?"

Piet nodded. Took a quick look around the bar then sat down. Hugo brought him a beer. "Good to have you back, Piet. Although I'm not sure for how long. A courier delivered something for you from Jack. That normally means you have a new case to work on?" Hugo passed the package over.

Piet peeled back the perforated opening strip and pulled out four copied case files, from the British police, and another file full of notes. As he sipped his beer, he glanced through the files Jack had obtained, and his notes on the four missing girls. Plus, the overview from his friend Bill, the retired detective.

*****

He gathered the files together and headed for the hotel dining room where he ordered a steak and mushroom pie with chips. Delighted he wasn't asked about allergies. Once done, he sat back satiated, gathered up his paperwork, then made his way back to his cottage.

Tired but determined, he spread the contents of the briefcase over his dining room table. Carefully matching each girl's hank of hair with her piece of jewellery and her photograph. Then he turned back to the four case files Bill Watson had given to Jack, along with Jack's notes and observations.

Listed here were the four schools the girls had attended, all in Cape Town, the address of where the girls and their parents had lived at the time and details of any siblings, if they had them.

He had to admit the British police had done a thorough job of trying to find the girls, but the police in South Africa had not been forthcoming. But to be fair, Piet concluded, there was little to go on. The girls had boarded their flights, had passed through immigration, then disappeared into another country.

The South African Embassy in London had, of course, been informed, but given the tumultuous times on-going in South Africa at the time, and no body had turned up, the first case of the missing girl, Anna-Marie, had no doubt been buried beneath all the other events going on at the time. The hand-over of most of the white South African staff working at the Embassy to their new government replacements took precedence over everything else.

From Jack's police detective friend, Piet now had the name of Zelda's boys, Marius and Tinus. He would contact his mate Bertie, ex-Home Affairs, who, as far as Piet was concerned, was the man he needed with his incredible network and databases all over the world. He would be able to dig around a bit and find out more about Zelda and her family with the surname Cameron.

But more importantly, Piet wanted to know more about the two boys she had taken to the UK with her husband. Where were they now? His gut instinct told him they could be linked to everything that had happened afterwards.

Perhaps it was one of her sons who had written the letter he was now holding in his hand, warning Zelda she was in danger. Telling her he was going away for some time. Perhaps one of them had left her the briefcase and told her to put it in a safe deposit facility where it would be safe.

He needed more information about them.

Why had Zelda cut them both out of her will?

Piet gave a cavernous, noisy, yawn and rubbed his tired eyes. No matter what Zelda Cameron had been trying to hide or destroy, Piet would find the official records and take it from there. He knew the *bleddy* British lawyer would tell him *fok* all else he needed to know. Waste of time was Mr *bleddy* Barrington-Smith, in his fancy suit.

Chapter Twenty-Five
London

The next morning Jack took the short train trip to Larkstown, hired a car, and booked into a nice-looking guest house in the centre of town, then set out for Zelda's last known address at The Gables.

It was only a ten-minute drive from the centre of the pretty village with its pastel-coloured houses, hump backed bridges, boutique shops, restaurants, and pubs.

His tyres crunched up the driveway to the front of The Gables. The building was yet another example of a modest country house now converted to apartments. He parked in the designated area and looked around.

Double oak front doors proclaimed the entrance with a discreet brass plaque embedded to the right of the doors partially hidden by climbing ivy, with the names of eight residents identified underneath. There seemed to be no security or caretakers' office available for enquiries. It didn't appear to be the place where one would randomly select a resident's bell to gain entrance. In cities it was quite common practice. But he didn't think the little upmarket town of Larkstown would lend itself to that sort of thing.

Jack contemplated his next move. He noticed a smaller cottage set slightly to the side of the main building, partially hidden by an ancient oak tree, and headed towards it. There was no name outside the door, but he could hear music playing softly inside. Taking a chance, he knocked tentatively on the door and waited.

The door swung open and a tall man, dressed in brown corduroy trousers, a well-worn tweed jacket with leather patches on the elbows, a crisp, blue-checked shirt and cravat at his neck, smiled in greeting. Clearly a military man with his ramrod straight back, even though he was probably well into his seventies.

"Ah, you must be the chap from the council?"

Jack smiled at him. "Good morning, sir. I'm not from the council. The name's Jack Taylor. I'm looking up a friend of mine whose aunt lives here. But forgive me, I must have knocked at the wrong door."

"My dear fellow, do come in. Delighted to have someone to chat to Cambridge or Oxford?"

"Cambridge, sir."

"Excellent. Name's Major Jordan, retired now, of course. do come in. Always good to see someone from my old alma mater.

"Now who is this aunt you're looking for? Everyone knows everyone here, although one doesn't mix, you understand. Just a nod of the head in greeting. One does not wish to intrude on anyone's privacy. That's why I bought this place. Old school types live here, know what's what and how to behave. Sometimes I take a walk around the grounds and chat to the estate manager. Nice fellow. Simon. Does a good job with the gardens and always around if you want something fixed. Been here for thirty years, he told me.

"May I offer you coffee, or perhaps?" he glanced at his watch. "A sherry?"

"Coffee would be wonderful, thank you."

The Major busied himself in the kitchen whilst Jack looked around the sitting room at various mementos of a well-travelled past. Major Jordan returned and handed Jack a mug of tea, then gestured for him to sit.

"Thank you, Major. You must have travelled considerably in your career with Her Majesty's overseas regiments?

"Indeed, I did. Some hellholes of course, Aden being one of them, but other memorable places. India. Africa, the Far East. Of course, things are decidedly different now. But enough of me. You?"

Jack hesitated for a second. He had one chance, and it was now. "I'm a journalist with the *Telegraph*. I've been with them for over twenty years now, initially based in London but now I live in South Africa. That's why I'm here, looking up an aunt of a friend of mine there. He lost touch with her years ago and asked me to pop in and see her. This was her last known address."

The Major sipped his drink. "Ah yes, Africa," he mused. "Best time of my life, Tanganyika, Uganda, Zambia, Kenya, what was then Rhodesia. I have fond memories of all those places. A very privileged lifestyle, sadly gone now. So, what was the name of the aunt your friend is seeking?"

"Her name is Mrs Cameron. Zelda Cameron?"

The Major frowned slightly. "Then I'm afraid you're too late, my dear chap. Mrs Cameron died two years or so ago. I bought this place from her estate. This is where she lived. Sorry, your journey seems to have been in vain."

He looked at Jack shrewdly.

"It seems a long way to come to look up a relative of your friend. Did you know Mrs Cameron by chance? It seems, as a journalist you have more than a passing interest in Mrs Cameron, or rather the late Mrs Cameron?"

Jack took a sip of his coffee. "I'm sorry to hear Mrs Cameron is no longer with us, Major. My friend will be most distressed to hear this news. I was merely going to be in the area and thought I would pop in and check on her."

The Major nodded his head. "I see. Not that I believe your story for a moment, especially as you're a journalist with one of our top newspapers.

"I was with Army Intelligence for most of my career and I can spot someone who isn't quite giving me the full facts and story. But be that as it may. I shall indulge you. Do continue."

Jack glanced around the room, uncomfortable that he had been rumbled so quickly. "So, Major Jordan, the place was completely empty when you bought it?"

The Major took a generous swallow from his glass of sherry. "There was an option to buy the contents. I bought a few things. Didn't have much of my own to furnish the place. Army always provided our homes, fully furnished, with a full household of servants. Not that one may call them that anymore, of course. Called soil technicians or household executives or some such other ridiculous titles."

He gestured around the room with his rapidly depleting glass of sherry. "So, a lot of this belonged to the late owner. I just had to add my own bits and pieces to make it feel like home."

Jack looked around the modest sitting room, trying to imagine Zelda living here with all her secrets and anxious thoughts. The Major had made the place his own with the pictures on the wall of horses and what looked like some sort of family estate. A group of men dressed in the correct attire for a day's pheasant shooting. The results lying in broken heaps at their feet, alongside a dozen or so working dogs. Books were lined up with some precision in a large bookcase with the watery sunlight filtering through the windows, Jack could see the quivering cobwebs festooning the books.

There seemed to be no trace of a woman's touch.

No lingering essence of the woman called Zelda Cameron.

Jack carefully put his empty mug down on a coaster on the coffee table. "Thank you, Major. It seems my journey was indeed in vain. However, the least I can do is visit her grave and pay my respects? I understand her husband was a doctor. He passed away here in the village from what I can gather?"

"No idea, my dear chap. Perhaps the local priest might be able to assist. Nice enough by all accounts. Catholic. Knows everything going on in the village. Sorry I couldn't help. But it would be difficult without you telling me the truth about why you are here."

Jack stood up and shook his hand. He reached into his pocket and withdrew a card. "Here are my details. Perhaps someone here at The Gables might have known Zelda? It would be, how can I put this, quite useful to have known a little about her last few years here."

The Major sucked in his breath, looking disappointed. "Doubt it, old boy, keep themselves to themselves here. Been living here myself for ten months, haven't had a conversation with any of the other residents. Not like the old days when one had one's club to go to, whether in Nairobi, Lusaka, or Salisbury, or even in London. Funny old life when I look back - everyone knew someone who knew someone you knew, no matter where you were posted. Not now of course, all that has gone.

"Too expensive to travel and belong anywhere these days. Not even allowed to have a dog or cat here for company. It seems to me the older you get the more is taken away from you. They do have a local taxi company who take the residents into town twice a week if they don't have their own car. Not giving into that, my boy, not yet anyway. Have my own car. Old but dependable, like me!"

Jack nodded in sympathy. "Oh, by the way Major, what happened to Mrs Cameron's things, the ones you didn't buy with the cottage, any idea?"

The Major shook his head. "No idea, old boy, everything was cleared out before I moved in, except for the things I purchased. The estate agency might know. Probably sold off what was of any interest and gave the rest to one of the local charity shops. Baker's Estates, they're in town, they should be able to help you."

The Major saw him to the door. "Thoroughly enjoyed meeting you, Jack Taylor. Perhaps I shall read more about Mrs Zelda Cameron in a story which I'm sure will appear in your excellent newspaper at some point.

"Have a word with Simon," he glanced at his watch, "should be taking his lunch break around about now. You'll find him down at the entrance gates, near his cottage."

Jack grinned at him, then climbed back into his car and with a final wave, made his way back down the drive. Loneliness, he surmised, as he watched the diminishing figure of the Major recede in his rear-view mirror, was the hardest thing of all to bear. Not something you ever think will happen to you. Especially as the Major had without doubt led an interesting and fulfilling life during his many postings abroad.

Jack drove slowly down the drive looking for the estate managers cottage. Having lived and worked here for thirty years, according to the Major, he would have a better idea of the last few years of Zelda Cameron's life.

According to the Major, Simon was more than just the estate manager at The Gables. He also handled any maintenance which may be required. He lived on the property himself and had done for over thirty years. He kept a close eye on the residents and who came and went. He helped them with changing bulbs high up in the ceiling, with blocked drains and any other things he could assist them with. Each evening he checked the homes were secure and first thing in the morning.

Simon, according to the Major, made mental notes of all cars which entered the property. He knew which car belonged to which resident. He knew the courier company that delivered their parcels, the home delivery from the various supermarkets in town and the local taxi company who ferried the residents into town twice a week for a couple of hours, then brought them back. He kept a close eye on who came and went.

The residents had a direct phone line to Simon and would call him with any assistance they may require. If they were going away on holiday, Simon would be there to carry their luggage to the waiting taxi and assure them he would keep an eye on their flats whilst they were away, even water their plants.

Simon knew everything that was going on. This was his patch.

He lived on the property himself, in a small cottage set back in the grounds with a workshop attached which held all the gardening equipment and everything else he needed to maintain the high standards residents at The Gables expected. It also enabled him to see who came and went on the estate.

Jack spotted him sitting on a bench eating a sandwich and made his way towards him.

"Hello Simon. Mind if I join you? I've just been having a chat with Major Jordan about one of the residents who used to live here. He suggested I have a word with you about her. My name's Jack Taylor."

"Take a seat, Jack, beautiful day, isn't it? Spring is coming and the gardens will look glorious when the daffodils and bluebells shoot through from their winter hibernation. It will keep me busy for a few months. Is Major Jordan a relative of yours perhaps?"

Jack smiled. "Nothing gets past you, eh! I'm here because a friend of mine, a relative of Mrs Zelda Cameron, wanted to know a little more about her years here at The Gables, see how she was doing. The Major, of course, couldn't help me much as he had never met her. I'm here, from South Africa, visiting my family who live in Somerset. The Major told me she had passed away, that you could help me, perhaps tell me a little about her last years here?"

Simon closed the lid on his Tupperware box, then lit a cigarette and blew a long stream of smoke into the atmosphere, looking thoughtful.

"Mrs Cameron didn't mix much with the other residents. She would phone me if she needed help with anything in her cottage. But I didn't know her well. A very private person. I would call a taxi for her when she went up to London every few months. I think she missed the buzz of her life there, apparently it was where she lived for many years when she left South Africa."

Jack pursued his line of thought. "Did she have any visitors here?"

Simon shook his head. "No. It must have been difficult for her with most of her relatives, I presume, living in another country. But she seemed quite self-contained, spent time in the gardens here, painting away."

Jack looked into the distance, composing his next question. "So, no visitors at all?"

Simon took a small square of tin foil from his pocket and stubbed out his cigarette, then squeezed the tin foil around it.

"Well, there was someone who came every year in September for about four or five years. He would stay an hour or two. He always brought a bouquet of lilies with him. I'd find them in the trash the next day. Obviously, she didn't care for them."

Jack frowned. "Why do you remember this so well. It was a long time ago?"

Simon glanced at him. "Well, yes, it was. Fifteen years or so."

"But you remember it?"

Simon nodded it. "Yes, I do."

"How so?"

"Well, the guy always came in a London cab, a black one."

Jack pretended to look puzzled. "A bit far out of London, a big fare for a cabbie. Maybe a wealthy relative who didn't fancy tubes and trains. I presume the cab parked then and waited for his passenger? Very nice fare indeed."

Simon nodded. "Yes, the cabbie parked under a tree and just waited for him. No, it wasn't that. It was the passenger."

Jack glanced at him. "Something odd about him? Is that what you're saying?"

"No, Jack, nothing odd about him. The reason I remember this so well is that a black cab arrived, quite late one night, but in February, instead of the usual September. In fact, I hadn't seen it for many years. That's why I remember all this.

"But what seemed out of the ordinary was he arrived the night Mrs Cameron died. Thinking about it afterwards, maybe it wasn't anything unusual. Perhaps she had asked him to call on her."

Jack frowned. "You think he had something to do with her death?"

Simon shook his head. "Oh, no, absolutely not. Impossible. He wore the same distinctive apparel as he always did. A cassock."

Jack grinned. "Nothing odd about that, Simon. If he was a priest maybe he had come to hear some kind of confession, or she knew she was dying and asked him to come to perform the last rites or something like that. They do that sort of thing you know, especially practicing Catholics."

Jack stood up and held out his hand. "Thanks for your help, Simon. I'll let my friend know about Zelda, he'll he glad to know her last years were happy here."

Simon shrugged. "I wouldn't say she was particularly happy, she seemed lonely to me, like most of the residents here I suppose. But glad I could help. Nice to meet you, Jack."

Jack climbed back into his car.

A priest came calling on the night Zelda died?

115

Chapter Twenty-Six

Jack had no trouble finding the ancient Catholic church in the centre of the village. He wandered through the double wooden gates and found a slatted bench to sit on. He looked at the many graves in front of him, then turned his face to the watery sun making its way over the village, buttoned up his coat and wrapped his scarf around his neck against the chilly wind. He closed his eyes and thought about his conversation with Simon.

The silence was soporific, peaceful. He opened his eyes and wondered about all the people lying down in front of him. Their laughter, their hopes, and dreams. The lives these people had lived, through wars, pandemics, untold happiness, utter despair, and, of course, the joy and happiness and that elusive thing called love, in all its guises. Who would remember them? Who would remember four missing South African girls?

He leaned forward, resting his elbows on his knees. Those four girls would not be forgotten. He was going to make sure of it.

He and Piet were going to find out exactly what happened to them.

His thoughts flickered back to the death of one of his friends, three months ago. He had been killed whilst covering a story in Iran. Because Christopher had had friends and colleagues all over the world, covering various stories, it had been impossible for all of them to attend his funeral. But with the miracle of technology and despite all the various time zones, it had been decided Christopher would have a "virtual" funeral.

There would be no black-clad mourners, shivering within the walls of Christopher's ancient home church, no long faces, no veils, no tears. All his friends and colleagues had sat in all those countries all over the world, with all the different time zones and watched the Memorial Service, courtesy of Zoom, in the comfort of their homes.

At first Jack had felt a little uncomfortable with the entire concept. But he had sat there in Hazyview, wearing just his shorts, with a single candle lit in remembrance and quite alone. With a glass of wine to hand, he had watched the entire service and decided Christopher would most definitely have approved. He had lifted his glass in salute and bid his own private farewell to his friend.

Exactly how Christopher would have liked it. As he would have liked to be remembered. A living breathing person, surrounded by friends and colleagues from around the world, all lifting a glass to him. Each one remembering him in their own way without the hundreds of years of trappings of a formal funeral.

No black veils, no freezing church, no conforming to what was expected.

Christopher would have loved how each of his friends remembered him – drink in hand, feet up.

To remember him the stories came thick and fast from all over the globe. A loving final gesture to a talented journalist friend who was no longer here.

It was the best funeral Jack had ever attended. Quite alone with his private thoughts and no protocols to follow.

He was brought abruptly back to the present as an elderly priest approached him.

"May I help you at all? I'm Father Gabriel."

Jack stood up, shook the man's hand, and introduced himself. "I'm on a visit here from South Africa. I'm a journalist and promised an old friend of mine I would call and pay my respects to an aunt of his who lived here in the village. Perhaps," he said innocently, "you'd be able to help me locate her? Her name was Mrs Zelda Cameron. She died a couple of years ago from what I can gather. I think, according to my friend, her husband was buried here as well. I would imagine they are buried together?"

Father Gabriel gestured for him to sit back on the bench and joined him, wincing slightly as he lowered himself down. "I've been here in Larkstown for over fifty years now," he chuckled softly. "I know everyone. The ones lying down here and the ones still upright!"

He frowned and glanced at the graves in front of him. "Yes, I do remember Doctor Cameron. Paul. Popular figure around town. Became involved with village life here when he retired from his practice in London. Rotary, fund raising, captain of the village cricket team etc. Good turnout for his funeral."

He glanced back at Jack. "Paul's wife, Zelda, was more of a private person, pleasant enough, but she didn't immerse herself in the community as her husband did. She attended church but not on a regular basis. Stayed in the village after her husband died, lived at The Gables until she too passed away, as you say, a couple of years ago now."

Jack stood up. "Perhaps you would be kind enough to show me where they're buried, Father?"

Father Gabriel bent down and plucked a few leaves from one of the graves. "Well, you see, that was the strange thing. There was no funeral for her here. I was expecting to perform the service and bury her near her beloved husband," he gestured to his left, "over by the wall there. But that didn't happen."

Jack stared at him. "So, what happened to her then? Where is she?"

The priest frowned again. "No idea, I'm afraid. I did, of course, make discreet enquiries. It would appear she had made private arrangements, through her lawyer, to be cremated and have her ashes delivered to a church in London somewhere. As I said - all a bit unusual really."

Jack nodded. "Indeed, it does all sound odd. But who can deny anyone their final wishes? Perhaps she had close friends or relatives her husband wasn't aware of. Or she contacted old friends in London after her husband died. Friends she met when her husband had his practice there and felt it was more appropriate to have them attend some kind of memorial service?"

The priest shook his head. "No. Zelda became even more reclusive after Paul died. Kept herself to herself at The Gables. I didn't see her very often in church again."

Jack wrapped his scarf more tightly around his throat, feeling the chilly wind. "Tell me, Father, did the Cameron's have any children?"

The priest ran his hand through his thinning hair and gave Jack a quizzical look. "You ask many questions Mr Taylor. Surely, this friend of yours would know if the Cameron's had any children.

"Being a journalist, as you told me, is there a story you're following? A story about Paul Cameron. Or is it Zelda Cameron you are more interested in?"

In front of a man of the cloth Jack had the grace to look contrite.

"I am following a story, Father. Zelda Cameron was not what she appeared to be. Something has become known. Some very disturbing information, in fact. There are a number people involved. People who have been waiting for answers to questions for over twenty years. I was hoping you might be able to help me?"

Father Gabriel ran his finger around the stiff, slightly greying collar, at his wrinkled throat. "We should seek shelter from the cold within the church, Mr Taylor. I'm not sure I can help you, but the good Lord tries to alleviate tormented souls when they are in need."

Jack entered the church, noticing the board to his left with notices of village and church events. It was colder than the weather outside. There were various religious booklets, a pile of hymnals piled haphazardly next to them. A wooden box for donations and the inevitable small candles available to all who wished to take one and move towards the dimly lit interior to place them and remember their loved ones. Here they too flickered and died in the frigid air permeating the interior of the church.

Jack could feel the history of the place, probably a few hundred years old. He imagined the thousands of people who had, over the years, trodden the cold stones beneath their feet and shuffled along the pews to find a space for whatever service they were attending, be it the normal service, a wedding, a christening, a funeral, Christmas, or Easter. It seemed the circle of life continued here, one way or another.

Even as a child Jack had disliked going to church. Compulsory, of course, at the schools he attended later. But he had always been frightened of the solemn aura of something he couldn't understand as a young child. People behaved differently; grown-ups threw aside their boisterous familiar selves once they entered church. Becoming humble and ordinary, almost subservient, as if there was something quite frightening about the place. As if they had to discard and shed the person they were, expensive clothes, titles or otherwise and become a shadow of themselves. It was powerful stuff and difficult to comprehend.

Now, as an adult, Jack understood it all. Having seen the absolute worst of humanity in his career and the catastrophic effect it had on the ones left behind.

Father Gabriel's church exuded that peace, hope and faith. A haven from the thousands of questions people asked themselves each day. A place, hundreds of years old, where generations had come to seek solace and answers. A place still steeped in silence. A place where no answers were given, and only blind faith prevailed.

Jack followed the priest and watched as he crossed himself with Holy Water, dipped his head and then made his way towards the alter.

At the front pews, he turned towards Jack. "Come sit, my son. I will help if I can."

Jack gingerly sat down on the hard pew feeling the cold permeate through his trousers. "You see, Father Gabriel, I think Mrs Cameron was involved in something, perhaps not of her making, but I may be wrong.

"Four children went missing some twenty odd years ago in London. They were never found. My partner and I have acquired information that these children were all from South Africa."

He loosened his scarf slightly. "Someone has asked us to ascertain what happened to them. I would like to be able to tell their parents, the truth about what happened to their children. Something I know you believe in Father? The truth that is."

Father Gabriel looked towards the altar as though seeking divine guidance, then he turned and looked at Jack, his small brown eyes behind his round smudged glasses, full of sadness.

"I know what you are asking me, Mr Taylor. I am sure you fully understand the confessional is a sacred place. Whatever is confessed there is between the confessor and God. The priest is merely the conduit. I cannot, under any circumstances, reveal anything about Mrs Cameron. Indeed, I'm not even permitted to divulge if Mrs Cameron ever made any kind of confession."

He stood up awkwardly. "I'm sorry, my son. I cannot help you."

Jack stood and glanced at the Confessional. Over the years it had become one of the things he could never come to terms with. He knew a confession was sacrosanct and the priest unable to reveal anything to any authorities, no matter how heinous the crime confessed to. It had confounded and angered lawyers, families of the bereaved, and the police for generations. Surely a priest had an obligation, not only to his Holy Father, but to society, to bring a killer to justice. A killer who had sat behind a curtained grill and confessed to his or her crimes. Someone who might go out and kill again?

But for a priest to reveal the identity of someone who had committed a crime would mean the priest would be abandoned by his church and cast adrift from everything he had dedicated his life to. Priests were known for their loyalty to the Church. Their loyalty was to their God and their utter faith He would mete out justice, come the day, to all those who had hidden behind the curtain and the grill and confessed to crimes no normal person would be able to comprehend.

Jack stood up and shook the priest's hand, then turned to go. "Thank you, Father Gabriel, for trying to help. I understand your situation although I have to say I have never understood how so much good in the church could overwhelm the generations of such evil existing each day. But that is between you and your God, I think.

"I am profoundly grateful I chose a different path. Mine is dedicated to finding the bad guys and making them pay *now* for what they did. I can't wait for your God to decide what should be done. What punishment should fit the crime. I'm doing something about it. I sleep well at night knowing I have done something to put things right. I'm not sure how you sleep, Father. Your burden is far greater than mine in that you can do nothing about it."

The priest prised himself upright with some difficulty. "Go well, my son. I will pray for the souls of the four missing girls."

Jack turned around slowly. "I said four children went missing, Father. I didn't say they were all girls.

"But you have answered my question about Zelda."

*****

Father Gabriel watched Jack Taylor as he left the church. He sank to his knees and crossed himself. Yes, he knew about the four girls. But he was powerless to do anything about it.

He had recognised her voice, of course, during the confessional. She had an unusual accent, and he had known who she was. But he had kept his eyes steadfastly in front of him and listened to her confession.

Father Gabriel also knew who had received her ashes.

Chapter Twenty-Seven

Jack turned left after leaving the church and made his way down the main street of the village. There were coffee shops, antique shops, clothing boutiques, banks, and a household name supermarket squeezed in between, almost in embarrassment at having to be amongst the more individual bespoke shops.

Finally, he spotted the estate agency he was looking for. Bakers Estates. He glanced at their window and whistled with surprise at the price of houses up for sale. He could buy an impressive vineyard in Franschhoek, under the heady blue skies of the Western Cape, for the price they were asking for a modest cottage in the village.

A harried looking young man looked up from his computer as Jack approached his desk. "May I help you, sir?"

Jack helped himself to the chair opposite the agent's desk and sat down.

He gave the man a friendly grin and introduced himself. "I'm here on behalf of a friend in South Africa. He wanted me to look up an aunt of his who used to live at The Gables? A Mrs Cameron?"

The agent sighed with disappointment. No sale coming up here.

Jack continued blithely on. "I've been out to The Gables and heard the sad news that Mrs Cameron passed away two years ago. I met the chap who bought her place from her estate, Major Jordan. He told me he had bought some of the contents of the house, but not all of them.

"I wonder if you could tell me what happened to any of her personal things. My friend would appreciate some kind of memento if that's at all possible to find?"

The agent frowned and tapped at his computer. "Ah, yes; here it is. Major Jordan did indeed purchase the house and most of the contents. The rest, as instructed by her lawyer, was sold off by auction and anything not sold was donated to a charity shop here in the village."

He looked up at Jack. "That's all I can tell you I'm afraid. There's a second-hand shop at the end of the road called *Remember Me*. The owner often buys up things from deceased estates. You might want to pop in there and ask him if he acquired anything from the estate. Friendly fellow called Sam Bates."

Jack thanked him profusely, then made his way through the meandering tourists until he found what he was looking for.

Remember Me, in keeping with the style of the village was not your normal second-hand shop piled to the rafters with dusty junk. It was small and the things for sale were tastefully displayed.

A man in his thirties, with a full head of curly brown hair down to his shoulders, no doubt the friendly fellow Sam Bates, looked up as the tinkle of a bell announced a potential customer.

Jack lifted his hand in silent greeting then proceeded to browse through the things on display. There were bookcases holding hundreds of books, elegant pieces of furniture, crockery, cutlery, glassware, a section of expensive looking second-hand clothing, framed pictures stacked against a table with spindly legs, pieces of old leather luggage and trunks, some stylish pieces of silver and a myriad of other things.

Sam Bates looked up from the chair he was busy re-upholstering. "Looking for anything I can help you with? It looks a bit crowded in here, but I know where everything is. Feel free to browse around unless you're looking for something in particular?"

Jack made his way to the owner's desk which was littered with things he intended to repair. "Are you Sam Bates?"

Sam nodded. "That's me."

Jack held out his hand. "Jack Taylor. Pleased to meet you. Perhaps you can help me with something?"

Jack explained why he was looking for any small thing from the estate of Mrs Cameron, thinking his friend would appreciate a little memento of his late aunt.

Sam scratched his head with the end of the end of the screwdriver he was working with. "She died two years ago you say? Phew, I've had a lot of things through my shop since then. Let me have a look. I keep a list of everything I purchase and who or where from. I also keep a record of everything I sell, of course. The VAT man doesn't care who owned what, dead or alive, just so long as he gets his cut. Now let's look and see what we can find."

Jack perched on the edge of Sam's desk as the man tapped away at this computer looking for his records of goods bought and sold.

Sam frowned at his screen. "Was it a Mrs Zelda Cameron who lived at The Gables?"

Jack felt a small kick of excitement. "Yes, that was her. Zelda Cameron."

Sam rubbed the stubble on his cheek and scrolled through a brief list. "I didn't buy much as far as I can see here. A few African carvings, masks, a nice silver tea service, a carved chest, um, and that was about it. Oh yes, and a couple of paintings. Water colours. I remember them quite well actually. Originals, not copies. Nothing particularly notable about them just country scenes, somewhere remote, but they had a poignancy about them. A sadness if you like, which was appealing.

"Nothing much left I'm afraid. I sold everything belonging to Mrs Cameron except for one painting which will be here somewhere. Let me look."

Jack followed him towards the paintings stacked against the spindly table and watched him sort through them.

"Ah, here it is. I've put a price of two hundred and fifty pounds on it but so far, no buyers. Your friend might like it?" he said hopefully.

Jack took the painting and stood it against the back of the table. To his mind it wasn't anything eye-catching, but it did have a certain nostalgia about it. It was a scene somewhere out in the bush, a low farmhouse, the ubiquitous water mill on its triangular platform, heavy skies promising rain and a hazy outline of mountains and hills in the background.

On his recent road trip from the north to the south of South Africa he had passed scenes like this dozens of times.

Sam stood next to him. "Looks like it could be Australia or Africa. With the chest and masks I bought from the estate I would say Africa, wouldn't you?"

Jack peered at the picture hoping to find an indication as to who the artist might have been but could find no signature anywhere. "Yup, this is definitely a painting of a farm somewhere in Africa."

Jack straightened up and pursed his lips. "Not sure there would be anyone interested in buying it though. But, as I said, my friend would like some kind of memento of his aunt and as this, according to your records, was part of Mrs Cameron's estate. Would you consider lowering the price?"

Sam ran his fingers along the frame of the painting. "The frame is of decent quality; I could use it for some other artwork I have. How about we take it out of the frame, and I'll sell it to you for a hundred quid?"

Jack held out his hand. "Deal. Easier for me to carry on the flight home without a frame."

Sam lifted the painting and took it to his desk. Selecting a sharp work instrument, he carefully eased the back off. "There you go," he frowned. "Oh, there's something wedged into the corner here. Judging from the backing of the painting it must have been here for decades," he peered at it. "Looks like an old photograph. Maybe relatives of your friend's family."

Jack stared down at the small black and white photograph of two little boys. They both wore long shorts and pale shirts, their hair hidden behind floppy sun hats. It was hard to see their features in the harsh sunlight. There was no background, no houses, just what looked like the empty bush. No grown-ups with their arms around them. Just two boys standing quite alone.

Sam handed Jack the rolled-up painting. "The photograph is free. Hope your mate finds it of some comfort. He might recognise the two kids. He'll need a good memory though; it looks decades old."

Jack gave him his credit card and continued to study the photograph. Why, he thought to himself, did the artist hide a photograph of two small boys in the back of a painting?

Had Zelda Cameron been aware of the photograph's existence? Or had she bought the painting not knowing what was hidden there?"

Or he mused, had Zelda Cameron hidden the photograph there and, if so, why?

Another thought crossed his mind. Was Zelda Cameron the artist? Unlikely thought it might seem, were these two boys her sons?

*****

Back at the guest house he pinned the painting to the wall with blue tack, took shots of it with his phone, then a couple more shots of the photograph of the two boys.

He spent the next hour sitting on his bed enlarging the painting on his phone and studying it. There had to be a signature somewhere, but he was damned if he could find it.

Next, he enlarged the black and white photograph of the little boys. He made the image as large as he could before it distorted. He reduced the size and studied the slightly creased images. They seemed to be about four or five as far as he could ascertain. Neither of them was smiling at the camera, in fact they were scowling at it looking distrustful and ill at ease. Now the photo was enlarged he could see they were both poorly dressed and neither wore shoes.

Their shorts and shirts looked too big for them and were shabby. The shorts frayed and held up by what he thought might be string. The waistbands curling over it, the shirts thin, one of them with a hole at the elbow. Their faces were gaunt and their bodies thin. They reminded Jack of images he had seen of children after World War Two wearing similar shabby clothes, their bodies thin from rationing and lack of healthy food to build them up, their faces gaunt and haunted.

Who were these children? What was their photograph doing wedged in the frame of an old water colour belonging to Zelda Cameron?

The lawyer in London indicated there had been no beneficiaries to her will. So, who were these boys? Why hide this photo in the frame?

Jack rubbed his tired eyes and slumped back on his bed. Nothing was making any sense, but his instincts told him there was a story here and it was all connected to the woman Zelda Cameron and her tenuous link with the four girls who went missing.

He needed to get in touch with Piet and bring him up to date on what he had discovered.

He wrote an email to Piet and sent it with the photographs he had taken. He copied Harry in, knowing if he didn't, he would have Harry bellowing down the phone asking where they were with the story.

It was seven in the evening; it was now dark outside. Jack took a hot shower, changed his clothes, and made his way back through the village. There were five pubs he had counted so far. He went for the one that looked slightly more up-market than the others. One that looked as though it had been there for hundreds of years.

He sat at the bar and looked around. It was charming and quite obviously a few hundred years old. Old horse brasses decorated the ancient fireplace, the fire glinting off the patina of what he presumed was the original implements used to keep the fire going, brass tongs, a coal scuttle, cracked old leather bellows, a poker, and brushes.

The modest bar was pitted and dark with age and he wondered about all the people who had sat there over generations, also nursing a beer, and wondering about where their life was going and with whom. He knew, instinctively, if the locals of the village went anywhere this is where they would come. This would be their local.

It might be a place where tourists would pop in for a drink. But this was, he was sure, an integral part of village life, where he would hopefully get to talk to the real people of the village; people who had resided here all their lives and knew a thing or two about the other people who lived here.

It amused him that every time the pub door opened all eyes swivelled to see who had arrived. It reminded him of the meerkats in Africa, up on their haunches, their eyes, and ears on high alert for any uninvited guest. He had to admit to himself out of all the little animals there he found them the most captivating and amusing.

He ordered scampi and chips at the bar, his mind going through what he had learned so far. His eyes scanned the people in the pub. He was looking for someone who had lived in the village for at least twenty years - someone who might have known Doctor Cameron and his wife Zelda.

He finished his excellent crispy scampi and chips and ordered another pint. He wasn't surprised to see Sam Bates come through the door. He raised his hand in recognition as Sam made his way through the now crowded but not noisy bar.

"Well, hello again, Mr Taylor. Still in town I see, but soon to be off, no doubt for some much-needed sunshine in Africa? A place I have always wanted to see and go on a safari. But until I find a priceless heirloom and sell it for a fortune, I can only dream about it!"

Jack smiled at him. "Come and join me. What will you have to drink?"

The barman slid a pint of beer across the counter. Clearly Sam was a regular and the barman knew what he liked.

Sam took a long gulp of his beer and wiped the foam off his lips.

"So, Sam, what did you do before you got into the world of second-hand treasures and people's secret pasts?"

Sam grinned at him. "I was a copper in London, like my old man before me. But I couldn't deal with the politics of it all. All that politically correct stuff, it tied our hands; I can tell you. Bottom line, I left in frustration and decided to open my own business here in the village. I prefer good people around me, friendly people. The police get a lot of flak from the public and I didn't like the hostility day in and day out. We didn't deserve it. You help an old lady across the road and the next thing there's a complaint against you for sexual harassment!"

He took another long swallow from his glass. "There are a lot of interesting people living here, even though they're mostly retired.

Here's a thing, Jack. In big cities the younger generation see an old man or woman shuffling along and dismiss them. They don't think about who that person might have been when they were younger, when they swung on swings, laughed, danced, fell in love, and had spectacular careers.

"We have an eminent scientist living here, authors famous in their day, people who did all sorts of interesting things during the war, both male and female, all hush hush stuff. A few military types who have travelled the globe and left their mark one way or another, not too far from London so they can go to their old clubs. This is their favourite pub. Here everyone is interested in each other, and they look out for each other. It's like a big family, not like the tourists who don't give a toss. There's a lot of respect and affection for all those retired types - they like it here. I like them here, sometimes I sit with them so they can re-tell their previous lives. As I said, we're like a big family."

Sam ran his hands through his curly hair. "Look here, Jack. In other cultures, they don't toss their old people out when they get old. The Indians, Chinese, Africans, Italians, the French, the Mexicans, and countless other places, they revere their old people. They look after them, keep them close within the family fold if you like. Respect them, learn from them. It's not like that here. Everyone here is proud to be British and proud of their history. You can see it, in all its glory, on Remembrance Sunday.

"Did you know on Remembrance Sunday all the veterans come in from all over the country to London for the march past the Cenotaph. There are assembly points for them. Lined up are hundreds of London cabbies ready to take them to the Cenotaph. They transport them, free of charge, and collect them after the service. It's a fantastic gesture from the cabbies. But I guess you know all this having worked in London.

Jack nodded. "But a lot of people don't. It's a real salute to the cabbies."

Sam took another sip of his beer. "So many young people today don't care for the elderly people who made it happen, gave them the life they now know. The life they enjoy. The terrible sacrifices their grandparents made during the war. Far too busy climbing up the corporate ladder, too busy making money. No, they hastily shove their old parents into care homes where they lose the will to live."

Jack nodded again. "Sad, but true. I guess if you have pots of money when you get old it's not so bad but, money or not, there is still the loneliness; waiting for the grandchildren to arrive for a visit, a telephone call or two. But the bottom line is they sit there alone, rich, or otherwise and wonder if anyone really cares for them anymore. Sadly, hardly anyone is interested in the life they lived. They must accept the frightening fact their life is almost over. That they are old and didn't realise it."

Jack took a sip of his beer. "Funny thing though, when a family pet gets old it's not shoved into a shelter, is it? No, they keep it going for as long as they can. Pity they don't feel the same way about their old folks."

Sam shrugged his shoulders in agreement then looked around the bar. "See that old chap over there with his ancient sheep dog?"

Jack spotted him and nodded.

"He was an eminent surgeon with rooms in Harley Street. When he retired, he came here to Larkstown. Came out of retirement for a couple of years and practised here as a GP before he retired again. His name is Edward Fellows. He's here every night, hits the whisky a bit more than he should. But we all watch out for him."

Jack straightened his back. Zelda's husband had been a doctor who had immersed himself in village life here. The chances he knew Doctor Paul Cameron were good. "He looks interesting Sam; I'd like to meet him. Maybe he knew Zelda Cameron's husband, Paul?"

Sam shrugged on his coat. "I have no idea. Must go. Got a date. I'll introduce you if you like?"

Jack sat down in front of Edward Fellows after he had been introduced by Sam. With a cheery wave Sam had left them to it.

*****

Doctor Fellows looked at Jack with interest, from beneath his bushy eyebrows. "So, Jack, what are doing here such a long way from home? You clearly don't live here. Not with that tan. Although I would hazard a guess you were brought up and educated here with your rather public-school accent?"

Jack gave Doctor Fellows a brief potted history of his life and childhood in the UK and his history with the *Telegraph.*

Doctor Fellows took a large mouthful of his whisky, rolled it around his mouth and swallowed. "Sam told me he had sold you a painting belonging to Doctor Cameron's wife, Zelda. So, being a journalist, I must assume you have more than a passing interest in collecting art. You're looking for information. You're after a story - correct? Something to do with the Cameron's I have no doubt?"

Jack looked into his beer and thought for a moment. "Yes. In your profession you have the patient and doctor code of ethics and confidentiality, but I do need help. Mrs Zelda Cameron might have inadvertently or otherwise, been involved in something I've been following. Tell me, was Zelda Cameron a patient of yours here in the village?"

Doctor Fellows gave an imperceptible shrug. "She was married to a doctor. Why would she have to consult me?"

Jack ordered another double whisky for the doctor. "Perhaps she didn't wish to discuss certain things with her husband? Sometimes it's easier to talk to a stranger."

Doctor Fellows leaned forward his eyes suddenly clear and bright despite the whiskeys he had consumed. "They were a complicated couple. An unusual relationship in some respects. Paul was a gregarious character, immersed himself in the life of the village here. Zelda was quite different, aloof one could say. Now suppose you tell me what this is all about?"

Jack knew this was the only chance he would get to find any answers. "The thing is Doctor Fellows, twenty years or so ago, four young girls from South Africa flew into London, all separately, over a period of some years. They were on their way to university. They all arrived in London and then disappeared. We have good reason to think they were murdered."

Jack ran his fingers through his untidy hair. "Something has come up which links Zelda Cameron with these four girls. I'm not saying she was involved in it, but before she died, she sent some information to my newspaper through her lawyer. There is a certain retired police officer in South Africa who she has asked to help her find out what happened to the four girls. She arranged for this information to be revealed two years after her death. It was a very compelling letter."

Jack paused a moment. "For her to do this leads me to believe she knew a lot more about these girls and what happened to them. This is the story I'm following. I need to find out what happened to those girls. Their families have waited a long and agonising time to find out what became of their daughters. Is there any way you can help us? I know so little about Paul and Zelda Cameron. It would help to know if they had any children - we need some kind of connection here?"

Doctor Fellows rubbed his face. "Four girls you say. You think they were murdered?" He looked shocked.

"No." Jack said. "We believe they were murdered. We have proof. But I need to know more about Zelda and her husband."

Doctor Fellows took another gulp of his whisky. "This must remain confidential, Jack. A doctor never discusses his patients with anyone. But if four young girls have been murdered...well, that casts a different light on things."

Doctor Fellows contemplated the contents of his fast-emptying glass of whisky. "Zelda Cameron is dead and so is her husband. That leaves the field clear, so to speak. If it brings whoever killed these girls to book, then I have no problem with telling you what little I know about the Cameron's. I have spent my entire career trying to save lives. It's the code I always lived by. But what you are telling me is deeply disturbing."

Jack sat forward, perhaps he would finally get some answers. "I found a photograph of two boys, a little faded, in black and white, hidden in the frame of a painting I bought, which used to belong to Zelda. Would you have any idea who they were?"

Doctor Fellows shook his head. "Zelda was physically unable to have children. Paul, her husband, did not want children. He was gay you see, and in those days, it was difficult for some people to deal with."

Jack frowned. "Okay. So, who were the boys in the photograph then?"

Doctor Fellows shrugged his shoulders. "I have no idea. Paul spent some years in South Africa, where he met Zelda. He was offered a position in London with a prestigious practice. He knew he would be more readily accepted if he presented himself as a family man. Don't forget we are talking forty or so years ago now. Image was everything.

"Zelda, from what I understand, wanted to leave South Africa for whatever reasons she had. They married there and came to England. Paul got the job, and he was remarkably successful."

Jack felt that familiar sizzle down his spine. He felt something else was coming here, something which may answer some questions.

Doctor Fellows drained his glass, stood up and shrugged on his coat. "From what I can gather not only did Paul Cameron arrive back in his country with a new wife, but Zelda brought two children with her. One must assume she had them before she married Paul. They were certainly not her own, most likely adopted.

"By the time Paul retired and came here to live in the village, those two children must have grown up and left home. I, myself, certainly never saw them."

Jack also stood up. "Do you think Zelda Cameron died of natural causes, Doctor Fellows?"

Doctor Fellows wrapped his scarf around his neck. "I had prescribed sleeping pills for her during the last few years of her life. She seemed agitated. Unable to sleep. From what you have told me about her possible connection with your four missing girls, I can understand why. Sometimes you get a sense of a particular patient. Zelda Cameron although appearing perfectly normal when I saw her, well, I felt she would make her own choices when she wanted to."

Jack rubbed the back of his neck. "I'm not sure I understand."

"You understand perfectly well, Jack. Sometimes a doctor, whether rightly or wrongly, helps a patient cope with things. Strictly against the law here, but not in places like Switzerland. It's not unknown for a doctor to assist a patient to get relief from unbearable pain. He signs the death certificate and that's that. All is in order."

"So, are you saying Zelda Cameron committed suicide?"

Doctor Fellows buttoned up his coat. "I'm not saying anything, Jack. I signed the death certificate, and her lawyer took over from there. As per her instructions her body was cremated, and her ashes taken to a church in London."

Jack shook the doctor's hand. "Thank you, you've cleared a few points up here. Everything you have told me will remain strictly confidential. You have my word on that."

Doctor Fellows touched his hat in farewell. "Good luck, Jack. I'm sorry I couldn't be of more help."

Then slowly he turned back to Jack. "Don't know if this will help, but when I was called to The Gables to examine Mrs Cameron and sign the death certificate, I did notice the fireplace was quite full of what were clearly papers, or documents which she had destroyed. There was an empty bottle of wine on the floor, next to her chair, and an empty bottle of sleeping pills. I discreetly removed them, I'm not sure what she was doing but she must have been deeply distressed about something. The place was in a bit of a mess.

"She must have been pulling out drawers, opening cupboards, as though she were looking for something else to burn.

"There was one other thing…Zelda nor Paul ever talked about their children. Obviously when I met them, there were no children in the household. That's quite normal, I suppose. But perhaps there was another reason?"

Jack thought quickly. "Did Paul ever mention the boys? Mention their names in conversation?"

The doctor shook his head. "Never."

*****

Jack returned to the guest house. He lay back on his bed and thought about his conversation with Doctor Fellows. The bottom line was Zelda Cameron was involved in the disappearance of the four girls. She had never had children of her own, and none with her gay husband. The marriage sounded as though it had been convenient for both of them.

Obviously when they left South Africa and entered the UK, their papers had been in order. They had brought two boys with them, with the correct papers. Marius and Tinus.

According to the lawyer, James Barrington-Smith, Zelda had left nothing to anyone. Why had she left nothing to her two sons? Why had she cut them both out of her will?

So, who exactly were the boys in the old photograph? Jack surmised they would both be in their late forties now, given Zelda's age when she died. That's if they were both still alive. Surely, they had to be her adopted sons.

So where were they?

Why had Zelda turned her back on them?

The fact that, as Doctor Fellows had said, Zelda had destroyed personal documents, left a lot of unanswered questions. The biggest one being he had said the place looked as though it had been thoroughly searched. Why would Zelda be pulling out cupboards and drawers in her own home. What had she been looking for?

Or it might have been someone else. That someone else could only have been her last visitor on the night she died.

The priest.

If she had destroyed papers and documents from her past, to hide whatever her involvement was with the missing girls, then why had she, through her lawyer, contacted Piet and presented him with the contents of the briefcase? Why wait two years after her death?

Jack threw back the blankets on his bed and went to stand at the window. He needed to get back to South Africa and, as Piet had suggested, start at the beginning. He had achieved as much as he could in the UK and although he had made some progress, he felt he could achieve more by going back.

He returned to London the following day to his room at the Draycott hotel.

He had, thanks to Bill Watson, the last known addresses of the four girls, their parents' names, and the names of the private schools the girls had attended in South Africa.

He called reception and asked them to book him on a flight to Johannesburg the following evening and a transfer to the airport. He would spend a few hours at the offices of the *Telegraph,* see if Stefan De Villiers had managed to come up with anything with his research on similar stories, then have lunch with Harry and bring him up to speed on things so far.

Then he called Piet in Hazyview. "*Jeez,* Jack, thought you were never coming back. Come on, my man, we have work to do. What have you got so far for me?"

Jack tried to stifle a cough because he knew Piet would blame it all on the damp lousy weather in the UK. "I couriered you copies of all the four police files plus all the other information. I'm booked on the flight tomorrow night, should be with you by lunchtime.

"I'm then going to Cape Town to try and find the parents of the girls and somehow gain access to the private schools they all attended. I have a plan for that. I've done a lot of research and made a list of the schools the girls attended. I recognised their uniforms from our photographs and matched them to the schools."

Piet grunted. "Better be a good plan, my friend. The one thing those posh schools hate is bad publicity, even though it might have been years ago. They must justify the mind-buggery fees they charge. No scandal, no stain on their impeccable academic history, producing the future leaders of the world. Good luck with that one, Jack. What's your plan?"

Jack stifled another cough. "I'm going to visit each school, looking for a suitable one for my 'daughter.' I shall ask all the right questions…and then a few they might not like.

"However, we're talking about twenty or so years ago, so chances are it might not be as easy as I think. The Heads of school will have changed, teachers will have moved on. All the pupils who were there twenty years or so ago may well be mothers themselves and no doubt scattered all over the world. If they're still in Cape Town, they might have their own girls already listed for a placement at the school they attended.

"That, Piet, will be my starting point. Then I'll move onto the parents of the four girls, if they're still around and try to locate any siblings. Anyway, it's where I'm going to start. I'll see you tomorrow."

Chapter Twenty-Eight
Cape Town

Jack had returned to Hazyview for three days and brought Piet up to date on things so far and his own observations and speculations, before flying to Cape Town.

Piet had decided he would not pursue any of his own investigations until Jack returned and he had more to work with – now he had absolutely nothing.

Jack hired a car at the airport and made his way to the guest house he had booked in Constantia, one of the upmarket suburbs on the outskirts of the city.

He unpacked his leather travelling bag then pulled a map of the city from one of the side pockets. He knew his friends laughed at him in this age of technology. But Jack liked his maps, he liked to spread them out and study the areas he was in, follow all the back roads with his finger. Of course, he could get all the same information by using his phone or laptop. But a good paper map was all Jack needed to get a feel for wherever he was. Folding them back into shape was more of a challenge.

He pulled his notepad from his shirt pocket and checked the addresses of the four private girls' schools, then checked the addresses of where they had lived. Only one school was near the city centre, the other three were in the southern suburbs where he was now.

Anna-Marie Cloete, the first girl who went missing in 1997, had attended a private school near the city centre. Her parents had lived in Sea Point. He had the address of the school and their then home address from the police records Bill had given him.

He had already phoned the school and made an appointment with the Headmistress on the pretext he would like to enrol his non-existent daughter in the school. He checked the time. He would need to leave now to keep his appointment with Mrs Chambers.

Jack parked in the space reserved for visitors, straightened his tie, and patted his hair down. He looked at the impressive building which housed the school, Table Mountain providing a magnificent backdrop.

The school grounds were immaculate, dark green benches were dotted around under the shade of old heavy trees. Groups of girls in their brown and yellow uniforms were gathered there, others walked quietly across the quadrangle to a separate building which Jack presumed would be the dormitories or other schoolrooms.

He paused for a moment and watched the girls. What did life hold in store for them? They lived in a beautiful country; been given the finest education a private school could offer. Many of them would go on to make a name for themselves, one way or another. Others would crash and burn within relationships. Dashing any high hopes and the enormous amount of money their parents had invested in them.

He knew prestigious girls' schools would give the pupils everything they would need, a fine education and the skills they would need once they left. But no matter how prestigious a school was they would never be able to help those girls cope with relationships with boys, or with falling in love.

Relationships, he surmised, would not protect them. Some, of course, would marry well, travel the world, shine in whatever career they had chosen, but others would go through the heartbreak of a broken relationship which would affect and taint everything else they attempted for years to come.

Squirrels scampered across the lawns in front of him as he made his way to the main building of the school. One of the girls directed him to Headmistress' office.

Jack knocked tentatively on the door and waited before the door was opened and a tall woman, in her late fifties, her grey hair pulled back into what looked like an uncomfortable knot.

"Good afternoon, Mr Taylor, I'm Mrs Chambers. Do come in and take a seat."

Jack did as he was told and sat down feeling slightly nervous. The situation took him back to when he was a schoolboy and been summoned to the headmaster's study.

"Now, Mr Taylor, tell me a little about yourself, then we can move on to discuss your daughter," she glanced down at the paperwork in front of her. "Victoria, isn't it?"

"Yes, Mrs Chambers. Victoria. I've done quite a bit of research of your school and its excellent record for turning out young ladies with impressive academic results. You must be congratulated on your school's fine reputation."

Mrs Chambers gave him a hard look. "Yes. Our reputation has been well earned, Mr Taylor. Things have changed over the last fifteen or so years. We have embraced technology, as one must. The girls don't carry around heavy bags of books as they used to. They all have laptops to work with."

Mrs Chambers was watching him carefully and Jack thought he knew what was coming next. She crossed her arms across her chest and gave him a hard and hostile look.

"As I was saying, Mr Taylor. Technology has indeed changed the world we now live in. It offers all sorts of information. Now tell me, why you are here? I know you are a journalist; you work for the English newspaper the *Telegraph*. Like our school you have an impressive track record, with you it is for tracking down stories, which you refer to as cold cases. You now live here in South Africa. You are unmarried and most certainly do not have a daughter called Victoria."

Mrs Chambers raised an eyebrow. "So, perhaps you will tell me why you are here and what you are looking for."

Jack wasn't unhappy with the way the conversation was going. It wasn't in his nature to be untruthful, but even so, he felt extremely uncomfortable to have been rumbled in such a short space of time.

"Well, Mr Taylor? I'm waiting for an explanation."

Jack put both his hands up in submission and shrugged. "I'm sorry for the subterfuge Mrs Chambers. You're quite correct. I am a journalist; I do live here, and I don't have a daughter called Victoria.

"However, my intentions are honourable. I know a school with such a fine reputation for excellence as yours has, does not want anything from the media to tarnish that reputation."

"Oh, for goodness sake, Mr Taylor," she said testily. "Please get to the point, will you?"

Jack took a deep breath and looked at the formidable woman sitting in front of him. It was now or never.

"Mrs Chambers, in 1997 one of your young students, Anna-Marie Cloete, graduated and was accepted at a university in the UK. She boarded an aircraft bound for London. We know she arrived safely; the authorities confirmed this. However, Anna-Marie disappears from all records at that point and has never been seen again."

"And your point is, Mr Taylor?"

Jack leaned forward in his chair. "My point is this, Mrs Chambers. During the past few weeks, my partner and I have irrefutable evidence that Anna-Marie not only disappeared without trace. She was possibly murdered.

"I'm here because I want to know exactly what happened to Anna-Marie. Plus, there were three other girls who also went missing under the same circumstances. We believe they were also possibly murdered. There is a connection between these girls, a link. I want to find it."

Mrs Chambers looked shocked. "Anna-Marie was murdered! Dear God, this is extremely hard to understand or accept…" her voice trailed off.

Jack could see how visibly shaken she was. "Do you remember her at all, Mrs Chambers?"

Mrs Chambers stood up and went to look out of her window. It was open, the warm air filling the room. Jack could hear the faint calls of girls, shouting and clapping. A sports event, no doubt.

She turned back to Jack. "Yes, I do remember Anna-Marie," she said softly. "I've been involved with the school for over twenty-five years now. It would seem impossible for you to understand, but I remember every girl who attended this school under my tenure. I remember Anna-Marie, she didn't stand out in any way, she was an average student, good stable background. But she worked hard and earned her place at a university in the UK."

Mrs Chambers felt for the beads entwined around her neck. "Of course, we heard about her disappearance. But there was no follow up by the police here, they were busy with other things at that time. I thought she'd been found. But you say not."

Jack sat back in his chair. "Do you have anything you can give me to help find out what happened to her?

Mrs Chambers shook her head. "I expect you'll want to speak to the family and the relatives of Anna-Marie? But, Mr Taylor, you will be wasting your time. Something like this invariably changes the dynamic in a marriage or relationship.

"I understand the parents of Anna-Marie split up, some years after their daughter left. This happens quite often when a child disappears. There's anger, a lot of grief and, of course, the blame game, but I do not know where they might now be."

Jack stood up and held out his hand. "I'm sorry for the subterfuge Mrs Chambers, but I had my doubts you would see me if I had told you the real reason for my visit."

Mrs Chambers stood up looking visibly shaken. "Your apology is accepted, Mr Taylor. Trying to find out what happened is extremely important. I must say I am deeply shocked and I'm sorry I couldn't have been of more help."

Jack gave her his card. "Should you recall anything, anything at all, please get in touch."

Mrs Chambers looked at him, without glancing at the card. "So long ago, Mr Taylor…it's doubtful I will be able to assist you. It's hard to understand how this could have happened. I hope you find whoever was responsible, it will be difficult after all this time. Almost impossible I would think."

Jack shook her hand. "I will find who was responsible, Mrs Chambers," he said softly. "It's something I'm particularly good at."

Chapter Twenty-Nine

Jack made his way through the busy traffic towards Sea Point, where Anna-Marie's parents had lived. He found the address he was looking for and managed to find a parking spot not too far away from the address he had.

It was an imposing block of flats called Surf Crest, with an outstanding view of the ocean. He checked the names of the residents listed to the right of the entrance. The Cloete's name was there. He pressed the buzzer for 402.

A soft female voice answered. "Yes?"

Jack knew he was in for an emotional meeting with Anna-Marie's mother, if indeed it was her voice who had answered the intercom.

He cleared his throat. "Are you Mrs Cloete, ma'am?"

There was a slight hesitation. "Yes, I am. Who is this?"

"My name is Jack Taylor; I work for a London based newspaper. I wonder if you would spare me some time?"

Mrs Cloete was quiet for a few moments. "Is this something to do with my daughter Anna-Marie?"

Jack took a deep breath. "Yes, ma'am it is."

A loud buzz sounded, and the front door opened silently. Jack made his way to flat 402. Anna-Marie's mother was waiting for him when he got out of the lift, her face expressionless.

Mrs Cloete was a woman in her mid-sixties and well dressed. But the loss of her daughter had stripped and claimed her face, which was now heavily lined with skeins of grief.

Jack showed her his press credentials. She smiled bleakly and held the door to her flat open. "Please come in, Mr Taylor."

The little flat was immaculate, a cream lounge suite with a heavy wooden coffee table. A flat screen television. A bookcase crammed with books and a shelf displaying, he assumed, photographs of her family.

Jack sat down but Mrs Cloete stood rigidly by the window and looked out over the endless blue sky and the vast expanse of sea in front of her, her arms wrapped tightly around her.

"Have you found my daughter, Anna-Marie, Mr Taylor? Is that why you're here?" she said softly.

Jack stood up and went over to her. "I'm sorry Mrs Cloete, we haven't."

Mrs Cloete rubbed her arms. "She's dead, Mr Taylor. My little girl was taken from me. I haven't heard anything from her for twenty years. I've never been able to come to terms with it. We only had one child you see. Anna-Marie. It's impossible to believe she would be nearly forty now and perhaps I might even have had a grandchild."

She walked over to the photographs displayed on top of the bookcase, then handed one to him. He recognised Anna-Marie immediately from the police photograph and the contents of the briefcase, standing with her mother and a man.

Jack tapped the photograph. "This was Anna-Marie's father?"

Mrs Cloete nodded. "Yes. Losing our daughter had a catastrophic impact on our lives. We were not wealthy, Mr Taylor, but we both worked hard so Anna-Marie could go to a good private school and then on to university in the UK. The fees were extremely high. We spent the rest of what we had trying to find her when she disappeared in London. We hired a private investigator, but he produced nothing."

She placed the photograph reverently back on the bookcase, then came and sat down opposite him. "After five years or so my husband, Sean, left me. He didn't want to be in South Africa anymore. He was convinced someone here in this country was somehow involved in the whole thing.

"Sean moved to New Zealand and met someone else. He married her and now they have three children of their own. He moved on, you see. So much easier for a man. They lose something for whatever reason and then go on to reinvent themselves, sometimes with breath-taking speed. Unfortunately, a woman is not like that. Especially when there's a child involved. The mother is left with the debris of her life. Left to find some way of dealing with things that have been taken away from her."

She clasped her hands tightly together in front of her. "I very much doubt he thinks of Anna-Marie. But I do. Every single day. It's the not knowing, Mr Taylor, that's the hardest thing to bear.

"When something like that happens, friends rally around with their hollow words and empty promises of hope Promises that my daughter will be found. But, as the years went by, they didn't know what to say."

She twisted her hands in her lap. "They wouldn't say her name or talk about her because they thought it would upset me.

"Eventually they drifted away, continued with their lives, their children safe at home. I found it easier without them, to be alone with my own memories, it didn't hurt so much…"

Jack knew what he was going to do next with the girl's mother would not make thing easier.

He knew instinctively he could not confront Anna-Marie's mother with what they had found in the briefcase. It would bring her perilously close to a complete breakdown.

He leaned forward and took her hands in his. "Mrs Cloete, I know this is hard for you, but there were another three girls who suffered the same fate. They also disappeared over a period of five years. They were all from Cape Town and all of them went to private schools here."

He paused for a moment trying to gauge her reaction. "We're determined to find out what happened to them. We have an excellent team following up every lead to find out not only what happened to your daughter but the other girls as well."

Mrs Cloete freed her hands from his and wiped her eyes. "Anna-Marie is dead, Mr Taylor. Someone took her. If she was still alive, she would have been in touch with me. We were extremely close. All I ask is that when you find the person who took her, you'll let me know the circumstances surrounding her disappearance. I need to know what happened; I need to know the truth."

Tears cascaded down her cheeks, seeping through the lines on her face.

Jack looked at the broken woman in front of him. "I give you my word when we have the full picture of what happened all those year ago, you'll be the first to know."

Jack rubbed the back of his neck, this part of his job he had never enjoyed. "Was your daughter involved with anyone? A boyfriend perhaps? Is it possible someone was waiting for Anna-Marie when she arrived in London?"

Mrs Cloete fingered the gold chain around her neck. "No, Mr Taylor. She had boyfriends and plenty of friends, of course. But no-one she went out with would cause her any harm. Something happened to her in London. We saw her off at the airport on a direct flight with SAA and that's all we know."

She picked at the skin around her thumb. "We didn't hear from her for a couple of days, but we put it down to all the excitement of being in London. I wasn't particularly concerned. We had booked her into an inexpensive hotel, recommended by the travel agent here, on the Earl's Court Road. She was to take the Heathrow Express into London then a taxi to her hotel. After waiting two or three days I rang the hotel to make sure she was alright and settled. Mobile phones were new at that time and Anna-Marie didn't have one."

She wiped at the thin sliver of blood on her thumb with a tissue. "That's when I found out Anna-Marie had never checked in. I panicked and phoned the police here, but there was nothing they could do because she had left the country. They suggested I get in touch with the South African Embassy in London.

"The Embassy was extremely helpful asking for her details which they promised to send on to the police in London. The police there needed a full description of her. They needed a clear photograph of her, the name of the hotel, which flight she had been on etc. They appointed a liaison officer, in London, who would pass on any information to us here in Cape Town. But there wasn't any information to pass on. Anna-Marie simply vanished."

Jack already knew the flight details and where the girl was going to stay in London from Bill Watson.

He watched Mrs Cloete's face carefully. "I'm not here to write a big story, to cause you any more grief - all I want is some answers. As do the parents of the other girls who went missing. But more importantly we need to find the person who was responsible for their disappearance."

Mrs Cloete pointed to a door to the left of the sitting room. "I haven't touched anything in her room. Twenty years is a long time, but it's all I have left here now of my daughter. You're welcome to look if you think it might help?"

Anna-Marie's bedroom was typical of a young teenager. Posters on the wall, a chair piled high with discarded clothing. The bed with cuddly toys, all sitting erect, waiting for the Anna-Marie who would never come home. A cupboard door was open, the hangers bereft of clothes, as Anna-Marie had left them as she packed for her big adventure. A hockey stick leaned forlornly against the back of the cupboard beside a tennis racquet.

Jack made his way back to the living area. Mrs Cloete was once again staring out of the window, twirling her necklace through her fingers.

"Mr Taylor, I understand you not wanting to reveal too much of your investigation but there is some comfort knowing the case has been re-opened. Tell me, are the police involved now?"

Jack shook his head. "My partner and I are investigating this without the knowledge of the police here or in the UK. Having said that my partner is a retired police detective. We want to collect as much information as possible before going to the police. Piet feels we'll work faster on our own using our own contacts.

"We have enough information to go out there alone and find out what happened."

Mrs Cloete frowned. "So, what information do you have, Mr Taylor? Surely, I have a right to know? Why the sudden interest in Anna-Marie? What have you found?"

Jack shifted in his chair. "The information was in a safe deposit box at a bank in London which belonged to a South African woman. She passed away two years ago leaving strict instructions that two years after her death her safety deposit box could be opened but by only one person. That Mrs Cloete was Mr Piet Joubert, my partner. The ex-police detective.

Mrs Cloete shook her head. "I can understand now why you wish to work with Mr Joubert and not with the police. So, are you suggesting the woman who owned the briefcase was involved with my daughter's disappearance and the other three girls?"

Jack nodded. "Something along those lines. Things are not entirely clear at this point. I think she got caught up in something, perhaps not of her making. We're following every lead we have.

"Tell me, Mrs Cloete. Did Anna-Marie have any distinguishing marks? A birth mark, or anything else physical which someone might notice. Any tattoos or body piercing we should know about?"

She gave him a half smile. "No, nothing. These private schools are extremely strict about piercings and tattoos. Obviously, unless they were boarders, they would be able to do whatever they liked at the weekends. Torn jeans, tattoos that only lasted a day or two and whatever jewellery they wanted to wear. Anna-Marie didn't have tattoos or body piercing, but she did have a favourite piece of jewellery she would wear when not at school. It was a silver and black ring, nothing expensive, but she loved it."

Jack looked at his notes. "When Anna-Marie left school, did she travel at all, before leaving for university the following year? What did she do with her time before leaving the country. Did she stay here in Cape Town?"

Mrs Cloete smiled at him. "As I said, my daughter and I were close, we wanted to spend the months before she went to the UK together. She found a job as a waitress here in Sea Point, there are so many restaurants here. She wanted to make some money before she left for university. So, no, she was here all the time, working and meeting up with her friends when she could."

Jack glanced at his watch and stood up. Without any doubt now, Anna-Marie was one of the victims, verified by her silver and black ring. He knew he couldn't say anything about this. His years as a cold case journalist had taught him one thing. Telling a mother, father, brother, wife, or children, the person they had waited for was dead was always the hardest thing of all. He had done it many times before but only when he had the hard facts to back it up.

Anna-Marie was dead. But he wouldn't be able to tell her mother that. He needed to find the girl's body.

"I'm afraid I must leave now. I'm sorry I can't tell you more, but you can rest assured Piet and I will follow this case through and find out who took your daughter."

He handed her his card with his South African contacts. "If you think of anything at all which would help us then please contact me. Even if it's just to talk about your daughter. That would be alright as well. It might help you a little to talk about her."

He looked briefly around the sitting room. "I don't like to think of you sitting her alone day after day. Memories should be shared; I'd be happy to share them with you, there must have been many of them, and stories of your daughter as she grew up. She deserves to be remembered for those – it's what she would have wanted."

Mrs Cloete squeezed his arm in silent thanks as she walked him to the front door of the flat then turned to him; the tears spilling down her cheeks.

"Thank you for continuing to search for the truth."

Jack seeing her distress, instinctively put his arms around her. In situations like this he knew the touch of another human being, although not taking the terrible loss away, could ease the pain, albeit briefly. He didn't care if it was politically incorrect or could be misconstrued as sexual harassment, or whatever other title society wished to bestow on it. It was instinctive with him.

This woman was dying inside from loneliness and unanswered questions.

"We care about what happened to her as much as you do. You're not out there on your own with a forgotten daughter. We'll find out what happened. I promise."

Chapter Thirty

The following day Jack had appointments with the Heads of the three schools attended by Chantel Jameson, Elizabeth Balfour, and Suzanne Clifton, the other three girls who went missing.

In these cases, he introduced himself as a journalist wanting to do a story on some of the top girls' schools in the country.

There was no resistance. Until he started to ask questions about one of their pupils, Chantel, who had gone missing all those years ago.

The Headmistress at the school in Rondebosch, Mrs Barker, had only been head of the school for the past ten years. Of course, she had heard the story of Chantel who had disappeared in London. But with her years of experience with young female students had concluded that Chantel Jameson had probably met someone and planned to meet up with him in London. It wasn't difficult to assume she had run off with some boy.

Jack had asked if he might have the address of Chantel's parents. But it seemed, having checked her computer, Chantel's parents and her older brother had emigrated to Australia to start a new life, four years after Chantel had left South Africa. Mrs Barker had no other information she could help Jack with.

Two down - two to go.

Elizabeth Balfour, the third girl to go missing had attended a school in Constantia. He used the same cover story as before then asked the headmistress if she recalled a student called Elizabeth Balfour.

Miss Tibbs was only in her early fifties and assured him she had no recollection of Elizabeth, who had gone missing so many years ago. She was of the same opinion that parents did not always know what their daughters were thinking or feeling and who they might have met up with.

"You must remember, Mr Taylor, all those girls had been brought up in tumultuous times, dangerous times politically. South Africa was desperately trying to show the world they were worthy of acceptance into the global family. Young girls at that time were forming their own opinions, making their own judgements.

"They had been suffocated all their lives by political media headlines, they were not oblivious to the plight of their futures. They listened to conversations their parents had around the dinner table…and they agreed. Or didn't.

"Personally, Mr Taylor, I wouldn't blame any young girl who wanted to be part of a bigger world, a more glamorous world, to want to escape it at the first opportunity. Leave it all behind and have a new life without politics and crime and without the hostile and vitriolic comments about Apartheid and the inherited part they undoubtedly had played in it. Whether it was true or not. It was difficult to defend a situation which had not been of their making, but something they had inherited. A heavy load to carry for a young girl looking for a fresh start in life."

Miss Tibbs cleared her throat. "It's not unusual for someone to want to reinvent themselves. You've told me four girls went missing over a period of five years. All boarded a plane here in Cape Town and were never seen again."

Miss Tibbs paused for a moment. "It happens all over the world, Mr Taylor, it doesn't necessarily mean they came to any harm. These four girls who went missing, well, their bodies were never found. There could be numerous answers to the questions you are looking for. For instance, how many girls, or boys come to that, have disappeared over the years, and never been found?"

Jack thanked her for her time and stood up. "I'd like to speak to Elizabeth's parents, if that's possible?"

Miss Tibbs shook her head. "I'm sorry, I don't have their personal information now, it was a long time ago, Mr Taylor. I'm sure wherever they are they won't want to have such a traumatic time revisited. It's a dreadful thing to have to go through as a parent. I don't think it would add to your article on one the finest girls' schools in South Africa," she paused and looked at him shrewdly. "If this the story you intend to write, which I somehow doubt?"

Jack knew he had been rumbled once again.

"You see Mr Taylor; I did a little research myself. I like to know about anyone who wishes to interview me. You are a highly regarded journalist with your newspaper. Your speciality is what they call cold cases. It doesn't take a genius to work out the story you are currently pursuing. Clearly you have uncovered new facts pertaining to and linking these four girls. This is very disturbing, not only for the families of the girls involved but also for the schools they attended."

She stood up slowly and came around her desk, smoothing down her skirt. "The reason I can't give you any information on Elizabeth's family, Mr Taylor, is because her parents are no longer with us. The house they lived in is now a trendy restaurant here in Constantia. Elizabeth was their only child and when she disappeared, they spent every cent they had on trying to find her…including selling their house."

Miss Tibbs bit her bottom lip. "They took their own lives. They had nothing left. It was some kind of pact. If they couldn't find out what had happened to Elizabeth, well, they didn't want to be here anymore."

She turned her head away from him and looked over the school grounds. "I'm quite sure you've done a great deal of research into these four girls but there would have been little to find in any of our local newspapers all those years ago. Just a paragraph somewhere overwhelmed with all the other dramatic headlines during those wretched times."

She walked to her office door and opened it, then turned to him, taking his proffered hand in hers. "I hope you find the truth, Mr Taylor, and I'm sure you will. I trust the personal information I have given you about Elizabeth and her parents will remain between the two of us. Should you use this in your story I would ask you don't mention my name?"

Miss Tibbs reached for a tissue from her skirt pocket. "You see, Mr Taylor, Elizabeth's mother was my sister."

Chapter Thirty-One

Jack parked in the designated area of the last school on his list. The grounds of this Claremont institution, like the other private schools, were immaculate. The frontage of the main school was built in the old Dutch style with its gracious curves and green shutters. There were security guards at the entrance and a sweeping driveway with a circular fountain, where parents navigated to park their cars to collect their children.

He sat watching the chattering girls pouring out of the buildings, carrying books and laptops, their young voices calling to each other, car doors banging, mothers of weekly boarders opening boots and packing away week-end gear. Dogs barking from the back seats of expensive, highly polished cars.

Jack waited until the parking area emptied out and the children had gone home for the weekend. He made his way to the main entrance of the school.

His meeting with Caroline Tibbs had opened a door he had been hoping for. She was closer to the story he was following than any of the other Headmistresses' he had met. She had a close personal connection with Elizabeth and her family. Caroline wanted the answers as much as he did as to what happened to her niece.

He made his way, following the signs to the Headmistress's office and knocked on the door. There was no response.

"Are you Mr Taylor?" He turned and saw a young girl of around sixteen with an impressive array of various badges attached to her uniform.

"Yes. I have an appointment with the Head."

The young girl held out her hand. "I'm Thandi. Head Girl." She indicated the badge on her blazer proudly. "Sorry. Mrs Palmer had to cancel your appointment. She sends her apologies. I believe you're writing an article for your newspaper about the best girl's schools in South Africa?"

Jack shook her hand. "Hello Thandi. Well, now I'm here perhaps you'd like to show me around the school. I believe this one is renowned for turning out brilliant athletes?"

Thandi tossed her long-plaited hair back and grinned at him. She had the look of so many of the other young, privileged, girls in South Africa. Fresh faced, healthy, and happy. He thought back to his years in London and the school children and young adults he had encountered in the poorer areas of the city. Sullen, angry, disillusioned, kicking at life as though it were already a disappointment with no hopes or dreams for a brighter future.

Thandi led him down long corridors of the school. Framed photographs of girls who had left their mark and gone on to make their names in the world of academia, sports, science, and other fields of excellence, lined the walls.

Thandi paused at one of the photographs. "This is Suzanne Clifton. I think out of all the girls who attended this school she certainly was the star!"

Jack stopped and took a closer look. Holding a huge gold cup high in front of her, her hair hidden with a tight cap, water cascading down her body, she looked every inch the champion she was, or was hoping to become.

Suzanne Clifton - the fourth girl who had disappeared without a trace. Her body toned and muscled by the brutal training sessions she must have endured for years to be the champion swimmer she had become.

Thandi chatted on as Jack took some pics. "First, she represented the school, then the Western Cape, and then South Africa. Long before my time, I wasn't even born then. But she is a bit of a legend at this school even today. The world wasn't interested in South Africa at the time, everything was muddled up with politics then. But a university in the UK saw her incredible potential and offered her a place."

Thandi used her sleeve to wipe off the glass frame then straightened it reverently. "Apparently, she had to give up her citizenship here and become British. Here's another photo of her. She had lovely hair, didn't she? This was at some event or other."

Jack took another shot. He hadn't missed the thin black strands encircling her wrist. He enlarged it quickly.

An elephant hair bracelet.

Thandi laughed. "She wanted to compete in the Olympics and the only way to do that was to renounce her citizenship, so she did."

Thandi frowned. "As far as I know she was given a tremendous send-off from the school before she went to chase her dreams. I'm not sure what happened after that."

Jack smiled at her. "I'm sure she went on to become a world champion swimmer."

Jack suddenly bent forward. There was a thin dark line high up on her right hip. "Surely that's not a tattoo I can see?"

Thandi laughed. "It's highly unlikely, no body piercing, tattoos, or anything like that allowed at this school. Strictly forbidden. But it does look like one doesn't it? Maybe it's one of those things that washes off. Or a piece of seaweed?"

Jack laughed. "Probably a piece of seaweed if tattoos are strictly forbidden."

Thandi looked up at him. "Anything else you would like to see, Mr Taylor?"

"Thank you Thandi, I'm sorry I didn't get to meet your Head Mistress, but perhaps another time?"

He paused. "Tell me, Thandi what are you going to do when you leave school?"

Thandi tossed her beaded plaits over her shoulder. "I'm going to study medicine; I already have a place at a university in Kenya. That's where I come from. My father is the Ambassador here in South Africa. I want to be effective in my own country. I know if I applied to other universities both here and overseas, I would be accepted. But it's not what I want to do.

"I've been given more opportunities in my life than most of my fellow Kenyans. But Kenya is my home. I can be effective there, instead of being swallowed up in some other prestigious university. It's important to me. It's what I want to do with my life."

She looked at him shyly. "A little like you, I think. You're a journalist, but I think you don't go after a story for the sake of it, to blow people's lives apart. I feel, like me, you want to fix things that have gone wrong. Follow things and try to make sense of it all, try to help people?"

Jack smiled at her astuteness. "You will make a wonderful doctor, Thandi. Wanting to make a difference, wanting to help - it's a gift. There's more to life than making a name for yourself and accumulating a lot of money. It's the legacy you leave behind.

"In the end money and power mean absolutely nothing. It's people who count. Caring about people. But I think you already know that."

*****

Jack went back to his car and enlarged the photographs he had taken. He concentrated on the thin black line high up on Suzanne's right thigh. She had obviously finished a race and won it. Her black costume riding high on her legs before she had pulled it down, as swimmers do when they emerge from a swimming pool. He didn't think there would be any seaweed in a freshwater pool.

But it was just a dark line that dipped slightly. It could have been anything. Maybe a birthmark.

He enlarged the shot of her wrist as she accepted yet another award. There was no doubt that she was wearing an elephant hair bracelet. Her long blonde hair cascading around her shoulders.

Suzanne Clifton. The fourth girl who had disappeared. A hank of her lovely hair cut off and hidden in a small velvet bag inside the briefcase Piet Joubert had been made custodian of.

Jack had done as much research as he could on all four girls, but the internet hadn't thrown up much. However, there was a little more on Suzanne Clifton than the other girls.

She had been a champion swimmer and been prepared to give up her South African citizenship to chase her dreams in the international world of sports. It was a brave move, but she had had no choice. South Africans in those days, no matter how talented they were, were still tainted with the history of their country's past. International schools and universities were wary of taking them on, not wishing to be seen to be siding with the county's bleak and bloody past, by accepting a white South African into their prestigious hallowed halls of academia and years of excellence.

Suzanne had clearly had to make an emotional and difficult decision. But her ambition to be an Olympic champion had overridden her passion and love for her own country. Obtaining British citizenship had not been difficult. Both her parents and grandparents, from what he had gathered from the British police files, had been British.

From what Jack had gleaned from the internet was that her parents had refused to give any interviews to the press and quietly disappeared themselves. Suzanne was their only child. The address he had for them in Bantry Bay, a prestigious location for the very wealthy, had long gone and had now been turned into an apartment block where units sold for millions of Rands.

*****

Jack put his car into reverse but was distracted by the tapping at his window. Thandi smiled at him. "I think I may have found someone you might like to talk to Mr Taylor. Lucky you hadn't driven off!"

Jack lowered the window. "Really? A member of staff perhaps? The Headmistress is back and willing to see me?"

"No, Mr Taylor. This is far more exciting. I had almost forgotten about Mrs Hammond!"

Jack smiled at the animation on her lovely face. "Mrs Hammond?"

"Yes, Mrs Hammond. Any girl who has ever attended this school knew the formidable Mrs Hammond. She wasn't a teacher here, she was the house mother, for the boarders, but of course she knew all the girls. When she retired the school allocated a flat for her behind the boarding school. She's still here. Must be well into her eighties now. I thought she might be able to help you with the history of this and some of the other private schools in Cape Town. That's what you want to know about isn't it?"

Jack climbed out of his car. "Will she see me, do you think?"

Thandi laughed. "I think she'd be delighted to see you. She knows more about this school than anyone else. She loves to have visitors. The girls still go and see her, she's a bit of a treasure."

*****

Jack knocked softly on the door of the flat. A commanding voice called out.

"Come!"

Mrs Hammond, despite the heat of the February summer, was sitting in a reclining chair, a soft blanket covering her legs. The flat was comfortable, but compact, full of memorabilia of years gone by. Every surface was filled with framed photographs. Large windows looked out over the back of the school and the grounds beyond.

Mrs Hammond still showed the shadow of what she had once been. Her white hair caught back in a simple ponytail, her face soft and accepting of the age it had brought with it. She gestured for Jack to sit down. He noticed her nails were well manicured, with the feathered touches of make-up on her cheeks and lips. Nothing overt. Just a woman who was not going to let go of who she had once been, not for any audience, but for herself.

"Thank you for seeing me, Mrs Hammond. I understand you're a treasure trove of history of the school?"

Mrs Hammond laughed and looked at the clock on her mantelpiece. "I'm delighted to meet a journalist from the *Telegraph*. Always has been my favourite newspaper. Now, how about a gin and tonic?"

She gestured to the silver tray on a side table. "If you wouldn't mind doing the honours, Mr Taylor. I love to look out over the school grounds at this time of the day with a gin and tonic, lots of ice and a slice of lemon. It brings back many memories."

Jack busied himself mixing the drinks.

"I met my husband here. He was the caretaker of the grounds. Big, strong, and so terribly attractive. Blond and tall like you. I looked after the girls, and he looked after the grounds they would walk upon. He was irresistible. I'm not saying it was love, it was a powerful attraction.

"Does that shock you Mr Taylor? I think that kind of attraction far outweighs love. Healthier somehow without all the emotional baggage."

She took a sip of her drink. "You look at me now and you see an old lady well into her eighties, don't you? I don't see myself like that. I only see me, as me. I see me with all my young memories."

She twirled the ice and lemon in her drink with a manicured finger. "If you think you're old then you get old; sink into the whole thing. I might not be able to race across the grounds of this school into the arms of the man who was truly my caretaker. But I sure as hell am not going to sink into the pit of old age and give up.

"Now, Mr Taylor, I'm going to call you Jack. You can call me Margaret. What is it you are looking for? Thandi mentioned briefly you are writing about the top private schools in Cape Town. Is that so?

"Rather a long way to come for a story which will hardly make headlines around the world?"

Jack smiled at the woman in front of him. She was no fool and he knew he would be caught out immediately if he pursued that story line.

"Just the truth will do Jack. I've been the house mother at this school for forty years, dealing with girls of all ages - I can spot someone who isn't telling the truth."

Jack held up his palms in a gesture of resignation. "Okay, Margaret. You've got me. I'm following a story of four girls who went missing from private schools here in Cape Town around twenty years ago. One of those girls was a pupil here."

Margaret took a sip of her drink and nodded. "Suzanne Clifton. Yes, I remember her well. One of the best swimmers this school, even this country, ever produced. There was much speculation when the school heard she had disappeared, it seemed impossible to imagine she had given up her dream of the Olympics and decided to do something else – impossible. Why are you following this now, so many years later and more to the point, the other girls as well? There must be some kind of new evidence that has surfaced after all this time. I'm right, am I not?"

Jack hesitated for a moment. "Yes, unfortunately you're right. We have evidence all four girls didn't just disappear, they were murdered."

Margaret reared back slightly and shakily put her glass down, some of the contents spilling onto the small round table next to her. "Dear God, that's shocking news. Terrible news. Have you any idea who was responsible? Clearly you have proof that links the girls together. Even after all this time?"

Jack put his drink down and rubbed the side of his face. He had made little or no progress in Cape Town. He knew a bit more about each girl and her family but apart from that he had no new leads, no ideas as to what to do next. He hoped Piet had been digging deep with his search for more information on Zelda Cameron. She *had* to be the vital connection they were looking for.

He had kept Piet and Harry as up to date as he could with what little information he had been able to garner so far. They were as disappointed as he was with the slow progress he was making.

Sitting in front of him was a woman who knew everything there could possibly be to know about how an all-girls school worked. Margaret had forty years of experience under her belt, dealing with parents, teachers, and the girls themselves. She knew how the engine of the school turned. The rules and regulations, the traditions. She had seen hundreds of girls pass through its doors and watched them go out into the world, well-educated and equipped with the skills they needed to make a success of their lives.

Margaret was watching him carefully. "You're wondering if you can trust me with the information you have. Let me tell you something, Jack. Parents, teachers, visitors, and the girls themselves, have confided in me over the years. You wouldn't believe the things that go on behind closed doors.

"What happens in some of the homes of the hundreds of girls who have attended this school over the years and indeed the private lives of some of the teaching staff. Some of it beggar's belief. But not something I wish to discuss. Nothing is ever as it seems is it Jack, as you have without doubt discovered over your years of being a journalist?"

Margaret took a deep breath. "What you have told me has stunned me, I have to say. But you need to know a little more about how a girl's school is run. There must be something which ties these four girls together, a common denominator. I'd like to help you."

Margaret looked at him shrewdly. "Whatever you tell me, if you are prepared to do that, will remain between the two of us. I may be able to come at this from a different angle. But to do this I need all the information and details you can give me."

Margaret took an unsteady sip of her drink. "Obviously at the time these girls disappeared the police were involved both here in South Africa and the UK. It seems to me you are investigating this on your own now and don't wish to have the police involved at this stage. Would I be right?"

Jack looked at her. Margaret was right. He didn't know how an all-girls school operated. The private schools the girls had attended were all somehow connected, this he couldn't ignore.

She would have some useful input, open some different avenues to follow. She had been in the private school system for decades. He knew, from his own research, and personal experience at his own schools, there were associations, unions, and other organisations schools belonged to. Over and above this, private schools were competitive; inter school competitions, sporting challenges where schools went head-to-head to be the champions.

Therefore, many of the teachers over the years would have known each other from their interaction with each other and their pupils, socially or otherwise, and through their various conferences and associations.

He had no chance of infiltrating any of these associations. But sitting right in front of him was someone who could.

He knew how a boys' public school in the UK worked, but amidst a sea of hundreds of young girls in a different country was something else altogether.

He quickly made up his mind.

"What I'm going to tell you, Margaret, will be very disturbing. You're right we haven't involved the police, either here or in the UK, with what we've discovered. My partner is an ex-detective who worked for the police in the Eastern Cape for most of his life, as a cop. We have worked on a few cases together, very successfully, over the past. Both of us are based in Hazyview. We want to solve this case ourselves with the contacts we have both here and in the UK.

"I've worked for the *Telegraph* for the past twenty years, mostly on cold cases. I met Piet Joubert when I was following a case about a young child who went missing in the Eastern Cape many years ago. I fell in love with the country and here I am, still working for the same newspaper but based here and not London."

Margaret waved her glass in front of her. "Right, Jack. Let's have a refill and get down to business. Let's see if I can help you."

For the next hour Jack went through the photographs on his phone, showed her the contents of the briefcase and giving her the background on Mrs Zelda Cameron.

Margaret sat back in her chair, a single tear coursed its way down her cheek, she groped for a tissue up her sleeve, swiped it away and tucked the tissue back. "Oh God," she whispered softly. "I hope it was quick, and they didn't suffer. Suzanne was such special girl."

She took a deep breath. "Of course, we heard about the other three girls who went missing. But everyone had their own opinion on where they had gone to.

"You see, Jack, girls can be devious, secretive, have their own private dreams. It was mostly assumed they had plans to meet up with some boy somewhere in Europe or the UK. You'd be surprised, or perhaps not, at how many girls just want to get away from their parents. Even dislike them.

"They want their freedom and if it's offered, with a promise of love and romance - well, they take it. I think this was assumed by most of us, parents, and teachers alike."

Margaret covered her face with her hands, then took a shaky sip from her glass. "But it was none of these things, was it? I know our Suzanne most certainly didn't run off with anyone. She was determined to be an Olympic champion. That's all she thought about. I'm assuming none of the parents are aware of this new evidence?"

Jack looked down at the floor. "No. Only Piet and I, the newspaper and a UK retired detective know what we think is the truth."

Margaret looked at him. "It seems to me your Zelda Cameron is the key to all of this. Your starting point is here in South Africa, as you know."

She glanced at all the photographs cramming her bookcase. "It will surprise you to know that when I left school, I joined the police here.

"Then, over time, we could see the changes coming, the anger of the people couldn't be ignored. I didn't rise to any great dizzy heights, but I was tenacious. I loved my job and believed in what I was doing. I was the keeper of the files if you like. I had to keep a record of which files could be officially closed after a court case. Which ones were ongoing and, as you would call them today, cold cases where there was not enough evidence to convict anyone."

Margaret eased herself out of her chair and reached for a black and white photograph on the bookcase, blowing the dust off she handed it to Jack.

"This is Tom, my caretaker, my darling husband who never got old... I knew as a young white female police secretary, there would be no future in the police for me. Tom had been a game ranger, his life was the bush, the animals.

He liked that animals just got on with what they had to do. No politics involved, but even he could see his world was going to change. So many private lodges and reserves belonged to white people…there was resentment there. Many owners weren't even South Africans. They lived overseas and employed managers to run their lodges."

Jack listened as she told him her story. "I saw this position here advertised and applied for it. The position was for a geography teacher for the little ones. Even the private schools could see the troubles coming. Someone with my background, I knew the country like the back of my hand through my work, might be an asset in the days to come. Tom was reluctant to leave the bush and the animals and move into a city like Cape Town. But there were opportunities for him here as well.

"Not only did he accept the position of caretaker, but he held classes to tutor the girls about the bush and the animals. Took them out in groups into the bush and taught them about the unique country they had been born into. I think he opened a world the girls had never even thought about. He was a wonderful photographer as well, being a ranger."

Margaret blew gently on the glass and frame then wiped her sleeve over it. "Then one night he went into one of the townships to attend a meeting. He was the keynote speaker on poaching, which was beginning to rear its ugly head, as the township people grew angrier, hungrier, and more desperate."

She came and sat down again. "After that meeting, as he got into his car, an angry mob set upon him. They burnt him alive."

Once again Jack was reminded of the tumultuous and violent past of this country. It had come a long way at a terrible price. But he still believed it had a future, as bright as the sun and stars that shone above it.

"I'm sorry to hear what happened to your husband – a horrible story."

Margaret waved her hand dismissively. "It was a long time ago. I didn't marry again or have children." She smiled sadly and looked across at her photographs. "But I filled my life with other people's children, and they certainly kept me busy. With my background I knew the country well and I had found something quite inspiring to do. I loved to teach the little ones about their country. The vastness of it, the breathtaking mountain ranges, the hills, the valleys, the coastline, the deserts, and the oceans. So that's what I did. Then ended up as the house mother, looking after the weekly boarders."

Jack ran his hands through his already untidy hair. "Thank you for your time, Margaret. Now you know the story I'm following, you may think of something which could be helpful. I seem to have made little progress with any of the schools or the relatives I've met."

He reached into his shirt pocket and handed her his business card. "With your police background, your geographic knowledge of the country, and the years you've spent here at the school, perhaps you'll think of something which I've missed completely."

Jack flipped through his notebook. "I know so little about girls' schools here in South Africa, in Cape Town. There seems to be a tight group of people who move in the same circles. Networking they call it now."

Jack looked out of the window. The ancient oak trees filtered the last of the sun across the immaculate lawns, as they had done for over a hundred years. Watching silently over the thousands of girls who had passed below its benevolent boughs.

"Tell me Margaret, the staff, not just the teachers, but the other people who work here. There are obviously many others. Groundsmen, catering staff, housekeeping, security staff, plumbers, carpenters, the in-house doctor. Contractors who look after the general up-keep of the building."

Margaret nodded. "Yes, indeed, that is so."

Jack rubbed his tired eyes. "There are other ways these girls could be connected. Brothers attending private schools both here and all over the country, introducing their sisters to their friends. Girls and boys mixing socially, out of school, with all the inter-school activities.

"A careful watcher, knowing what he's looking for would have no trouble integrating into any of these schools. Finding what he was looking for."

Margaret swirled the depleting ice in her drink. "There are male teachers at all these schools, teaching music, coaching sport – any number of subjects. Then of course, there are the exchange students, going off for a month to learn the ways and languages of another country – France was always a popular choice with schools like this. Who knows who they met there? Who was watching?"

Margaret glanced at the card briefly then put it carefully down next to her half empty glass. "I shall most certainly give it some thought, Jack.

"Should you have any questions, please call me, won't you?" She fumbled under her blanket, retrieved her cell phone, and gave him her number.

"Perhaps, if you have time before you head back to Hazyview, you'll care to take tea with me here?"

Jack smiled at her. "It would be a great pleasure, Margaret, I'd like that very much."

Chapter Thirty-Two

Jack returned to the guest house and made his way into the garden where three tables nestled under the old oak trees. He ordered a beer and a toasted cheese and tomato sandwich then sat and watched the squirrels darting across the lawns, his mind on the various conversations he had had with school staff and relatives. He had come up with no new leads. All four stories about the girl's disappearance had been identical.

He sipped his beer and munched his way thoughtfully through his sandwich, pondering his next move. Maybe Piet had come up with something on Zelda Cameron; he would call him when he got back to his room.

His visit to Cape Town had produced nothing of any significance. He was no closer to finding out what happened to the girls and Piet had not made any progress with Zelda Cameron, having had little or nothing to go on in the first place.

All they had were four missing, dead girls. A killer in London who knew what he was looking for when the girls made their final journey. recognised them at Heathrow, as they recognised him, and the tenuous connection with Zelda Cameron.

Chapter Thirty-Three

Jack ordered a light breakfast and checked the time. He wanted to speak to Margaret Hammond, the house mother. Now he had even more questions he needed answers to.

Jack called Margaret Hammond and said he would be returning to Hazyview the next day, but perhaps she could help him with a few more questions?

"My dear, Jack. I would be delighted to see you again. A little short notice to take tea with me."

Jack laughed. "I've arranged a little surprise for you, for the help you've given me. Shall we say three? In your rooms?"

*****

At three that afternoon there was a discreet knock on the door of Margaret's flat. A large silver trolley on wheels, guided by a waiter resplendent in a turban, white uniform, and a vivid red sash, followed by Jack, glided into the room before placing it at the picture window opening onto the grounds of the school and the ancient trees.

The immaculate member of the staff from the Mount Nelson hotel, lifted the silver domes with a flourish, displaying cucumber and salmon sandwiches, a Victoria sponge, freshly baked scones with strawberry jam and clotted cream, and tiers of exquisitely baked cupcakes. The silver tea pot glittered in the afternoon sun, begging to be poured, to let the prisms of light capture the essence of the rich golden liquid.

Margaret inclined her head to the waiter and watched him pour the tea, another waiter spread an impossibly white napkin over her blanketed knees then discreetly left the room.

Margaret clasped her hands in her lap and surveyed the feast which had been laid before her. "Oh, Jack. What a lovely, lovely surprise! But my goodness there's enough food here for twenty people!"

Jack grinned at her. "Yes, I know. Thandi helped organise this for me and once you've had your fill, and me of course, the waiter will remove the trolley, re-fill the cake tiers, and deliver it to the orphanage the school supports. The little ones are beside themselves with excitement."

Margaret poured the tea and daintily helped herself to an assortment of sandwiches and delicate cakes; Jack did the same.

"Yes, Jack, so many little ones without parents. The school has always offered as much support as possible. Few of them are adopted. Most couples want a baby, which is understandable. There's no demand for the toddlers."

She bit delicately into her scone. "So many young girls pregnant before they even reach their teens. What hope is there for the baby when they're not much more than children themselves? The babies are left outside churches, hospitals, sometimes just left in the bush."

She reached for a cucumber sandwich and another scone. "Of course, it's different in the rural areas, quite different. Lots of grannies and aunties who just gather them up and do their best. But in the cities? Well, families in the townships can barely feed their own. There's no back up system, no government help. They have no future. Their only choice is to make their own way and that, unfortunately, pulls them into the world of crime and gangs in the townships. We do our best, but it will never be enough I'm afraid."

Margaret placed her half-eaten scone back on her plate. "There are good people here, Jack. People who still live a gracious and privileged life, wanting for nothing, who take these little children in, feed them, and shelter them. You won't read about them in the newspapers. They run little unofficial, and unregistered orphanages, not in the city centres, of course, there would be hell to pay for that from the neighbours.

"No, these are people who live out of town, who have the space, the time, and the compassion to give something back to the country that has given them so much. They look after the little ones – black, white, coloured, Indian, Chinese – it doesn't matter.

"These places are under the government radar, Jack. Not registered as a business or a charity. They're not doing anything wrong – they just want to help."

Jack suddenly lost his appetite, and he could see Margaret felt the same. He lifted the silver bell from the tray and rang it.

Within seconds Thandi appeared with the waiter. "All done here Mrs Hammond? Mr Taylor?"

They both nodded. "Thank you Thandi," Jack stood up. "I'd give anything to see the kids' faces when they see the trolleys come in!"

Thandi smiled. "Why not come with me then, Mr Taylor? It might make a nice little article for your newspaper, along with some photographs?"

Jack shook his head. "Unfortunately, I don't have the time, Thandi. I must get back to Hazyview. But it has been a pleasure to meet you and thank you for organising all of this for me."

He held out his hand. "I wish you well with your future. I'm sure you'll make your country proud. You are going to be a fine doctor, Thandi."

Thandi ignored his hand and gave him a hug. "You must come and visit Kenya sometime. It's the most beautiful place in the world. I'll look out for you!"

"As I shall look out for you. But I think I'll look for you out in the bush, in some rural area, looking after the less fortunate?"

Thandi looked at him. "Yes, that's where you'll find me, it's where I want to be."

Jack smiled at her retreating back, the beads in her plaited hair clicking softly as she followed the waiter out of Margaret's rooms.

He sat down again. "I'm afraid I have more questions for you Margaret."

"Fire away, Jack. I'll do my best to answer them."

He pulled out the notepad from his shirt pocket and flipped the pages back. "So, at the end of their school year the matrics have their results, most of them having already applied to various universities both here and overseas. Correct?"

"Yes indeed, Jack. That's how it works."

Jack leaned forward, his elbows resting on his knees. "To mark the occasion, the matrics have individual photographs taken and these are then put on the school notice board where parents and relatives are invited to come and order copies. Underneath each photograph would be the name of the girl – correct?"

Margaret nodded. "Yes, quite correct."

"So, anyone could come into the school and study the photographs and decide how many copies they would order. Now being the house mother for all those years, I'm assuming you would have been there to see your girls on the next step of the journey, am I right?"

Margaret nodded. "Indeed, I was. Watching the girls I had looked after, taking their first brave steps into their future."

Jack flipped through his notes again. "Do you recall the name of the particular photographer the school used?"

Margret frowned. "That's a tough question, Jack. Of course, I remember that time of the year. It's an emotional time for both parents, students, and teachers. I remember lots of photographs being taken, but I'm afraid I can't remember the name of the photographic company or any photographer.

"However, I would hazard a guess it couldn't have been the same company or photographer at all four schools. Perhaps the company had a dozen or so photographers covering the end of an academic school year. Impossible to know."

She patted the blanket covering her knees. "I know where you're going with this. You think someone studied those photographs and chose the girl they wanted?"

Jack shrugged. "Wouldn't have been difficult. He could have made up any excuse for being there. No-one would have questioned who he was."

"But you're missing something here, Jack. Having been accepted by a university, both here and overseas, there would have been a gap where the girls would have worked as waitresses or done an internship somewhere. They may have travelled. Gone overseas earlier until they entered university. That will be your problem. Where were these four girls before they left the country, if they did? It's called a gap year – and that is your gap. How did this person track the girl he wanted, followed her for nine months or so, then snatch her at the airport?"

She smiled sadly at him. "It would be impossible Jack, absolutely impossible. The girls could have gone anywhere in the world for nine months or so and then taken any airline from anywhere to get to their university, wherever it might have been."

Jack frowned with frustration. "But you would have had a list of girls here somewhere in the school and which university they had applied to go to and been accepted?"

Margaret bit her lip. "With the technology today, yes, it's possible. But you're talking over twenty years ago, my dear. Once our girls leave the school, that's it. We are unlikely to hear from them again.

We're too busy with the next intake of girls. I'm sorry, Jack. I can't help you and I don't think anyone else will be able to either."

Jack made a note in his book. "Okay, one final question. I know the school is very strict about tattoos and body piercing. However, when I enlarged the photograph of Suzanne with her bathing costume holding a golden cup up, I noticed a mark high up on her leg, I'm thinking despite the strict rules of the school it might have been a very small tattoo. Is that possible?"

Margaret smiled at him. "Yes, it was a tattoo, well hidden. I noticed it at one of her final sporting events. She had had to give up her South African citizenship to further her career. It was a small outline of the map of South Africa, a reminder of who she was and what she had had to give up. I didn't mention it to the school. She was leaving, and we were all enormously proud of her."

Chapter Thirty-Four
Hazyview

Piet lifted his arm in greeting when he saw Jack coming through the doors of the Hazyview airport, off his flight from Cape Town, a broad smile on his face.

"*Jeez,* Jack. Thought I was going to have to take over the whole case and go it alone, whilst you swanned around Cape Town with all the rich folk. Wouldn't have been a problem really…but, hey, nice to see you. I've stocked up your fridge so we can get down to work as soon as you've had a shower and unpacked. *Braai* is good to go, beer chilling."

Piet turned off onto the dirt road leading to Jack's cottage. "Opened the place up for you and left Hope on guard. She's either stretched out on your bed or standing guard near the *braai* trying to look important." He shook his head in despair as he switched off the ignition and got out. No sign of his dog.

Jack was pleased to be home. Sure enough, Hope was stretched out on his bed, gave a weak wag of her tail, turned over and went back to sleep.

While Piet busied himself preparing their dinner, Jack took a long hot shower, changed his clothes, and poured himself a beer. Then went to join Piet at the fire. He sank into a padded chair and sighed with relief watching as Piet prodded and poked the hot embers.

"Thought we might have something a little different tonight, Jack – a Smiley. Been cooking for hours, should be ready in about an hour. Normally we just peel off the tinfoil and tear away at the sheep's head – smiles an' all. No salad or potatoes."

Jack looked at him with horror. "Listen, mate, even your dog isn't interested in your choice of menu tonight. No wonder she's in the bedroom. I'm not eating anything like that, okay?"

Piet's shoulders lifted with laughter. "Okay, okay, just kidding. Lighten up my friend. Meat's ready to cook; ribs, steak and chops. I nicked a garlic loaf and salad from the hotel to go with it. Now, I've put Zelda's briefcase in your office laid everything out on that table of yours.

"Whilst I cook, why not go through everything. All your notes, my notes, photographs and whatever else you have accumulated on your trip to the girls' schools. Then, when we've eaten, we can study everything and see what we have before we decide what to do next. I'm keen to get going on this one, Jack. Can't move this end without more information. I have a lot, but not enough to approach Bertie with."

He threw the chops on the hot fire. "We need to know exactly who Zelda Cameron was, or whatever her name was before she got married. Where she lived and who was the father of those children?"

*****

Jack worked studiously for the next hour, putting together as much as he could, using his highly tuned journalists mind trying to make sense of what was in front of him. The thick hanks of hair belonging to the missing girls, their personal jewellery. The background of their families, the history of their schools and which ones they had attended, the dates of their departure from South Africa on a ticket to nowhere and their photographs.

The notes he had made of the interviews with the priest, the doctor, Major Jordan, Simon, the estate manager at The Gables, and the original painting of a farm somewhere… this he pinned to the top of the board. This was where it had all begun, he was convinced of it, so many years ago.

The meeting with Barrington-Smith, Zelda's solicitor in London, he had recorded and transcribed and pinned this to his fast-filling board of facts. Finally, he pinned up the letters from Zelda, the one from the unknown author who had warned her about the danger she was in, and the one she had written to ask Piet for his help.

That bothered him.

The two years Zelda had demanded be waited, after she died, before doing anything? The other thing that bothered him was why her ashes had disappeared to a church in London. It made no sense to him at all.

Jack sat back in his office chair – basically, to anyone else, this woman Zelda Cameron never existed. There seemed to be no record of her birth or her life. She had died on the 27th of February 2016.

So, if she did indeed have two adopted children – where were they? Had either of her sons attended any kind of memorial service for her in London?

She had most definitely been involved in the disappearance of the four missing and now dead girls.

He placed the copies of the British police records into the investigation next to each girl's hair and jewellery. Then he stood back and stared long and hard at the crowded board and table.

Without Zelda Cameron's given name, where she was born and where she had lived. They had nothing to go on.

*****

Piet and Jack sat around the dying embers of the fire. For the past two hours they had argued, speculated, and come up with various scenarios on how to find this so-called Zelda Cameron. Without her name before she married, even Piet's close friend, Bertie would not be able to help them without more information.

Jack poked at the fire. "Did you try Bertie, Piet? He might have some suggestions?"

Piet shook his head. "I can't go to him with a favour like this without more information. It would be like you asking a mate for the whereabouts of a John Smith in London. I value Bertie's help. He's never let me down – but I don't have anything for him to work with, absolutely nothing."

Jack's phone vibrated on the table, and he snatched it up. "Jack Taylor."

"Hello Jack, it's Margaret Hammond speaking. Sorry, it's a little late to call."

Jack smiled down the phone, he had taken quite a liking to the feisty Margaret Hammond and was grateful for all the help she had given him with how private girls' school were run.

"Hello Margaret. I trust our little orphans enjoyed their tea party?"

She laughed. "Oh, my dear, you have no idea how much it meant to them.

"But that's not why I've called. Those four girls, especially Suzanne, and Zelda Cameon have been on my mind since you told me the story about them. But it's Zelda Cameron who bothers me the most."

Jack reached for his ever-present notebook.

"At first, I didn't really consider the painting you showed me on your phone. I know you think Zelda might have been the artist. Be that as it may, because of the photograph you found of the two little boys. But it's also possible she wasn't the artist. Perhaps it was a friend of hers, a relative. Or something she bought because it reminded her of something."

Piet was listening intently to the conversation on speaker. "Anyway, the fact you found the photograph might have nothing to do with the painting itself and who painted it. But obviously it meant a something to her if, and I repeat, if, she did indeed hide the photograph there."

He heard her cough delicately. "I have studied the photograph you took of the painting. I think I mentioned I used to teach geography to the little ones, before I became house mother. Well, dear Thandi managed to blow up the image of the painting and printed out a copy of it for me, so I could see it quite clearly."

Jack took a sip of his beer. "What are you thinking here, Margaret?"

He heard the tinkle of ice in a glass. "Well, I recognise the mountain range in the painting. I know it's not clear, but I truly believe that mountain range is in the Eastern Cape. It's not a distinctive range of mountains like others here in the country, the Drakensberg, Twelve Apostles etc. What does make it different is the cascade of light coloured, but dense, forest that enhances its side."

Jack and Piet leaned forward. "I remember telling the children there was a mountain range in the Western Cape called Sleeping Beauty, or something like that. For the life of me I could never make out the shape of anyone sleeping or otherwise.

"But your painting was done in the Eastern Cape. It's a huge area, as no doubt you know. But this little mountain range is near a place called Molteno."

Jack picked up the phone, his foot jiggling with anticipation. "You're absolutely sure about this Margaret?"

"That's what they look like to me, of course no artist paints like a photograph, there are always little discrepancies. But if it is a picture of a real place, this is where I would start looking. I do hope this will help you and your police officer friend, Piet."

Piet was already scrolling through his phone, suddenly galvanised into action.

"Margaret, thank you. This is important. It could be the key to everything. You may have given us a starting point to try and find out who Zelda was, how she was connected to the girls, and what happened to them."

Jack bid her goodnight, turned off his phone and sat back with a broad smile on his face. "Well, it's a start, Piet. Where the hell is Molteno?"

Piet was busy with his phone. "Eastern Cape, my friend, Eastern Cape. Sort of near Bloemfontein, but it's a massive area. Packed with history, very Afrikaans, hundreds and hundreds of small-holdings, farms, lots of agriculture and a range of unknown mountains – should be a piece of cake to find *Tannie* Cameron's roots, hey? Especially as we don't know who she was…"

He looked at his watch. "Sorry, my friend, need to get back to the hotel. We have a small group of VIPs staying, with their bodyguards and such like. Need to make sure Shaka is on the ball. Hope, we know, will exude confidence with her guard dog capabilities. We know she's totally useless, but those *okes* don't know that.

"I need to clear a few days with Hugo. Seems to me you and I will be spending some time wandering around hundreds of farms looking for a woman who doesn't exist. Might be gone for months."

He sighed dramatically and rubbed his cheek. "Don't suppose they do first class on flights to places like Bloemfontein? Or, maybe, after your recent most enjoyable trip around the country you fancy another run at it – only take fourteen hours or so to get there. I can borrow one of the safari vehicles from the hotel. Lots of fresh air. Keep the costs down so Harry won't start bellowing at us?"

Jack looked at him in horror. "You must be joking mate. Those bloody vehicles of yours don't even have any windows, air-conditioning, or roof covering. The way they crawl through the bush, without, I might add, much in the way of suspension, it will take us weeks to get anywhere. So, the answer is a definite no – and there is no first class. So, it's down the back for you and down the back for me.

"Clear a few days with Hugo and I'll organise the flights. Bloemfontein you say? Is that the best airport?"

Piet nodded.

"Right, leave it with me. I'll make sure we hire a decent car so we can visit hundreds of farms with absolutely no idea where we will be going or who we're looking for. Sound good to you?"

Piet called his dog and made his way to his car. "You thought your last trip was long? You have no idea. See you tomorrow. I'll call in around lunchtime, providing there are no dead bodies lying over Hugo's pristine lawns, with Zulu spears pinning them to the ground. Lock the door to your office if you go anywhere. Don't want your Zulu housekeeper to discover your chamber of horrors. Night Jack."

*****

Jack smiled as he cleared up the plates, Piet's dry humour had that effect, he extinguished the fire and returned to his office. He rummaged through a drawer until he found his pile of maps of South Africa. Finding the one he wanted, and a large map of the entire country, he pinned them next to his board. Then stood back and blew out his cheeks.

He moved closer to the small regional map. The whole map was peppered with what looked like very small towns, or *dorps* as they called them here. He cross checked the references and found the small town of Molteno, right in the middle of all the other small towns, surrounded by what looked like thousands of miles of nothing, but had to be the small-holdings and farming areas Piet had mentioned.

It seemed, from the research he did now on the internet, that it was all about farming, agriculture, livestock, breeding, and farming in general. Along with a deep painful history of the Afrikaner and the British in that area, particularly the Boer War.

He closed his eyes briefly – it could be more than just a challenge than finding a lone female in a vast province – no doubt Piet would relish the possibility of blaming everything on the British and go banging on about it for hours.

He was about to close his computer down and head for bed when he saw that the biggest social, business and farming event on the calendar was due to be held in Bloemfontein in two weeks' time.

It was a huge event from what he could gather. Judges came from all over the world to evaluate the prize-winning livestock; cattle, sheep, pigs, goats, horses and chickens. It was big business and a massive social event with music, food, dancing, pig racing, kids' entertainment, and the more serious business of the buying, selling, and breeding of livestock. Held over a few days it attracted farmers from all over the country.

Jack rubbed his hands together. Perfect. Farmers knew other farmers. Breeders knew other breeders. Folk who had been farmers, or related to them would be there in their droves; generations of families who had lived in the areas for decades would all be there.

Someone, somewhere, must know who Zelda Cameron had been. Although the area was vast, Jack knew how tight knit farming communities could be, whether here, in the UK, Australia or South America.

All he and Piet had to do was find a woman who no longer existed, the unknown artist of a painting and a range of mountains somewhere in the middle of it all.

Not too much of a challenge then…

Chapter Thirty-Five

Piet and Jack arrived in Bloemfontein. Placards were all over the historic city advertising the biggest event of the year.

Jack had organised a hire car for them – keeping in mind the vast area without main roads they would have to cover in their search. The 4x4 looked sturdy enough to handle any kind of terrain.

By chance, he had been lucky enough to find a modest guest house, just on the outskirts of Bloemfontein, that had had a cancellation and he booked it. Most accommodation outlets were booked up on a regular basis for this time of the year.

Piet and Jack had worked out their strategy. Jack would go to the show with his British press credentials; they never let him down. Piet would act as his sidekick because he was Afrikaans and spoke the language. Piet would be invaluable in getting close to anyone of interest, someone who spoke the same language, who had the same history, the local farmers. They would feel more comfortable speaking to one of their own, rather than an Englishman with a distinct accent and scruffy hair. These people had long memories.

*****

After two days of looking at champion sheep, pigs, goats, cattle being led around the arena to be judged, or auctioned off, looking at tractors and farm vehicles and wandering around the food stalls, the intoxicating smells of *braai's* with their curling plumes of grey smoke, and watching the entertainers; Piet and Jack were getting nowhere. Exhibitors were too busy looking for the serious business going on to engage in any idle chatter.

Piet noticed Jack was becoming despondent. "You can't hurry these things, Jack. It's country living at its best. The show ends tomorrow, exhibitors and such like start to relax, their hard work is over.

We still have the equestrian events tomorrow, then it's all fall down as everyone heads for the beer tents and the entertainment and that, my friend, is where we will really start to work."

Jack watched the magnificent horses strut their stuff in the arena, there was trotting, dressage, the riders dressed in bowler hats and tails, international judges had flown in for the event. He was impressed. The show was up there with the best in the world.

Most of the riders were in their prime, young, and fit. In full control of their horses. The judges watching keenly. One of them caught Jack's eye. Older than the rest.

He wore a bowler hat, and must have been in his mid-seventies, a little aloof from the other judges, looking a little old fashioned somehow. He checked his programme. One of the judges, it would appear, was to retire after this annual show. His name was George Botha.

Meneer George Botha, according to the programme, had been born in the area, was a rider of note before he went into stud farming, at which he was highly successful. Then he sold his successful farm and performed in equestrian events where he became a notable competitor. This would be his final appearance in the world of horses.

The crowd roared, stood up and clapped as he departed the judge's tent.

Piet leaned over to Jack. "This is the end of his career. The way he wanted it. George is a legend in these here parts. Everyone knows him and has the highest respect for him. He's in his mid-seventies now and has decided this will be his grand finale."

Jack watched as the proud man left the arena. "That man, Piet, will know everyone. Breeders, farmers, locals and all the rest. We need to meet with him."

Piet nodded. "I agree. There's a party to be held in his honour, in the competitors tent. I think he might quite like a bit of a story about him in an international newspaper. Come on. We can get in easily enough with your credentials."

The competitors' tent was packed. It was impossible to get anywhere near George.

Piet studied the crowd. "This lot are getting stuck into the booze, Jack, marking the end of George's legendary career. Things will quieten down in an hour or two. Exhibitors will be loading up their animals and heading back to their farms. The crowds will start to head for home, most of them have long drives ahead of them. The visitors will party on before heading back to their guest houses or hotels, come, my friend, I'll introduce you to some authentic Afrikaans food from one of the food stalls. Then we'll come back and see if we can find George."

Jack nodded in agreement. "I don't want to eat anything with a smiling face, or a plate of worms, okay?"

*****

Two hours later Piet and Jack, having enjoyed an *al fresco* dinner of things Jack had never heard of, returned to the now equestrian marquee where George had bid farewell to his world of horses and the life he had always known.

There were a few people left, gathered around tables, sitting on bales of hay, discussing the show, the horses and potential breeding opportunities.

Jack shook his head. Once you were out of the game, whatever profession you might have been in – you were out of the game. Life moved on; business moved on…you were out there on your own with only your memories.

George was sitting quite alone in the shadows of the marquee. Still immaculately dressed in his old-fashioned riding attire. His bowler hat placed carefully on the chair next to him.

Piet nodded to Jack. "Let me handle this, speak to him in his own language. I'll introduce you as a British journalist, not sure how it will go down, but George, from my research, was an international figure as well, a top polo player, travelled the world. Judged horse shows everywhere, bred horses which became world champions."

Piet approached George, his hand held out in front of him, speaking to him in Afrikaans, although George spoke English perfectly.

Jack leaned forward after the introductions were made. "An honour to meet you, sir. I'm not sure where to begin with writing your story for our newspaper. If you will allow me to do so?"

George looked at him, long and hard. "There really is no beginning is there, Mr Taylor – only an end. I'm not going to give you an interview. Few people will be interested now I'm out of the game, as they say."

Jack saw the emptiness in his eyes. He was still a good-looking man, but it was more about the way he held himself, the confidence he had in himself, knowing he had been the very best he could ever have been, knowing he never would be that again, it had clearly left a hole.

Jack smoothly moved the conversation on. "You had a spectacular career. People in the equestrian world know your name. But what about who you were, your personal life?"

George lifted his glass of brandy and coke and took a large gulp. "I have never discussed my personal life, because, well, it's my personal life. Nothing to do with my career."

*****

George ran his fingers around his bowler hat, removing an imaginary speck of dust. "I was a top polo player, travelled all over the world, stayed at the best hotels in the world, beautiful women in abundance. Came close to marrying once or twice."

He smiled at Jack. "But you see, that wasn't to me a real world. All the immense wealth, the beautiful women, stunning hotels, private islands, yachts, private jets, it was a world which I was never comfortable with. I enjoyed it yes, of course I did.

"But I was a simple farmer from the Free State. I knew any woman I met who spent her time following the rest of the rich and famous on their endless glamorous social circuit around the world, attending all the international fashionable events, appearing in glossy magazines dressed in the very latest fashions, staying in outrageously expensive hotels on private islands – well, I didn't think any of them would hang around for long on a remote farm in the Free State.

"And I most certainly didn't want to spend my life living what I considered a facile and empty existence trying to keep up with the super-rich, who didn't know one end of a sheep from another, horses possibly. Sheep no. The only bit they knew was a lamb chop flown in by private jet from New Zealand to enhance their dinner that evening, on a private island in the Bahamas."

George turned to Piet, seemingly bored by the conversation. "Where are you from Piet? Not English obviously."

Piet looked at him in horror. "Definitely not. Born hereabouts in the Eastern Cape. I was a cop, retired now and in charge of security at a hotel in Hazyview. Helping Jack here try to find a farm in the area. He's looking for a South African woman who lived here decades ago. Someone got in touch with his newspaper and asked for help in trying to track down her relatives."

George took a sip of his drink and laughed. "Shouldn't be too difficult. Thousands of farms in the area. Your search could take months and months. What's the family name?"

They both shook their heads. "That's the problem, George," Piet said. "We don't know it..."

George's bushy white eyebrows crawled up his forehead. "You have an impossible task on your hands, my friends. What was this woman's first name, do you even know that?"

Jack looked a little embarrassed. "Zelda," he muttered.

George tried to keep a straight face. "Zelda, hey? Well, shouldn't be too difficult then, should it? It's one of the most popular girls' names in the country. Mission impossible, my friends. Over and above only having a Christian name, even if you did discover her family name, she may well have married and changed her name, married twice and changed it again. Might even live in another country or have died."

Jack sat back and reached into his pocket for his phone.

Piet anticipated his next move and held up his hand to him. He wanted George Botha's opinion before Jack revealed anymore, he wanted confirmation of the whereabouts of the farm, the area; over and above Margaret Hammond's observations of where she thought it might be.

He pulled his own phone out of his jacket pocket. "See here, George. You know this land better than anyone, married to it in a way. You've travelled this area with your background of farming, visiting farms and small holdings."

Piet scrolled quickly through the photographs on his phone until he found the one he was looking for. The painting which had belonged to Zelda.

Jack sat back and waited. Piet had his own way of doing things, he knew these people, knew the right protocols, how to approach the questions to ease out the answers.

Piet leaned forward. "This is the only thing we have which might lead us to Zelda, despite all the obstacles in our way. But it will take a man who is at one with his own land. Zelda owned the painting. If anyone will recognise where it might be, which area, it will be you, George."

George straightened his back, patted his immaculate riding shirt for his glasses then stared at the enlarged photograph of the painting.

He was silent as he cast his eyes over the image, taking in every detail.

He sat back and rubbed his eyes behind his glasses, shaking his head. "This could be anywhere, but wait a moment…" He leaned forward and studied the backdrop of the painting.

"This mountain range, it's slightly in the distance, a bit distorted. But it's the only mountain range in a particular area. Whoever the artist is they've captured the moody colour of the sky there and the unusual forest of trees cascading down its side. The Cape Dutch style of house? It's not common but it's slightly unusual."

George took off his glasses. "This, my friends, is without a doubt a farm near Molteno, a huge farming area. The mountains confirm this."

Piet and Jack looked at each other. Confirmation from Margaret and George.

George stood up, a little stiffly. "Time to bid you farewell, gentlemen. I wish you luck in your search for the mysterious Zelda."

Jack stood up. "May we give you a lift somewhere?"

George bowed his head slightly. "Thank you, but I have Goodness waiting for me, with the horse box. Been with me forty years. We're like brothers. Our love of the land and the horses have created a bond between us.

"He came with me all over the world, looking after the polo ponies – and me. He's the closest thing I have to a brother. Like me, he never quite understood, what I consider quite vulgar now, the immense wealth out there, for the chosen few, whilst the money may last and the owners make utter fools of themselves by flaunting it with bigger yachts, younger women. But even they cannot escape the inevitable, can they?"

Jack put his hand out. "I know you won't give me an interview for my newspaper on your life now, but perhaps, with your immense knowledge of this farming region, you might consider a short piece on what it was like, then, to be a simple farmer, in a world you had no idea was going to change so dramatically politically?"

George gave him a wolfish grin. "It will cost you another drink, my friend. And should I agree, it must be understood my name will not be mentioned? The barman knows where Goodness is. Ask him to take him some decent food and a drink. Also remind him to take care of my horse for another hour or two, okay?"

Jack nodded. "You have my word." He knew from long experience when someone retired from a spectacular career, and now retiring from the much smaller world of annual shows in the middle of the Free State, well, for them it would be good to know they had a voice, their opinion mattered. What would George do in the future? Sit in a creaking chair on his stoep, look up at the stars, with a horse or two and Goodness for companionship?

George still wanted to be something, despite his advancing age. Sitting in front of him were two people chasing a story and Jack could see he was not ready to throw his hat into the ring and disappear into obscurity.

Jack reached for his notebook. "Listen, why not invite Goodness to join us here for a drink?"

George gave him a small smile. "I think he prefers horses to people, feels more comfortable with them. They're more predictable…kinder."

Piet ordered another round of drinks and let the journalist take over.

George took a sip of his brandy and coke. "His father, Goodness's father, Kanu, and I grew up together, played together as kids on the farm. My Pa was a modest sheep farmer then, dabbled a bit with horses, but we were a poor family, living off the land, expecting nothing more.

"Kanu and I were also like brothers. When I was sixteen my Pa would send us off to various farms and small holdings, bloody miles away, in an old *bakkie,* bald tyres, black smoke belching out the back, to buy a couple of sheep or goats for our farm to enhance the breed. We worked alongside Pa on the farm. It was hard work. This area is unforgiving if you're a farmer. Miles from anywhere, the bitter cold of winter, the unbearable heat of summer, the droughts and all the disease that came with it, steadily killing off the livestock."

He shook his head at the memories of his tough childhood. "Kanu left the farm, married, and had children. I lost touch with him. Then one day this young African pitched up at the farm, that was Goodness, Kanu's first born. He was an absolute natural with horses. Kanu had died."

George rubbed his eyes and put his glasses back on. "My Pa had long gone by then, and I was making something of the farm. I had moved into breeding sheep and horses on a bigger scale. I was successful, as you know."

Darkness was descending rapidly outside, after all the events and the eating and drinking a silence was descending on the showgrounds. The staff clearing everything away. There was a stillness around the three men sitting around the table in the marquee.

George cleared his throat. "You see, my friends, I know exactly where the farm is you're looking for… it's where I met her. That's why I remember it so clearly.

Chapter Thirty-Six
Fifty years earlier…

George and Kanu had finally arrived at the farm. They knew the farmer had been expecting them, but obviously not when, given the great distances between the properties.

George dusted off his hat against his leg as he stretched. It was late afternoon, and the sun was sinking behind the mountain range in the distance. But he knew he would be given the traditional Afrikaans courtesy of a meal and a bed for the night, as would Kanu.

Unexpectedly there seemed to be some celebration going on. Several fires were already lit in the grounds of the farm. Curls of grey and white smoke were rising from several *braais,* the carcass of a pig turning slowly over a pit of red-hot coals, the smell intoxicating. There were large barrels of ice with beer buried deep and chilling, awaiting the thirsty farmers who had come from miles around.

Music drifted over the still night, traditional music with violin and concertina and the singing of farm folk with tales of their history. Dogs barked, children ran all over the place, playing their noisy games. The farm staff were shouting at each other cheerfully as they carried heavy plates of food and placed them on the long wooden trestle tables.

George sighed with delight. Celebrations, parties, were non-existent on their isolated farms. He knew they would both be welcome here. A traditional farm party was a rare thing in his life and his heart lifted in anticipation of a life away from sheep, disease, the penny-pinching, the punishing weather, and the frugal life his own family lived.

Parties also meant girls.

He looked around. There must have been over thirty adults here. So many children, *bakkies* parked any which way, lanterns everywhere lighting up the night.

They made their way to the main house, built in the Cape Dutch style, probably not how it looked hundreds of years ago, but the remnants were still there.

But it was not the children, the dogs, the food, or the staff that caught his eye.

There were teenage girls and boys. Their young fresh faces reflected in the flicker of the sunset and fire. They circulated, laughed, and flirted, their voices loud, lifted to the stars above them.

It was in the blood that ran through his veins. He was a farm boy; he was twenty-two years old. He knew, as well as he knew the sun would come up tomorrow, he needed to find a mate, a wife, to continue the tradition of the farm, of his people. He would need children to carry his name, his heritage, his stories.

It was expected. That's how it was.

*****

He didn't remember much about the night. The drinking, the singing, the music, the dancing, the food. He woke up on a cot bed somewhere in the house, his head ached.

He made his way to the sounds of a kitchen, gratefully accepted a large tin mug of coffee offered by the still smiling kitchen staff. Then made his unsteady way out to the main stoep of the farmhouse.

And that was when he saw her.

The debris of the night before had been cleared away, the fire a grey mound of smouldering ash. The farm was as it was before, the sun rising over the distant mountains, only the echo of goats and sheep calling in the distance.

The guests from the night before had either made their way home through the pitch black, or were asleep in the back of their vehicles, or scattered around the homestead finding a bed or sofa where they could. But now they were all gone.

She was sitting a little way from the main house, an easel in front of her, a paintbrush poised over something she was working on, looking into the distance at a world, it seemed to him despite his hangover, which held her imagination.

She was young. Her back straight, her body blushed by the early sun filtering through the generously leafed tree she was sitting under. But it was her hair that caught his attention. The same sun had caught the streaks of gold in her thick straight blonde hair which tumbled around her shoulders and down her back.

In his twenty-two-year-old mind he knew he was looking at a girl he had been waiting for. A girl from the farmlands, a girl who knew how it all worked in the land of farmers. Someone who had grown up in the world of harsh extremes. Someone who might fit into his life in the future.

He was smitten. She was beautiful.

His head cleared as he made his way towards her. He crouched next to her and introduced himself.

She nodded to him and returned to her painting. George swallowed as he looked at her work. "A farm in Africa, hey? It's good. You've captured the feel of the land, the light, the isolation. I like it."

She turned and looked at him again, but there was an emptiness in her large brown eyes.

She turned back to her painting. "I want to remember this place as it was when I was a child. I like to think in decades to come it will bring some joy to someone who wants to remember it too. I will remember it. But for all the wrong reasons."

George cleared his throat, totally captivated by her. She had the look of so many girls born in this land. No make-up, no fancy clothes, her skin soft and clear, her thick, long, blonde hair untouched by chemicals or sharp scissors. Her large brown eyes clear and wide, unassisted by colour from a box. But, yes, empty. As though the future had already presented itself and she didn't like the look of it.

George was mesmerised. "Are you one of the guests here or part of the family?"

She put her brush down and turned towards him. "I feel like part of the family. I've known them most of my life. But, no, I'm not. I don't have a family anymore. I spend a lot of time here, always have, but it will never be enough for me. I have other plans for my life – and it won't be on a farm in the middle of nowhere."

George felt his heart sink. She wanted far more than he could ever offer her.

"What will you do then? Where will you go to find this other life?"

She packed her brushes and paints away, dismantled her easel and stood up. "I don't want to be remembered for anything. I'll go somewhere else, get out of this country with all its memories, that's all."

George knew this was a girl who would not be a part of his future. He could see she had set her sights on another life, somewhere far away.

She would not be interested in a simple farm boy. He stood up, dusted his hat on his trouser leg and put it on.

"I wish you well then as you pursue your dream of another life. I might read about you sometime in the future when you become a famous artist."

She tossed her hair back and looked at him. "Perhaps…but I hope not."

She turned her back and walked away. "Hey," he called out to her. "What's your name? Where do you live?"

"My name?" She turned, a tentative smile curving her mouth. "My name is Isobel. I don't live anywhere in particular. It was all taken away from me a long time ago. I plan to make another family in a place far away where no-one knows me."

Chapter Thirty-Seven

George leaned back in his chair. He stabbed a finger at the shot of the painting on Piet's phone. "This is like the one the girl called Isobel had been painting when I met her early that morning. But, of course, there are thousands of similar paintings all over the country. None, I would imagine, very collectable.

"Certainly, I never saw the name of Isobel, whatever her surname might have been or would become, being auctioned off for large sums of money."

Jack sipped his beer. "Any idea, George, what happened to this girl who clearly stole your heart the moment you set eyes on her?"

George flicked a moth off his bowler hat. "No, Jack. Her name was Isobel, that's all I remember. No point in pursing something you know you will never have, is there? It's funny though, a young man never forgets the first girl he was attracted to, had hopes for – love at first sight and all that romantic stuff, not that she felt the same.

"There was an emptiness about her. I thought about her often over the years and wondered where she was living, what she was doing."

Piet ran his hands through his hair. "Don't suppose you remember the name of the farm then – long time ago?"

George grunted. "No, I don't remember the name of the farm or the family who owned it. But I might be able to help you. You see my father was a meticulous accountant as well. He recorded every purchase of every animal he ever bought. Back at my place I have shelves of ledgers where he recorded all these things, down to the last chicken.

"All hand-written, all faded over time, but all the transactions will have been faithfully recorded. Where each animal was purchased, which farm, where it was and the name of the farmer who sold him the livestock."

Jack tried to still his foot which was beginning to twitch with the familiar sensation that he was finally onto the story he had been pursuing. Here was the link they had been looking for.

"Would it be possible for you to help us then, George?" Jack asked. "We have to find the name of both that farm and the woman we know as Zelda." He took a deep breath. "You see, this story is much bigger than we have told you. There are four girls involved, all four girls went missing, and were, we believe murdered. We need to find out what happened to them. We believe the link is a lady called Zelda and we know the story started here, in this area."

George crunched the last of his ice, from his drink. "Then, gentlemen, why don't you tell me this story?"

Chapter Thirty-Eight

George lived twenty minutes from the town of Bloemfontein. His home was modest, comfortable, and packed from floor to ceiling with the memorabilia which told the story of his life.

When they arrived the next morning, George greeted Piet and Jack and invited them into his home. "I must say what you told me last night has shaken me. To think it may well have started right here in my homeland takes a bit of getting used to."

A tall African man glided into the modest sitting room. "This is Goodness, gentleman. You must excuse me; I have some business to deal with. Goodness will take care of you."

Jack and Piet stood up and shook the African's hand. Goodness narrowed his eyes as he shook hands with Piet. "Police, *neh*?"

"Yes, Goodness. But retired now. We need your help with the ledgers of George's father. We're looking for the name of a farm which Mr Botha thinks you might be able to help us with?"

Goodness straightened his back. "If you wish for coffee, you will find it in the kitchen. I will seek this ledger Mr George has asked me to find for you."

Piet made the coffee and carried it out to the stoep. They could hear George on the phone somewhere else in the house.

Goodness appeared carrying a heavy ledger. "Mr George will not be long on the phone. But I will try to help find what you are seeking."

He opened the heavy canvas cover of a large ledger. "This was the year, when Mr George was just twenty-two years of age, when he went to visit three farms to buy the sheep, goats and cattle for our farm, with my father, Kanu."

Piet and Jack leaned forward, looking at the pages which mapped out the life of a Free State farmer so many years ago, the handwriting neat and precise.

"This farm," Goodness pointed his finger at the tiny annotations, "is where George lost his heart for no reason, my father told me this. He remembered it. They bought sheep there and as you can see chickens and cattle."

He ran his bony finger across the page. "The name of the farm was *Die Oudekraal*. The farmer we bought the sheep from was *Meneer* Barnard. This place, this farm, was two maybe three hours from this place called Molteno.

"If it is still there you will find it. If it is not, then you will have had a long-empty journey to nowhere."

George came back into the room rubbing his hands. "So, my friends, did you find what you were looking for?"

Piet stood up, taking a last look at the piece of history laid out in front of him. "Yes, I think so. But tell me, I know it was decades ago and you remember the girl, Isobel. But do you remember meeting the farmer Mr Barnard, who sold you the livestock?"

George looked at him in astonishment. "You must be kidding, right? There was a huge party there when we arrived, people all over the place. The business with the sale of the livestock had been done before with my Pa and the farmer. The livestock would have been penned and waiting for us, the paperwork and proof of pedigree done weeks before.

"Kanu would have had the livestock loaded into the *bakkie*, no reason to meet the farmer, although if I had I might have found out the surname of Isobel. But, hey, we were only the farm hands loading the animals and we had to start the long road back to our own farm. I was suffering from rejection and a hangover from hell. Don't remember much, only the lovely Isobel.

"My advice would be to contact the local council in Molteno and ask about this farm. They should be able to look it up and give you directions. If it's still there. Lots of farms have been sold for what they could get for them. This talk of taking back the land for the people has spooked them."

He ran his hand fondly over the old ledger on the table. "Recently a world-famous country house and one of the most famous game lodges here, was returned to the people who claimed the land was theirs. They wanted it back. The government complied and promised all sorts of compensation for the owners of the country house, who had built up their international brand in tourism all over the world; The government promised they would take over not just the land but the business, keep it going, buy all the assets, keep the staff and management on."

George looked into the distance. "The government gave the land it was built on back to the people with the promise of buying the place as a going concern and purchasing all the furniture and fixings. Well it never happened. The government never paid for the actual hotel, its fabulous reputation, the millions that had been spent on it. The owners had invested their whole lives in it."

He leaned forward and took a sip of his coffee. "The government reneged on their promise. There was no money paid for the actual business, so the owners auctioned everything off and walked away. What else could they do? The cancellations came in fast and furious from all over the world. The hotel was finished.

"Now I hear the place has been stripped of everything, the private pools green with slime or empty – the fine English furniture which graced each room – well, there's nothing left – all gone. Before long, the bush will reclaim it and it will be as though it had never existed. But the people would have what they considered their land, back. But the game lodge is still going, so that's something."

He rubbed his neck and moved in his chair, his back quite clearly giving him some sort of pain.

George looked at Piet and Jack. "People around here are not sure of their place in the country anymore. People don't want to invest in something which might not give them a return in the long run and this country is desperate for overseas investors."

Chapter Thirty-Nine

After breakfast the next morning, Piet and Jack were on the road, heading towards Molteno. It would take them around four hours. Both were quiet, working through the information they had accumulated so far. Piet had found a place in town where they were able to transfer Zelda's painting from his phone and have it blown up and laminated to a decent size.

The town of Molteno was small, dusty, hot, and quiet after Bloemfontein.

Piet looked around. "Let's find an old guest house, not one of these fancy ones, Jack. The older the better to dig a little deeper into the past residents of this here town. Let's grab lunch then visit the municipality and see if we can locate the exact position of this farm called *Die Oudekraal*.

"I'm thinking it could be another two or three hours away, depending on the state of the farm roads. Can't be sure it still exists."

Jack nodded in agreement. "We also need to come up with some feasible reason why we are making a visit to this farm, Piet."

Piet shrugged. "Ag, don't worry, my friend, I'll come up with something. You might be a bit of a problem though with your English accent. Obviously don't belong in these here parts. But leave it up to me, hey. Go buy a baseball cap to flatten down that hair of yours – okay?

"Let's check in somewhere, find a quiet corner and go through what we've learned from our new friend George. Then we can find a pub somewhere and get a bit of a feel for the place. Might be an idea not to mention what we're doing here until we've seen the farm. Small town people are suspicious of strangers – we'll visit the farm, come back here to Molteno then ask around a bit."

*****

Early next morning Piet and Jack were once again on the road looking for the turn off to the farm called *Die Oudekraal*.

Following the instructions of the cheerful, rather large, lady at the municipal offices in Molteno, they found three signposts at a four-way intersection an hour from town. One sign indicated the road they had just travelled, two obviously led to other farms in the area and the fourth was the one which would lead them to the farm called *Die Oudekraal*.

Its sign was made of some kind of cheap metal, battered, and bent from the elements over many years, the name barely legible. The two bullet holes didn't enhance its appearance.

Piet turned down the badly maintained road. The vehicle bucked and rocked, swerving around the deep potholes of the bush road. "Could be a bit of a rough drive, Jack. I'll try and keep the speed up so we can skim the corrugations, might have to brake now and again for some big potholes, maybe the odd sheep or cow along the way. Probably string us up if we kill one of their livestock."

Another beaten, barley legible sign announced they were now entering the private property of *Die Oudekraal*. A bleached skull of a buffalo lay at the foot of a wooden pole holding aloft the modest sign to the farm. Underneath written in red paint was another sign clearly warning the public to KEEP OUT. PRIVATE PROPERTY. TRESSPASSERS WILL BE SHOT.

Jack had been trying to study Zelda's painting but gave up as it shuddered and shook beneath his hands. He put it back in the large envelope from the photographer's shop. Instead, he turned to look out at the Barnard's farmland. There was nothing much to see, just miles and miles of scrubland and some birds of prey hovering on the thermals high above a peerless blue sky – even the land looked fallow, no signs of farming of any kind.

"Tell you what, Piet, let's stop for a while. The guest house packed food for us. I need to get out and stretch my legs and I'm hungry."

Piet didn't bother pulling over, he just stopped right in the middle of the dirt road, clouds of billowing dust settled like talcum power behind and over the vehicle. "Good idea, could do with a break myself, feel like my arms are being torn out of their sockets with driving this road, so long."

They both got out, stretched, walked around the vehicle, and looked around. There was utter silence, only the ticking over of the hot engine of the vehicle.

Jack removed his baseball cap and shook it, then took off his sunglasses and wiped the film of dust from the lenses, using his sleeve he rubbed it across his dry gritty eyes. "Why," he said softly, "would anyone want to live out in this isolated desert of a place?"

Piet was busy foraging in the back seat for his much-anticipated picnic. He pulled the plastic box out and placed it on the bonnet of the vehicle. He flipped the clips and opened it, peered inside, then frowned.

"Okay Jack don't think you'll enjoy your picnic. Not quite egg mayonnaise and cress, like the fancy hotel in London, but it will fill a hole or two. We have two dried sandwiches, contents unidentifiable, two sticks of biltong, two apples and two *koeksisters.*"

Jack stared at the contents. "I think I'll just stick with the water, thanks. What's a *koeksister* when she's at home anyway?"

Piet grinned at him. "One of the finest things to come out of this country, my friend. A dessert fit for a king. Try one, it'll give you a bit of energy, which you look as though you need." He hauled one out of the box and handed it to Jack.

Jack examined its orange plaited shape then sank his teeth into it, chewing tentatively, then turned his head and spat it out on the dirt. "Jesus, that's pure bloody sugar, Piet, I can feel it worming its way towards my unsuspecting teeth and already boring holes into them. It's like the rusks your country is famous for, breaking your teeth whichever way you bite. I'm thinking there must be plenty of wealthy dentists in this country. I'll stick to water, thanks. Come on, let's get this show on the road. I'm not enjoying myself very much at the moment."

He looked around in despair. "Why, oh why, does a farmer need so much land and not cultivate it Piet? We've been on this farmer's private road for over an hour and not a lettuce leaf, or cabbage, in sight. What's the point of having so much land and doing nothing with it?"

Piet chewed on a piece of biltong. Jack was a first-class journalist; he had rarely seen him angry or despondent. A little depressed sometimes when one of his budding romantic relationships hadn't quite worked out, but he was normally cheerful, excellent company and with that unique sense of British humour, which Piet secretly enjoyed but would never tell Jack that.

"What's bothering you, my friend?"

Jack shook his head. "This country. You have a hot-headed young politician making a name for himself now. He wants to kill the *Boer* farmers and take their land with no compensation, no payment of any kind. He has a massive following with all the millions of people in this country who had such high hopes things would be different when Mandela came into power. Nearly three decades later nothing has changed for those people. They still have no land, have nothing to farm, nothing to hope for – but this young politician has hit at the heart of things.

"The white people, he tells his followers, own the farmlands. His people, the Africans, want the land back. They want to own something; they want to farm as well. They want back, what they consider is their land.

"We have driven for well over an hour now on this farm which belongs to the Barnard family. The land is lying fallow. I'm looking at this through the eyes of a journalist, Piet. I'm not agreeing, or disagreeing with the way things are, the history of this country. It's not my country, it's yours.

"But surely," he waved his arms across the vast openness, "if the land is not bringing in an income to the farmer, he could afford to give some pockets of it to the people who have nothing? He wouldn't even notice they were here. But it would give some families a chance to have a little land of their own, to farm and provide for their families. Plus, it might take some of the sting out of the rhetoric that hot-headed politician is spouting. Might give the farmer a little insurance in the future? He gives away some of his land, in good faith, and gets to keep the working, cultivated part he lives on."

Jack sighed with the despair of it all. "Perhaps if the farmer let some families grow vegetables and things they could pay him back, not with rent, but with produce. It's possible Piet, isn't it? This place is so vast the bloody farmer wouldn't even be able to locate them."

*****

Piet knew, to an outsider, this is how things looked. He thought about how he should answer these questions.

He knew that Jack was aware of all the progress farmers in other parts of the country were making, those who had come to terms with the changes in the politics of the country. In the Western Cape in particular. Wine farmers had given land to their workers, given them the use of their equipment, taught them how to produce award winning wines. Other farms across the country had done the same, given land to their workers.

After all the workers were the ones who had worked the land for decades, knew exactly how to grow things, harvest things, sell things. Had been with the farmers families for generation after generation, were *part* of the family.

It had worked.

Piet picked up speed to negotiate the deeply rutted dirt track. "See here Jack, I don't disagree with you, not at all. It is the only way forward for this country; the land must be shared.

"I don't agree with the politician you refer to. He wants anarchy in this country, the infrastructure is already crumbling. Desperate people have nothing to lose, so they will back him.

"But it must be done legally, and I fear this will not be possible. I know you see here hectares and hectares of land which is not being used and not producing anything. But the Afrikaner farmer is something different altogether.

"For generations, his people have lived on these farmlands. Far away from the bright city lights. It's all they have ever known – cut off in so many ways from what is going on. They are simple people, at one with their land, content with what they know.

"They wake at dawn, work their land and animals, and sleep when it gets dark. It's simple and enough. They marry their own kind, have their families, work the farm, then pass it down to the next generation."

He braked slightly to let a dozen or so Guinea Fowl scuttle across the road, then grinned. "Those birds are so quick, hey, you can never run them over. I tried it for years, never got one.

"Anyways, as I was saying. This is the farmer's land, their land legally, registered decades ago in the correct way. They were born here, and they will die here. Yes, your arguments about sharing the land are valid. But, my friend, not to these die-hard farmers. They live in a bygone world. It's their land and they will never give it away. They fought for it and worked hard for it. It belongs to them. They are fiercely possessive about it. Their country has changed – but they haven't.

"Yes, there are farm murders now, but still they will never give in or give up what generations of their families have worked so hard for. They are aware of your politician, of course they are. In defiance, and to hold on to what is theirs, they've upped their security.

"They are armed and ready for any event. They keep in touch with each other by radio, check with each other if anything looks suspicious. Just like the farmers in what is now Zimbabwe did. They look after their own, watch out for each other and guard their land fiercely.

Piet wiped the dust from the windscreen with his sleeve. "See here Jack, this is all they know, farming. This is all they have ever known. What must they do, hey? No-one is buying farms now. Even if they were thinking about selling, where would they go? What would they do." he said grimly.

"I doubt few of them have passports even if they did have the opportunity to leave the country and certainly don't have any hard currency stashed offshore somewhere."

Piet veered to the right to avoid a large pothole. "I'm not talking of the wealthy farmers here, with their thousands of heads of pedigree animals which they breed and export all over the country and around the world. Some of those pedigree bulls sell for millions of rands as you saw at the show."

He glanced at Jack. "I'm talking about your everyday farmer scraping a living and keeping his herds going so he can still feed his family. I'm not talking about your average couple plus two children, I'm talking about huge extended families, of grandparents, aunties, brothers, sisters, and cousins who were born on the farms, grew up there and then, when just young boys and girls they would muck in and work the farm as well. They spend their entire lives there. It's all they know Jack."

Jack swiped viciously at a persistent buzzing fly, caught in the interior of the vehicle, not saying anything, just listening.

"These farm people are not ignorant, Jack, but they don't have the sort of background you were privileged to have had. They are simple folk who want to live a quiet life, work from dawn to dusk, read their bibles on Sunday and leave the rest up to God to sort out.

"I bet George was happier pottering around on his land, running his stud farm here, then he ever was sitting on some *larney* yacht in Monaco, drinking champagne and listening to the inane chatter going on around him, longing for the peace and tranquillity of the African bush where everything stays the same."

He pointed ahead. "Enough of politics, my friend, because up ahead I can see farm buildings. Let's focus on the job in hand and find out who this Zelda woman was. Let's hope the farmhouse was in better shape when she lived here if she did. It's looking a bit run down from what I can see."

Chapter Forty

Piet slowed down as he nosed the vehicle towards the front of the house. Anyone would have seen the cloud of dust billowing behind them from miles away and no doubt watching the vehicle and wondering who was in it and what they wanted, brandishing their guns, in case it was trouble.

Six large dogs advanced with intent, and they didn't have dolphin smiles like Piet's Labrador. The six circled the vehicle, baring their teeth, hackles up and barking, not friendly in the least. They looked big and tough and not a wagging tail of welcome between them.

Jack looked nervously at the dogs, they were here to do a job and if that meant ripping him apart as soon as he put a leg out of the door he was going to pass.

Within minutes a large African woman appeared from the side of the house. In a torrent of Afrikaans, peppered with one of Jacks favourite words, *voetsek,* which seemed the one call all dogs and cats understood. She yelled at the dogs who put their tails between their legs and skulked off to the shade of a large tree. Their unfriendly eyes trained on the two strangers who were now alighting from the vehicle.

Piet removed his battered cap and smiled in greeting at the large lady standing with her hands on her hips. She looked rather more frightening than the dogs.

Piet spoke to her in rapid Afrikaans, explaining they would like to speak to *Meneer* Barnard about a family member of his who had asked them to call on him. He introduced himself and she told him her name was Graceful, although she looked anything but.

Jack kept a straight face. He was astonished at how parents had come up with these names for their children. But he liked it. He was unsure of her age, he had always found it difficult to guess an African's age, especially if they were clearly fond of their food. She could have been anywhere between sixty and ninety with not a tooth in her mouth.

Graceful turned to Jack, her eyes narrowing with suspicion. "*Engels, neh*? Then she pointed at Piet. "*Police, neh*?"

Piet tried a charming smile, one he rarely practiced. "Not anymore, Graceful. See, this is my friend Jack, he is helping try to find this relative. He is from across the sea, but he lives here in our country now." All this was said in Afrikaans.

Graceful frowned. She was not impressed and looked slightly worried about these two men in front of her. Then she smoothed down her stained white apron, adjusted her headscarf and indicated they should follow her into the house.

To say the house had taken a battering from the elements over the years, was an understatement. And there was clearly no money to maintain the place. Maybe the artist who had painted the place so many years ago had caught it at its best.

They mounted the creaky bleached wooden steps to the front door. Inside it was dark and cool. She pointed at a large room to her left. "I speak little English, Mr Yak from over the sea. But I try for you are guest in this place. I make coffee for you both."

She bustled off towards what had to be the kitchen somewhere. Jack looked around the large sitting room. The shutters were closed to keep the heat out. The floor was cement and scattered around were skins of long dead animals. The furniture was heavy, dark, and old. The stuffing oozing out of the corners of the cracked leather armchairs.

An enormous square wooden table, which looked as though it was made of old railway sleepers, squatted in front of the chairs, pitted with age, cigarette burns, and countless stains left by wet glasses. The walls were adorned with stuffed and glassy eyed heads of kudu, impala, and other antelope.

In one corner was what Jack could only call a wireless. Low and squat it held a record player and records in their sleeves stacked next to it. There was no sign of a television or any computers. There were four or five faded paintings on the walls, of farms, animals, and farm scenes and two large oil paintings of fearsome looking ancestors with long beards and hostile eyes.

Despite Piet telling him generations of families had lived here it was eerily quiet. There was no sound of any children, no sound of anything – just silence but for the ticking of an ancient clock perched on top of the mantelpiece of one of the largest fireplaces Jack had ever seen. It was big enough to park a small car in.

Graceful bustled in with a tarnished tray and placed a tin mug in front of each of them. No doubt, he surmised, as he peered at the dark brown contents, it was loaded with sugar. Jack thought of his teeth. If he wasn't careful, he'd end up like Graceful with none. Following in the wake of Graceful was the delicious smell of something cooking. It reminded him of his mother's kitchen.

He looked at his watch. Coming up to midday. Lunchtime he guessed. The farmer must be due soon. Perhaps the place would fill with family members coming back from a hard morning working and the sense of desolation would be dispelled.

Graceful started to build the fire to warm up the room before the family returned, at least that's what Jack presumed. "The men will be back when the sun is going down. They will wish to speak to you of this person you are looking for. Who is this person?

"I was born here. I know everyone on the farm, and hereabouts." She lowered herself into the chair with a sigh of relief, propping her swollen feet on a low wooden stool. "What is this you are carrying, Mr Yak. I will give it to my boys if you wish?"

Jack slid the laminated photograph out of the envelope and handed it too Graceful.

She frowned as you looked at it, then smiled widely. "Here is our farm. Where did this come from? I'm liking it very much. Who is painting this picture? Is it for old Graceful?"

Jack nodded. "A gift to you from us. Perhaps if the family won't be back until much later you might be able to help us. We will have to leave shortly, we have a long journey back to town."

Graceful nodded as she stared at the photograph. "This will be looking very fine here in this room. Now, what is it you are wishing to know?"

Piet moved smoothly into the conversation. "My friend Jack here, he writes for a famous newspaper over the sea. He would like to write a story about this farm and the people who lived here."

Graceful looked immensely pleased and proud but puzzled. "This farm?"

Jack smiled at her. "Yes, this farm. I have heard that many years ago this was a big family. You speak good English. Did you go to school in Molteno?"

Graceful's large body rippled with laughter. "No, Mr Yak, too far to go for small children. Then, when I was young, there were many farms around here. A cousin, I am thinking it was a cousin, Miss Izzy, would come sometimes and teach the little ones of the staff, the children from other farms and our family here how to read and write.

"Miss Izzy, I am thinking made this picture of the farm. She liked to do this and teach the children with paint and brushes, but they only made a mess."

Graceful peered at the photograph again. "*Ag,* this picture is being done by Miss Izzy. Always she is putting this small yellow flower at the bottom in the grass, so no one is seeing it."

She looked fondly at the photograph. "I was already grown from child to woman. But I too wished to learn, and I would sit with the little ones. The teacher lady was nice, lovely hair. The colour of corn and long, like pictures you see in magazines for selling shampoo."

Jack smiled at her imagination and waited for her to continue. "If it was winter, we would sit in the big office of the family where there was a fire to keep us warm. In the summer when it was very hot, we would sit under the tree," she paused and stabbed at the photograph. "This tree which is still standing here and have lessons there."

She sighed loudly. "It was many years ago now. The farm was a happy place for all relatives and friends. She gestured around the empty room. "Now they have all gone. The young ones when they grew older wanted to move to the big towns where there was much money to be made, more so than in farming. They had learned this from the teacher cousin. The old people died and then soon not many people left to work the farm.

"*Mama* Barnard, she left here when she was young, leaving two small children. My own *mama* said I must look after the little ones, there was no-one else. Their *papa* was too busy with his work on the farm. The teacher cousin still came to the farm to teach the few children left. But one day she came no more."

Graceful rubbed at her eyes. "*Papa* Barnard soon became tired and lonely without his wife. There was much drinking at night. His sons did not fill his heart with love anymore. Then one morning I brought him his tea, before the sun rose, and he was dead in his bed."

Graceful stared at the photograph. Re-living the days when life on the farm was quite a different place. "There was only me," she said softly. "I could not leave the children, so I stayed with them."

She smiled at her visitors. "I am still here. Still looking after them. They are good boys but have no wives or children. Life now on the farm is hard. There is no time to look for a wife to come to a farm which is too old to work well. There is no money to make this place look like the picture you have given me.

"*Eish*. My boys are not young anymore. Too old to make a family to keep this place when they have gone. But I will stay with them until my time comes. Then, when their time comes, the farm will belong to no-one. There is no-one left to give it to."

A tear rolled down her round cheek and Jack felt his heart squeeze. It was a sad story of days gone by when life had been full and happy for the simple folks who lived on this farm and the farms around the area.

He remembered the story George had told him of the night he had spent here with all the laughter, good food, music, and the communities of farmers who had gathered.

Graceful was a good woman, despite any dreams she may have had of her own future, she had dedicated her life to looking after the children she now called 'her boys' and clearly, they loved her and had made a place in their hearts and their home for their surrogate mother.

Jack glanced at Piet and let him take over. "We would like to know about *Mevrou* Barnard?"

Graceful narrowed her eyes and looked at Piet. "*Eish*. Why you want to know this? She left many years ago?"

She levered herself, with some difficulty, out of her chair. "Come with me."

Piet and Jack followed her out through the kitchen where the delicious smells were coming from. A small dusty path led a little way to the right.

Graceful stopped and opened a rickety gate.

"Here she is."

The family graveyard was immaculate, well cared for, and there she was.

Zelda Barnard, wife of Andreas, born 1940 died 1975.

Graceful wiped a tear from her eye with the corner of her grubby apron. And here, you will see her husband's grave. *Meneer* Barnard. *Eish*. He was loving his wife. His life empty when she was gone. Then too much brandy and sadness took him as well."

Jack and Piet glanced at each other. Jack pulled the creased black and white photograph from his shirt pocket and handed it to Graceful. "Are these Zelda's children?"

She peered at it myopically then handed it back to him. "No. I know my boys since they were born. These are not *Mama* Barnard's children. These are not my boys, not Tinus and Marius."

Piet stared down at the grave trying to hide his surprise. "Tell me, Graceful. Did Zelda like to paint pictures as well?"

Graceful shook her head. "No, it was sewing she is liking and working in the office with all the family papers and business things to do for the farm."

Piet nodded. "This Miss Izzy, the teacher, do you know her family name? Where she lived?

Graceful frowned. "This Miss Izzy, she was a strange one. She was young but already old. A young woman laughs and smiles, talks to everyone. But this Miss Izzy, she spoke little, always so sad. I am thinking she was hurting inside from the thing that happened to her."

She looked at them both, then at the photograph of the painting. "When sometimes we had many friends and family coming here for a gathering, when there was singing and dancing and good food, some relatives would bring their own food and kitchen staff to help us in our own kitchen. Making the food for the people outside we would *skinner* about who we worked for and talk about our own families. I am remembering now someone talked about the girl Izzy, for she was just a girl then it would seem, a child maybe.

"Her family lived on a farm somewhere not so far from this place. Those *skollies* came in the night with their guns. They are tying the family up, taking all of value from the farm." She shuddered at the memory of the story,

"They killed the father and mother and the boys. Miss Izzy's little brothers it was said."

She wiped her eyes with her apron then carefully smoothed it out before she continued. "This was the sadness she was holding inside herself."

Piet rotated his aching shoulder. "What happened to her after that?"

They had left the graves and returned to the sitting room. Graceful rubbed the arm of her worn chair.

"At this time when these bad people killed her family, it is said she was sitting with the cows in a shed, waiting for a mother cow to give birth. These bad people did not know this, they burned down the farm and left – this is the story I heard in the kitchen, but many, many seasons ago.

"I am remembering seeing her parents before those bad people came. They sometimes came to this farm with the little girl, Miss Izzy, and the baby brothers, when there was a gathering here. They were good people, like my boys. The children played with the other children not knowing what was waiting for them.

"Then for many years after her family were killed, I did not see her, only when she was grown up and came back to visit the farm and teach the children this painting.

"*Eish,* such sadness to carry. Then, as I am telling you, she left. I am not knowing where she went. The farmer next to the burnt farm bought her land, this I am thinking is why she is leaving with her money from the farm."

Chapter Forty-One

Piet and Jack arrived back in Molteno in the late afternoon. They both agreed a hot shower was in order before they arranged to meet up again for a well-deserved beer before hunting down a decent steak house where they could fill their empty stomachs.

Jack headed for his room anxious to spend at least an hour brushing his teeth to remove all the sugar coating them. But over and above that he had been stunned to see Zelda's grave.

The story of Miss Izzy was heart-breaking, but, as he had learned, it was a story which had repeated itself over and over again on these lonely remote farms.

So, who exactly was Zelda Cameron who had left for the UK decades go? Clearly, she was not the Zelda buried in the simple family graveyard.

All they had to do now was untangle the web and find out the identity of the person who had reached out over the years asking for help from Piet?

The woman calling herself Zelda had arrived in the United Kingdom with a new husband and two small boys – Tinus and Marius. All the paperwork, according to his ex-policeman friend, Bill Watson, had been in order.

What was not in order was the fact Tinus and Marius were still there on the farm.

So how were they all they linked to the disappearance of four young girls in Cape Town?

Jack put down his splayed toothbrush and took a hot shower, sluicing all the dust from his hair and tired body.

*****

Piet was waiting for him on the *stoep* of the guest house, already downing his beer, beads of moisture sliding down the bottle. Jack ordered his drink.

"Make it quick, Jack. I need food so I can think straight. This case is getting complicated. Nothing seems to fit so far. But things are starting to add up. We just need to figure it out and I need a big steak and chips to kick my brain back into gear. Let's go."

They found a steak house in the middle of town and ate ravenously. Piet leaned back with a sigh of satisfaction. "So, my friend, what have you come up with after scrubbing your teeth until they squeaked with relief?"

Jack flashed him a smile. "I think we are making progress, finally. Zelda Cameron was clearly not Zelda Barnard. Her two sons are alive and well and living on the farm. According to my ex-police detective in London, when the so-called Zelda Cameron entered the United Kingdom, she did indeed have two boys with her and a new passport with her now married name. The father was not Paul Cameron, her then husband, as I learned from the retired doctor in Larkstown. And our Zelda was unable to have children. So where did they come from?"

Piet picked at the last chip on his plate. "The immigration officials, in those days, didn't have the technology they have today. So, it's highly likely the papers were given only a cursory glance, husband, and wife and two small boys. British husband returning from abroad with a new wife and family. In those days they were not looking for terrorists, it was simpler then."

Jack nodded in agreement. "Okay, so far so good. So, if the real Zelda died on the farm leaving two little kids, which, as we know, are still there. Where the hell did this woman get two other kids from?"

Piet chewed on another cold chip and frowned. "Graceful told us a relative or cousin, with long blonde hair came to the farm to give lessons to the farm children, she called her Miss Izzy. Both you and I know this could only have been the woman called Isobel, who George fell for. The woman whose family had been taken out when she was a child."

Jack wiped his plate with a piece of bread, soaking up the last of the juice of his steak. "You mean Miss Izzy of no fixed address?"

"Yes. Isobel. George told us he met her under a tree, and she was painting, said she had long blonde hair remember? She was the one who painted the picture, Jack. That's the connection – Zelda and Isobel. The two boys? I have no idea at the moment – but they are key to this story somehow, both of them, or one of them.

"I need to get hold of Bertie as soon as we get back to Hazyview, put him to work and see if he will dig into his impressive database and find anything which might help us. He'll be able to track down a bit of history of the Barnard family, the boys, and their mother Zelda. It would have been useful to have their ID numbers especially Zelda's, but I knew if we had hung around 'til the sun went down at the farm and they came home, well they were probably the size of rugby players, hungry and tired.

"They would have sussed me out as a cop and you a *bleddy* Englishman and told us nothing. I didn't think the car hire company would have appreciated bullet holes in their vehicle."

"True," Jack agreed.

"That useless *oke* of a solicitor gave me bugger all to work with. I need her surname, her maiden name, birth certificate, her marriage certificate. Bertie needs more information before he can start digging for us," Piet said.

"Come on let's take a wander around this town and see if we can find some residents. The older the better. They must have a local watering hole where they meet up. These farming types always have a favourite place where they gather."

*****

It wasn't difficult to find where the locals hung out. It was a low building on the edge of town, old, dusty and in need of some serious restoration. Farm trucks were parked haphazardly on the pavement outside, their sides spattered with mud and dust and plenty of dents and scrapes on the paintwork.

They entered the gloomy depths of the pub; the smell of stale beer and cigarettes was overwhelming. Obviously, the No Smoking signs were of no consequence to them. Heads turned as they made their way to the crowded bar. Piet lifted his hand in greeting to no-one and found two hard bar stools vacant at the far end of the counter.

Piet ordered two beers from the surly bartender and sat back to survey the local inhabitants. They were all big and burly and aged from anything from their early twenties to some old timers who could have been any age, their faces weathered and darkened by the elements.

The barman slid the beers across the counter, slopping some of the contents on the counter with no apology. Piet thanked him in Afrikaans.

"So, *Meneer,* you *okes* tourists? Not much to see in this place except the Ouma's biscuit factory, which should take ten minutes. Nothing else of interest."

He paused. "Also, you're a cop and your mate is *Engels.* So, what you doing here, hey?"

Piet scowled at him. "My friend here is a highly respected journalist working for an English newspaper. He is writing an article about rural South Africa. About the farmers who have lived here for generations, an historical piece.

"I'm showing him around, introducing him to the courteous and warm locals," he said sarcastically, "who own the farms hereabouts. I was born in the Eastern Cape and yes, I was a cop, but retired now."

The barman moved away looking unimpressed and tended to his customers, no doubt whispering to his patrons about who they were and what they were doing here.

Jack grinned. "How come everyone sniffs out you were a cop, Piet? Is it your grumpy face or what?"

Piet looked highly offended. "It's my face, grumpy or otherwise. Like your wild hair, my friend, nothing I can do about it. Also, in this neck of the woods, it's easy to work out you're a *bleddy* Englishman as soon as you open your mouth. These people have a long memory and the older generation still hold grudges against the English, the Boer war and all that."

Jack laughed. "Okay, let's try and change all that. There's a table of elderly gentleman over there near the window. Let's go and chat to them. Let me see if I can change their minds and prove the British are fine decent people, despite history."

Piet snorted then grinned. "Why not. I'd like to see you do it. These old *okes* blame the Brits for everything. But we need that information we're looking for."

The six elderly farmers looked up as Piet and Jack approached. Their faces hostile and suspicious. Piet pulled up two chairs and they both sat down. He spoke to them in Afrikaans, explaining Jack was doing an historical piece on the area and would appreciate their input. With great relish he told them Jack was an Englishman.

There was a long silence. Jack indicated to the barman he should bring another round for the six men. They nodded, unsmiling, as the barman brought their drinks over.

Jack smiled brightly, although he was a little daunted by the stony looks, he was getting. "So, gentleman, tell me a little about yourselves, your history here in Molteno."

One of the old timers leaned forward. "Maybe you should be telling us what you were looking for at the Barnard's farm this morning, *neh*?"

Jack smiled warmly at him, although he was surprised the news had spread so quickly. "Oh, well, it seems it's one of the oldest farms in the Eastern Cape. I thought it would add to the story I'm writing. I wanted to get a feel for what life was like for a farmer and his land over the decades. The hardships they had to endure, the isolation of living in remote places."

Oom Hansie, who had asked the question, leaned across the table.

"You *Meneer* Taylor are a journalist. Your friend here is an ex-cop, or still a cop. We may live out here in the sticks, but we are not stupid. You may be writing a story about this area, but I think it is another story you are interested in. The Barnards? How so?"

Jack looked at Piet. He was out of his depth. Piet smoothly took over the conversation. "Another drink, gentlemen?"

The drinks were delivered. The old farmers were staring to loosen up, they were not as hostile as before. Piet continued in Afrikaans. "See here, gentlemen, you are right. A person who was related to the Barnard's has come into an inheritance in England. We are trying to find her – that's all. Nothing criminal here, no-one has done anything wrong. But we need to find this woman.

"We think she spent a lot of time on the Barnard farm, teaching the children of the farmers. We understand she liked to paint and was quite good at it."

Piet scrolled through his phone until he found the shot of the farm painting. "This painting was bought by someone in England. We have traced it back to the artist herself. We need to find her to tell her the good news of her inheritance. Her name was Isobel. But we can't find her. Don't even know her family name. She spent a lot of time on the Barnard's farm from an early age apparently."

All six men around the table were silent, looking at *Oom* Hansie. He sucked in his breath and whispered, "Isobel."

With a shaking hand he took a sip from his drink. "Isobel was my cousin. Her family had a small farm." He stopped for a moment; his eyes hard with anger. "Bastards came in the middle of the night and wiped her family out. She sold the farm to a neighbouring farmer and went to live in Queenstown."

He swiped his hand across his eyes. "She died there – so young. They never found her body. A neighbour said she had told them she was going to the bush for a few days, to paint. She never returned."

Hansie took a deep mouthful of his drink. "I'm thinking it was what she wanted. After her family was murdered, she always carried a gun with her…"

Piet leaned across the table and squeezed his arm. "What was Isobel's family name Hansie?" he said softly.

"Her name was Isobel Kruger."

*****

Piet and Jack were having a nightcap on the patio before retiring for the night.

"You going to tell old George about what happened to Isobel, Piet?"

"*Nah,* sometimes it's better to leave things as they are. It was a long time ago. Let's leave George with his dreams and memories of the girl called Isobel Kruger."

Chapter Forty-Two

Back in Hazyview, Piet and Jack transcribed all their information, everything they had learned on their trip to Bloemfontein and the farm in Molteno, to Jack's wall chart in his cottage.

They had been disappointed to hear of the death of Isobel Kruger – she would have had valuable information to convey for their investigation. But she had gone as well. Given the story they had been told about her from Graceful, he thought perhaps she had chosen the way she wanted to go.

Another dead end.

*****

Piet perched himself on the side of Jack's desk and stared at the board as he sipped at his beer. "Okay, my friend, it's time to ask Bertie for his help. We have quite a bit of information now. All we need are some dates and correct names of the people so far, some proof. Then we can move on. I still can't see the connection with Zelda Cameron and Isobel Kruger except they must have been quite close, therefore I'm thinking they were a similar age. She went missing around the same time as Zelda arrived in the UK, yes?"

Jack nodded as his eyes swept across the board. "Yup. So, no body, no proof Isobel did die is there? What if Isobel and Zelda were the same person Piet?"

He glanced at his watch. "That's what I'm thinking as well, my friend. Better get back to the hotel, I need to put some time in there and earn my salary, see if there are any problems. I'll leave you with your school board of information and see you in a day or two, hey."

Jack stuck a ready-made meal in the microwave but didn't bother transferring it to a plate. He stood there, scooping his pasta out of the container it came in and stared at his board.

They had achieved what they had set out to do. Follow and find the trail this Zelda Cameron had left for them. Why did she do that? What did she want Piet to find? What was the connection between a farm in the Free State and the four girls who had been murdered in London?

He frowned, it was looking at him, willing him to find it. Isobel and Zelda – that was the connection? But Zelda had died when she was thirty-five.

Isobel had access to the Barnard farm, taught the little ones. Because of the nature of life on those farmlands it was obvious Zelda and Isobel had grown up together, they must have been a similar age. She had filled a much-needed gap when Zelda died, a familiar figure comforting the two boys, along with Graceful, as well as she could.

But then, according to Graceful, she had suddenly left the connections she had with the farm and, according to the old farmer Hansie, she had moved to Queenstown, before dying a mysterious death herself. But he had his doubts about that as well.

Jack took a sip of his coffee and looked at the board again. Concentrating on the passport photograph of Zelda Cameron. She looked quite ordinary, with her solemn face and short hair.

This, in his opinion, was Isobel Kruger. How easy it would have been to swap identities with Zelda after she died. She taught the children on the farm. Teaching in the office in the bitter winter months where it was warmer, according to Graceful.

She would know where the private papers, the ID documents, birth certificates, marriage certificates were kept in the office. It would have been easy to take whatever documents she needed to re-invent herself.

Isobel had left the farm abruptly, according to Graceful.

But she hadn't taken the two boys with her. They were still there, middle aged now, still working the farm they had inherited.

Somehow, this Isobel Kruger had acquired two little boys and using Zelda's documents, left South Africa, and moved to the United Kingdom with her new husband and the boys – the boys in the photograph.

This had to be the key as to why she had approached Piet. She could not have known him personally, that was impossible. Therefore, she must have read the articles in his newspaper on the cases he and Jack had solved together here in South Africa and Kenya. That's how she must have known his name, and reached out from her grave, asking for his help to put something right, which had obviously gone so horribly wrong with her plans, and her hopes for a new life in another country. Plans, he imagined, she had been making for years.

Plans that had somehow eventually led to the missing girls.

His eyes travelled back and forth across the board, looking for some kind of thread to link things together. The only thing that jumped out at him was the fact that religion, so far, wove its way through, like invisible stitching.

The Catholic church.

The last person to see Zelda Cameron alive was a Catholic priest. A Catholic priest who had visited her at least once a year over four years.

Who exactly was he and where did he come from?

Chapter Forty-Three

Piet waited patiently for Bertie to pick up the phone. "Hey, Bertie, my man, how are you?"

There was a short silence. "*Jeez* Piet, I hope this is a social call. I'm flat out now." He sighed audibly. "But knowing you, you want me to find something for you and won't give up 'til I find out what it is you want me to do now? Something simple perhaps?" he said hopefully.

"*Ag*, Bertie, you know you're the best in the business and have access to information both here and around the world with your network of databases. Should be a piece of cake for you, take an hour or two at best. You can use those algae things you know all about that most of us don't understand, can't even spell. Thought it was one of those things for cleaning the slime out of a swimming pool."

Bertie sighed again. "Algorithms, Piet, algorithms. Get with the tech world, my friend, you're lagging behind here. Artificial Intelligence is coming sooner than you think. It'll change the world like the internet did. Give you answers to anything you want to know just like that. Be like chatting to an old buddy like me, hey."

Piet snorted. "Well then, Bertie my friend, I shall make the most of you until that happens and when it does, I'll just speak to a robot, instead of you. Probably be a helluva lot quicker as well."

Bertie laughed. "Now what is it you want?"

Piet cleared his throat, knowing he was going to ask Bertie to do a lot of digging for him. "See here, Bertie, I need information for a case Jack, and I are working on.

"Four young South African girls went missing over a period of five years, twenty years ago. They got on flights to London and were never seen again."

He paused for effect. "They were murdered, Bertie. This we know. It all started with a woman called Zelda Cameron, although we're sure that wasn't her real name. She died in the UK two years ago. She sent me a letter and asked for help – now I'm asking for yours, Bertie."

He heard Bertie suck in his breath. "*Jeez,* Piet. Give me what you have, and I'll get cracking on it."

Piet updated him on the contents of the briefcase and the information they had, or thought they had. "Thing is Bertie, I need to know as much as you can find on this Zelda Cameron. Zelda Barnard died in 1975. Jack and I went to the farm where she lived and died, leaving two small boys, who are now middle-aged men."

Piet cleared his throat. "I need information on the following people.

"Zelda Cameron. Doctor Paul Cameron, a Brit who worked here for a while, married who he thought was Zelda Barnard. They then left the country to live in London, taking two little boys with them. We need to know their real names and who the parents were. Because it wasn't the good doctor or as far as we can tell, or the woman he married."

"We think Zelda's real name was Isobel Kruger who supposedly died somewhere out in the bush in Queenstown forty or so years ago. I have no more info on her, where she was born, or where she lived, but presume it was somewhere near Molteno.

"Her family were murdered on a farm, she was the only survivor. The farm was sold, and she moved to Queenstown where she disappeared, out in the bush somewhere, body never found. She apparently committed suicide, according to one of the local farmers in Molteno, he was her cousin. So, we must take that as so."

Piet rattled off the names of the four girls, their ages and the other information Jack had gathered on his trip to Cape Town.

"Jack has an old contact who was a detective in the UK. Retired now, but he gave Jack some information on the girls but not much else, it was over twenty years ago.

He told Bertie that Doctor Paul Cameron had returned to the UK with a new wife and two kids. Their passports were in order. "I want to know where those kids are, Tinus and Marius, where they came from, their names on a birth certificate. Middle aged men now, of course, and anything else you can find. Can do?"

Bertie was quiet for a moment. "So, Piet, you're asking me to find out about people who kept changing their names in the middle of the Free State forty years or so ago – right? Plus, two small boys who left the country with this Zelda and you have no idea where they came from? And this Zelda is actually dead?

"*Jeez*, piece of cake really – thought you were going to ask me something hard and complicated. Anything else you would like me to do? Go shopping for you, wash your car, clean your family silver? Something a bit more challenging perhaps?"

Piet laughed. "You're the only one who can find out this information for us, Bertie. Jack and I are a bit stuck here now. We need answers before we can hunt down who killed the girls. I want to find him."

"Okay, Piet, this will take a lot of work, but I'll see what we can get from the UK, on their databases. Maybe dig a bit deeper than Jack's old detective mate in England. With all this data protection crap, it would be impossible for most people to get the information they need.

"But as you know we tech geeks, as you call us, can dig a lot deeper and faster with our exclusive club members all over the world. We all have access to each other's databases. But I have to say this will indeed be a challenge. But I'm on it now, Piet. Give me a few days and let's see what we can come up with, so long."

Piet snorted. "How long before these *bleddy* artificial robot peoples take over from humans, Bertie? Thing is we need this information now. Do your best to speed things up, hey?"

Chapter Forty-Four

Jack poured his first cup of coffee of the day and wandered out to the veranda. A fine mist of rain was sweeping across his garden. A welcome cooling change in temperature from the brutal heat of summer.

He shrugged on the light jumper he had around his shoulders and sat down sipping his coffee. The birds normally swooping across the garden were huddling for shelter amidst the branches of the trees, looking bedraggled and cold as they hunched up and tucked their heads down.

The silence and lack of distraction helped him with the questions he was seeking answers to. Bertie would be the key to many of them, but they would have to give him time to unearth the information they needed.

He looked up at the sound of a car coming down the road towards his cottage. He was pleased to see it was Piet. Maybe he'd come up with something.

Hope bounded out of the back seat and rushed towards him, shaking herself vigorously. Jack looked down at the new layer of wet fur he had just acquired and sighed.

"Come on Hope, let's find you a stick of biltong to chew on whilst I pour the boss a cup of coffee. Keep off my bed, you hear me?"

"Morning Piet, coffee coming up, take a seat. I'll get it for you."

He returned with a steaming mug and handed it to Piet. "Early for you to visit. Nothing going on at the hotel to keep you busy?"

Piet took a noisy mouthful of coffee and sat back on the cushioned seat. "*Nah*, most people checked out this morning, game drives cancelled once they looked at the weather. Bugger all to see in the bush when it's like this. But a dozen or so guests checking in after lunch. No doubt they too will moan about the weather and anything else they can find fault with.

"Anyways, thought I should let Hugo know about the story we're after. I've been away for quite a few days this month; thought I should tell him why. Once he heard what we were up to he said to take as much time as I needed. He's a good *oke* even if he is English."

Jack drained his coffee and slid his mug across the table. "Well, we can't do much more until we hear from Bertie. Unless you've come up with anything?"

Piet frowned. "See here, Jack. I'm thinking this Isobel Kruger might not have gone straight to Queenstown when she abruptly left the farm thereabouts in Molteno. I'm thinking she was in Bloemfontein for a while planning her next move. A city where no-one would have known her.

"It's not easy to nick two kids off the streets without someone noticing. It would have been in the papers, big police search and all the rest of it. So, I'm, thinking it was there she carried out the next part of her plan.

"So, I contacted an old police buddy of mine in Bloemfontein. Retired now of course. But he was a young serving officer there forty years ago. I explained the situation to him. He assured me that as far as he could recall there was no such case of two kids being nicked.

"He said he would have remembered something like that. As I said it would have been a big case with a lot of police involved, especially if the kids were brothers and being white it would have been a big, big story. Their family would have made sure of it."

He threw the dregs of his coffee across the lawn. "So, here's what I'm thinking, my friend. I'm thinking those boys were taken from an orphanage.

"There's a Catholic orphanage in Bloemfontein, run by the church nuns I think this Isobel visited the orphanage, maybe taught the kids to paint or something. Then she carefully chose two of them who were the right age as the Barnard boys paperwork stated. Then she took them. She was a Catholic, right? So, she would want two catholic boys, like her dead brothers. So, that makes sense to me."

Jack put his hands on his head and stared into the distance. "Yup, that makes sense, but would have been difficult to accomplish. Again, you can't just take two kids from an orphanage and hope no-one notices."

Piet nodded and chewed his lip. "That's true, hey. But supposing Isobel formed some sort of relationship with those two boys. Once she had picked out the ones she wanted, she spent more time with them than the others.

"The nuns noticed this and were happy someone was taking such an interest in them. Isobel persuaded them to let her take them home with her for the odd weekend. Nothing unusual about that. Then one weekend she doesn't return them."

Piet wiped his sleeve across his mouth. "What could the nuns do about it? No doubt the boys had been dumped at the convent when they were very young, so no parents, no names, no relatives. They would have taken them in, of course."

"Perhaps," Jack murmured, "the nuns were grateful someone had seemed to care for the kids and were thankful there would be two less mouths to feed. It's possible they did nothing about it. From that photograph of them, they certainly looked like orphans, poorly dressed, malnourished, scowling at the camera. I think you might be onto something, Piet."

Piet tried not to look to smug. For once he had one up on Jack. "I ran this theory past my old police buddy. He thought it was a good fit as well. He told me the orphanages in the city, including the one at a convent, had been taken over some years later by a government body under the banner of Child Welfare. The kids were institutionalised, and they took responsibility for them.

"It would be impossible now to find out which orphans went where; I think we would be wasting our time. But if you agree, my friend, then I think we should go along with that scenario."

Jack nodded, remembering his conversation with Margaret Hammond about orphans and how they were dumped outside churches.

"So, Isobel nicks the kids and takes off for somewhere no-one knows her. Part two of her grand plan would be to then find a husband, wouldn't have been too difficult. George, our polo player, said she was a real good-looking girl.

"She meets Doctor Paul Cameron, who might have been her doctor, who knows, perhaps they were friends, they make a deal of some sort. He's looking for a ready-made family to gain the respectability he needs, being a gay man, to nail the job he's been offered in London. A marriage of convenience as they say."

Jack refilled their coffee mugs and Piet continued with his theory. "Isobel uses Zelda's personal documents, chops off her hair to look more like the Zelda in the passport, uses the birth certificates of the Barnard boys, Tinus and Marius, and leaves the country."

Jack slowly nodded his head thinking it through. "It's a good fit, Piet. It makes a lot of sense to me. Good thinking."

Piet glanced at his phone on the table. "Bertie should at least be able to find their marriage certificate in the system. He's had three days now to dig around. Doesn't normally take this amount of time, but I did give him a long list, so long."

His phone beeped he snatched it up and quickly read the message, then looked up. "Bertie. Said he'd call at five – make sure you're around, hey. What are you up to today anyways?"

Jack's foot began to jiggle and he steadied it with his hand. "Bit of shopping to do, need some other things from town. But will be here at five."

Piet stood up a smile spreading across his face. "Okay. See you just now then. Get some meat. We'll have a *braai*. I'll grab a salad from the hotel."

Jack looked up at the weather and frowned. "In the rain, are you kidding?"

"*Ag,* don't be such a *wuss*. South Africans in your country *braai* in shorts and *takkies* when there's three foot of snow outside, or it's chucking it down with rain, which seems to me is most of the *bleddy* time. Then they get to work on a *braai* with an umbrella over their heads."

"That may be, mate, but the neighbours think they're nuts. But if it makes them happy to have a *braai* in a howling gale with rain lashing down, why not?"

Piet laughed. "See here, its tradition, my friend, *braai* on Sunday. Isn't that what Harry was banging on about when we went to his *larney* white man's club. Tradition is everything?"

Jack shook his head in despair. "It's not a white man's club, Piet. It's just called Whites."

Piet flapped his hand. "Whatever. Deeply offensive and racist name for a private club, not so? Wouldn't survive a week here in this country with a name like that. Would've been torched."

He looked at Jack from under his thick eyelashes. "Tradition is why the Zulu's wiped out a whole regiment of English soldiers. What were they thinking, hey? Bright red jackets in the bush, sun glinting off their shiny buttons. Sitting ducks, they were.

"Should have worn bush gear, khaki, blended in. But no, they stood out like those red post boxes I saw in London. Fine soldiers by all accounts – but so much for your tradition. The Zulu's wiped the lot of them out. Blending in, that's what it's all about, become part of the landscape."

Jack scowled at him. "Bugger off Piet. I'll see you later."

Piet whistled for his dog and strode to his car, his shoulders shaking with laughter.

Chapter Forty-Five

Jack stood with an umbrella over his head and poked at the sausages on the *braai* which spat against the sweeping rain. The garlic bread was fine, wrapped in its tin foil, away from the elements. He thought longingly of a pasta dish cooking in the oven and a nice warm fire going in the sitting room.

But he was determined to show Piet he was not going to be beaten by the elements; a strong wind had now added to the uncomfortable cold and wet evening.

Piet pulled up half an hour before Bertie was due to call. He rubbed his hands together as he approached the fire, Hope bounding along beside him, her nose twitching with anticipation. "Smells good, my friend, let's throw the steaks on and eat quickly before Bertie calls. I'll go get the plates and chuck some dressing on the salad." He looked at Jack's face. "What?"

Jack frowned at him. "Okay, I'm going to put my foot down. I'm not sitting out here in the windy wet and cold weather to eat. We'll cook the steaks then move inside. I've got a fire going to warm the place up. If you want to sit out here on your own, be my guest. But I won't be joining you."

Piet threw the steaks on the fire. "Okay, okay, I agree the weather is *kak*. Let's eat inside if you insist. Grab a glass of wine and wait for Bertie's call."

Jack cleared the plates away, threw another log on the fire, filled their glasses with red wine and settled down in his chair. Piet put his phone on the table. Jack pulled his notepad out of his pocket.

They were ready for Bertie.

On the dot of five the phone rang. Piet snatched it up. "Bertie, my man, what have you got for us. Jack is here, the phone is on speaker."

Bertie cleared his throat. "*Ja*, I can hear that. Anyways, this is what I have managed to find out for you. Not as much as you might like but I gave it my best shot considering the time span of forty years.

"Okay. We have the ID number for Zelda Barnard. We have her birth certificate, her marriage certificate, and the birth certificates for her two sons Tinus and Marius. But no death certificate.

"But that's not unusual for those folks who live in the sticks in the middle of nowhere in the Free State. They consider it a private matter and as she was the only wife of her husband, Andreas, they buried her on their farm and didn't bother to report it to the authorities. Probably thought it was a waste of time and none of their business.

"You said you saw her grave and the housekeeper confirmed it was her. So, we must take it as so. Her husband didn't marry again. I don't have the date of his death. But he was without a doubt buried out on the farm himself and this wasn't reported either being family business and no-one else's. Probably didn't want the tax man sniffing around looking for his cut."

Jack and Piet glanced at each other as they listened to Bertie tapping away on his computer.

"Now. This Doctor Paul Cameron. He was a Brit with a licence to practice in South Africa. He was a resident of Queenstown. A Permanent Resident of South Africa. No problems there. We have the marriage certificate confirming he married a Zelda Barnard, which is a bit of a problem because she was dead at the time.

"It's not an unusual name, neither Zelda nor Barnard. So, it was possible she just had the same name, hey? But from the background you've given me on the story you are following, I would say this is not so. Zelda Barnard died when she was thirty-five. Her two boys, according to their birth certificates were then five and seven."

He cleared his throat and continued. "Now comes the interesting part. When the other Zelda married the good doctor and moved to the United Kingdom, her two boys, according to their birth certificates, were five and seven. Now, in those days the children were only stamped in the passport of the mother. Not all the hoops to jump through today, what with the child trafficking and so on."

Bertie continued. "Next, we come to Isobel Kruger. Born in Bloemfontein. We have all her information, and it checks out. However, according to our records she moved to Queenstown and then we have a blank. She was listed as missing, all those years ago, but now is presumed dead. Circumstances unknown."

Bertie cleared his throat again. "As I said before a Zelda Barnard entered the United Kingdom with her married name, Zelda Cameron. The two boys, registered in her passport were called Tinus and Marius. A year or so later Mr and Mrs Cameron changed the names of the boys, legally by deed poll, to Tom and Mark. No doubt to make them more English sounding to fit in with their new British lives.

"But keep in mind that although the boys' ages would have been registered in the mother's passport it doesn't necessarily mean they were that age. Could have been younger. You think they may have been orphans so they could have been any age, but obviously young kids to match the paperwork."

They heard the click of a lighter as Bertie lit a cigarette. "Mrs Cameron had to ensure all the information tied in with the papers she had stolen from the real Zelda Barnard. So, briefly, I would say the so-called Zelda Barnard was indeed Isobel Kruger. I could find nothing more about the boys who would be men now. No record of either of them doing any time in prison. I checked that as well.

"Everything about the four missing girls checks out. ID numbers, family history and so on. We have nothing to add to that."

Piet and Jack glanced at each other, disappointment showing on their faces.

Bertie tapped away on his computer. "Now, there is only one undertaker in the town of Larkstown. As you know it's impossible to get any information from them about anyone who died unless you are next-of-kin. It doesn't matter if you are a brother sister, cousin, or whatever, again it's the Data Protection law. They will disclose nothing.

"So, my man in London, who has little regard for that particular law, found the name of the undertakers who took care of your Mrs Cameron and basically hacked into their records and learned that your Zelda was cremated, and her ashes delivered to a Catholic church called Saint Theresa's in a place called Islington. So that might help."

"That's it, that's all I have for you. Over and out."

*****

Jack took a sip of his wine. "Well not much more to go on unfortunately, Piet. Except we now know the adopted names of her two sons. Tom and Mark Cameron. Why she cut them out of her will is a big question.

"Let's go and have another look at the board, Piet. I want to read the letter from Zelda Cameron again. Something is niggling at my brain. One thing that doesn't fit is the priest who visited Zelda every September with his unwanted lilies and was Zelda's last known visitor on the night she died, in February."

Piet stood next to Jack as he once more ran his eyes over his board, then he unpinned the letter Zelda had sent and read it carefully. "Ah, this is the bit which has always bugged me." He read it out.

The man who entrusted it to me, not the owner, carries a heavy burden of guilt as he is unable to reveal who it once belonged to. It is his cross to bear, as it is mine.

He is still in danger, if he still alive, with the knowledge he must hold within. The owner of the briefcase knows where to find him but probably feels safe enough after all this time. However, now I have handed this over to you Inspector Joubert, I know you will pursue this story of the missing girls, and this person I loved so much, will once again be in danger.

Like him I know exactly who the owner of the briefcase is. Like him, I also carry a heavy weight of guilt for the part I played.

The person who is responsible for the girls' disappearance and I fear their murders, is still out there somewhere.

The reason I instructed my lawyer to send these papers and the briefcase to you two years after my death, is because the person I hold close to my heart will have returned from his hiding place.

Piet frowned at him. "What are you thinking here, my friend?"

Jack tapped the side of his glass. "My thinking is there is a lot of catholic language in this letter. This could be because Zelda was Catholic. But there must be more than that. This story has the Catholic Church running all the way through it. Look, this person she fears for, she says he knows who the killer is but is unable to reveal anything. He knows who the briefcase belongs to, as does Zelda, but can't say. The only person a murderer can confess to murders to is a priest. And a priest is known to be visiting Zelda.

"My gut feel is Zelda is talking about her two boys here. I think one of them is a priest."

Piet nodded slowly. "Yes," he said softly, "now things are beginning to make sense. We need to find that priest, not that he will tell us anything. It's possible then the other brother went to this Catholic church, made his confession, and left the briefcase with his brother. That's how it ended up with Zelda. He had no-where else to hide it."

Jack picked up the thread of Piet's train of thought. "So, the priest delivers the briefcase to Zelda on the night she died? No, that doesn't stack up. She wouldn't have had the time to arrange for a courier to deliver it to her lawyer. So that doesn't work.

"The problem here, Piet is we don't have a time frame to work with. Why did this priest visit Zelda on four or five consecutive years, in the same month?"

Piet shrugged. "Well it wasn't her birthday, that's for sure, you can see that from the copy of her passport.

"Maybe Zelda knew she was going to die and called the priest to administer the last rites and say goodbye to him?"

Jack nodded. "Okay, let's take another look at the other letter from the briefcase, the one for Zelda from someone warning of her of the danger she was in."

We have discussed the missing girls on many occasions but have been unable to do anything.

The person responsible left this briefcase for me to find. So confident was he that I could never discuss it, or the contents, with anyone.

I shall be leaving London for an indeterminate time, in a place where no-one will find me. I shall be safe. However, I cannot take the briefcase with me. I cannot take anything with me. Therefore, I have no choice other than to leave it with you. My suggestion would be that you go through the shocking contents then keep it in a secure place...

Jack took a sip of his wine. "The writer of this letter says he cannot take the briefcase with him, he can't take anything with him. To me it sounds like a priest, a Catholic priest. If he can't take anything with him wherever he was going then it must be a retreat somewhere, or possibly a remote mission, somewhere he would indeed be safe."

Jack tapped his pen against his teeth. "Or the briefcase was delivered to Zelda's lawyer years ago and just sat there in a safe deposit box."

Jack could feel his excitement building. "Both Zelda and this person knew who the owner of the briefcase was. One of her boys. She left nothing in her will to either of them. If one were a priest and I'm starting to lean that way, he would have no need of any earthly

227

trappings. The other one – if she knew was the killer – well, she was not going to leave him anything was she?"

Piet rubbed his hands together looking pleased. "So, what's the next move, my friend?" He was getting a bit fed up with all this priest business.

Jack flipped through his notes. "A priest came the night she died, which one we don't know. I'm not saying he killed her, but what I am saying is he wasn't there to administer her the last rites. Oh no.

"Doctor Fellows told me the place was in disarray when he went to sign the death certificate the next day. Drawers and cupboards open. Someone had been looking for something. That someone was a priest, and he was looking for one thing and one thing only – the briefcase.

"Zelda must have been dead. She knew he was going to come looking for it. She took a whole load of sleeping pills along with a few glasses of wine and killed herself."

Jack slammed his fist on the table with frustration. Hope looked up in surprise, then sank her face between her paws, unused to hearing angry voices.

"For Christ's sake, Piet, why couldn't Zelda just tell us what she was thinking. What she knew? Why did she leave this trail of bloody secrets and cryptic remarks for us to follow? Or more to the point, for you to follow?"

Piet shook his head. "Listen, my friend, I hear what you're saying. But getting angry is not going to get us anywhere. Zelda had her reasons for leaving us this trail. Maybe it was her religion, or her tragic past. But if it leads us to who killed those four girls then that will be enough. She would have done what she set out to do."

Piet leaned against the wall. "See here, Jack. That priest, if it was the same one, visited Zelda every year, over four or five years, not so?"

Jack nodded as Piet continued. "He visited in September with his bunch of funeral flowers, right? This is what I'm thinking. If you look at your board, you will see all four of our girls were killed in the month of September. This is why he came, every September, after each one of the girls was killed.

"He wanted her to know what he had had to do to punish her for whatever she had done to him. He brought his little blue velvet pouch with a photograph of the girl he had killed, a school photograph, family photographs, with her name, a lock of her hair and a piece of her jewellery as proof, even her passport."

Jack frowned. "So how exactly did our killer obtain family photographs of the girls?"

Piet sipped his beer. "Friend of the family? Waiting at the airport in London, they would have recognised him if this were so? But this is not so, my friend. It is highly unlikely he would have known all four of the girl's family so intimately, especially as they all went to different schools."

Jack glanced at his watch. "I'm going to get hold of Harry. Bring him up to speed on what we're thinking so far, then ask him to send Stefan around to Saint Theresa's church in Islington and see what he can find out for us. Even though the priest went away for a while he might well be back by now. Not that he will tell us anything, confessions being sacred. But once we have his name, we'll have the name of the other brother."

Piet stood up. "Better get back to the hotel. Need to check a few things."

*****

Jack reached for his phone, it would be around six in the evening in London and Harry would be making his way home, he called his mobile.

Harry's voice boomed down the phone. "What is it, Jack? I'm not in a good place now, so this had better be good. You're dragging your feet on this story. I need results, you hear me, and where is my next column from you?"

Jack laughed. "Why are you so grumpy, Harry? It's almost April over there, place is blooming with cheerful nodding daffodils and bluebells. Spring is in the air, people peeling off layers of clothes in anticipation of some warm sunshine. Putting their striped hired deckchairs out in the parks trying to catch a bit of a tan, lambs frolicking in the fields."

Harry was silent for a moment. "I'm sitting at the railway station, in the rain I might add," he said sourly. "There are no trains going anywhere. Train strike. Lord knows when I'll get home. So, yes, I am bloody grumpy. Where are we with the story?"

Jack brought him up to date. "Look, I need Stefan to go and check something out for us. I want him to go to Saint Theresa's church in Islington and see what he can find out about a parish priest who presided there, given what I've just told you. Soon as possible? Also need to know if this priest left to go overseas somewhere for a few years or so, and if he did, where did he go? Doing missionary work somewhere maybe? Thought I would run this past you first rather than contacting Stefan myself."

Harry's mood changed. "Sounds like you both are finally making some good progress, old chap. Has all the makings of a cracking story. Keep at it. I'll get Stefan to follow up with the church in Islington tomorrow. Don't forget your weekly column, old chap, deadline coming up for it. Cheerio."

Chapter Forty-Six

Stefan De Villiers found the Catholic church of Saint Theresa's in Islington, no problem. Jack had given him an update on the story they were trying to unravel and what they were looking for now.

Harry had been quick to send Stefan on his way to uncover whatever he could from the secretive world of Catholic priests.

The church was small, old, and dark, but nevertheless a quiet haven from the roaring traffic making its noisy way through the streets of Islington. When Stefan entered, there were three other people kneeling in prayer.

Stained glass windows, some of them cracked and broken, no doubt by vandals, Stefan thought, were covered with grime from the passing traffic, and tried valiantly to allow any shafts of sunlight to penetrate their once vibrant colours. Alcoves held statues of saints and angels lit by flickering candles.

At the alter a young priest was dressed in a cassock with a simple cord tied around his slim frame. Silently, he was going about his business of getting ready for the next service. He stood back, bowed his head, crossed himself and turned to look at his few worshippers. He nodded to the young man sitting in the front pew. Not on his knees but watching him.

Stefan thought he was somewhere in his mid-twenties but already losing his hair. Far too young to be Zelda Cameron's son, so definitely not the right priest. He had an open friendly face as he advanced towards Stefan.

"Good afternoon, my son, welcome to God's house," the young priest said. "Do you wish to make a confession or are you here for some quiet contemplation, away from the chaos of the outside world? You are most welcome here. I am Father John."

Stefan smiled at him, quickly re-arranging his story in his head. "Good afternoon, Father. I'm here looking for my brother, he is, or was a priest here. I was wondering if you might be able to tell me where he is? Perhaps he will be along later? We lost touch some years ago. Like me, he was South African, but I really need to talk to him?"

Father John gave him a questioning look. "I see, my son. It's tragic when a family member loses touch, but how can I help?"

Stefan raced ahead with his lies. "You see our mother died two years ago, and I think her ashes were sent here, perhaps there is a plaque or something in remembrance of her? I would like to pay my last respects. I would very much like to have my brother with me when I do?"

The young priest nodded. "I am the only priest here and have been for the last two years or so. There is no other priest. So, this pilgrimage will have to be done by you alone I'm afraid. But I can check your mother's details for you, my son, if you are quite sure her ashes were sent here. Perhaps you would give me her full name and date of death?"

Stefan had memorised everything for this moment. "Her name was Zelda Cameron, she died in 2016, in February. Her request was to have her ashes sent to this church. She died in Larkstown, here in the UK. Her ashes were delivered here so she could be close to her dear son, as I said, my brother the priest."

Father John frowned. "Are you quite sure she is here. Your mother? Surely your brother must have let you know when she died?"

Lying to a priest about his past did not sit well with Stefan De Villiers, but for the greater cause of finding out what happened to the four girls he was quite sure God would forgive him. Even so it didn't sit well with him.

"The thing is Father John, at home in South Africa, I'm a game ranger. So, my life is spent out in the bush showing tourists on safari the glory of God's gift of nature and the animals. There is no internet. No way of keeping in touch with the outside world…"

Father John looked at him shrewdly. "We may be priests, my son, but it does not mean we are not observers of people and their ways. I think you might like to make a confession," he nodded towards the confessional to the left of the nave. "To confess why you are here? You are far too young to be the former priest's brother. Please keep in mind you are in God's house here. It would be a sin for you to not tell the truth. For you lack the colour of someone who spends his time out in the bush as a game ranger."

Stefan shook his head. "All I am asking is you show me where Zelda Cameron's ashes are. If there is any plaque? I need to talk to the priest who was here when her ashes were delivered. It's important."

Father John gave him a long, cold, hard look. "Clearly this Zelda Cameron was not your mother and the priest you are looking for is not your brother. Your story has too many holes. You are not telling the truth."

Father John stood up. "However, this seems to be important, in what context I have no idea. But there is nothing in the church rules that forbids me from showing where Zelda Cameron's ashes were scattered. If indeed this was so. But you do have some dates which I will check for you. Just give me a few moments whilst I look her up. Meanwhile may I suggest you get on your knees and pray for forgiveness for not telling me the truth. Or you might like to make a confession after all?"

The priest walked slowly away, his back stiff with anger, towards a dark alcove which must have led to where the church records were held. Stefan cursed Harry and Jack for making him lie to a priest, but comforted himself with that they were edging closer to someone who had taken four young girl's lives.

A few minutes later Father John returned and stood in front of Stefan.

"Yes, indeed, the ashes of Zelda Cameron were delivered here to the church. She wanted them to be scattered in our Garden of Remembrance by her son who was the priest at the time. She specifically asked there should be no plaque put up in her memory and no flowers under any circumstances.

"However, her son, Father Cameron, abruptly left this church, for personal reasons, around the time her ashes were delivered. There is no record of where he went."

Father John frowned. "What is unusual is that her ashes are still here. They haven't been scattered. We adhere very strongly to the wishes of the deceased, which would suggest her ashes arrived after her son left. The ashes are being left for him to scatter on his return. But I have no information as to whether or when he will return."

Stefan absorbed this information. "Father John, this information is of paramount importance. I respect all the rules and regulations of the Catholic church, truly I do. I'm not here to harm anyone but I need to know the name of the priest who the ashes were sent to. Can you tell me that?"

Father John took a deep breath. "His name was Father Mark Cameron. I never met him; he was gone before I arrived. That is all I can tell you."

Stefan gave one more push. "Tell me, Father John, did Father Mark spend some time overseas, perhaps as a missionary?"

Father John looked annoyed. "Enough. I cannot tell you where he is. Now, good day to you."

Chapter Forty-Seven

Stefan had been furious about having to lie to a Catholic priest to get the information Jack was looking for.

"I understand your need for as much information as you can get," he said tightly. "But lying to a catholic priest, even though my intentions were good, well, it was very uncomfortable, Jack. It didn't sit well with me and please don't ask me to go back and ask him any more questions because I won't. I can't. Halfway through my questions I realised he had seen through me, that's when I had to lie about being a game ranger etc."

Jack had winced at the anger in Stefan's voice. "Listen, Stefan. We can't let religion and niceties get in the way of finding the killer of those four innocent girls. It goes with the turf. I'm sorry you found it offensive, and I understand. But let's keep our eyes on the end goal here.

"You've done well; we now can move forward with the story. That's what you must keep in mind if you want to be a successful investigative journalist. You must put your own personal feelings aside and swim in the same sewer criminals swim in. You've done a great job; you didn't like it but it's what we journalists do. Prise information out of people for the greater good."

*****

Jack wandered around his garden, working through the information Stefan had given him.

Father Mark was Zelda Cameron's adopted son, or at least the one she had brought up as her son. He had a stepbrother called Tom. This they knew without any doubt.

They were finally making progress. They had the name of the potential killer and the owner of the briefcase.

But they had no proof it was Tom Cameron. None whatsoever.

An idea started forming in his mind. Although the murders had occurred over twenty years ago it was possible someone might remember something.

It had always astonished him how this happened, but it did. Something triggered a memory buried long ago and people recalled something unusual happening. Either at the time they had dismissed whatever they may have seen or had chosen not to come forward for whatever reason. There were many people who had witnessed things but didn't want to become involved with any police investigation. Perhaps they had been in a place they were not supposed to be, with someone they shouldn't have been with.

Jack decided to draft a short article, one not to be printed under his byline. No.

It would have to be written by a relative. He would have to get their go-ahead. He considered the relatives of the girls' and felt Anna-Marie's mother was the best candidate. He didn't think she would have any problem with a cry for help for information about her daughter's disappearance, one with a photograph of her daughter alongside.

He made his way to his office, glancing at his board packed with information, then sat down and wrote his article.

Over twenty years ago, in 1997, my daughter Anna-Marie Cloete went missing. She was on a flight from Cape Town in South Africa to Heathrow, London. According to the records at the time, Anna-Marie arrived safely, however she then disappeared. Despite the efforts of the police, she has never been found.

Twenty years is a long time. But not a day goes past when I don't think of Anna-Marie and wonder what happened to her. For a mother to lose her child the pain is unbearable, the despair haunts me, but I still hold on to the thought that one day I will see her, hold her, and talk to my Anna-Marie again, even though there has been no word from her all this time. Not a single word. I still have hope – it's all I have.

My Anna-Marie was a beautiful young girl with her whole life ahead of her. Someone must have seen something; someone must remember something. Despite all the appeals for information at the time, no-one came forward. I beg you to search your memory. Any tiny bit of information might be the key to what happened to Anna-Marie Cloete.

If you could not speak then, maybe you can now. Perhaps you are a parent yourself? Look at your children and try to imagine the despair at losing one of them and not knowing what happened.

I can't let go of Anna-Marie. I need to know what happened to her.

My daughter is not just a face in a crowd, a statistic. She had her dreams and hopes for a future just as your children do. I miss her terribly; I so desperately want her back. I want to hold my little girl again, even if it's only once more.

All this has been taken away from me. So, please search your memories, come forward. I beg you, please, come forward with anything you might remember, anything at all that can help me find my beloved daughter.

Jack read through what he had written, picked up the phone and called Anna-Marie's mother.

"Mrs Cloete?"

"Yes, Mr Taylor," she said breathlessly. "Do you have any news for me, anything at all?"

Jack rubbed his eyes. The longing in her voice, the hope in it, was still raw. "We are making progress, Mrs Cloete. But, no, I have no further news on your daughter. But I thought a letter from a parent printed in the newspaper and appealing for information might bring something up. To put this through, I need your permission, I need you to sign it off. Let me read what I've written, see if you approve?"

He read it out to her. Surprised by the lack of reaction over the phone.

"What do you think? The letter could be out in a day or two alongside Anna-Marie's photograph, the one we used before."

He could hear the hope seeping from her voice across the African miles. "Yes, alright Mr Taylor, I'm happy with that. Maybe, just maybe, someone will come forward."

Chapter Forty-Eight
Tuscany

The old man stroked his long white beard and leaned on his crook. He looked out over the gentle rolling hills of Tuscany; in the distance he could see the familiar ancient turrets of the monastery. Serene and silent as they had been for centuries, bathed in the afternoon sunlight of an Italian summer.

He looked at his flock of fat white sheep grazing where he could see them and watch over them. He liked the peace of his animals. They asked for nothing except to be able to graze all day and a warm barn to sleep in at night. They didn't care what they looked like, what they looked like to others, didn't care how old they were or what the future held. They needed nothing; just the God given grass they could graze on and, at the end of the day, and the gentle guiding hand of the shepherd leading them back to their barn, next to his modest dwelling.

The shepherd, was a simple man himself. He had lived in this place all his life, he had never been on a train, visited a big city, or watched television; he had no idea how the world was changing so rapidly with its new technology, had no idea of the chaos going on around him in the outside world. He didn't even have a watch. He told the time by the light in the air and the colour of the sky. The change in the seasons by the mood of the landscape, the colour of the leaves on the trees and the cooling of the air early in the evening. Like his flock he was content with what he had been given. He needed nothing more.

A devout Catholic, he would sometimes deliver the carcass of one of his beloved sheep to the monastery in appreciation of letting him use their land for grazing. Having taken the vow of silence, the monks had only crossed themselves and bowed their heads with a gentle smile at his gift.

Some months ago, when the young lambs were huddled next to their mothers, he had noticed the light skinned monk. He could see this monk was not Italian, his skin was too pale. He did not know the landscape he trod so relentlessly every day. This person, he thought, came from another land, far away.

The monk in his cassock, a rope tied loosely around his waist, walked the hills for many hours. This was not unusual for the monks living or taking to a retreat in the monastery. Although he knew they had their duties to perform within the ancient walls of the monastery, it was not unexpected to see a lone monk taking to the hills now and again in quiet contemplation.

But this one intrigued him. The pale skinned one. He took to walking in the hills, no matter the weather. Unlike the other monks he had seen who looked around drinking in the beauty of the Italian countryside, at peace with themselves, this one, his cassock lifting in the breeze with his movements, looked only at the ground. A man, he thought, who was deeply troubled. For many months he had watched him come and go but he still had not seemed to find the peace and tranquillity he was seeking.

He thought the other monks at the monastery would have noticed this lost soul within their midst as he would with a troubled sheep. He knew instinctively if one was behaving differently from the rest, one who was restless, unwell, or troubled by something. Normally this sheep would end up adorning the tables of the penitent monks.

He puffed contentedly on his pipe and stroked his beard. The pale skinned monk was walking the hills again. The sheep were moving slowly through the grasses.

He stood, picking up his crook, and made his way to the path he knew this monk would take. In his loneliness, for the shepherd had picked this up, perhaps he would like someone to walk with, not speaking, of course. The man would not speak Italian and had taken the vow of silence of that the shepherd was quite sure. But the presence of someone else on his lonely walks might bring him some comfort.

The shepherd fell in step with the pale monk, who looked taken aback by his sudden presence. He greeted him in Italian, not expecting a reply.

The monk looked at him in surprise and the shepherd saw the torment on his lined face, the hollow emptiness in his gentle brown eyes. He was not a young man, but he was not old either. The shepherd indicated they should walk together. He decided he would talk to this monk, knowing he would not understand a word he was saying. But living in a world of silence at the monastery, the shepherd thought the sound of another voice may heal the troubled soul he was walking beside.

*****

Father Mark walked silently beside the old shepherd. His tormented soul finding some comfort there with the simple shepherd's gesture of companionship and the gentle words of Italian he didn't understand.

He so desperately needed to talk to someone. What he had held within for so many years was burning his very soul.

Father Mark knew the time had come, but not with the shepherd for obvious reasons. He would have to find someone and then watch as the only world he had ever known, disintegrated before his very eyes. Then his world would be over. Taking him with it.

Chapter Forty-Nine

Father Mark Cameron was indeed a very troubled soul. The weight of what he knew and the terrible truth he had to carry, but could not divulge to anyone, had brought him to his knees in despair.

He had chosen to become a priest as a young boy. Not only to escape his abandonment at an early age, but because he needed something to believe in. He knew, when he was living in the orphanage, that he was destined to be alone for the rest of his life. His mother had left him outside the Catholic church, promising she would be back the next day and take him home.

She never came back. No-one wanted him.

He had tried to remember her name, but the only name he knew was 'mother.' Even now he couldn't remember what she had called him. The nuns had only called him "my child," as they did all the others without names. 'Come, my child, we must eat now' or 'Come, my child, we must pray now.'

He had liked the order and discipline of life with the nuns. He had felt safe there, cared for, unlike so many of the other little ones who were heart-broken, bewildered, and angry. Unable to understand how they had been abandoned by their mothers, or why. The babies, of course, thrived. They had no memory of anyone. They only knew the comfort of a loving nun's arms. It was all they needed then.

As they grew older, they adapted to an institutional life. The only life they had ever known. Although, he thought now, they would have had questions as they grew older and went out into the world.

Some of the orphans were luckier than the others and were adopted. Some were taken into foster homes. He thought there had been around thirty babies and children at his orphanage, white, black, and coloured. They went to school there, gaining a basic education which would help them adapt to life in the outside world when the time came.

He had liked helping in the church, finding it peaceful and tranquil as he went about his simple tasks of polishing the silver goblets, with his little hands, tidying the hymn and prayer books. Dusting and polishing the pews, removing the burnt-out candles. The nuns called him their little altar boy.

Even then, at such an early age, he knew this was the road he wanted to travel.

He wanted to be a priest.

He remembered the young woman who came to the convent to give painting lessons once a month. Like the rest of the orphans, he too, had to attend his lessons, over and above helping in the church.

He had noticed the young woman who came to the church each time she came to the orphanage, before the painting classes began. He knew in between her prayers; she had been watching him.

He didn't care much for painting. But he saw the loneliness even at that young age, of the young woman who taught them about colours, landscapes, shape, and form. Her name was Miss Izzy. She had long blonde hair which she tied back in a loose knot. Her voice was gentle as she encouraged her young pupils to look beyond themselves and see a different world through painting. A bigger world with all its beauty. A world they had never seen but now could start to imagine.

There was another boy in the same class as him. He didn't know his name. The boy took no interest in painting, refusing to even try and lift his paintbrush. He seemed fixated on Miss Izzy.

After the lesson the boy would help her clean up the room, wipe down the messy paint splotches, wash out the jam jars of discoloured water, wash the paintbrushes. It seemed to Mark she liked him. Saw something in him.

It was only so many years later he realised what she saw in this boy who liked to wash the paintbrushes, was irrevocably damaged, like so many others there.

Then one day, after Miss Izzy's painting class, the Mother Superior had summoned him and the little boy who helped wash the paintbrushes and told them Miss Izzy would like to take them both to her home for the weekend.

Even then Mark had been hesitant. He knew the weekends were busy in the church and he wanted to be there to help with the familiar, centuries old, rites and prayers he had become so familiar with. But he had no choice.

Miss Izzy took the paintbrush boy and the altar boy away from the convent in her car.

For the first time in his life Mark was seeing the outside world of busy streets, cars, crowds of people and a place far away from the peaceful one he had grown to accept and love.

He had looked at the boy next to him in the back of the car. His face had lit up at the noise, the endless traffic, the throngs of people hurrying along in their daily lives, the busyness of it all. His breathless excitement as he pressed his face to the car window, misting his view before he wiped it away with his sleeve and kept watching as another world unfolded before his eyes.

Miss Izzy had taken them both to her house, which was small and basically furnished and seemed empty of anything which might have belonged to her. Leaning against the wall, next to the front door, was a small painting of what he thought might be a farmhouse set amongst an endless view of the bush with mountains in the distance.

He had seen pictures like this in books the nun, who taught geography had shown the children. She had taught them about the great oceans of the world, the different countries, cultures, and language. To him it seemed very big out there.

Like the nun, Miss Izzy had chatted away to them about places around the world neither of them had ever heard of. She talked of a place called London, of beautiful ancient buildings, big red telephone boxes, and red buses which would take you all over the city to see the wonder of it all.

She had bought them snacks they had never seen in their lives before. Crisps, biltong, koeksisters and then supper. They had both stared at her in wonder at the new world she was describing to them. One boy more animated than the other.

Her house was some way from the town they had passed through, surrounded by bush and dusty roads. She had asked them to come outside because she wanted a photograph of them.

Mark remembered that moment quite clearly now. Neither of them knew what she wanted as she held the camera to her eye.

Chapter Fifty
London
2018

Joe McNeil was sitting out in his garden enjoying the last of the afternoon sunshine. His two daughters were playing and splashing in the blow-up pool he had bought for them. His wife was busy in the kitchen preparing the food for their barbecue later, singing along to a song on the radio.

He took a sip of his tea, leaned back, and closed his eyes relishing the warmth of the sun on his ravaged face.

Life was good, better than he could ever have expected given his background of poverty, drugs and growing up on a council estate outside of London. His days of living on a dilapidated barge buried deep in the undergrowth of the river Thames seemed like a different life now. He had survived those years by selling drugs and taking them himself.

Then one incident had changed his life. The girl who had appeared on his barge huddled in the corner, begging for help. Although he had been smoking dope for most of that day, the shock of her dying in front of his eyes had shaken him more than he had imagined possible.

After sliding her body back into the Thames, he had smoked a bit more, snorted some cocaine and passed out on his bunk.

He knew for a fact that the drugs he had supplied over the years had undoubtedly left more than a few people dead after an overdose. But he had consoled himself with the fact it had been their choice, not his. He had just been selling a commodity which had been in high demand, like other drug dealers around the city of London. A bit like people supermarket shopping, he had reasoned at the time, it supplied things people needed and wanted to buy.

Eventually he had been caught and busted by the cops. After serving five years in prison, he had decided to change his life. Try and make things better for himself. There had been a lively business going on in prison, drugs were available, smuggled in, paid for, and exchanged.

He had looked at his future and saw nothing but more of the same. His life was going nowhere. But the image of that young girl had stayed with him.

"Daddy, daddy, look at me! I can hold my breath in the water. Watch me, daddy, watch me!"

He opened his eyes and watched his two daughters playing and cavorting in the pool and smiled. Who would have thought? Him, Joe McNeil, now a respectable businessman with his own modest hardware shop, married with two children. He hadn't touched drugs since he came out of prison. It had been a long hard road to recovery. But he had done it. Meeting Belinda, his wife, had been a turning point for him. They had been in the same drug rehab programme and together they had fought their way through that world, fallen in love, and eventually married.

He had worked hard whilst out on parole. Stacking supermarket shelves, packing bags of groceries at the till, washing cars, mowing lawns. Then working in a hardware store doing the same thing, but gradually he had gained the trust of his boss. He was hard-working, friendly with the customers, willing to do anything to improve his life. Gradually he became the assistant manager, learning about stock, accounts and how to run the business.

Finally, he had accrued enough knowledge to step out on his own and start his own little hardware store and here he was now, living in his modest house with a wife and two children.

He took a deep breath. He had been given a second chance and taken it with both hands.

He reached over to the table next to his chair for the newspaper. Time for a beer and a catch up on what was going on in the world. He shook the paper and started to read.

On the front page was a photograph of a young girl laughing into the camera. Next to it was a letter from a mother whose daughter had disappeared, twenty years ago and her poignant pleas for any information.

Joe looked up and watched his daughters playing, splashing water at each other, and shrieking with laughter. He tried to imagine what it would be like if one of them disappeared without trace. His heart squeezed at the very thought of it, and he shuddered. Trying not to imagine his beloved daughter being tipped into the icy river of the Thames and being swept out to sea.

The mother's letter was heartbreaking. Once more his thoughts went back twenty years when the young girl had appeared on his barge. He had never given it much thought then, but of course, she would have had family somewhere. A family who had had to grasp the fact their daughter was never coming home again. There had been no second chance for that young girl.   He felt sick to his stomach.

Maybe it was time to give something back. The newspaper had said any information would remain anonymous. What did he have to lose?

He stood up abruptly. His mind made up.

*****

Someone else was reading the same article. He frowned slightly. Damn, after all these years. Then he grinned. No problem there. This pathetic letter from the mother of one of the girls, well, he had the power to put her out of her misery.

He pondered making an anonymous call to the newspaper himself, play a bit of a game with them. But, no, he would put Anna-Marie Cloete's mother at the top of his list for a visit when he returned to Cape Town. She would be grateful he had called on her.

She would have to go, of course. Once he told her what he had done to her daughter. But judging by the tone of her article in the newspaper, he would be doing her a favour. Just like the other girls he didn't want her to suffer any longer.

It would be a good and kind thing to do.

He stared at the photograph of Anna-Marie. Such a pretty young thing then. Today she would be heading into her forties, her looks beginning to go, trying to cope with her adult life with all its problems.

He had saved her from all of that.

Chapter Fifty-One

Joe McNeil's call was picked up by the special line at the *Telegraph*. "I need to speak to someone about a girl, um, one I think went missing years ago, like what you said in your newspaper today? This'll be a secure line, yeah? No names. No tracing of calls?"

"Absolutely sir, nothing you will say will be recorded or traced," her soothing voice replied. "We guarantee that. Let me put you through to Stefan De Villiers. He's handling any information relating to the disappearance of Anna-Marie. We appreciate you coming forward. It's a brave thing to do and very much appreciated."

*****

Stefan picked up the call with a sigh. The phone hotline had been ringing all day, mostly nutters who had some theory on what had happened to Anna-Marie and wanted some kind of reward. But so far, he had written them all off. He'd rather have been down the pub watching rugby with his mates.

Wearily he answered the incoming call. "Stefan De Villiers."

*****

Joe almost lost his nerve but thought back to his girls playing in the pool and ploughed forward. "Um, this call won't be recorded, yeah?"

Stefan assured him it wouldn't be but turned on his recording device, nevertheless.

Joe took a deep breath. "You see, something happened twenty odd years ago. I've never spoken about it before. But I read the bit in your newspaper about a missing girl from South Africa?"

Stefan sat forward in his chair, knocking some files off his desk. His thoughts of rugby and his mates down the pub instantly forgotten. This was not another nutter. He sounded as if he knew something.

Joe, his voice shaking with nerves, coughed and cleared his throat, then continued. "See, I was living on a barge in the Thames. Not a high point in my life, living rough as I was. I was heavily into drugs at the time, dodging the coppers until they busted me. Did me time in prison, yeah. But I'm clean now, got me own little business, wife and two kids, yeah.

"One night, I can't give you a date, couldn't even remember me own name at the time. Well, this girl appeared on me barge. Huddled in the corner, naked except for her knickers. I took her down in me cabin. She was in a bad state. I covered her in a blanket but within minutes she croaked on me."

Stefan let his breath out slowly as the anonymous caller continued. "I was into drugs, as I told you, not thinking clearly. I took her back up to the deck and put her back in the river where she appeared from. Didn't report it 'cos I didn't want the cops crawling over the barge and discovering me stash of drugs, I would have been busted for that. Probably accused of killing the girl, you know what I mean? Given her an overdose or something."

Stefan was on full alert. "Did she say anything to you before she died?"

"Yeah. She was muttering about something black. Not sure what she was talking about. Maybe she had a black boyfriend who did her in. Maybe it was her surname, dunno."

Stefan paused for a second. "What did she look like. Can you remember?"

"Yeah," Joe said softly. "I can. She was young, very young, tanned. Her body was athletic looking. She had long hair, not sure what colour 'cos it was wet. Odd hairstyle though, long on one side and chopped short on the other."

Stefan pushed him, keeping his voice calm. "Anything else you remember?"

Joe paused. "You sure I can remain anonymous? Don't want the coppers on me doorstep tomorrow. I've done me time, done with coppers, I'ave."

Stefan assured him he could. "So, is there anything else?"

Joe paused for a moment. "Yeah. She had this kind of tattoo high up on her left, or maybe it was her right, thigh, not sure what it was, can't remember clearly. But it looked like a sort of map."

The phone went dead in Stefan's hand.

Stefan turned off the recording with this man, his heart beating fast. He checked through all the notes in his file on Jack's case. Jack had suggested that one of the girl's had a tattoo high up on her thigh.

That girl had been Suzanne Clifton. He remembered the contents of the four velvet bags spread out on Harry's desk. All found in the briefcase, with the hanks of hair and pieces of jewellery. According to Jack she had been a champion swimmer in South Africa, heading, hopefully towards the Olympics and, according to Jack, she had a tattoo high up on her leg.

It was a fit.

They had found Suzanne Clifton.

Chapter Fifty-Two

Jack and Piet were sitting out on the veranda of the cottage, watching the sun set behind the hills, the sky a palette of gold, pink and red, a masterpiece of heavenly art.

They sipped their beer in comfortable silence. The grey wisps of smoke indicating another *braai* tonight.

The garden was silent and peaceful. Squirrels scampered across the lawn, the birds swooping and soaring as they made ready to return home and roost.

The tiny buck, the dik-dik, was now a familiar figure as she came silently down to the stream on her dainty legs and black hooves to drink.

Her large expressive eyes rimmed with dark lashes, watched carefully, before she dipped her head to drink; the fading sun glinting off the tips of her feathered ears and horns. The last of the evening light casting a dappled shadow across her deep chestnut and tan coloured hide, allowing her to blend effortlessly with her environment. Then with a flick of her dark tail she was gone.

Jack sighed with pleasure as he looked around his garden. Here in South Africa was the closest he had ever felt to nature, after living his entire working life in London. The only wildlife he had seen there had been a marauding fox, his big bushy brush sweeping the air as he crashed dustbin lids off looking for food.

When he'd lived in London surrounded by the world of crime which he'd lived in as a journalist, he would make his way home at the end of the day, through the traffic. The teeming endless crowds also making their way home.

The packed tube trains, the grim expressions on the faces of the commuters and the final walk home, mostly in the rain and dark to his small flat. He would order a take-out and sit in front of the television to catch up on the news. The rain slashing against his dark windows. The thoughts of the day, despite the current world-wide news, endlessly working through his head.

There, there had been no escape from the world he lived in.

But tonight, with Piet, was a welcome respite from the chaos going on in the world. The heartbreaking case they were dealing with and the tumbling thoughts going back and forth through their heads.

For a brief moment it was a peaceful world, here in Jack's garden, where nature was at its absolute best and the real world seemed a million miles away.

This, he thought, was better than any anti-depressant, blood pressure pills or any of the other pills which doctors dished out to people who simply couldn't cope or understand the world they were living in. Finding it too much to deal with as they faced each day and the next and the next and the next, and all the days to come where they could not escape from the suffocating reality of their life.

Jack had opted out of the so called 'rat-race' – and found a place where he could live a life full of beauty and peace and still be a journalist for his newspaper. Authoring articles out of Africa, thanks to the miracle of technology.

The case he and Piet were working on now was distressing, complicated and frustrating. But sitting out here in his garden, with Piet by his side, he knew they were making progress.

Jack took careful aim at the mosquito busy dining out on his leg. He slapped it viciously and sat back, then started to scratch vigorously.

"*Ag*, Jack, I don't know what it is, but our mozzies here most surely love the blood of an Englishman. It must be sweeter than we tough South Africans, hey. Easier to digest maybe? Put a bit of toothpaste on it that'll stop the itching."

Piet eased himself out of his chair and prodded the *braai* where the embers were red and hot. Hope looked serious as she watched the heat rising from the coals. If she didn't look too interested, a piece of meat might come her way.

Piet threw the meat on the grill and the smell every single South African in the entire world knew so well, rose into the air. Yes, they had their barbecues in America, all over the world, in fact, but somehow their own was different. Perhaps it was the essence of the African wood they used. Certainly, a gas barbecue was simply not the same.

It was said certain aromas could bring back emotional memories, long buried through a lifetime. But to a full-blooded South African there was no other aroma which could bring them right back to their childhood. Bringing the memories with them of the place they had called home.

Jack's phone rumbled on the table. Stefan. He put it on speaker.

"Hey Stefan, how's it going. Any response from the article we published?"

"I tried to call you last night, Jack, but there was no reply. Where were you? Hot date or something?"

Jack grunted. "Bloody power went off for seven hours, so no internet, no emails. Phones went down as well. Why didn't you call this morning then?"

Stefan's voice was vibrating with excitement. "Because, Jack, your article was in this morning's paper and Harry instructed me to be at the end of the anonymous hotline for the entire day, just in case knowing Anna-Marie was a South African someone came through speaking Afrikaans which no-one else speaks here."

"But, apart from all the nutters that came through, one after the other. We got a hit. We have a witness. We know what happened to Suzanne Clifton."

Piet knocked over his glass as he leaned forward eagerly. Jack's foot began to jiggle, as he felt the excitement crawling down his spine.

Stefan turned his recorder on and paused it. "I have the entire conversation here. It tells us everything. Here it is."

Piet and Jack listened; their faces expressionless as they looked at each other.

"Play it again Stefan," said Piet. His voice husky with emotion.

Stefan complied.

When the anonymous caller rang off, Jack sat back in his chair and took a shaky sip of his beer. Trying to imagine the scene of Suzanne crawling up the side of the barge, terrified, begging for help and then being returned to the icy waters of the Thames for the last time. It was heart-breaking to imagine.

Jack could hear Harry bellowing Stefan's name. "Look, guys, Harry's on the warpath about something. I've given you all I have, so far. I'll brief him on the call."

Jack took a deep breath and blew out his cheeks. "Excellent work, Stefan. Thanks."

*****

Jack watched Piet as he silently tended the *braai*. Stabbing at the sausages with unnecessary force. A few minutes later he walked slowly down to the stream and stood there looking at the water. Hope picked up a stick and trotted down, placing it at his feet. She sat next to him leaning her body against his leg sensing he needed some comfort.

Piet stroked her head, then came back and slumped into the veranda chair, rubbing his eyes with the back of his hand.

"What do you think, Piet? It's a big breakthrough."

Piet narrowed his eyes. His face hard. "It's good news, of course, now we've found out what happened to one of the girls but not how.

"Remember Suzanne was a champion swimmer, young and extremely fit. So, my thinking is the killer drugged her with something, put her in the water, but when she hit the icy water, the cold overcame some of the effects of the drug. It must have been dark and somewhere in the Thames where there was little or no traffic or people around. She must have been terrified. Incapacitated by the effects of the drug the killer gave her and the shock of the icy water, plus the darkness, and she did the only thing that came naturally to her.

"She swam."

Hope barked anxiously. Flames were rising from the fire. Piet hastily leapt to his feet, removed all the meat, and covered it in tin foil and shoved it in the warming drawer in the kitchen. He came back and stood looking out at the dark night, spattered with dark clouds, hiding the stars. Was this the final glance at the world Suzanne had seen? On some squalid barge?

Jack kept quiet and listened as Piet, clearly upset, continued. "Suzanne somehow ended up near our drug addict's rotting barge, no doubt hidden in the undergrowth and had just enough energy left to climb up and collapse on his deck. He finds her, no doubt bombed out of his head. But within minutes she dies, and he puts her back in the river. Jesus…"

Piet bowed his head for a few moments, then continued. "In my experience this is how the killer operated. Snatched the girls. Took them somewhere. Did whatever he did to them. I don't want to think about that now. Drugged them then waited 'til it was dark before disposing of them in the river where they would have been swept out to sea. Never to be seen again. Turns my stomach, Jack. I'm used to dealing in the world of crime, as you know, but mostly hardened criminals.

"What happened to this young girl, my friend, is something quite different. What chance did she have when she started swimming. Her instinct for survival was strong. Unfortunately, not strong enough."

He took a gulp of his beer and swiped his mouth with his hand. "My thinking is this, Jack. The killer took all four girls over five years, he used the same *modus operandi*. He met each one of them at the airport. They went with him willingly, that's the puzzling part. Why would the girls go with him so willingly? Where did he take them? How did he recognise them at the airport? How the hell did he know which flight they would be on?

"I'm thinking he kept them somewhere for a while, not weeks, not months, only a few hours. How do you hide someone for just a few hours?"

Jack searched his mind and came up with nothing. "I don't know, Piet. If he took them to where he lived, someone would have noticed. But no-one noticed anything. A young girl from South Africa, overcome by the big new adventure she was excited about and embracing, given her background, would surely have questioned being brought to some man's home.

"She would have been frightened. She might have gone along with being picked up at the airport. But surely must have realised something was quite wrong with where she was then. She would have shouted, screamed, made some kind of noise if she was being bundled into someone's house. Someone, next door neighbours, people walking past would have noticed?"

Piet stood up and paced around the veranda. "See here, Jack, that's not what I think happened. This is what I'm thinking."

Jack watched as Piet stopped his pacing and sat down.

"I'm looking at things differently, Jack. You lived in London. The way of life in the city there was so familiar you didn't see things as perhaps a tourist would. Things a tourist would see, like me when you took me on that *bleddy* awful tour of London, which might have been nice if the sun was shining but was *kak* in the rain and cold, but whatever."

Jack leaned forward. He had seen that look on Piet's face before. He was coming at this case with a completely different point of view - as a detective.

Piet took a sip of his beer. "Why would these girls have gone with a stranger? Someone they had never met before but seemed familiar to all four of them?"

Jack shrugged. "Well, whoever met them knew their names. No doubt had them up on a board with the hundreds of other transfer companies. The girls were surprised but happy to have someone meet them and take them to their hotel – except, as we know, they didn't. What are you thinking here, what have I missed and you've picked up?"

Piet stared into his drink. "What I noticed in London was no different from any other tourist visiting for the first time.

"It was the traffic. The familiar things any tourist has seen when planning a trip to England. Apart from the famous buildings, the bridges and so on, a few of the iconic things were red buses and taxis. The endless traffic weaving their way through the streets of London.

"How could anyone remain anonymous in a city like London, Jack?"

Piet now had Jack's full attention. He had missed something, but Piet hadn't.

"Because, my friend, the one thing is this. If you see something often enough, where you live, you accept it as so. In a way, you register it being there. It's familiar, always has been. You don't give it a moment's thought.

"When Harry hailed a taxi to take us to his fancy club, it was a moment or two before a taxi came along with its light on which I knew was then available. If the light wasn't on then the taxi wasn't available, not so Jack?"

Jack nodded. He finally knew where this was all leading.

"It was right in front of us, in full view, and we didn't see it. A London cabbie can drive all day in London with or without his lights on. No-on takes a blind bit of notice. It's so familiar. The lights are on for business or they're not. Londoners don't look at the driver or his passenger if the light is off. They wait for a taxi with the light on."

Piet rubbed his face. "And that, my friend, is how I think he did it. He was a cabbie. A London taxi driver, blending in with the London landscape. With his light off, knowing no-one would give his cab a second glance, he caught each one of our girls. He didn't need to take them to any house. He had them right where he wanted them. In the back of his taxi with the light off."

Piet stood up and paced around again. "Our anonymous caller said, before the girl died, she had whispered the word 'black.' She wasn't talking about her surname, or a black man – no. She was talking about a black cab. One of the most familiar sights in London.

"A black cab – with a killer driving it."

Chapter Fifty-Three

Jack and Piet finished eating. Although neither of them had much of an appetite, Hope was delighted. She waited until they had both left the veranda then helped herself to the generous amount of food they had left on their plates.

Jack and Piet, once again, searched the board of their investigation looking for another thread which might lead them to another angle.

Jack's thoughts came back, again and again, to the girls' when they arrived at the airport in London. "Okay, Piet, the London cabbie makes sense; he waits at the airport for the passengers, he has their name on his board. The girls see their names, no doubt surprised, but presumed their parents had arranged a surprise for them."

Jack paused, thinking on his feet. "Instead of taking a bus, a coach, or the Tube. There waiting for them is someone who had been booked by their parents to take them to their hotel. Hell, he even has their names up on a board. What's not to trust about that?"

Jack turned on the lamp and the whole board lit up so they could see it more clearly. "This is what is wrong here and we have to dig deeper."

Piet looked at him. "Like what and where?"

"See here, mate, a London cabbie does not go inside the airport to collect his passengers. Passengers, once they have cleared immigration and customs, must go outside and queue up with hundreds of other passengers for a taxi. They're all sitting there with their lights on, open for business.

"A London cabbie must have a special tag to line up outside the airport to pick up passengers. It's the law, always has been. You can't just queue up there, hop out of your taxi, snatch a girl from the arrivals hall and make off with her. That most certainly would not go unnoticed by the other cabbies, or any CCTV cameras– impossible, it would never happen.

"Those London cabs move every few minutes. Impossible for any cabbie to be in the queue and not move."

Piet thought this through. "Okay. But suppose a London cabbie, using his pass to be allowed to pick up passengers from London airports, decides he wants to go pick up his mom or a friend, or a relative? Obviously, from what you're telling me, he can't wait in the queue, he must go inside and pick up his dear old mom? Right so how does he do it, Jack?"

Jack tapped his pen against his teeth. "There is only one way. He would have to have the official tag to access the airport. However, if he is picking up a relative or friend, he wouldn't be waiting in the queue. You're right about that. No, he accesses the airport with his official tag, then turns off his light and parks in the multi-storey parking lot. All legal, no-one will question a black cab parked with his lights off in the airport parking area.

Piet looked impressed. "How do you know all this Jack? Been doing some research and not shared it with your partner?"

Jack gave short laugh. "I lived in London and travelled frequently by taxi. I know how all this works, I must. A black cab is an integral part of the London scene, as you so rightly said. Although they seem untouchable, with their impeccable historic record, well deserved and, I hasten to add, well earned. Well, someone will find a way to abuse the situation, and this is what we have here.

"Our London cabbie was indeed a licenced cabbie. He must have done what they call The Knowledge. He must have had all the licences and legal requirements needed to do his job and have the required pass to pick up passengers at all the London airports."

Piet snorted. "You mean the *okes* who bicycled around London for four years in the *bleddy* awful weather? *Jeez,* still can't get my head around that, hey. But whatever, go on."

Jack ran his finger over the photograph of Suzanne Clifton on his phone. "This is what I think. Our cabbie, with the correct legal tag and paperwork, drives to Heathrow, parks with his lights off in the multi-storey parking area, picks up his board with the name of one of our girls, then waits in the arrivals hall and collects her, tells her he is indeed a London cabbie, but is parked in the parking area, as he can't wait in the queue outside the arrival's hall.

"Our young girl knows nothing about how all this works. She follows him out towards the parking area and gets in his London cab...and why not?

"Any traveller to London will know about the black cabs. Just like any traveller to New York knows about their yellow cabs. So, what has she to fear? From her point of view, her parents have organised a kind surprise, London cabbie to pick her up and take her to her hotel.

"Of course, she gets in. What a wonderful introduction to London – a real London taxi with a real cabbie driving it. All paid for by her parents.

"The cabbie, no doubt a friendly sort of fellow, stows her luggage, leaves the parking area, and off they go heading for the city. He chats to her asks about her dreams and hopes for the future. Knowing full well she was not going to have one.

"But," Jack said sadly, "they were going nowhere. Not to her hotel. Our cabbie had other plans. He would, of course, know London like the back of his own hand. He would know where he could park. Some isolated part of London, under a bridge somewhere. No-one would take any notice of a taxi with his light off parked somewhere. If anyone had noticed, they would think he had stopped there for a nap or to eat his lunch. Nothing unusual about that, lots of them do it for a short break from driving."

Piet blew his cheeks out. "He kept her in that taxi. Did whatever he did with her, then when it was dark, he slid her into the river. He killed her.

"But here's another question. Maybe he wasn't a cabbie at all my friend, he borrowed a cab from a buddy for the day?"

Jack shook his head. "Highly unlikely. If a genuine cabbie got caught doing that, he would lose his licence immediately. After working for four years to get it and then making good money with fares and tips. Well, it would be, like I said, highly unlikely. Also, he would have to give his so-called buddy his licence to display and other official documents. No cabbie would jeopardise his career to do some buddy a favour for the day."

Piet nodded writing that scenario off in his mind.

"The question is this, Piet. How did he know their names? How did he know what they looked like when he chose his victims. Which flight would they be on. Who fed him that information?"

"*Ja*. He knew specifically what he wanted, Jack," he said thoughtfully. "Young, long, blonde hair, and from South Africa."

"Father Mark and his brother were both born here. Their mother, or adopted mother, Isobel, was also born here. She with the long blonde hair."

Piet stared down at his new safari boots. "He must have come to South Africa before he started his killing rampage. He must have had his plan in mind as to how he was going to get what he needed. He had identified the private girls' schools. Probably using the same story you used, about wanting to put his child there. He must have come back every year to select his next victim."

Piet frowned and looked out over the tranquil and now dark garden. "But how did he know which flight the girl would be on when she left for London? Still can't work that out, Jack.

"See, here's a gap year, as they call it. The girls didn't leave school and jump on the next plane to London. They leave school in November. The intake for a student into a university in the UK begins in September the following year. So, unless they go to a local university, they either travel somewhere or find part time work as a waitress or something like that. They wait until they can travel to start university. So how did this so-called cabbie, if you're right, know which flight they would be on?"

Jack shook his head. "That's what Margaret Hammond, the house mother, told me as well. Anna-Marie didn't travel anywhere either, she worked as a waitress in a local restaurant, saving money for her trip to the UK. Okay, let's come at it a different way.

"Some of the girls may have chosen to go to university in South Africa. But the four schools these girls attended, are expensive. So, I am assuming, given the turbulence in the country at that time, the parents opted for an expensive education in the UK, with a better, more secure, future for their daughter."

Jack was warming to his theory. "You see, at around that time, when the new government was firmly in place here, with their new policies on education etc, the private schools and universities were under a great deal of pressure to allow what they called the 'disadvantaged' into their schools and universities. White people were worried about the future of their children. They might think getting a degree from, say, Potchefstroom University, just wouldn't cut the mustard on a future CV, but a degree from a British university would be recognised immediately."

Piet scowled at him. "What's *bleddy* mustard got to do with anything, hey?"

Jack laughed. "Just a British expression meaning, well, not good enough."

Piet glared at him. His eyes hostile. "What are saying, my friend? That our universities are not good enough for rich people? Some of the finest brains in the country were educated at our universities and don't you forget it, hey. *Jeez...*"

Jack held his palms up in a gesture of surrender. "Okay, okay. It's just that the University of Potchefstroom, which may be excellent, doesn't quite have the same ring as say Oxford or Cambridge University. Hate to tell you this, but if anyone outside of South Africa, was looking at a CV and that came up, the first thing they would ask is 'where the hell is Potchefstroom.' See what I mean, mate. It doesn't have the same cache."

"*Ag*, don't know what you're talking about, man. Mustard and *bleddy* cache. Anyways, I need to go back to the hotel and check everything's alright. I'll leave you with your fancy words and posh accent — and the washing up."

Piet called his dog and stomped off towards his car. Jack smothered his laughter. Yup, it had been an intense day and Piet had definitely lost his sense of humour.

He made himself a cup of coffee and took it though to his office with the enormous boards and the dozens and dozens of bits of information they had accumulated so far.

They needed to find the two brothers. Tom and Mark – Tinus and Marius.

Another call he was going to make was to his old detective friend Bill Watson. Somewhere there must be a list of all registered taxi drivers in London. He wanted Bill to see if there was one registered called Tom Cameron, he could pretend to be a disgruntled passenger and wanted to report him.

If this was also Data Protected and Bill could come up with nothing, then he would ask Piet to ask Bertie if he could hack into the Taxi Associations data base and find out that way.

Then another thought struck him. When London cabbies retired, they sold their cabs stripped of all the official badges the law demanded. He remembered reading somewhere of celebrities, not wishing to be recognised and wanting to travel freely around London without being hounded by photographers. Few people knew Prince Phillip himself had one. With the cab light off and wearing a flat cap he could drive anywhere without being recognised.

But Jack somehow thought a celebrity or even Prince Phillip himself did not fit the profile of who they were looking for.

He frowned. It was possible then, that their focus on a London cabbie, with all the right tags and paperwork, might not have been a cabbie at all. It was possible he had bought a cab from a retired cabbie and driven around in it and captured the girls' that way?

Well, there was only one way to check that. He would call his mate Bill Watson and see if Tom Cameron was indeed a licenced cabbie.

Bill called him back, two hours later. "Yup, Jack, he is indeed a registered cabbie."

Chapter Fifty-Four
Mark

Miss Izzy took them to a place called Queenstown. It was a big place and, for Mark, confusing. Far away from the life he had known. They had lived in a little cottage on the outskirts of the town. She had bought them new clothes and shoes and told them they now had a new life outside of the orphanage and she would give them names. Marius and Tinus Barnard, but she would call them Mark and Tom, she also gave them their birth dates.

Mark didn't have a problem with this because he didn't know what his real name was anyway, but at least he knew his birthday now, even though Miss Izzy couldn't have known what it was and probably made it up. Tom was two years older than him. But he was thankful. He wouldn't be an orphan now but a proper little boy with a home, a full name, and a birthday to look forward to each year.

Mark as he now called himself was brought up with the Catholic faith and this he still practiced. He knew the paintbrush boy, now called Tom, was not happy. He was given to unpredictable outbursts of anger. He never smiled and pulled away from Miss Izzy if she tried to put her arms around him. He rarely spoke and would shut himself away in his room, refusing to participate in any of the lessons Miss Izzy gave every day.

Mark was puzzled by the behaviour of his adopted brother, his big brother, Tom. Why was he not happy to finally have a home with a kind person like Miss Izzy?

Nervously, he had asked him. "Why are you so angry Tom? Miss Izzy is a good person, she looks after us, she's given us a home and teaching us things about the world. She's a good Catholic like me. You should be happy for a second chance. We now have a name and a birthday to look forward to!"

Tom had launched himself at Mark, punching and kicking him. "She's a whore. Like my mother was," he screamed at him. "I don't want to be a Catholic. I don't want to be here. I hate her and I hate you. She should be punished for what she did. She stole us. Don't you see that?

"My mother was going to come back one day and take me home. I know she was. I was waiting for her. But Zelda stole us and now my mother will never be able to find me!"

Mark had backed away holding his eye which was beginning to swell.

"Fuck off, Mark, with your religion and your God. He doesn't exist. You're stupid to think he does. Go on, you idiot. Introduce me to one person who has ever seen this God of yours? Go on, show me someone!"

The tears spilled down Mark's cheeks. "Perhaps, Tom, he doesn't want to be seen by non-believers like you." He wiped his nose with the sleeve of his shirt. "I see him everywhere. But I fear for you. I fear you will not have a good life. A life, yes, but an angry one where there will be little love but much torment."

Mark backed toward the door as Tom picked up the lamp next to his bed and hurled it at him. Mark quickly left the room and heard the lamp crash against the closing door.

Thus began a new chapter in the life of the little boy called Mark and his angry brother Tom.

Chapter Fifty-Five

London was even bigger than Queenstown, much bigger with so much traffic and noise. But over the years Mark became used to it and accepted it. His mother, as he now called Miss Izzy had a new name too. Mrs Zelda Cameron.

Both boys attended the local Catholic school. At the age of eighteen Mark started his journey to becoming a priest. A road he knew he had always longed to travel.

He accepted his calling, spending several years of education in the seminary before ordination to the priesthood. It required a deep faith, a sense of calling to serve God and a commitment to a life of celibacy and a strong moral character.

Mark had finally found his way.

When Zelda's boys left home, she gave them their British passports as she knew they would both need them at some point in their lives. But she didn't give them their birth certificates which she had stolen from the farm when the real Zelda died.

*****

Tom chose a different path. From the age of twelve he had found a different world. He worked hard, delivering newspapers, running errands, shop lifting, assisting old people across the roads and relieving them of their purses when they had collected their pensions. Blending in with the crowds in the crowded London streets, watching out for the unwary and helping himself to their handbags, purses, and jewellery.

But Tom was not stupid or unintelligent. He watched the world around him in London and found the perfect solution as to how he would make this Zelda Cameron pay for what she had done. In his distorted mind she had turned into the mother who had dumped him on the steps of the orphanage.

As his so-called brother entered his new life as a priest. Tom relished living in London on his own. He found a job as a courier, winding his way through the streets of London on his motor bike. After three years he knew London like the back of his hand and found the solution he was looking for. It was then he had planned his so-called mother Zelda's punishment.

His next choice of career would give him the perfect cover for what he had been planning for so long.

He lived in a cheap room in London. He never kept in touch with the woman called Zelda or his pious brother. He cut them both out of his life.

He was street smart and worked out, at an early age, that his so-called adoptive father, the doctor, had a life of his own which didn't include him, his brother, or Zelda. He despised the man.

In the quiet shadows of his troubled mind, untouched by empathy, Tom harboured a cruelty that set him apart. He found pleasure in the suffering of others, animal, or human. The malevolence left a trail of hurt and pain in his wake.

The look on a pensioner's face as she searched for her stolen purse with shaking hands. The tears scattering down her face, not knowing it was safely in his pocket adding to the pile of money he was busy accumulating and with his new career he was making plenty.

He revelled in the power he felt when inflicting harm. A power that set him adrift in a world he had already turned his back on. He would make his own world until he had wrought as much pain and suffering as he could on Mrs Zelda Cameron.

In the chaos of his mind, he was not going to cause harm. No, he was a saviour. Saving young people from the agony that would surely be inflicted on them if they lived too long. He would show them what pain was and they would be grateful to him for saving them from a lifetime of it.

He didn't want angry young girls who had already given up on what life had given them so far, who would be grateful for the quick release he could give them if he put an end to their misery.

He didn't want girls with bodies covered in ugly tattoos, with studs in their noses, mouths, ears, or eyebrows, with strange, coloured hair, or worse, shaved heads. Although it had given him a couple of ideas as to how he was going to do things. No, he didn't want that.

He wanted beautiful young girls who had lived a privileged life where they had been given the best of everything life had to offer. Their unblemished bodies young and tanned, their hair glinting with the gold bestowed by the glorious sun of his homeland.

The girls he chose would have to be perfect, with no idea what was waiting for them when they left the safety and comfort of their family homes. He didn't want them to have to go through life with all its unpredictable twists and turns. He wanted to save them from that. A noble and good thing to do. They would be grateful to him for saving them. Keeping them young and beautiful forever.

He knew he had a vicious streak. He knew he was unpredictable. But he could put things to right now.

Yes, of course, he would have to kill them. But it would be a gentle killing. He would be kind to them and tell them why they had to die. He would relish the beauty of their smooth, tanned skin and silkiness of their golden hair.

He would control their lives, their destinies. He would explain to them why it was necessary and for their own good; why he didn't want them to go through the life he had had to endure and how it had twisted him and left him with no roots or family. He would tell them what his mother had done to him and how she had abandoned him.

No, it was a good thing he would do. The young girls he would choose would never be abandoned by anyone. Not by a mother, a boyfriend, a lover, a husband, her children, or anyone else they loved. But most importantly they would never have to leave their child on the steps or an orphanage and lie about coming back to fetch them.

He would ask them about their childhoods, where they lived, about their siblings, where they had travelled as a family. He would ask about their pets, their friends. Encourage them to show him family photographs, ask them questions as he relived their lives in his head, imaging himself within such a loving family.

Then he would kill them.

But he wouldn't be out of control, not at all. He decided there would be four girls, and he would be their saviour. Just one a year would be enough. But they had to be South African, blonde, and pure, with an accent he knew so well.

He had been born in South Africa. He remembered little about it, only that it was big and in the summer it had been hot. At night, through his young eyes, the skies had been painted with the glitter of stars. So perfect. The winters had been cold. It had been a brutally cold day when his mother had left him, promising she would return with warm clothes for him.

She had never returned. But he remembered her accent.

He didn't want any of his girls to go through something like that. But he did want them to be South African. The only thing he remembered about his mother was that she had been young with thick blonde hair.

His chosen girls would have to be something like that. He would save them from ever having to make the kind of decision she had had to make.

Apart from this he didn't want his chosen girls to ever hate their mothers. He wanted them to be happy and grateful for everything they had been given.

He had worked out how he would do it. Once done, he would visit the woman he hated more than anyone in the world.

Zelda Cameron.

He would show her the results, the proof of how he had saved these girls from a life of misery. Perhaps then she would realise what a nice little boy he had really been, as nice as his brother the bloody priest, who, in his mind hadn't done so very much. No, he would be the one who would save souls. He would leave proof of this – something his brother would never be able to do.

Sure, his brother had spent a year here or there on some mission somewhere, but the rest of the time he had been handing out thin biscuits and a sip of wine or waving his pot of smelly incense over his congregation. As far as he was concerned his brother was a complete and utter waste of time and did nothing for anyone except promise them some glorious afterlife, of which he could offer no proof of at all.

If you're going to promise someone a life floating around the clouds somewhere, when they died, at least back it up with something.

When he had saved his lovely girls from a life of potential misery, he would present his so-called brother, the priest, with results that would make sense. Not some nebulous promise of nothing.

It would be his one and only gift to his adopted brother. Let him make what he would of it. He would have the proof in front of him and be unable to do absolutely anything about it. Then he would disappear, and his pious brother would never see him again.

Zelda would be gone chasing her other son's promise of another life. Dead. He would make sure of it.

He himself would be pursuing another life and it wouldn't be up in the bloody clouds.

He would finally give himself the gift he had been waiting for. His reward. He would have sent the girls on their way, but the ultimate prize still awaited him.

He wanted to see the devastation he had caused. Wanted to see the faces of the parents of the child he had taken. Wanted to see the unbearable pain he had caused.

Just as his mother had caused and broken him all those years ago.

Chapter Fifty-Six

Tom eased his vehicle out of the lock up where he kept it. It had taken a long time for him to come up with how to make Zelda Cameron pay for what she had done. But today was the day.

As he drove, his thoughts went back to how he had come to this point in his life. His memories of being abandoned at the orphanage in the Free State by his mother. He had waited and waited for weeks after that, convinced she would come back. She had told him he would only be there for the day because she was going into town to buy him some new clothes.

He had sat down on a bench in the garden of the orphanage, although he didn't know it was one at the time, and waited and waited until it got dark, and a nun had approached him. He remembered the look in her eyes, sadness, and compassion as she took his hand and led him inside.

Every day after that he went back to the bench in the garden, so his mother would have no trouble finding him when she came back to take him home.

But she didn't.

The little paintbrush boy finally gave up hope and replaced it with a seething anger. He was not popular with the other children; he didn't play with them or talk to them. He was given to wild outbursts of anger, and unpredictable behaviour.

The other children were wary around him and kept their distance, afraid of him and his need to physically hurt anyone who came near him. His anger came from realising his mother had thrown him away. If she had loved him, she would never have done that. But worse, he didn't even know what his name was anymore or how old he was.

They were forced to attend church every day and that was when he noticed the boy helping the priest with his duties. There was a calmness about him, an acceptance of where he was. He looked as though he had found another life within the safety of the walls of the orphanage.

The months passed quickly and although the boy had not one single friend, he had to attend classes like all the other boys and girls.

The painting classes with the *auntie* who came to teach them was of no interest to him, but he watched Miss Izzy. She didn't force him to paint but let him make up for that with cleaning up after the class was over, emptying the cloudy glass jars and washing the paint brushes.

The nuns had noticed the little paint brush boy, for that's what they called him, was less aggressive when he was with Miss Izzy. They had been worried about him and the way he isolated himself from the other children with his unpredictable anger and fury. But they knew from years of experience that the boy had been severely impacted by his mother's abandonment of him.

Then, one day, the nun had told him that he and another boy had been invited to go home with Miss Izzy for the weekend. He had climbed into the back of the car, surprised to see the gentle little boy who helped in the church – the altar boy.

Miss Izzy had taken them to her home. The paintbrush boy had glimpsed a world he knew he wanted to be part of. Somewhere he could make his own life, away from all the memories of the one so far.

The altar boy only knew he didn't want to be part of that world.

Early the next morning, Miss Izzy had bundled them into her car and driven them away to a big city, chatting to them about all the things she wanted to show them. She told them she was going to adopt them, give them their new names.

Tinus and Marius.

Miss Izzy had told them she was going to be married to a doctor, who would be their stepfather and they were going to live in London where they would be a real family.

The boys had glanced at each other. "Which one am I, Miss Izzy?

She smiled at the paintbrush boy. "Your name is Tinus Barnard, and your new brother will be called Marius Barnard. Your family name will be Barnard, like mine. But once I am married, we shall call you Tom and Mark Cameron.

*****

The years passed swiftly as Isobel adapted to her new life in London. Her husband, who only knew her name as Zelda, led his own life as she knew he would. He had been honest with her about his sexual preferences. All Isobel had ever wanted was to replace her little brothers who had been killed on the farm. She knew she would never have children of her own. But the two little boys had filled a gaping hole in her life. Filled the empty void of her dead brothers, replacing them with two orphans who were now the children she could never have conceived.

*****

Tom, making his way through the London traffic, had flashes of his childhood. London had been a shock, with all its noisy traffic. Nothing like the orphanage in the bush. But he had embraced it and began to visualise how his future might be.

Although overwhelmed by his change of life it took him some time to realise why he had been drawn to Miss Izzy.

She reminded him of his mother. In his mind she became the woman who had abandoned him. The woman, his mother, had long blonde hair. That he did remember. His hatred of his mother built up. When he looked at this Miss Izzy, he only saw the distorted image of his real mother. The woman who had dumped him, unwanted, outside the orphanage. The memory of her retreating back was seared in his memory.

The two brothers thrived in London. Tom was clever, devious, he knew how to make a buck or two. He saw his brother Mark moving serenely into his new life knowing exactly where and what he wanted to be. They had never been close, not like real brothers at all. He could tell under the serene alter boy's pleasant face, Mark didn't like him at all. Mark made Tom feel like there was something wrong with him.

Chapter Fifty-Seven
Cape Town
1996 – Twenty two years earlier

The priest waited patiently as the passengers boarded the aircraft en-route to Cape Town. He found his seat in economy, apologising to the young girl who was already seated, as he squeezed past her.

He could see he was not what the young girl had envisaged as a travelling companion for the next twelve hours. He looked at the tattoos on both her arms, the blue stripe of colour through her hair and her jaws moving as she chewed her gum, her body moving in time with some kind of tinny music he could hear coming through her cheap earphones.

He would most certainly not be engaging her in any conversation. He opened his bible and lost himself in a different world.

When dinner was served, he crossed himself and gave thanks to God for what looked like a paltry meal, then turned off his overhead light and went to sleep. He had a busy day ahead tomorrow.

*****

He liked the reverence shown to him by the public, even the grim looking immigration officials at the arrival's hall had looked at him with respect and smiled; especially when he called them 'my son'.

The priest hired a car at the airport and made his way to a modest chain hotel where he checked in. He spent the rest of the day wandering through the city and shopping malls, enjoying the nods and smiles from people. Such a friendly place, Cape Town. It was good to hear the remembered accents, the laughter, and loud voices as people of all colours chatted to each other as they shopped. The Rainbow Nation as Mr Mandela now called his country and his people, with all their diverse backgrounds, were revelling in the new dawn in their history.

The following day he entered the school in the late afternoon when he had observed most of the parents and relatives had come, chosen the photographs they wanted and left. There were photographs of each girl filed neatly in envelopes, in a long filing box, on the reception desk.

The ones pinned to the board, from what he could gather, belonged to the school, and would be moved into the archives once the orders had been taken.

He approached the senior girl at the desk who looked up and smiled at him. "Hello, Father. May I help you with something?"

"My child. My name is Father Mark. One of my fellow priests in London has asked me to come and order his niece's photograph. He's missed spending more time with her as she was growing up here. But there is much one must give up, gladly I must add, to follow the Lord."

He fumbled in the folds of his cassock and looked intently at his list, then turned to look at the lines of photographs of the matric girls, with their names written beneath them.

He spotted the one he was searching for. "Ah, here she is. Anna-Marie Cloete. Her uncle told me she has been accepted into an overseas University. He's so proud of her. I wonder what she will do when she leaves school here before she enters university. Probably travel for nine months. Travel broadens the mind, a wonderful experience. God bless the child and her good fortune."

The girl smiled at him. "No. Way too expensive. I know Anna-Marie. She's going to get some part time work, a waitress or something, before she heads for Edinburgh University in September next year. It will be hard for her mom. They're very close."

The priest nodded. "Yes, it's the price you pay for giving your daughter so much, then you must watch them fly away to begin their own lives. Anyway, my child, may I take one of these for Anna-Marie's uncle? Unfortunately, I'm leaving on this evening's flight back to London, so won't be able to order and pick it up later."

"Of course, Father Mark." Her fingers moved nimbly through the envelopes before she pulled one out. "Here we go. I'll pop it into another envelope for you. No charge. I'll order more for her family."

The priest frowned slightly. "My child, may I share something with you? You see, my fellow priest is rather estranged from his family here. Some of Anna-Marie's family found it hard to accept he was going to leave the country and follow his own path...but he was particularly close to Anna-Marie when she was a toddler. I cannot say anymore. But perhaps I may trust you not to mention this to the other members of her family? It will mean so much to him. He does not wish to cause any more anguish for his family here."

The young girl looked at him sympathetically. "Of course. I'm happy I can help. How kind of you to do this for him."

He grinned as he walked back to his car, then sat and looked at his photo.

Yes, she would do nicely. Very nicely indeed.

Chapter Fifty-Eight
Hazyview
2018

As Jack unpacked his weekly shop, he began to despair about the Zelda Cameron case.

He needed time out. He needed to go somewhere and clear his mind for a few hours. He kicked off his shoes, poured himself a glass of ice-cold wine and wandered down to the gurgling stream at the bottom of his garden.

Sitting on a warm rock he swished his feet around in the tepid water, the sun glinting off the ripples as it made its unhurried way to wherever it was going. Unlike him, he thought. He felt he was going nowhere fast enough with his story.

His phone rumbled in his pocket. Hugo.

"Hi Hugo, what's up?" He could hear loud voices and laughter in the background. Obviously, Hugo's bar was as busy as usual.

"One of our guests called from his room, and asked if either you or Piet was around. I sent Shaka over to his room to check all was alright. Didn't seem to be a security issue. Piet won't be back from town for an hour or so. Want me to let my guest know to expect you anytime soon?"

"Who is this guest, Hugo, what's his name?"

There was a shout from the bar, followed by loud laughter. "Sorry, can't remember off hand. Look, must go, busy as hell this afternoon. Shall I give our guest your number maybe?"

Jack hesitated. "No, it's okay I'll be there in half an hour or so, see you then. Thanks Hugo."

Jack felt his heartbeat speed up a fraction. Whoever it was wanting to see him, or Piet, was clearly not a local if he was staying at the hotel. Few people knew he and Piet worked together on various cases, only Hugo as far as he knew.

He threw the dregs of his wine glass into the stream and sprinted across the lawn to his cottage. He would have a quick shower, put on some long trousers in case the mozzies were about, which he knew they would be, and head for the Inn. But first he called Harry in London.

"Jack, my boy, what news do you have for me. Come on, I'm waiting for some progress on this story?"

Jack sighed. "Something might have come up. There's someone at Hugo's place, a guest, who has asked Piet and me to meet him there. I need to check if anyone has been asking for us? Stefan can help. He's the only one on the staff who knows Piet and I work together on stories…"

Before he could finish his sentence, Harry's voice boomed out over the intercom. "Stefan! My office. Now."

Jack flinched and held the phone away from his ear. A few moments later he heard Stefan's breathless voice. "Hey, Jack, how can I help you?"

"Hi Stefan. Has anyone called the office asking about me or Piet?"

Stefan laughed. "Yes, someone did call, said he was on his way to South Africa. He knew both your names and wanted to know how he could contact you. So, I told him to try the Inn in Hazyview. He had a South African accent, not strong, so I could see no harm in passing on the info. Hope that was okay Jack? Anything to do with South Africa is passed to me now. Sorry, should have checked with you first, but it seemed legit to me."

Chapter Fifty-Nine

Jack pulled up outside the Inn, the place was certainly busy, the car park full. Before he could open his door, Shaka loomed up from behind a large car.

"Ah, Mr Yak. I am watching out for you. Someone is here to see you and Mr Piet. He is in room 240. Mr Piet is still to come back. This man is saying he will meet you at five. He is busy with some things but will see you in the garden near the pool."

Jack slid out of his car and frowned. "So, I have to have an appointment with this person, Shaka?"

Shaka gave him a wide grin exposing his perfect white teeth. "Yes, Mr Yak. He is busy with someone more important than you and Mr Piet.

"This person is being sent by God. He is wearing a dress."

*****

At five, Jack was sitting a little back from the pool, under the shade of a large, dark green umbrella, the sun throwing shadows across the grounds as it prepared for its departure.

A shadowy figure emerged from room 240, the skirts of his cassock moving in the slight breeze. Jack stood up and watched the priest's hesitant approach. He held his hand out.

"Good afternoon, Father. My name is Jack Taylor, but you already know that. Piet Joubert is on his way. Ah, here he is now."

Jack raised his arm and beckoned Piet over. Piet looked at the priest and Jack saw his shoulders slump.

*****

Piet sat down abruptly and looked at the priest. "I must tell you Father, I'm done with priests, the Catholic Church and all its secrets. What's your name?"

The priest bowed his head. "For the moment, I am Father Mark. I have come a long way to see you both."

Piet scowled at him. "So, for the moment you are Father Mark? Then what will you turn into. Father Tom?"

Jack watched Father Mark as he flinched at the anger in Piet's voice. He had a gentle face, a gentle manner. Piet's aggression was a little out of place.

"I am Zelda Cameron's adopted son. My name was Marius Barnard. I have been a priest since I was eighteen. It's the only life I have ever known and loved."

Piet and Jack looked at each other, then turned their attention back to Father Mark.

"Go on," Jack said gently.

The priest stood up. "I can't go on, not as I am. If you want the truth, I shall tell it to you. Please bear with me for a moment or two. I will be back shortly."

They both watched him as he slowly walked back to his room. "Now what, Jack? What's he going to do next?"

Jack looked down at his hands. "I think he's going to do something he could never have imagined. He's about to give up a life he loved. The only life he has ever known."

Piet stared at him. "You think he's going to top himself then, is that what you're thinking? If he is, I hope he doesn't make a mess of the room."

Jack retrieved his beer from the table and took a sip. "No. For him it's something far greater than that. Suicide would never be an option, not with his faith. Let's wait and see. I think I know what he's going to do."

It didn't take Father Mark more than a few minutes to do what he had to do next.

He came out of his room dressed in a simple shirt, and trousers. The cross was gone from around his neck. He made his way back to them. His face full of despair as he carefully sat down.

"The four girls you are looking for. I know what happened to them. But for me to tell you I must relinquish everything I have ever believed in. But I truly believe it is the only way forward for me. The truth must be told, and the person must be punished for what he did to them and their families.

"What I must tell you, I heard in confession. It is my vow never to reveal what I hear in confession. It is one of the most sacrosanct vows a catholic priest makes. To break the seal of confession, to violate the law of the church, I will be excommunicated. For years I have struggled with the knowledge I have. Trying to find a way around the seal of the confessional. But there is no way around it. My life as I have known it will be over."

He reached for the familiar cross on his chest, then returned his empty hand to his lap.

"I will tell you what I know, what happened and who Zelda Cameron really was. But in return I ask this of you. I ask you don't involve me in any police investigation either here or in the UK. I will not be returning there again. Zelda is dead and you have the briefcase I gave her. I must ask you to give me your word on this?"

Piet looked at the broken man in front of him. So far, they hadn't involved the police. The priest had made a huge sacrifice by agreeing to tell them what they so desperately needed to know.

Piet looked at Jack who nodded his head. Then turned back to the priest. "You have my word. Jack agrees with this decision."

Jack and Piet leaned forward in their chairs. Finally, they were about to learn the truth about what had happened to Zelda and the girls and where the connection was.

Chapter Sixty
Father Mark
1995

After years at the seminary learning the ways of the church and being ordained, Mark was sent by the Vatican to Ghana, to a remote village where he would establish a small church, clinic, and a school for the people. He had told Zelda he would be away for some years, and it would be impossible for him to be in touch.

Before he left, he went to his childhood home, in London, to say goodbye to the only mother he had ever known. She had sat him down. "I have something I must tell you, Mark.

"My real name is Isobel Kruger, not Zelda Cameron. Zelda died years ago and is buried on her farm, close to a place called Molteno. We had been close since we were children. Her two boys still live there. Marius and Tinus. Middle aged men, now of course. But I stole their identities, just like I stole you and your brother."

Mark had not been shocked. He now lived in another world. He understood how frail the human spirit could be and why people sometimes did the wrong things, followed the wrong path.

It was then that Isobel had told him the story of her own childhood, the murder of her parents and her two little brothers, how she had stolen the papers from the Barnard farms and then taken him and his brother from the orphanage and, using the stolen documents, had brought them into the UK all those years ago.

Isobel continued. "I realised after some years that my little brothers could never be replaced. But I loved you, Mark. You were easy to love, kind and gentle. You will always be my son, no matter what. Tom, unfortunately, inspired no feelings in me, although I tried over the years to love him. I haven't seen him, or heard from him, since he left home nine years ago now. I have no idea where he is or what he's doing.

"You see, darling, there was something wrong with him. He was always so surly, so angry, nothing made him happy no matter how hard I tried. My life is much calmer since he left."

Father Mark said nothing.

"I wanted to tell you all this because you are going far away and who knows what may happen. But I did want you to know where you were born, where you came from and how you came to live in England. And I hope that you can forgive me for taking you out of Africa."

He nodded, as she held him close. "Goodbye, my little altar boy. I'm so very proud of you."

Two years later in 1997 Anna-Marie went missing.

*****

Father Mark eventually returned to London, via Rome, where he had learned he would have a new parish in the London borough of Islington, St. Theresa's.

By that time Zelda and her husband had moved from London. He was eager to see her again and, through his stepfather's old practice in London, obtained her telephone number.

His stepfather, she told him, had died and she now lived in a place called The Gables, in Larkstown.

"Then I shall take the train there as soon as I can. I'm longing to see you."

There was a slight pause, not what he expected. "Mark, you mustn't come here. Please, for my sake, don't come here. Things happened whilst you were away. Terrible things I can't talk about."

He was totally unprepared for the bombshell which would explode in his face some years later.

Chapter Sixty-One

He waited in the queue until the last person left the church then made his way to the Confessional. The light was on the priest was waiting for him...he could not see him, nor could the priest see who was to make their confession. A grill and a curtain gave complete privacy. He placed the slim briefcase next to his leg and rubbed his hands in anticipation.

The priest offered the ancient words to the penitent before he began his confession.

Tom smiled, he was about to blow the priest's life apart, knowing he would not be able to do anything about it.

"Forgive me, Father, for I have indeed sinned."

There was a pause. Had Mark recognised his voice? Whatever, the man told him to confess all, and that was exactly what Tom was going to do.

"So, we finally meet again. I've been wanting to talk about this for years now. Finally, I can do this knowing there is bugger all you can do about it.

"Let me start with my first girl, Anna-Marie Cloete."

Over the next two hours Tom described, in detail, how he had gathered the information on the four girls he wanted and how he tracked them before killing them.

Firstly, he had travelled to Cape Town and selected a girl who reminded him of his mother. She had to be beautiful and have long blonde hair. He visited the first school on his list. He didn't want anyone who looked tired, angry, or disillusioned before their time, so he went for the private schools and selected them from there.

It was far easier than he had anticipated it might be. He went in November each year, for four years. Young girls were leaving school, they had chosen the universities they wished to attend and had been accepted.

He perused the board of girls and chosen the one he wanted. The name printed underneath. A few chosen words of interest elicited the name of the university they would be attending the following September. All he had to do was wait.

When the time came, it only took a simple phone call to the admissions office of the university to obtain their arrival dates.

Tom had no problem at all learning of their flight details, using some excuse of being a relative who would be collecting them from the airport, or a friend who wanted to welcome the new student with a welcome hamper, or perhaps a few necessities he would like to deliver to the young girl who would be taking up residence on campus. The information was given quite happily and the dates they would be arriving.

A final call to the offices of SAA in London to confirm which flight the girl might be on, using a plausible excuse about forgetting what day he was supposed to be picking his niece up and couldn't double check with her parents because they were on a cruise, but he had promised he would collect her, and take her to university. Could they help?

*****

He had eased his taxi out of the lock-up, made quite sure his welcome sign was on the white board, written in large black print, and could not be missed. He turned off his light as he made his way to Heathrow then parked in the multi-storey parking, reaching for his board.

The girls had walked right into his arms. Every one of them. Thrilled with this unexpected treat when he had told them their parents had organised this lovely surprise.

He had looked at them with envy. So perfect, so privileged, so trusting.

He knew he had to save them, keep them the way they were, untouched by what the future would do to them. He had never had that choice. It was the right thing to do.

Over the four years he had used the same method. He collected them from the airport, chatted to them as he put their luggage in the taxi, then he had taken them for a trip around London, showing them all the sights, all the wonders of London and its history.

The girls had been full of excitement, chatting away to him. He was a South African, he told them, now a registered London cabbie, he showed them his licence. Even more reason for them to trust him.

And they did.

He showed them around the city, then stopped at a crowded pub for lunch, wanting to show them all the old traditions of London which he knew they would never again experience.

Over a typical pub lunch, he had asked them about their life, their growing up in Cape Town, their parents and their siblings and the pets they had left behind, where else they had travelled to. They chatted easily without fear.

Eventually, he knew, they would have to go to the ladies' room. He slipped the pill into their drink and waited for them to come back.

Then the games would really begin.

Games he would tell individually.

*****

Anna-Marie sat back in the taxi. Her luggage at her feet. Tom had told her he wanted to show her London by night, her parents had hired him for the day, then he would deliver her to the hotel she had been booked into.

Anna-Marie had begun to feel drowsy as the afternoon light over the city began to fade and found it hard to keep her eyes open.

"Probably a bit of jetlag and all the excitement, luv," he had called from the driver's seat. "Close your eyes for a while. I'll take care of you."

Anna-Marie had slumped sideways in her seat unable to keep her eyes open. Tom drove on, glancing at her occasionally to make sure she was asleep.

He drove towards the Thames; it was quite dark now. He found the overgrown path down to his favourite spot under the now disused and abandoned bridge and turned off the ignition.

He grabbed a black garbage bag from under the seat and climbed into the back of the cab to watched Anna-Marie as she slept. He reached for her backpack and removed her travel documents, confirmation of her booking at a hotel on the Earls Court Road, her passport, which he slipped into his pocket, a small set of keys which he would need to open her suitcase, an envelope with her admission papers to the university, and her wallet. There was nothing else of interest, so he placed them in the black garbage bag.

He opened her suitcase and spent time going through the contents. He pocketed the envelope of family photographs, some in frames, some not. Her clothes and other personal effects were of no interest to him. He emptied the suitcase and added the contents to the rapidly filling black bag, walked to the seat next to his in the front of the taxi and placed the empty suitcase on the floor of the vehicle, along with the contents of the black bag, then he returned to the back seat where Anna-Marie was now stirring. He slid the black and silver ring off her finger and pocked that as well.

"Have a nice sleep, luv?"

Her eyes opened; she looked around in confusion. "Why is it so dark? Where am I?"

Tom flipped the soft passenger light on. "You're right here with me, Anna-Marie. Safe and sound, but I'm afraid not for long.

"Let me explain. I don't want anything bad to happen to you. I don't want anyone to hurt you, let you down, or treat you badly. There are a lot of cruel and bad people in this world. I should know, my mother was one of them. She dumped me when I was little more than a toddler. Abandoned me on a church doorstep in the Free State.

"She never came back, see. I don't want anything like that to happen to a lovely young girl like you. You do understand, don't you?"

Anna-Marie had panic written all over her face, she began to cry and begged him not to hurt her as she shrank back in the corner of the cab, kicking her helpless legs against him.

"I'm not going to hurt you, luv, you won't feel a thing. I can see you're very frightened and I don't want you to start screaming and getting hysterical.

"Now, I'm going to give you a little injection to calm you down, then I want you to take your clothes off. Here we go."

She struggled against him, with no energy left in her. "No, no, please don't hurt me." He plunged the needle into the smooth skin of her arm. "Now that didn't hurt did it. No point in screaming, my girl, no-one will hear you.

"Now take your clothes off."

Speechless with terror Anna-Marie did as she was told. He could tell she was already feeling the effects of the injection. Her movements were slowing as she fumbled with her clothes. Then she was naked before him. Naked and afraid. Without the will or the strength to fight.

Then she gave in and closed her eyes, the tears still running down her cheeks.

Tom sat for a while, admiring her smooth skin. Briefly he stroked her thick blonde hair. Reaching behind him he withdrew the kitchen scissors and a square of tin foil. Grabbing a handful of her hair he hacked it off, placed it tidily on the tin foil and rolled it up.

He checked his watch and turned off the passenger light. Time to say goodbye. He placed a light kiss on her lips, opened the passenger door and pulled Anna-Marie out of the cab.

It was pitch black now, the tide was right. He carried her down to the river and slid her still warm body into its icy depths. He caught a brief glimpse of her naked body before she was gone.

He lifted his arm in farewell then made his way back to his cab. Putting the clothes, she had worn into the black bag. He put four bricks on top, enough to give it some weight. He started up his vehicle and made his way to another remote spot a few miles further on. There he disposed of the black bag with its contents and watched it sink without a trace.

The suitcase he would get rid of on his way home. There were plenty of waste containers all over the city, he knew the one he would use, it was in a disused yard and would be deserted at this time of night. There would be no identification tags on that suitcase, no tag from the airline.

He drove back to his lock up, parked his cab, lowered the door so no one could see him and tidied up the back seat. Using a held hand vacuum cleaner, he captured the few strands of blonde hair that had fallen to the floor. He looked with disgust at the wet patch where Anna-Marie had been sitting. Tomorrow, he would take the cab to a valet service and that would remove anything he may have missed.

Father Mark said not a word.

"So, that's how I did it – clever hey. Same procedure for all four girls. They all tried to fight back but they were drugged, so not much of a problem.

"Suzanne put up a bit more resistance, she was stronger than the others, kicking and scratching at me, but she was no match for me. She had a tattoo on her thigh, ugly looking thing, looked like a map of South Africa, so she wasn't so perfect. Wouldn't have bothered with her in the first place if I'd known about that. Anyway, I didn't wait for the drugs to kick in, just chucked her in the river.

"Oh, by the way, it was you in your dress that gave me the perfect alibi. People are polite to priests, aren't they? I wore mine each time I visited the schools in Cape Town to choose my victims. Used your name.

"Anyway, I have my mementos of those four lovely girls, photographs, piece of jewellery, hanks of their hair and their passports. Every year in September, for four consecutive years, I visited Zelda Cameron, always at night, and I would take along the proof to show her what I had done. I drove there in my cab wearing a cassock with a big cross around my neck.

"No-one took a blind bit of notice of a priest arriving in a taxi to visit a resident where she lived. I always parked under a big tree, light off, no-one would have known I was the driver, would they?

"Zelda Cameron was terrified of me. It was good to see I must tell you. I threatened to kill her too if she repeated anything I told her. Threatened to tell the world she had stolen me as a child. She's the one who broke the law, not me. I didn't leave her any of my trophies, couldn't leave her with any evidence, but I always took her a bunch of white lilies, you know those funeral flowers?

"She could never be sure what night I would arrive in September, but a taxi engine has quite a distinctive purr, she heard that and knew I was coming for her."

Father Mark heard him yawn. "Anyway, just wanted to bring you up to speed as with what I have been up to over the years. I only killed four girls, I'm not sure they were dead when I tossed them in the river, but they would have drowned anyway. I continued with my job as a cabbie, of course. Now I'm planning to retire to somewhere nice and warm.

"I have a little unfinished business to attend to. I saw the article in the newspaper from the mother of Anna-Marie, think I might call on her. Can't take my briefcase with me because that would be too dangerous now, wouldn't it?

"So, I'm going to leave it with you, and you won't be able to do anything but hide it. Just as you won't be able to say a word about the conversation we've just had.

He laughed. "You turned out to be a useful brother in the end, didn't you Mark? Gave me someone I could unburden myself to. Will you and your God forgive me now? A couple of Hail Marys and my soul will be saved?"

Father Mark didn't know what to say.

"No? Oh well, never mind. I still hate you, anyway."

Father Mark heard his brother leave the confessional. He put his head in his hands and leaned forward, the tears trickling through his fingers as he tried to absorb the appalling confession Tom had given.

He had found himself unable to follow his teachings and forgive the man the other side of the confessional. That was a sin too.

Having composed himself he rose from his knees and found the briefcase Tom had left for him.

It was not unusual for people to leave something behind after confession. The normal procedure was to try to identify the owner and return whatever they had left. But in this case, he knew he would have to hide the briefcase somewhere in the church or in his own spartan quarters. But not before he looked inside.

He now knew why Zelda had not wanted him to visit her. She was frightened for his safety and for her own.

Tom had dressed as a priest, used his name, to stab at the heart of her, and threaten Mark. It made him wonder what Tom's ultimate plan might be.

Chapter Sixty-Two

The gardens of the Inn grew dark and quiet as Jack and Piet listened to the story told by Father Mark.
Clearly the man was upset and now he had broken his vows by revealing Tom's confession. The only life he had ever loved was over.
Piet leaned forward his face showing his anger now he knew what had happened to the girls, and why Zelda had left such a difficult trail for them to follow. He was going to hunt down Tom Cameron, whatever it took, and however long it took.

Jack looked at the soon to be defrocked priest, with compassion. "Father Mark, I know there are some life-changing implications from what you have told us here today, but you were still wearing a cassock earlier. Has the Church already been informed of what you have done?"
Father Mark's face crumbled as he held back his tears. "Yes. The wheels are already in motion to remove me from the Catholic Church."
A waiter appeared silently through the shadows of the trees asking if they would like to order anything.
Jack looked at the distraught priest. "As you can imagine, there are many questions Piet and I still have. We should order something to eat and drink? Have it out here in the garden, away from the others inside?"
The waiter returned with the menus and waited for them to choose what they would like.
Father Mark looked at the menu with disinterest. "I should like the fish. It is Friday and that's what we eat on a Friday. Perhaps I may have a double whisky to go with it?"
Jack and Piet ordered the Inn's famous steak and mushroom pie with a side order of salad and chips, two beers and a double whisky, the priest declined the chips but also ordered a salad.

The three men sat in silence as the waiter busied himself with laying the table and placing a lamp in the middle along with a bowl of sweet-smelling frangipani. The food and drinks arrived, and they ate in silence. All three consumed with their thoughts. Father Mark pushed his half-eaten meal aside and stared out into the night.

After the waiter had removed their plates and cleared the table Jack was the first to speak.

"Did you ever hear from Tom Cameron again?"

Father Mark shook his head. "No. The years went by and I, like Zelda, thought he had left the country, he had hinted as much to me when he was telling me what happened to the girls.

"Zelda came to London to see me. She was very distressed. I told her Tom had been to see me, she guessed he had told me everything, but knew I was unable to do anything about it.

"I told her about the briefcase he had left in my keeping and that I had seen what it contained. She was horrified.

"Of course, Tom had shown her his trophies after he had killed the girls, arriving by taxi, and wearing priest's robes, mimicking me. They are not difficult to get hold of. Theatrical companies and such like need costumes and there are suppliers who specialise in this type of thing."

He had told Zelda that he didn't want the briefcase in his church, tainted with such evil which he felt defiled the house of God.

Zelda said she would take it. It would be safe. As far as she was concerned Tom had left the country and would not be a threat to either of them anymore.

But her main concern was that Mark would become embroiled in it all. She knew that someone would have noticed a priest visiting her in September for four consecutive years.

Reluctantly Mark had retrieved the briefcase and placed it in her care advising her to place it in a safe deposit box somewhere.

Father Mark bowed his head. "My mother, Zelda, had not looked well on that visit to London. She had aged considerably and seemed frail; her mind fragmented, she blamed herself for everything, but it was the four girls being killed that broke her. We both agreed it would be wiser and safer for us not to meet again. We didn't have any idea where Tom was or what he might do next.

"Zelda blamed herself for everything that had happened. She had brought the paintbrush boy to London to give him a new life within a loving family, not realising the evil he would unleash so many years later. The shattering grief he would inflict on the families of the girls he killed."

Father Mark had called her over those last years. Two days before she died, she told him the briefcase had been sent to her lawyer in London and as per her instructions, had been placed in a safe deposit box.

She also told him Tom was back, from wherever he had been and wanted to see her. She was frightened. She knew, without doubt, he wanted the briefcase. She warned Mark to leave the country, to go somewhere where no-one would find him.

Father Mark looked up at the stars as though seeking some assurance there; some proof that things would go on despite the evil which had touched so many lives.

"I left the country some days later and entered a retreat in Italy, in Tuscany. I was troubled and needed time to think. But I also knew I could not go on carrying this terrible burden of proof.

"When I returned, I learned my mother had died. Her ashes had been delivered to my church. She had wanted to be with me and have her ashes scattered in the Garden of Remembrance."

Piet and Jack remained silent as he continued. "It was then I made the hardest decision of my life – and why I'm sitting here in front of you tonight. I've now lost everything. But Tom is out there somewhere. You need to find him because I don't think he's satisfied with what he has done. I think he wants to see the results of what he did.

"He wants to see how much damage he caused – he wants to imagine how his birth mother would feel and look, after what she had done to him by leaving him on the steps of the orphanage.

"He wants to see the faces of the mothers, the parents, of the daughters he had killed. That's something he can do now, after your article."

Piet looked up quickly. "You think he's in Cape Town? Is that what you're saying?"

Father Mark nodded. "Yes. I think he's in Cape Town."

*****

Piet scrambled to his feet and moved away to another table, his phone pressed to his ear, his fingers drumming on the side of the chair.

"Hey, Bertie. Need you or one of your robot buddies to find something for me. I need that info now. It's urgent, you hear me?"

Bertie sounded sleepy. "*Jeez,* Piet, it's one in the morning. Just got into bed, can't it wait?"

"No," he growled into the phone. "It can't. I need you to check on some arrival and departure dates over twenty years ago for a Tom Cameron. Also, if he returned to South Africa any time since 2000 – can do?

"He's our killer, Bertie. He took those girls, and he killed them. I'm going after him. We think he's in Cape Town and I want him."

He heard Bertie tapping away on his computer but didn't hang up. He wanted that information, and he wanted it now.

"Okay Piet. I've found him, although I think you have the wrong man. A Thomas Cameron flew into Cape Town four times every year from 1996, always during the month of November, he stayed three days each time before leaving the country. There is no record of him coming back here until two months ago. He entered the country each time on a British passport.

"But you're wrong about this *oke,* Piet. His profession is listed as a Catholic priest. He couldn't be the Tom Cameron you're looking for, impossible."

Piet snorted. "Oh yes he is, my friend, he's exactly who I'm looking for and I'm going to find him, you hear me!"

*****

Whilst Piet was on his phone, Jack flicked through his notebook before looking at Father Mark again.

He took a deep breath. "A priest visited Zelda on the night she died. A source disclosed to me she had been burning personal papers and documents. Also, he said the cottage was in disarray. Drawers, cupboards etc. had been ransacked. The priest, my source assumed, had gone through the place looking for something.

"It must have been Tom then, dressed like you. He was looking for the briefcase. My theory is Zelda knew he was coming to retrieve his evidence and intended to kill her.

"I'm sorry to tell you she took her own life. By the time Tom arrived at the cottage, Zelda was dead. It will be a difficult thing to accept, Father Mark, but I also think she wanted to protect you, and this became her only course of action. A mother's love is a powerful thing and although her own life had been fraught with tragedy, it was you she thought about in the end – not herself."

Piet joined them again. "You're right Father Mark, Tom Cameron is here in the country." He glanced at his watch and looked around the grounds. Only a few of the hotel rooms had lights on. The bar and restaurant were now closed. He briefly glanced around the dark grounds catching a glimpse of Shaka in the shadows keeping a close eye on the three men seated at the table.

Father Mark stood up wearily. "I will wish you goodnight, gentleman. I have much to think about and I must pray for my mother's soul." He gave a sad smile. "Perhaps God will still listen to me."

He walked slowly back to his room. Shaka loomed up out of the bushes.

"All is well, *sah*?" he said to Piet.

"Yes, all is well but I want you to stay close to the priest's room. He has many troubles."

Shaka grinned at him, his white teeth gleaming. "Is it perhaps so, *sah*, it is because he is no longer wearing his dress and the heavy necklace of this Jesus person, who does not wish to be seen by anyone?"

"Something like that, Shaka, something like that. Just keep an eye on him – okay?"

The next morning Father Mark had gone.

Chapter Sixty-Three

The next morning Jack was up before the sun. He made his way to his office and, as he sipped his coffee, he updated his board of notes and photographs.

It was all coming together at last. He looked at the four hanks of hair lying next to each girl's photograph and a piece of their jewellery.

He checked the time. Harry would be at the office now, he always arrived early.

"Jack, my dear chap, how are you? And no, I don't want to hear what a glorious day it is in Hazyview. Birds singing, lions roaring and all that other good stuff. I want to know where you are with my story?"

"We've made a lot of progress, Harry. Just a few more things to tie up and you shall have your story."

He brought Harry up to date and told him about the visit of Father Mark and what they had learned.

"Splendid, Jack. First class news. Terrible story. The priest has made the ultimate sacrifice. He's a brave man and I take my hat off to him. Poor fellow, I wonder what he will do now he has been cast out into the wilderness? Sad and tragic this tale may be, but it will make a cracking good story for our readers. So, get on with it, old chap, will you. Must dash, meeting in ten minutes. Cheerio."

Jack made himself some more coffee and a piece of toast then sat down and began to write up the story of the four girls. He decided he wouldn't use the real names for the Cameron family or list St. Theresa's church.

Neither deserved the morbid curiosity of the public who liked to see 'where it all happened.' He himself had little time for the strict and rigid rules the Vatican placed on their priests which forbade them to reveal what they knew.

But he had the greatest respect for Father Mark who had been brave enough to come forward with the truth. He wondered what would happen to him now and where he had gone.

Chapter Sixty-Four

Anna-Marie's mother made herself a sandwich for dinner. She sat out on her little patio and watched the seagulls wheeling and crying as they made their way home. People were jogging and running along the seafront, dogs running along on leads. Boys played with rugby balls kicking them back and forth on the grass. Couples, hand in hand, strolled along, mothers with babies in strollers, old people, arm in arm, taking their usual evening stroll.

It was a beautiful still evening, the sea was calm, the sky reflecting shades of gold, yellow and red as the sun made its sizzling way into the sea. The lighthouse in Mouille Point, which she could see to her right, turning slowly as it guided ships in and out towards the docks as it had for generations.

She took her plate into the kitchen and washed it down; it joined her solitary mug on the draining board.

Lights began to glint from the hundreds of apartments facing the ocean, the main road beneath her filling with commuters on their way home or heading for one of the many restaurants and bars that filled the city of Cape Town.

She was surprised when the buzzer alerted her to a visitor. She pressed the answer phone. "Yes?"

"Is this Mrs Cloete? Anna-Marie's mother?"

"Yes, it is. Who is this?"

"My name is Father Mark. May I see you if it's convenient?"

She felt her heart squeeze. A priest had come to call – it could only be the news she had been dreading.

"Yes, of course."

The priest was waiting for her when she opened the door to the flat. "Do come in, Father Mark." She held the door open for him indicating he should enter. "You have news of my daughter?"

He smiled at her. "Indeed, I do. I have good news."

Anna-Marie's mother clutched her throat. "Have you found her then? Is she alive?" Her heart pumped with hope.

"Do take a seat Father."

Tom looked at her face, ravaged with grief and smiled. This was exactly what he wanted to see. How he wanted his own mother to look like now.

"Perhaps you might like some tea or coffee, Father?"

He shook his head. "No thanks. Pretty little thing, Anna-Marie, wasn't she? Lovely hair. You look quite a lot like her, but much older, of course, at least she'll never get old."

Mrs Cloete frowned; something wasn't quite right here.

"You know what happened to her then? Did Jack Taylor send you? I know he's been following the story. Have you met him?"

Tom looked at her innocently. "Never heard of him. But I do know about the other three girls. Look, I find in situations like this, as a man of the cloth, it's sometimes better to lie down, somewhere familiar, like Anna-Marie's bedroom, it will give you comfort when I tell you what happened to your beloved daughter."

Anna-Marie's mother was no fool. This was no priest.

Suspicion prickled her skin, no, this man in front of her was not a priest. She closed her eyes briefly. If he knew what had happened to her darling Anna-Marie, she had to know. Whatever the cost.

She led him to her daughter's bedroom and quietly lay down on Anna-Marie's bed.

He smiled at her. "Yes, your daughter is dead, but I did give her a nice tour of London before I killed her. Would you like to hear about her last few hours before I dumped her in the Thames?

"She had a lovely last day, a tour of London, lunch at a pub, then more things to see before I took her down to the river. She cried a lot, but soon calmed down after I sorted her out. I told her a little about my life as an orphan here in the Free State, what my mother had done to me. How she had never loved me. You were close, you two, she did tell me that. In fact, she said 'Mommy' a couple of times before I killed her. Should be a comfort to you. Lovely girl. Nice to be loved like that."

Anna-Marie's mother closed her eyes, feeling a burning anger surging through her body. An avalanche of fury she had not felt in all the years she had waited and prayed for her daughter to come home. She lunged at him, her hands clawing at his smiling face.

He pushed her roughly back on the bed. "Bit of a fighter, hey, just like your daughter."

Panting she lay there looking at him, the tears of rage running down her cheeks and into her hair. "Whoever you are, you are a disgusting human being. You are not worthy of love; do you know that? If I had been your mother, I would never have left you on the doorsteps of some orphanage. No, I would have taken one look at you and drowned you at birth. You will never be loved by anyone – ever.

"You are vile, despite your priestly clothes. You are totally unlovable, evil, and ugly. Your mother saw that – and that's why she dumped, you, got rid of you. She saw something in you and didn't want to be part of it. She probably hated you as much as I do. Maybe she had another child and gave him all the love and care in the world – loved him very much, as I loved my daughter."

She laughed hysterically. "Good for her. Do what you want, and I hope you rot in hell. I will be with my child soon. That was your plan, wasn't it?

"There is no one waiting for you, *Mark*. There never was and never will be. But there is someone waiting for me, and I want to be with her more than anything else in the world."

She felt the savage sting in her arm and then only blackness.

Chapter Sixty-Five

Jack saw the cloud of dust lit from within by the bright sunshine making its way up his drive. Piet lifted his arm in greeting, his dog with her ever-smiling face raced towards him as though she hadn't seen him for months.

"Morning Piet. Hello Hope. Got your message from Blessing at reception. So, Father Mark checked out at the crack of dawn. He told me housekeeping had found his cassock laid carefully out on the well-made bed?"

"*Ja.* Blessing had called a taxi for him and off he went. At least he paid his bill before he departed. Listen here Jack, I know you think I was tough on him, and I was. I wasn't pleased to see him there at the hotel sitting with you in the garden. But I have thought about things."

"Without him we would still be chasing our tails. He was brave and broke all the rules of the church, but having given it much thought, the hardest thing was he betrayed himself and everything he believed in. That takes courage."

He sat down and Jack poured him a coffee as he continued. "The bottom line is he gave us all the information we had been searching for, at a huge cost to himself. Without his courage to confess to us, we would still be going around in circles. He didn't need me to be so hard on him and I'm sorry."

Jack stroked Hope's head as she waited hopefully for her usual large stick of biltong. He gave it to her as they made their way to Jack's office and his board of notes and photographs.

"I've updated everything, mate. Now all we must do is find Tom Cameron and nail him." He swept his arm across the board. "We have every piece of evidence we need to have him arrested and sentenced to a long time in prison and, as a white man, that's not a good place to be in Africa."

Piet ran a practiced eye over the board, which he had done hundreds of times in his career when looking for motives and witnesses in the many cases he had handled during his work as a police detective.

He ran his hand through his short hair and down the side of his face. "With all the evidence we have now, what will you do? Will you let the families know what happened to their daughters? Before it would be my job, but I don't have that responsibility anymore, thank God."

Jack leaned back against the wall; his ankles crossed as he thought about this.

"It's too soon, I think. We need to find this Tom Cameron and get him arrested before we release any information to the families and relatives. There will be legal procedures, as you know. He will be extradited to the UK where the crimes were committed. Before that happens, he will be imprisoned here.

Piet nodded. "But what about Anna-Marie's mother? You know her better than any of the other relatives. You have a way with words. Perhaps you should tell her regardless?"

Jack stared at him then hit his forehead with the heel of his hand. "Dear God! Tom Cameron is in Cape Town! Father Mark implied he might be here in the country to see the results of what he had done."

Jack stabbed at the numbers on his phone, his heart beating rapidly as he waited for the call to be picked up.

There was no reply from Mrs Cloete.

He looked at Piet in despair. "Mrs Cloete rarely goes out. She should be at home; she always has been when I've called before."

Piet knew where this was going. "Look, calm down, my friend. Let me make a few calls. I'll get someone to go around and check she's alright. Give me her address again."

Chapter Sixty-Six

Inspector Kleinman, from Special Branch in Cape Town, took Piet's call. They had known each other for many years. Whilst Piet had lost his place in the swiftly changing police force in the Eastern Cape, the young man he had trained there, Elias Kleinman, had risen rapidly through the ranks and was now based in Cape Town.

Elias arrived at the block of flats in Sea Point and buzzed through to number 402 owned by Mrs Cloete.

Piet had briefed him succinctly on the case they were following and asked him to check on one of the victim's mothers.

Elias Kleinman waited and rang again. Another resident came through the door and seeing the men at the door asked if he could help with anything.

They showed him their badges and said they were checking on one of the residents. A relative had called from overseas and was anxious when they couldn't get a response to his call. Was there a caretaker who could help them?

The young man was clearly in a hurry. He scrolled through the numbers on his phone. "Yes. Here he is, his name is Wiseman, he should be able to help."

Elias phoned the caretaker. "Police here. Just need to check on one of your residents. A Mrs Cloete."

Wiseman took them to her flat and rapped on the door. There was no reply. "When did you last see Mrs Cloete, Wiseman?"

He frowned. "Not for a week or two, sir. She rarely goes out."

"Any recent visitors Wiseman?"

"No, sir, not that I recall. Perhaps she's unwell? Let me open the door for you, I have emergency keys to all the flats."

Mrs Cloete was not unwell. She was dead.

Inspector Kleinman and his sergeant slipped on their latex gloves. They found her in what looked like a child's bedroom. The heat of the flat and the buzzing of the blue flies, leant an unpleasant air to the place.

Mrs Cloete looked strangely peaceful. She lay there with her arms across her chest.

She was covered with a cassock; a heavy cross was bound tightly around her neck. Between her hands was a framed photograph of a young girl.

Inspector Kleinman sucked in his breath. "Seal the place off, sergeant. Get forensics in. Post someone at the entrance of the building. I want to know everyone who comes and goes here. Get some officers to interview every resident in this building, also the staff who work here. I want names and addresses of every one of them."

He looked at Anna-Marie's mother. "You can't just walk through the front door of this building, as we saw, you have a key if you're a resident, or you are buzzed in by whoever you have come to see. Mrs Cloete let the person who murdered her in. She must have known him or was expecting him."

*****

Inspector Kleinman having his team in place at the crime scene called Piet.

"Not good news, Piet. Mrs Cloete is dead. Murdered. I have a full team in place."

Piet slammed the phone down. This had Tom Cameron written all over it. Not only had he killed four girls, but he had a few more deaths to add to his list. Zelda Cameron, the parents of Elizabeth Balfour, who both committed suicide after they failed to find her, and now Anna-Marie's mother. And, in many ways the ending of another life, that of Father Mark.

He called Jack that evening and conveyed the news. "Listen here, Jack. I'm going to Cape Town tomorrow. I'm going to find Tom Cameron. This I can tell you now. I have contacted people who know where to look, know where to find. You carry on with the writing of this story and I will give you the ending. Don't call me, you hear. I won't need your help."

Jack stared at his dead phone. He had never heard Piet sound this way before. It wasn't just fury he had heard in his voice. It was something worse and it had all started with the opening of the briefcase and what he had found inside.

It was personal.

He wandered down to his stream and watched the slowly moving water. He thought about Anna-Marie's mother. Her utter faith in him to find the truth of what happened to her daughter. He had let her down.

The dik-dik appeared through the shadows of the evening. He had never been this close to where she appeared every evening when she came to drink from the stream.

She lifted her head, quite unafraid at seeing him there, and looked at him.

Their eyes met and for a moment he thought he was looking at something else, someone else in those brown eyes. Was it possible?

She dipped her head and drank from the clear water. Then with a flick of her short brown tail she turned to leave then stopped and looked back at him. Then disappeared into the bush.

He didn't know it then, but it was the last time he ever saw the exquisite dainty buck with her soft brown eyes.

*****

The memory of the last sighting of her stayed with him for years. He had seen something he didn't quite understand. But the dainty dik-dik had connected with him somehow or connected with something much bigger than him.

Once, on safari, a Shangaan tracker had told him that, in their language, the word 'goodbye' didn't exist. It was, he said, too final. "See, Mr Yak. This is a word we do not know. We say 'Ita vonana siku nrwana.' It means "until we meet again." Jack had liked that.

He hoped Father Mark had finally found somewhere where he could be at peace with himself. Impossible though it might seem.

Chapter Sixty-seven

Piet met with Inspector Elias Kleinman at a coffee bar on Long Street in Cape Town.
Piet had not been to the city for years and was surprised at the hundreds of bars, restaurants, back packer hostels, small guest houses and takeout food places. Mingled in between were night clubs, sex shops and no doubt drug dealers and prostitutes too.

During the day the tourists filled the famous street, but at night the locals came out to play, it was not considered a safe place to wander around on your own as a tourist.

The Inspector had swiftly followed up on any leads to the killer of Mrs Cloete, but his department was swamped. Some areas like the Cape Flats were controlled by gangs of criminals and an almost no-go area, as was Manenberg. Murders were committed there every day. His case load was overwhelming.

Crime was out of control in many areas of the city. Places where even the police were careful to avoid.

The Inspector blew on his coffee and took a cautious sip. "Not much to go on I'm afraid Piet. This Thomas Cameron is in the country legally now, his visa runs out in a couple of weeks, but nothing to stop him for applying for an extension, or he could nip across the border, re-enter, and get another three-month visa. He has no car registered to him and we have no address for him.

"My thinking is he stays somewhere in the city and uses a taxi. He won't be in the suburbs; there you need wheels to get around. I think he's planning not to extend his visa. He's going to get as far away from here as possible. He'll know we're looking for him. There was a small article on the murder of Mrs Cloete in the Cape Times. He knows her body has been found.

"He won't hang around for long. We have alerted the airports here, but, as I say, he could nip across the border by car to Swaziland, Botswana or Zimbabwe and simply disappear."

He patted his pocket and drew out a document. "This is a copy of his passport, it's all we have to go on at the moment."

Piet took his first look at Thomas Cameron. Middle aged, hair slightly thinning, small dark eyes and a thin mouth. He felt the fury and the anger boiling once more in his body as he thought of what this man had done to the girls and their families.

The Inspector continued. "We have circulated his photo around, as discreetly as possible, but, as I said we are stretched to capacity with not enough manpower to move as quickly as we would like."

Piet stared at the photograph again. "I'd like to get involved with this Elias. I *need* to get involved. I can help you, and I need your help."

The Inspector looked at him shrewdly. "You were a damn good cop, Piet and we could do with some help, especially as you have told me, all the victims, those young girls were South Africans. However, it will go against all the rules, as you know. You're not a cop anymore."

Elias took another sip of his coffee. "But nothing wrong with someone searching for his buddy is there?" he said innocently. "With a photograph of him?"

Piet grinned at him. "Thanks, my friend. This has been my case from the word go. I have all the proof you need to convict him when he's found. But it might take years before he goes to trial, as you said, you have bodies piled up in the morgue and mountains of other cases. It will be my pleasure to help you out here."

He paused. "As we both know, Tom Cameron can only be tried and convicted of the murder of Mrs Cloete. The four girls were killed in another country, so it will fall under a different jurisdiction. But we'll worry about that later, shall we? Might not even come to that…"

They both stood.

"Ah, one other thing, Elias. I have contacts as you know, but always useful to have another number or two. You know other folk who, shall we say, move in different circles to us. You know what I'm saying?

"Your three daughters must be all grown up by now," he paused. "These four girls never had that opportunity. They were snatched and killed. Imagine what the parents went through when they couldn't find their daughters, and now Cameron has killed the mother of one of them and doesn't give a *fok* what anyone feels if he thinks he's got away with it. Can't have that now, can we Inspector?

"I've known you since you were a young cadet. You and I have both seen too much of what one human being can do to another, know what I'm saying? This scumbag could kill again. He could leave the country and disappear, like the girls did. Get away with it again."

Piet held out his hand. "I need a phone number. I don't care about a name."

The Inspector hesitated. "I can't do that, Piet. I'm a cop, and proud to be one. There may be corrupt officers in the force, but I'm not one of them."

Piet chose his words carefully. "You have a murder case on your hands, a brutal one. I've told you I have indisputable evidence about the killer's other victims. Do this for me, Elias, and I will give you all that evidence.

"It will be one of the most sensational cases this country has ever seen, and you will have solved it. Your career will know no bounds. But more than that you will be able to give the family and relatives of all the girls, the desperate answers they have been seeking for over twenty years.

"It will be the right thing to do, Elias. Think of your girls. Think of the ones he killed."

He paused for a moment. "I need someone who knows where to look in the city, someone with a good network. Not a private detective, no, someone who moves in a much darker world than that. I don't need a name.

"Now, will you give me a number?"

Chapter Sixty-Eight

Piet spent the next day's trawling through one bar after another. He was dressed in jeans and a t-shirt. Emblazoned on the front with the slogan 'I love London' with a big red heart. Jack would love that he had thought sourly.

He still wore his battered cap and a pair of non-prescription glasses hoping he looked less like an ex-cop. But he couldn't change the look on his face, although he tried to look friendly as he went from bar to bar, showing the photograph of Tom Cameron. From the upmarket ones at the Waterfront to the less salubrious ones in the city centre.

He had his story ready. Looking for his brother who seemed to have disappeared somewhere in Cape Town, whilst on holiday. He went up and down the streets of Green Point, Sea Point, De Waterkant, gradually closing the circle of possibilities to Long Street.

He spent every night, late nights, showing the photo of his lost brother to busy bar tenders, waiters, street walkers and night clubs. He was not going to give up.

The phone call Piet had been waiting for came four days later, from an unknown number. He had sent the passport photo of Tom Cameron, on his phone, to the contact Inspector Elias Kleinman had reluctantly given him.

The caller had agreed a price for the initial job Piet needed to be done, which was to find Tom Cameron wherever he was in the city, where he stayed and the places he went to hang out in the evenings.

"This person you are seeking," the gruff African voice whispered now.

"We know where he is, where he stay, where he drinks. You want we kill him? It'll cost extra."

Piet replied immediately. "No. You tell me where I can find him. But I will need other help. I need transport for a long drive when I take

307

him. No violence is required. You, or someone, will drive us north out of the city, to a remote place. Then your services will no longer be required."

*****

Piet was staggered at what the underworld was charging these days for a job to be done. But he had to agree to the terms and conditions, being so close as he was to catching the killer.

Piet would not disclose the intended destination, but it included a drive of around six hours to and six hours back, including petrol. Another hefty expense.

The gruff whispering African voice continued. "The man I send to you has no name and will not be talking to you, you understand? I give you a number to call when you are ready. You tell him what you want, where you will be and what time you want him.

"He will wait inside the vehicle with the parking lights on. He will follow your directions to this place you want to go to. But no conversation you understand, white boy?"

Piet took a deep breath still wondering how he was going to get this expense paid by Harry. "Understood. Now, you listen to me," he hissed down the phone. "I will be armed. I want your driver to be armed as well. I need him as a bodyguard. Is that quite clear to you?"

The man agreed and upped his price.

"Now give me his *fokkin'* number and tell me where you want the money paid."

Harry would pass out when he got the bill which Piet would include in his expenses to the newspaper, under the nebulous clause of 'miscellaneous expenses' with no receipts to back it up.

*****

It had been agreed the money would be delivered to a fast-food outlet in Observatory, a vibrant area of Cape Town which attracted artists, musicians, startup tech companies, music studios and tattoo artists. Once a poor part of the city, it was now considered trendy to live there with its bars, restaurants, and small shops. It attracted young people, who couldn't afford to live in the city itself.

At an agreed time later that night, Piet would deliver the money to the owner of a small, modest Italian restaurant. Once the money had been counted, he would be given an envelope containing all the information he needed to corner Tom Cameron.

Chapter Sixty-Nine

Tom Cameron, Piet read from the information in the envelope, had a cheap room at the bottom end of Long Street. He went to the same bar most nights of the week and stayed there until the early hours of the morning.

*****

Piet watched Thomas Cameron enter the gloomy depths of a seedy night club at the wrong end of Long Street. Tom made his way to the bar and ordered a drink. Piet looked to the bartender who nodded at him before pouring Tom's drink, then busied himself with polishing the glasses behind the bar.

Piet tried to supress the boiling anger he felt, which overrode his satisfaction at having finally run his quarry to ground. He put his anger to one side. Then the coldness set in.

The bar was poorly lit, with music made to throb but made faint by the speakers being somewhere distant.

Piet sipped his mineral water and watched Tom Cameron take a drink from his glass before he swivelled around on his bar stool and looked at the other three people in the bar. His eyes finding Piet who was looking his way.

Piet lifted his glass in a friendly gesture and smiled at him. He watched Tom as he slid off his stool and made his way towards him. The bile rising in his throat.

"Mind if I join you? I noticed your 'I love London' t-shirt. Are you from London?"

Piet shook his head. "No, but I've been there recently."

His mouth went dry as he held out his hand to envelope one of the hands which had caused so much devastation in their time. He had spent some years with Jack and his British accent, and knew how to tone down his own, without using the usual South African colloquialisms.

Piet took a sip of his drink. "Where are you from, you sound English with a bit of a South African accent perhaps?"

Tom swayed, seemed to have trouble focusing. "Yup, born here. But I've lived in London most of my life. Just in Cape Town tying up a bit of unfinished business."

Piet tried to look interested. "Oh, what sort of business?"

Tom looked at him, his eyes narrowed suspiciously. "Nothing much. Bit bored now, to be honest. Not that it's any of your business. You?"

Piet patted his pocket. "Actually, I'm looking for someone." He took a fold of paper from his pocket. "Maybe you can help me?"

He unfolded the paper and flattened it out before turning it for Tom to see.

Tom looked down. His eyes went wide, his jaw went slack.

Piet stared at him. Then nodded at the bartender who disappeared immediately to make the phone call he had been paid a considerable amount to make, along with slipping a pill into Tom's drink.

Piet sat back in his chair watching Tom's shocked face as he stared at his passport photograph, then he leaned forward, unable to keep his anger under control any longer.

"I've been looking for you Tinus Barnard, or Tom Cameron, or whatever the *fok* you call yourself now. Looking for a long time. I happen to have the briefcase from Zelda with all your trophies in it. You're busted, you bastard. There is no hiding place now. No place to run and hide. Nowhere."

Tom reared back in his chair, eyeing the door.

"Now you listen to me Tom Cameron," he hissed. "I'm not going to arrest you or call the police. What I'm going to do, as you did, is let you experience what those four girls went through when you took their lives. You hear me?"

Piet glared at him. "Don't even think about making a run for it. I have everything covered. We have someone waiting for us outside and he looks like a cruel bugger to me, but then he is a killer. Just like you."

Piet watched the blood drain from Tom's face as he tried to get his head around what was happening. Tom attempted to get up and Piet pushed him back into the chair.

Piet smiled tightly at him. "Take a look around at the last bar you're ever going to see. The bartender slipped a little something in your drink. Nothing to knock you out, because that would have been too easy, no, you see I want something different. You're going to take a ride in a taxi. Nothing as smart as the one you drove in London, I have to tell you, but a taxi nevertheless.

"I want you to be aware of what is going to happen to you. I want you to feel everything those four girls felt, in their drugged state, and didn't understand, or feel much, of what was happening, or going to happen. Except their terror as they looked into your eyes before you killed them."

The bartender was back. He gave Piet the thumbs up.

Piet continued. "I'm not going to tell you what will happen next. But I think you can work it out. It was your *modus operandi* was it not? Only what I have planned for you is something a bit different – a little more African if you like."

Piet stood up. "Shall we go? Our taxi is waiting outside – with the meter running…We have a long journey ahead, but unlike the girls' you won't be having a tour of historic sights, bit more of a bush experience really. A real taste of Africa, a safari. People dream of going on safari, not sure if you will enjoy it much."

Chapter Seventy

They were far away from Cape Town, having driven through the night. The taxi bumped through the thick bush then stopped at the edge of the river.

For the duration of the journey, like his victims, Tom Cameron had no idea where he was. Groggily he looked around. All he saw was a wide river lazily making its placid way through the surrounding bush. Fear snaked through his body. The river.

Piet pulled Tom from the vehicle. "Now, I'm going to make a fire and brew some coffee. I want you to remember this day. It will be a memorable one. Well, for me anyway. I see the drugs we gave you are wearing off. That's good because I want you to be clear headed now."

*****

Tom Cameron looked around in terror, his bowels beginning to liquify. He had been drugged, like the girls, and now here was the river.

Piet looked at him dispassionately. "The fear you will feel will be far greater than any of your victims. Don't try to run. There is no place to run. My driver is armed as am I. He doesn't care who he shoots or why. Mean looking bugger isn't he, not much of a conversationalist. Maybe someone ripped out his tongue for some reason.

"Now, Tom Cameron, I want you to go and sit on that rock there and think about what you have done."

Swallowing nervously, Tom moved over and put his back to the river to sit on the rock Piet had indicated.

"You are going to tell me what you did. Confess all. You know all about that don't you? Your adopted brother being a priest when you told him about the girls you killed? He told me all about it. How you snatched them from the airport, showed them the sights of London, then drugged them before you threw them in the river."

Piet poked at the fire as the coffee warmed. "Yes, he told me all about it. He had to tell someone, unburden his soul. You destroyed him, but I doubt you care much about that."

Piet poured two tin mugs of coffee and gave one to Tom. He looked up at the sky then down at the river. "Another beautiful day in Africa, hey? The river reminds me of the Thames in a way. I was over there not so long ago looking for the killer of the girls – looking for you.

"The Thames is impressive, not so? Looks placid, a bit like this one, but underneath that calmness it can be very dangerous, with the tides going in and out. Our rivers are not tidal as you may remember from when you were a young innocent boy with the whole of your life in front of you, unfortunately there's not much left of it now."

Tom looked around in terror. "Listen, mate, I've got plenty of money," he stuttered. "Maybe we could make some kind of deal?"

Piet ignored him and took another sip of his coffee as he looked out contentedly over the bush. Across the river he could see a small group of impala bending their necks to drink, keeping a wary eye out for any predators. Their rhythmic lapping sending ripples across the smooth surface of the water.

Suddenly they scattered from the water's edge in panic.

Piet finished his coffee. Tom had not touched his and he didn't see the silent rippling of the water behind him.

*****

It slid out from under a ledge in the river and with lighting speed the massive Nile crocodile erupted from the water, its powerful jaws snapped shut around Tom Cameron's torso.

His scream echoed across the bush as its serrated teeth tore into his flesh, the crocodile's jaws clamped like a vice, preventing any escape. Tom fought back in a desperate futile struggle, his face a mask of pure terror, shock, and pain.

As Tom was pulled back under the water, disorientation and panic overwhelmed him, then the crocodile began its death roll, spinning its hideous body with a brief flash of the whiteness of its underbelly in a macabre final dance of death. The water turned turbulent, churning with violence and blood; a blur of motion before the crocodile sank beneath the surface, slithering into its depths, taking Tom Cameron with him.

Then, only silence. The river calm and serene once again, as it made its silent steady journey through the tangled bush.

Piet stood up and threw the dregs of his coffee into the bush. He retrieved Tom's mug from where it had fallen by the rock.

He looked at the taxi driver. His face was impassive – he had clearly seen worse.

"*Ag*, guess he didn't like the coffee."

*****

Piet checked into a guest house in the small town where he had asked to be dropped. Tomorrow he would call the Inspector and let him know Tom Cameron had indeed left the country. He would courier the briefcase and the evidence it contained to the Inspector, as promised.

As he sat out on the veranda of the guest house he looked up at the stars. He felt no guilt for what he had allowed to happen. Nature had taken care of everything.

He thought of the crocodile making its way back to its den where Tom Cameron would lay amidst all the other rotting flesh. Sometimes an air pocket in a crocodile's den allows the victim a few more minutes more of life. The pain of the attack would be excruciating. Death as inevitable, but those minutes would sear even a rotten soul.

Piet hoped Tom would see its yellow eyes and hideous head moving silently back towards him. He hoped Tom Cameron would realise that there was truly a price to be paid for evil.

Chapter Seventy-One

Jack met Piet at the airport, in Hazyview. His smile widened when he saw the t-shirt he was wearing.

"Ah, jolly good to see you promoting the delights of London, Piet. Never thought I'd see the day."

Piet gave him a withering look. "I'll burn it at the first opportunity. You can trust me on that."

Piet threw his scruffy bag into the back seat of Jack's car. "We need to go back to your place, Jack. I must do a few things, return promises I made. I need your help; I also need the briefcase with all its contents."

Jack slid behind the wheel. "No problems. So, you found him then, Tom Cameron? Harry will finally get his story. He'll be a happy man, Piet."

Piet grunted. "Not when he gets my expenses, he won't." Piet covered his eyes with his sunglasses. "Let's go and I'll tell you all about it when we get to your place. I need a beer, a shower and change of clothes, in that order. But no coffee."

Jack drove them back to his cottage. Piet, he thought was in a strange mood. But he stayed silent. Piet had his own way of doing things. He would tell him what happened in Cape Town when he was ready.

Jack busied himself with the pre-prepared pasta dish he had bought, tossed a salad, and slid the garlic bread into the oven. He stoked the fire he had made in the sitting room, opened a bottle of red wine, and waited for Piet to appear. It was dark and cold outside, he closed the curtains and turned on the lights.

Finally, Piet appeared.

"Thought you'd gone to bed, mate. What took you so long?"

Piet sat down and took a gulp of his wine. "See here, my friend, there's something I want to make clear to you. Zelda Cameron contacted me to help her with a problem she had, as you know.

"From the moment I opened that briefcase there was a connection. You and I both worked hard to follow the trail she had left. But I considered the case was mine, and mine alone, from that moment on."

Jack nodded. "Once a cop always a cop, Piet. I understand that."

"We're a team you and me, Jack. We work well together. But this case of Zelda Cameron is now closed. It must be handed over to Inspector Kleinman in Cape Town, the officer working on the case of the murdered Mrs Cloete, as I told you.

"For me to get the information as to the whereabout of Tom Cameron, I had to make a deal with him. I needed some contacts from him, not completely legit, but I shall get to that.

"We must send the briefcase and its contents to Inspector Kleinman. It then becomes his case. Agreed?"

Jack nodded, looking slightly puzzled. "Okay, I can live with that. Harry will be happy because it means we can publish the story – yes? It would help if you told me what happened to Tom Cameron and how you found him. I've got a feeling I might not like it much."

Piet grinned. "You can tell Harry I have some hefty expenses from my little trip to the Cape. *Jeez,* Jack it costs big bucks these days to get a bit of information, hire killers and such like, then there's car hire, bribes, hotel, and other stuff, oh, and a bit of a game drive as well."

Jack looked startled. "You hired someone to kill Cameron, is that what you're saying, then went on a game drive?"

Piet lifted his head and sniffed the air. "Something like that. Food smells good, let's eat and I'll tell you what happened."

*****

They carried their empty plates back into the kitchen and Piet retrieved his London t-shirt, throwing it into the fire and watching it burn.

For the next two hours Piet told Jack what happened in Cape Town, and how he tracked Tom Cameron down to a seedy bar in Long Street.

"You know how it all works, Jack. You've been down in the sewers of crime. You catch the person you are looking and hand him over to the cops, right?"

Jack felt his stomach curl. Clearly that wasn't what Piet had decided to do under the circumstances he had been faced with.

Piet's face was hard. "I wanted this killer to have, how you say in English – a taste of his own medicine? I wanted him to experience the terror he had inflicted on the girls. That's all I could see when I looked into his eyes. I saw what the girls had seen – evil, pure evil.

"We don't know if the girls were dead when he threw them in the river, I fear that they were not, but they would have drowned. Hard case to prove against Tom Cameron. No bodies, no proof.

"He threw them in the river, yes. You and I know that from Father Mark's account of Tom's confession, but a smart lawyer will argue that unless someone saw him do it, how could it be proven he was responsible for their deaths? Wasn't going to have that Jack.

"The case against Cameron, tried in a court in the UK where all this happened, would have dragged on for years, or, worse, be thrown out of court because of insufficient evidence. Cameron wasn't caught with the evidence; the briefcase, was he? No one saw him throw the girls into the river, no witnesses. He would have got away with it. I, personally, would not have been able to live with that."

Jack stayed silent. He didn't think he wanted to hear the rest of the story. But he was a journalist and they had both worked hard on this story – he had to hear the end of it. Piet was right, there was no solid proof that Tom Cameron had killed the girls.

"So, you didn't hand him over to Inspector Kleinman did you, Piet?" he said softly.

Piet smiled at him. "No.

"Okay, I didn't play by the rules, but rules are meant to be broken, not so? I wasn't prepared to go down the road of long-drawn-out court cases, which could take decades with things as they are in the country now. Waiting for years in prison was too good for him, if it could ever be proven he was guilty."

Piet stood up and prodded the remains of his t-shirt. He paced around the room. "I removed him from the bar in Long Street, to a so-called taxi, driven by a gangster, who was extremely expensive. Not sure how to get that bit past Harry either, but whatever.

"We drove north, through the night. When we reached a suitable spot in the bush near a river, we stopped, for a cup of coffee. It was a beautiful day, starting to get warm. I made the coffee and told Cameron to go sit on a rock and think about his sins. The river was wide, plenty of rocks warming nicely in the sun."

Piet took a sip of his wine and leaned back. "Cameron knew he had been caught. I reminded him of the crimes he had committed over the years. Must say he didn't have much in the way of conversation either. Didn't say a word, didn't even thank me for the coffee I made for him. Ungrateful bastard."

Jack was rooted to his chair. Trying to imagine what might be coming next.

The fire crackled and spat as Piet continued. "Suddenly, from nowhere, there was …

"*Jeez*, Jack, it was so quick, and the croc was massive. It came from nowhere and grabbed Cameron. There was a bit of rolling, thrashing, and screaming before the croc pulled him down under the water. Not sure if the croc drowned him, before taking him down to his slimy rotting den. Could be that was the case. A crocodile doesn't chew its victim, hey. It takes them and holds them under water until they drown. Then it drags you down to its den and leaves you there to rot before it devours you.

"Sometimes a crocodile doesn't get it quite right. You may come around and find yourself in a place of absolute horror. But the croc will return and eat you. Must be a bit scary seeing it slithering silently back towards you."

Piet shuddered. "Ugly buggers, crocs. Can't stand them myself. They lie around all day without moving, sunning themselves on rocks and such like, but when they move, they move fast.

"That's why I had the gangster with the gun with me in case there was another hungry croc lurking around. Didn't fancy being the special of the day on the menu.

"See, I know the area well, just as Cameron knew the Thames so well. Famous for crocs that part of the river, very dangerous. Horrible way to go."

Jack felt his stomach roil. But even he couldn't imagine the horror of those last few minutes of Thomas Cameron's life.

"See here, Jack, everything has a price. Africa is a beautiful and sometimes cruel place. She demands a price be paid for everything; she knows how to get justice. It's nature's way.

"Tom Cameron paid the price she demanded."

*****

Piet rubbed his eyes. "Time for bed for me, Jack. Need to get back to the hotel, my dog might even have missed me. Sometimes I prefer dogs to people. They're more honest, more open with their feelings. Give me a lift back, will you?"

Piet rammed his cap on his head. "Tomorrow we'll courier the briefcase to Inspector Kleinman. You brief Harry. He might have a bit of a problem explaining my expenses to the bean counters…

"Also, I ask that you don't mention Inspector Kleinman by name, and I think within your story of events, we don't mention Father Mark. Wherever he is."

Chapter Seventy-Two
Eastern Cape
2018

The road was long and dusty, the sun high in the sky and brutally hot.

He had taken the local bus to get to the place he wanted to be. He felt comfortable amongst the local passengers, as they laughed and shouted to each other.

Goats and bundles of belongings were tied precariously to the rack on the roof of the bus. Chickens squawked, pecking at each other, packed tightly together in their small cages, under the relentless noon day sun.

Clouds of choking dust followed the old bus as it belched out its cloud of black noxious fumes.

He was the last passenger. He had no luggage. Just a simple black book under his arm and a small hessian bag.

The young herd boy with his five goats watched him as he turned and made his way along the dusty road, his simple sandals leaving a brief puff of dust behind each step he took. The boy watched his slow and steady progress until he disappeared. It was unusual to see a white man walking in these parts, carrying nothing.

The boy knew of only one place where this white man could be heading.

*****

The elderly Mother Superior watched him make his way on the road that only led to their convent and church. She had lived there all her life, in this harsh and sometimes cruel part of the Free State. But she had known no other place since she had been a toddler.

The man staggered slightly as he made his way to the doors of the convent and orphanage.

He looked up at the familiar building, the only place, as a small boy, which had offered him comfort in a world that had not seemed to want him. The tears fell easily from his eyes, distorting the shape of his past.

Wanting him even less so now.

The Mother Superior opened the door, her wimple startlingly white against her round dark face as she looked at the shattered man standing before her.

"Come inside. You have had a long and difficult journey. I'll bring you some water."

He looked around as he sank wearily down on the bench inside the entrance of the orphanage he remembered so vividly. He held the hessian bag close to his chest. His bible he placed on the bench next to him.

The Mother Superior brought him water, then stood back, her hands clasped in front of her. "Perhaps you would like to come into the church. The one I know you remember so well?"

She smiled at the surprise on his face. "Yes, I remember you. But I don't know your name. You were only a little boy then, our little altar boy.

"You have lost your way. Once more, I think, as we all did when we were abandoned here."

He nodded.

She held her hand out. "Come with me."

Mark looked around and remembered himself as that little boy, and everything else that had come into what he hoped would be a simple life.

He entered the familiar confines of the church, fell to his knees, covered his face with his hands, and wept.

The Mother Superior waited a while. "You were a part of this simple church. Life can be cruel and not anticipated, through no fault of one's own.

"The Vatican is a closed community. They have their high technology there, as do all the churches around the world. Instructions and topical discussions. Decisions made, are sent around the world in seconds. Which priest is being sent to which parish and so on. We have here, in Africa, what we call the 'bush telegraph.' Snippets of news passed from parish to parish from visiting priests and nuns…"

She put her head to one side, a look of innocence on her gentle face. "We are isolated here, very little contact with the outside world, our internet is sadly lacking with very little signal, sometimes we have no idea what is going on for months and months."

She leaned towards him and helped him to his feet. "We will find work for you here. You have returned from a long journey.

"You belong here with us, little altar boy, yes, that's what we called you then."

She glanced at the hessian bag he was still holding close to his chest. "What is this you are carrying?"

Mark retrieved the urn from the hessian sack he had carried so far. "Her name is Isobel Kruger. She became a mother to me. Adopted me. I wanted to bring her home. You see this is where I first met her. Miss Izzy."

The Mother Superior nodded. "Ah, yes, Miss Izzy, I remember her too. We will look after her. You will both be safe here, together, with us.

"Of course, you cannot live in the convent, but there is a simple dwelling next to the church where you may live. Our church is open to everyone.

"I think God has forgiven you. That is why you have come home to us. But what shall we call you?"

"My name is Marius."

"Welcome home then, Father Marius, for that is what we shall call you.

"You shall have a place here with us."

Acknowledgements

I would like to thank the following for their unswerving support on this long and lonely road called writing. But seeing nearly 9000 wonderful reviews on Amazon, from readers all around the world makes me want to get started on my next story!

Thank you to the readers who took time to write the reviews – each and every one of you are special and I thank you for your support – sorry about the tears…

To be compared to John Gordon Davis and Wilbur Smith is a massive, and humbling, tribute, and thank you for that as well.

To my sister, Jackie who, as usual, held my hand every step of the way. As a librarian her input was invaluable having dealt with thousands of readers over many years. She knows what works and what doesn't.

Mark Baldwin, a friend of many years standing, for yet another stunning cover!

Michel Giradin, who is a legend in the safari business and has been for many years. Thank you, Michel, for all your amazing advice, without you I might have got some of my antelope in the wrong part of the country!

Brian Stephens for doing all that technical stuff required to get this book up on Amazon. I don't have a clue how to do that.

Ken Gerhardt for his photo of a Karoo farmhouse on the front cover. Ken is a photographer based in Cape Town

Finally, a big thank you to **David Styles** who gave me a fascinating glimpse into the life of a London cabbie. His book 'Everyone Is Entitled to My Opinion' is available on Amazon and great fun to read.

*****

If you enjoyed reading this book and would like to share that enjoyment with others, then please take the time to visit the place where you made your purchase and write a review.

Reviews are a great way to spread the word about worthy authors and will help them be rewarded for their hard work.

You can also visit Samantha's Author Page on Amazon to find out more about her life and passions.

Also by Samantha Ford:

The Zanzibar Affair

A letter found in an old chest on the island of Zanzibar finally reveals the secret of Kate Hope's glamorous, but anguished past, and the reason for her sudden and unexplained disappearance.

Ten year's previously Kate's lover and business partner, Adam Hamilton, tormented by a terrifying secret he is willing to risk everything for, brutally ends his relationship with Kate.

A woman is found murdered in a remote part of Kenya bringing Tom Fletcher back to East Africa to unravel the web of mystery and intrigue surrounding Kate, the woman he loves but has not seen for over twenty years.

In Zanzibar, Tom meets Kate's daughter Molly. With her help he pieces together the last years of her mother's life and his extraordinary connection to it.

A page turning novel of love, passion, betrayal and death, with an unforgettable cast of characters, set against the spectacular backdrop of East and Southern Africa, New York and France.

Amazon Reviews

"This book will keep you guessing; that's a good thing. I could barely put it down and one night dreamed about it so much I woke up and read more. It's unbearably sad in some places and wonderfully happy in others. Fantastic!"

"This book takes you on a safari round Africa. It is a compelling story with so many twists. It is beautifully and hauntingly told. The details and descriptions made me feel the heat, smell the ocean and slap the mosquitoes. Thank you."

"I loved The Zanzibar affair. I felt I was there sensing the smells, the sea and the warmth of Africa. The way she weaves the characters into the story is quite fascinating, leaving the reader spellbound and wondering where it's going to end. Always with an unexpected twist. A fabulous storyline and book which I could hardly put down. Highly recommended."

The House Called Mbabati

The Mother Superior crossed herself quickly. "May God have mercy on you, and forgive you both," she murmured as she locked the diary and faded letters in the drawer.

Deep in the heart of the East African bush stands a deserted mansion. Boarded up, on the top floor, is a magnificent Steinway Concert Grand, shrouded in decades of dust.

In an antique shop in London, an elderly nun recognises an old photograph of the mansion; she knows it well.

Seven thousand miles away, in Cape Town, a woman lies dying; she whispers one word to journalist Alex Patterson – Mbabati.

Sensing a good story, and intrigued with what he has discovered, Alex heads for East Africa in search of the old abandoned house. He is unprepared for what he discovers there; the hidden home of a once famous classical pianist whose career came to a shattering end; a grave with a blank headstone and an old retainer called Luke - the only one left alive who knows the true story about two sisters who disappeared without trace over twenty years ago.

Alex unravels a story which has fascinated the media and the police for decades. A twisting tale of love, passion, betrayal and murder; and the unbreakable bond between two extraordinary sisters who were prepared to sacrifice everything to hide the truth.

Mbabati is set against the magnificent and enduring landscape of the African bush - where nothing is ever quite as it seems.

Amazon Reviews

"It is a long time since I have been so absorbed by a novel about Africa. Reading it, I vacillated between willing it to last longer as I was enjoying it so much, and wanting to get through it to reveal the outcome. There can be no greater praise for this novel than its endorsement by the late John Gordon Davis, to whom the novel is dedicated. Anyone who has read any of JGD's novels, in particular his classic 'Hold My

Hand I'm Dying' will understand that Samantha Ford's novel is in the same league."

"What a wonderful story where you have a stormy love affair set in the heart of Africa. It twists and turns as the plot unfolds and you will surely shed a tear or two along the way. For those who have been on an African safari you will not put this book down. Such intelligent and beautiful writing."

"The book is captivating from beginning to end. It takes you on a riveting journey where the story develops and keeps you guessing. Loved it! Didn't want it to end!"

A Gathering of Dust

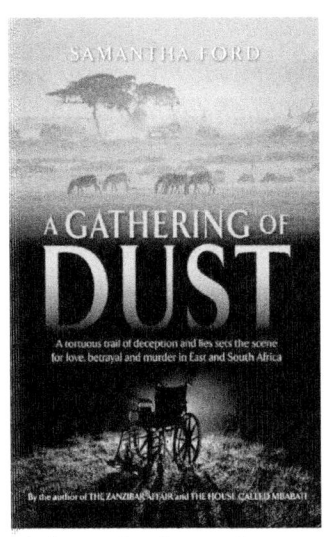

Through the mists of a remote and dangerous part of the South African coastline, a fisherman stumbles upon an abandoned car and an overturned wheelchair.

Thousands of miles away in London, an unidentified woman lies in a coma. When she recovers she has no memory of her past or where she comes from. As fragments of her memory begin to return, the woman has to confront the facts about herself as they begin to unfold. A disastrous love affair in the African bush: a missing husband: and a sinister shadowy figure who knows exactly who she is and where she comes from.

Tension builds as images and secrets begin to resurface from her lost past – rekindled memories that plunge her back into a world she finds she would rather not remember.

Set against the magnificent backdrop of East and Southern Africa. A Gathering of Dust is a fast-paced story of love, betrayal and murder scattered along a trail of deception and lies, with a single impossible truth, and an unthinkable ending.

Amazon Reviews

"What a writer this author is! So cleverly written and with twists and turns you never see coming. I am an avid reader and this authors books are the best I have read in a long time. Her books have everything, mystery, murder, romance, intrigue, suspense etc etc. Well worth a read."

"My husband knows when I am reading this author's books that there is little that will get my nose out of them. Her descriptives of even the simplest things create such a vivid picture. She has made me fall in love with Africa and her story lines are captivating and intelligently

thought out. I never want to finish one of her books only because I don't want them to end."

"Superb. Absolutely brilliant. I simply couldn't stop reading, turned TV off and just read and read, even ignoring my hubby. Can't wait to read the next book!!!"

"A gripping read, with many gut-wrenching twists and turns. I had trouble putting the book down to eat, sleep or work! Fabulous."

The Ambassador's Daughter

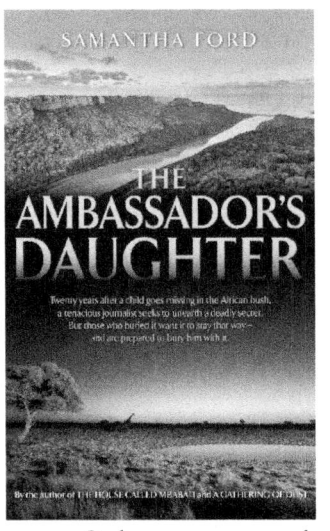

During a violent storm deep in the African bush, a child disappears.

Sara, the ex-British ambassador's daughter, and mother of the child, is arrested.

Twenty years later, journalist Jack Taylor, travels from London to the magnificent landscape of the Eastern Cape, in South Africa, where the unforgiving bush hides long-forgotten secrets of loss, hate, betrayal and revenge.

A staggering story awaits. A deadly secret threatens to destroy the lives of people who thought themselves now safe - a story which has fascinated the media for decades.

Only one person knows exactly what happened on that day - a nomadic shepherd called Eza - but can Jack find him?

Amazon Reviews

"This is simply the best book I've read in a very long time. This talented lady brings Africa alive. Wilbur Smith you have some competition..."

"A cracking good story with a totally unexpected twist at the end!"
John Gordon Davis – author of Hold My Hand I'm Dying

"Having read all Wilbur Smith's books, this author ranks up with the best of them. Best read I've had for years!" Peter C. Morgan

A Widow in Waiting

An accident in the Kenyan bush claims the life of Sir David Cooper, the Director of International Trade and Industry for the British Government -a man with impeccable credentials and an impressive family history.

Twenty years later at an auction on a remote farm in South Africa, a young woman discovers two boxes. One, a richly engraved Chinese puzzle box concealing things the late owner had clearly wanted to remain hidden; the other an antique silver box with an intriguing crest.

Jack Taylor, a journalist from London now living in South Africa, and his partner, ex-detective Piet Joubert once more join forces as they try to untangle the mysterious and tragic past of the two boxes and the people involved.

Set against the breath-taking beauty of Kenya and South Africa, this is an irresistible page-turner, laden with unpredictable possibilities. It takes the reader down a trail of deception, secrets and tragedy, culminating in a single impossible truth and an unthinkable ending, which even veteran journalist Jack Taylor had not seen coming.

Amazon Reviews

"Oh my word, what a story. Samantha really knows how to reel one in. Thank you so much for a gripping story. Didn't have a clue as to the ending."OK, so you've heard of Wilbur Smith, so why haven't you heard of Samantha??

One was a millionaire with mega-support, the other is equally as good (better??) when it comes to books about Africa (always with an International 'interest.')Samantha, however, is a dedicated "garret author" with no publicity/marketing Team, and so you can only get her books from Amazon. If you love reading, Africa, mystery.... and don't mind being obsessed with an **"I can't put it down"** *book, get onto Amazon now!" – Philippa J*

333

"Another fascinating book from Samantha. Her descriptions take you back to Africa! I could not put it down as I wanted to find out what happened! Great read from a great author." – Mrs Jacqueline A Lloyd

"Novel number 6 from Samantha will not disappoint another page turner with more twists & turns than a Rubix Cube, you have just no idea what jumps out at you from the next page. This author also cleverly takes us back to our verandas in Kenya & South Africa with our beers or gin & tonics watching the sun go down. Brilliant writing Samantha keep them coming." – Peter Morgan

Printed in Great Britain
by Amazon